/ w.

WHISPERS THROUGH THE HOUSE

WHISPERS
THROUGH
THE HOUSE

Laurel Means

NORTH STAR PRESS OF ST. CLOUD, INC.
Saint Cloud, Minnesota

First Edition, June 2011

Printed in the United States of America

Published by
North Star Press of St. Cloud, Inc.
P.O. Box 451
St. Cloud, Minnesota 56302

www.northstarpress.com

Contents

SPRING 1 EARTH

S HE COULD NOT LOOK DOWN TOWARD the rough, wooden coffin at the bottom of the muddy pit gaping open at her feet. Not down to visualize Bernard's shattered body within it. Lucy Dubois forced her mind instead to wander disjointed from the present moment. To drift off toward the distant lake, the stunted pine. To feel the eerie, spring-like warmth, so unexpected in this Minnesota March. To remember February's heavy snows.

Man that is born of woman, hath but a short time to live . . .

Bernard's short life . . . The minister's voice, forcing itself against her will. Lucy blocked it out with the sound of branches unloading clumps of snow, heavy thuds against the ground, against the coffin. Melting snow seeping into it. Icy water soaking the gray woolen suit in which her husband had been buried. A fine suit, not his, but belonging to his brother, Noel. Cold, icy water, numbing his hands, his feet. Hands—feet—which could no longer feel numbness, no longer caress her body.

Against her will she looked up, across the open grave, and glanced at the pitifully few knots of people. There was her sister Agnes, with her three children. Beside them a weak sunlight fell upon hatless men, upon a blond-haired pair, blond-bearded, tall and strong like Viking gods of old, the one with his hand upon the shoulder of the other. Both stared at her, forcing her gaze elsewhere.

Her cheeks burned and a strange tremor ran through her body. Quickly she lowered her head toward Bernard's coffin. How unseemly, how unthinkable, here at his very grave side, to entertain thoughts which should not be given place, dark secrets of the heart which bear no logic, no explanation; thoughts that needed forgiveness.

. . . we commend the soul of our brother departed . . . earth to earth . . .

Minnesota earth, this spring earth . . . Bernard now a part of it. A quickened breeze among the pines mimicked her quickened breathing. She resolved to not look up. She would only see Bernard's coffin, re-configure the shape of his face, his gentle hands. If only—

Now the minister's voice. . . . *grant him an entrance into the land of light and joy . . .*

Grant him . . . Her brother-in-law had summoned the man from a church up in Green Prairie. She hadn't been in any condition to protest or to make any of the arrangements. Noel Dubois, taking charge, as usual

"Ma, look at Martin! He's—" Her daughter Sabine's whispered voice, the pressure of her hand, startled her. Sabine was pointing at her younger brother, Martin. "Ma, he looks so mad. Know he's 'bout to cry, though. Won't catch me doing that." The last words thrust out in defi-ance. Sabine's anger assuming different forms from her own.

Indeed, Lucy's own anger was directed at God. His doing, taking Bernard. So unfair, to leave her, these children, so alone.

"Courage, *mon petit.*" Beside her Noel leaned down to whisper something to the boy, Martin's full, six-year-old anger at his father's sud-den death evident in his clenched fists, the backward thrust of his head.

Lucy was grateful he'd offered to take charge of the boys and hold baby Laurence in his strong arms. He was no substitute for a father, but a strength, a presence she needed, her children needed, however much she resented it. Laurence clung to his uncle, wide-eyed and confused, understanding little of what was happening, what had happened. He still watched the kitchen door for his father's arrival every evening after milk-ing time.

"Ma! Pay attention!" Sabine tugged again at her arm.

Grant to us who are still in our pilgrimage . . .

Pilgrims here . . . The words struck Lucy as strange, yet somehow meaningful. Those hatless men, over there, pilgrims unknown to her. Noel had earlier introduced them as his neighbors. That older man, she couldn't remember his name. Next to him a stocky, middle-aged man named Sep Holberg with three grown sons—those two blond Vikings looking like twins, the third brother shorter, darker. Furtively she watched them, strangely drawn, strangely shaken with emotions defying logic, almost immediately biting her lip, struggling to control such thoughts. How unseemly to stare at attractive men like that. To marvel at their manliness, their virile auras. And how sinful was it to feel comfort in her brother-in-law's strong and rugged physical presence beside her? And she, a new widow, with her husband's coffin at her feet?

Desperately Lucy forced her gaze away from those men to her sister standing near them, slight, frail, still with that strange, haunting look about her. Forced by Papa to marry—barely sixteen—Henry Morton, already old, a veteran, a grown family left behind. Only the occasional letter from them—Henry's son Wilson and his family, a farm near Winona. So strange how Agnes had inherited another family, neither his nor hers, after her own baby drowned, the family of another man—also drowned. Had they married? Agnes never spoke of him. Unexpected, what her relationship to Henry had become, changed through hardship and loss.

. . . we yield unto thee most high praise and hearty thanks . . .

Thankful for what? Bernard's death? Hardship and loss—hers and Agnes's. Did one ever get over it? High praise and hearty thanks, indeed! What price, spiritual consolation? How did one deserve it, or ask for it?

. . . that at the day of the general Resurrection . . .

With a shock, Lucy recognized those words signaling the end of the ritual. The minister was offering a final prayer, yet she could not seem to grasp the meaning of his mumbled words. Lost words, lost comfort. His hand signed a cross over the grave. His last words, his final *Amen* hung suspended over the hollowness of the gaping pit.

There could be no Amen for her. There could be no understanding of death nor comfort in its ritual closure. The man's words and gesture merely provided an instinctive alliance with something age-old. Perhaps it was wrong to deny that, yet she could not stop denying it.

"Come, Lucy," Noel's wife, Mary, broke into her thoughts and pushed her closer to the edge of the grave, "and you children, too. Take up a bit of earth—snow will do, the ground's still frozen—and drop it on your father's grave. When you do, say a prayer that the Lord will take his soul up into heaven, that he'll be in God's presence."

Hesitantly, scarcely understanding, the two reached down and picked up a handful of snow, Sabine's falling slowly through her fingers, melting before it touched the coffin. Martin's forming a ball which he obviously was preparing to throw down with the force of anger like a snowball. Hesitating, after a glance at his mother, he finally dropped it down onto the lid, where it hit with a dull, hollow *thunk*.

That sound pierced Lucy's consciousness. She was not prepared for it and stepped quickly back, unable to continue with the ritual.

"Come, come, Lucy. It's time to say farewell." Mary took her roughly by the arm. "Say farewell to your Bernard. You must do it. It's expected. What will people think?"

"How can I?" A tenseness formed around her mouth and descended down through her body. "I never had a chance—no one expected that wound to fester—he died in his sleep, I wasn't there—wasn't there at all, I never even heard him call my name—my name—couldn't go—lost—senseless—" Her words accelerated into a meaningless stream.

"Now, now, Lucy, calm down. Noel, at least, was with him. Such a simple accident, Noel said. Who would have expected a wound like that to be fatal? If only the doctor—"

Yes, if only, Lucy thought. Mary's words were wounds in themselves. Noel there beside Bernard's last moments of life. Not her. Yes, who would have expected it. A fall through the trap door of the barn loft. A shattered arm, thigh gashed. Festering, finally gangrene. A negligent doctor. Time lost. Husband lost. Life itself—what value now? Yes, how ironic, how unfair. A simple accident. Pitching hay from that loft a thousand times before. A moment's unsure footing. An instant of panic. The impact of pain. She'd relived her husband's shock, his panic, his pain, over and over again.

"Come, hurry up Lucy. People want to leave, but they can't until you make your final farewell." Mary's voice sharp, insistent, intrusive.

Lucy shuddered as she bent down and scooped up a handful of snow. She had no gloves. The icy coldness burned into her hand, yet she could not release it. A final act, one painful and difficult.

"Lucy—please!"

Mary nudged Lucy forward until she stood dangerously close to the edge of the pit. An instant thought—a fleeting desire to fling herself down to the very bottom, to press her body against the yellow pine lid, to sense Bernard's body beneath it. "Oh!" she suddenly cried out, her shoes sliding toward the edge, her body pitching forward, her hands digging into the snow.

Men on the other side of the pit instinctively moved forward, a tall blond Viking of a man rushing—impressions whirling around her in distorted shapes, sounds. Noel's strong arm caught her around the waist and pulled her back through the snow, it's cold heaviness clinging to her skirt and stinging the palms of her hands.

"*Ah, fais-toi l'attention, ma belle-soeur!*" exclaimed Noel, setting her on her feet beside him, still holding Laurence within his other arm. "Steady, steady, hold to me."

But she was far from steady. Leaning heavily against Noel, she slowly opened her hand and crumbled the cold snow until it fluttered down, the flakes glittering mockingly in the weak sunlight.

Again, Mary, annoying, insistent, glancing at Noel, then Lucy. "That's right, dear. Let it go." She guided Lucy away from the grave's edge. "Now come. Time to leave."

"So hard to leave. I wasn't there."

Now this moment at Bernard's grave would be her only goodbye. She could never again lie together with him in the bed where he'd died, feel the warmth of his strong body become a part of hers. Never work along side him broadcasting the seeds along the furrows of the fields, never move with him as together they scythed the newly ripened wheat or bundled the rye shocks.

Martin was running up the path to catch up with Agnes's younger son, Tom. Both cousins were near the same age, long since bonding, now pelting each other with snowballs. Boys' sorrow denied—for the moment.

Agnes embraced her. "Ah, Lucy, Lucy," she cried. "*Quel douleur, je suis desolée.*"

That moment brought an emotional connection, a sudden recall of their childhood in Quebec, their language of the heart, rarely now the language of the tongue. Yet in the shock of that emotion, Lucy seemed unable to bring needed words forward. An emptiness, loss, like so much else. She could do nothing more than hold her sister closely, a close, trembling embrace conveying what neither could articulate. Their mother, father, brothers moved away years ago to Shakopee, bringing a sense of isolation to that family nucleus so essential to immigrant communities

In a desperate attempt to regain control of her emotions, she turned to Agnes's elder son, Abe. "You and Jane best get your mother up to your buggy. Don't let her get chilled. She's already shivering with cold."

"But Auntie Lucy—" Jane sounded concerned.

"Don't worry. I'll be all right. Noel and Mary are looking after me. Go on, now. We'll get together again soon." She watched as Agnes, supported on each side by son or daughter, slowly walked up the sloping path toward the cemetery gate. It was a pity her husband, Henry, had not come, possibly due to chronic ill health. Yet in some way it was a relief. Lucy had always found him difficult and unsympathetic.

She watched as Tom said goodbye to Martin and ran on ahead to join his mother just as they reached their buggy. How fortunate Agnes had the support of her stepchildren, now that Henry wasn't well and turning most of the family business over to Abe. And how fortunate the mill and brickwords were prospering. Perhaps Wilson, Henry's grown son, could be persuaded to move here. Yes, she'd write to him. Who would have thought what Henry's life would be like, eight–ten years ago? Another minute and Agnes's buggy pulled away. Once again Lucy felt a sense of loss, a different kind of loss, one deeply rooted in the past.

"Excuse me, missus." One of the caretakers, hired by Prairie Lake Church to maintain the cemetery, waited to say something to her. "With all respects, missus," he said, touching his hat a little and resting on his shovel. "Will all respects, we must get on with our job, 'fore it gets much colder—wind coming up again, now that the sky's clouding over."

"You go on up there with your kinfolks now, ma'am," said the other. "Me and Jake, here, we like to do our job in private. Easier on everybody." He put his hand under Lucy's elbow and guided her over a low snow drift. Turning back toward the grave, he muttered, "Sure was a big job, digging this grave. Ground so frozen, had to use dynamite. People oughter not be allowed to die in winter, not here 'bouts, for sure!"

People oughtn't be allowed to die in winter . . . Nor ever, Lucy thought. Why Bernard? Why now? As she came up to the road, she looked at the big freight wagon Jake and his helper had used to bear Bernard's coffin to the cemetery, its team tethered to the gatepost and pawing impatiently to get away. The wagon had been made into a makeshift hearse. Some ragged-looking ostrich plumes were fastened to the horses' head harnesses, the wagon bed was empty except for the folded black velvet cloth used for covering the coffin. The empty space was hardest to accept, and a shudder went through her body.

That sensation made her aware of the heavy weight of her bonnet, a widow's bonnet with black silk flowers and a veil. A horrible thing, she'd had to borrow it from Jack's widowed mother, old missus Johnson.

"You've got to look proper," Mary had cautioned. "Respectable."

But there hadn't been time to acquire proper widow's weeds. As it was, Lucy's only suitable dress was an old, dark blue cotton with white flowers, little protection against the cold. She hoped the fine black woolen cloak loaned by Mary covered most of it, and pulled it around her more closely as she slowly made her way up to the main road.

"Now then, Lucy, in you get," said Noel as he helped her up the two metal footrests. "*Voila*, sit between Sabine and Martin. Sabine, pull that buffalo robe over the knees of your *maman*. It's getting colder—you feel it?"

"Where's Laurence?" Lucy asked in alarm.

"*Eh bien*, would you look at that? He's up there in Mary's lap, already dropped off to sleep."

Glancing at her older son and daughter, Lucy was struck by how pale and silent they were, most likely more bewildered than grieving. The grief would come later. Would that—could that—be true of herself?

"Hy-up, hup! You lazy nags, *allons-y*!" Noel shouted to the horses, struggling to pull the heavy surrey through deep, muddy ruts. "Don't feed you for nothing!" He flicked his whip over the horses' rumps several times, and the surrey lurched and swerved slowly forward, the one horse turning his head around several times with such a sad, reproachful look that it made Martin shriek with laughter. His hysterical laughter seemed to break the heaviness settled over them, the scenery, the weather.

"Oh my, look how dark it's getting," exclaimed Mary. "That sky's completely clouded over. Looks like more snow. See if you can hurry the team, Noel. We're only half-way home to Little Sauk. See, there's Lucy's cabin up ahead. Don't—" She broke off, whispering the rest. He responded by whipping up the team to a sudden spurt forward.

It wasn't hard to understand Mary's message. Don't let her see the cabin. As if not seeing it would help. "Slow down, Noel!" she cried. "Stop, pull in by the barn!"

Mary glanced back in surprise. "Why on earth, Lucy?" she asked. "Surely you don't mean to go back in there tonight, do you? That empty house? No, no, we can't let you stay there all alone. Out of the question!"

"Stop, I said." Lucy threw off the buffalo robe and stood up unsteadily. Noel was forced to draw back on the reins. The procession behind them also slowed.

"No, no, keep on going Noel!" Mary insisted. "Don't you know, we agreed they'd all stay at our place for the next few days, at least, until we get Lucy's future sorted out."

"Stop! Please pull in here!" Lucy was emphatic and not a little annoyed at the suggestion that they intended to sort out her future. "Stop the team, I'm getting out! I need to go home. Please, Mary—I know it's difficult to understand. But that's what I need most right now."

"*Non, non,* Lucy . . ." Noel began.

"Truly, I know what I need," she repeated. Concerned at the anxious expressions on the faces of Sabine and Martin, she added, "It's all right. Trust me." Then to Mary, "You can take the children, I'd be grateful for that. Being with their cousins will be best for them."

"No, Mama," protested Sabine. "You can't stay all alone here, that old empty house, Pa gone! I can help, really I can, I promise."

"Do what I say, Sabine. You and your brothers. I'll be quite all right. I want to walk a bit before going into the house. I need fresh air."

"All right, then, no point in arguing with a woman like you," commented Noel, adding some mutterings in French. Reluctantly he reined the team over to the left side of the road and waved the procession behind to go on ahead. "Get back home as you can, Reverend Simons, before the weather breaks," he shouted as the minister's phaeton drew up alongside.

When he hesitated, Lucy said, "It's all right, sir. I've some things to tend to here." To her relief, the man merely looked questioningly at her, slightly raised a hand in benediction, and urged his horse forward. Several other wagons followed, and Noel waved each one on with some explanation or other.

The Holberg men, however, stopped and pulled up alongside. On the way to the cemetery earlier, they'd offered to take Josie, Raymond, and Sarah, the oldest of the Dubois children, in their buckboard. The two youngest had been left at home with Hannah, Noel's hired girl. Josie immediately started to jump out.

"What's the trouble, here?" Sep Holberg asked. "No, Josie, girl! Not yet. You stay right here in the wagon."

"Lucy insists on going back to the house, Sep—and alone," Mary said, shaking her head. "Won't be persuaded otherwise."

"What about the children?"

"They're coming home with us," Mary answered.

"Well, then," he pointed out, "let the older ones ride here with their cousins. We'll just squeeze up a bit." He turned to one of his sons. "Mattias, bring them over."

"Do it ourselves," protested Sabine, her continued disappointment obvious. "Think we were babies or something?"

As the girl started to climb over the side of the surrey, however, one of the tall, blond Vikings, the one apparently called Mattias, took her in his arms. "Wait, miss," he said.

Lucy caught her breath. There he was standing beside her on the road, her daughter in his arms. This one the tallest brother, with a blond beard setting off ruddy cheeks and hazel eyes. The rough wool of his cream-colored jacket sleeve brushed against her hand as he settled Sabine more comfortably against his broad shoulder. The sensation was a strange one.

"Fair amount of mud, miss," he commented to Sabine, then smiled. "Wouldn't want you to fall into it, now, would we?" As he turned back toward the Holberg wagon, he added with a different kind of look, "My condolences, ma'am. Sure am sorry 'bout your loss. If there's anything we can do 'round your place—seed time coming up, for one thing."

Lucy was relieved he didn't seem to expect an answer. She could not think of one.

With Sabine still protesting in his arms, Mattias Holberg strode across the muddy ruts and set her down gently beside Josie in the Holbergs' buckboard. A weird-looking wagon, Lucy couldn't help but notice. It had a wide blue stripe painted along one side, as if they'd either run out of blue paint or changed their minds.

Martin had already climbed up over the rear wheel and was arguing with his cousin, Raymond. "You're hogging those warm bricks. Move your big, smelly feet over."

"Bricks ain't still warm 'nough to matter," Raymond pointed out.

"Well, then, you're taking too much of the fur robe."

"Stop it, you two," Josie interjected. "Room enough for you both. Now move over. Here's Sabine. Looks like she's freezing. And not another peep out of you, hear?"

Looking at her daughter, Lucy knew it was more than the cold. She'd felt rejected. Lucy realized Sabine needed her now, more than ever, but she could not deal with that, not just yet. She had her own needs, and those began with being alone for a space of time in the house she had shared with Bernard.

Noel gave a sigh of resignation. "*Eh bien*, Lucy, stubborn woman that you are, at least let me give you a hand down." He turned, unlatched the surrey door, and steadied her as she stepped down into the bank of melting snow alongside the road. "And at least let me stop by the Johnsons's on the way to see if they're back from Twin Falls. I'll ask if Jack can help you out next few days with the chores." Flicking the reins, he added, "Also send my hired hand, John Wold. That is, if he's not too busy, if he's not—"

The rest was lost as he paid attention to keeping his wheels out of the deeper ruts. "*Mon dieu*—oh Lord," he shouted back, "deliver me from bad roads and determined women!"

Lucy moved out to the middle of the muddy road, watching them slowly disappear from sight, first the Holberg wagon, then Noel's surrey. Silence permeated the gathering dusk. No animal sounds emanated from the barn. Increasing cold had stopped melting snow from dropping off the branches. Even the wind had died.

She glanced at the house, its windows dark, the snow on the short path up to the front door unbroken except for footprints made by her and the children earlier that day as they walked away from the house toward Noel's waiting surrey on the way to the cemetery. Now she had to retrace those steps, back into the darkness.

She opened the door—it was never locked, never had a key—and stepped inside, shuddering at the cold chill in the air which struck her forcefully. The fire in the kitchen stove was out, no fire in the parlor fireplace. For an instant the feeling reminded her of her wedding night, when Bernard had first brought her to this house, only a small, log shack of a homestead cabin then. Cold, with no whispers of its own yet, only the promise of their bodies together and the children who would come.

She went into the parlor, unable to force herself to light the oil lamp or even kindle a fire. Not bothering to take off the borrowed cloak or her shoes, soaked through from melted snow, she threw off the borrowed widow's bonnet and sat down heavily on the hard horsehair sofa. For some time she simply stared out the window into the growing darkness. Her body felt heavy as lead. It will do you good to cry, Mary had told her. But she could not. Tears—impossible.

Instead, memories. Flooding sounds and images gathering in the corners of the room, distant whispers coming from all around her. Fragments of thoughts, bits of memory, truncated re-enactments of events, little ones, big ones. Seeing Bernard's moment of tenderness when he presented her with a packet of sweet-smelling soap, bought at West's as an anniversary present

Still, she could not force back others. Shouts, screams from the barn when Bernard fell. Seeing him lying there, twisting in agony. Her frantic efforts to drag him home, lift him onto the bed. Running down the road, all the way to the Johnsons's, getting Jack to ride into Long Prairie for a doctor. The doctor's shaken look, seeing Bernard's shatered arm, bleeding wound. *I'll have to come back with more instruments,* he said, *some other medicine.*

That terrible accident, Bernard's agony . . . Her horror replaced by anger each time she thought of Doctor Maynard's failure to return in time to save Bernard's life. She wondered what had happened to him, how many patients he'd allowed to die. A graveyard full of Maynard's tombstones.

It wasn't until she began to shiver from cold that she realized she'd been sitting there for a long time, that her hands and feet felt frozen. The carriage clock on the mantel striking eight came as a shock, a jarring reminder that there were things she needed to do, that time was passing. How exhausted she felt, pressed down by all the events of the last few days, her mind numbed by today's ordeal at the cemetery. And she needed to go to bed, not the high carved bed in which Bernard had died, but to Sabine's bed, up in the loft.

In the morning, Jack Johnson appeared at the back door. He stopped in the mud room just long enough to stamp snow and wet slush off his boots, hang his Hudson Bay jacket on a peg, and throw his leather cap with the earflaps up onto the shelf

"Mornin', Missus Dubois," he said while holding his hands over the cook stove to warm them. "That brother-in-law of yours stopped by our place down the road late yesterday after the funeral. Sorry me and the missus couldn't be there, offer our condolences. Been in Twin Falls, sister Dotty took a turn for the worse, had to get a neighbor, old widow Dunlop, stay with her a spell. And today's chores of my own took me som'at longer this mornin'," he added, shaking his head. "Still got a few more of my own waitin' when I get home."

"So kind of you," Lucy began. "But you shouldn't think you've got to—"

"No, no, don't mean that, exactly. Be glad to, glad to. Can't expect you and the children to do eveything. They with Noel Dubois?"

"For a day or so, yes. Until I get things sorted out." Yet instinctively she wanted them with her, to make the house seem less empty. The children—Bernard's gifts to her.

"Well, ma'am, best get started. Time's passing faster'n a jackrabbit." Jack took down his jacket, pushed one arm through the sleeve.

"Oh, please, wait, Jack. At least let me offer you some breakfast first."

"Well, thanks kindly. Already ate, but coffee'd be fine." Still half into his jacket, he sat down at the table. For several moments he sat thoughtfully spooning sugar and a dash of salt into his mug of coffee. Then, in a rush of words, "Say, meant to tell you, that far field of yours, them fifty or so acres down longside the river?"

"Yes?"

"Well, that old river's been rising since the thaw began this spring. It's not a good year. Now it's well over the banks and coming up past the line of trees. At this point it's 'bout ten feet or so up into the field."

"But it does that every spring. Bernard doesn't—" She paused, corrected herself. "Bernard never worried. Water goes down in a few weeks—least by planting time."

"No, this is different somehow," Jack said, "more serious. Reason is, a lot more water coming down from rivers up north, Red River full of ice jams. When they go, then you've got a great rush of water. Old Sauk River here can't handle it. Big floods expected next few weeks, hear tell."

"What can I do about it?" This was not something she was prepared to deal with.

"Well, reckon not much you can do," Jack answered with a shrug. "Law of nature, man has to sit back, take it best he can. But I'll tell you this. You won't be able to sow that field, not this spring anyway. Not sure, either, 'bout some of them others."

He set down his empty mug firmly. "Well, got to look after a few things in your barn, then get myself home. Lots more to do my own place, so I'll just be off."

After Jack left, Lucy sat down to think, difficult because of a kind of numbness in her head. Sometimes it felt like packed cotton, no room for thoughts, for feelings. Talking out loud to herself seemed to help. "Those bottom fifty acres gone this year, the best acreage on the farm," she began to mumble. "Depended on that rye crop. Now let me see, that's worth—" She couldn't remember, her mind was a blank. "Oh, Bernard . . . if only Bernard were here . . . he'd know how to reckon—if only—"

In the far back recesses of her mind, however, echoed the words of Mattias Holberg, as he held Sabine in his arms, transferring her from Noel's surrey to the Holberg wagon the day of the funeral. If you ever need help . . . if you ever need . . . But the gap between her need and his offer was still too far, impossible to bridge.

It was late afternoon the next day when Noel brought the children home in his big buckboard. Although Lucy was glad to have them back, she was aware of their uneasiness, as if home now seemed to them a different place, their father's absence imposing a an unfamiliarity upon everything. Sabine and Martin seemed strangely silent or spoke in hushed voices.

Several nights later, like so many nights since Bernard's death, it was hard to sleep. Lucy still could not bear the memories of that bed with its high, carved headboard. Their marriage bed, his deathbed. She'd taken instead to sleeping on the horsehair sofa in the front parlor. Hard, unyielding, hostile to sleep. She drew a shawl over her nightgown, slipped on her boots. She wandered around the kitchen, parlor, avoided the small lean-to bedroom they'd added off the kitchen, a room so small the big bed dominated it. Finally it got so cold that she was forced to pull up a kitchen chair and huddle next to the kitchen range, its last few embers dying out by the time the mantel clock chimed four.

She was still there when Jack came in for his usual cup of coffee.

"Well, missus," he remarked, "you sure look flagged out. Had a bad night?"

"It's all right," Lucy replied. "Just thinking about things."

"That's for sure. A lot you must be thinking 'bout just now. Hate to mention this, but just discovered your milk cow appears to be drying up. Don't know what's wrong, have to get old Dahlgren in. He's good with cattle. May be all right come calving time in the spring, though. Dunno."

"You've already done so much, Jack, I hate to—" She knew what she wanted to ask him, but hesitated, rearranging knives in the sideboard drawer to gain enough courage. "Say, do you think you might ask the Holbergs for help? One of them—Mattias I think—offered." It was difficult to imagine the others had names.

"Well, guess I could do that. Them Holbergs're pretty busy now though. But you know, I'm thinking, too, you shouldn't be here alone now. I'll bring my missus along with me tomorrow. Maybe she can give you a hand 'round the house, with the children and all . . . I'll ask her to bring a can of milk or two. We've got plenty."

"Thank you, Jack. Very kind of you, I'm sure," she said. "But don't worry, I can manage all right."

I can manage . . . how many times had she had to say that over the past few days? She'd said it often enough to convince herself that it was true, but now, after last night, she was not so sure.

Nevertheless, she admitted she was grateful when Marika Johnson came along with her husband the next morning. "The missus'll stay here through the day with you," he said. "Help with the washing. Other things. The missus is a good one for making bread and such." He smiled, his lop-sided smile. "Things you women folk do best."

Later that morning, just as she and Marika had finished folding laundry out of the basket, Lucy heard the sound of wheels and horses in the barnyard. Again, that strange tremor down her spine. The Holbergs! They'd gotten Jack's message. With quickened gestures, she smoothed back her hair, took off her apron, then waited for their knock on the mud room door.

It did not come. Instead, there was a loud rapping on the front door. She opened it to find a stranger standing there, his buggy tied up at the porch. Without being invited, he stepped into the hall.

"Be assured, missus Dubois," he said, taking off his coat and hanging it on one of the pegs along the wall, "that I'm working in your best interests. Name's Elias Smith, land office in Park Rapids." His gray hair and neat moustache, and blue eyes behind steel-rimmed spectacles inspired confidence. "I am genuinely interested in your property. I represent a well-established real estate firm."

"But sir, " she insisted, anger rising, "who has passed the word that this farm might be put up for sale? It certainly did not come from me. There is no reason for me to sell, no reason at all."

"Such things get around, you know, but, be that as it may," Smith replied evasively, "let me assure you, now is a most excellent time to do so."

"Why now?"

"Do you have any idea how much this area has grown in the last decade?" he asked. "Since the war, there have been hundreds of settlers, snapping up all the best land. In fact, there is very little good land like yours left, good, rich bottom land, with much of the clearing done already. So many of the old homesteads have now been broken up into smaller and smaller parcels. You have a lot of acreage here and, why, you could sell your land in an instant, and for a good price."

"For how much, then?" she asked, hoping that her tone sounded casual enough to imply disinterest.

"Well, then, ahem, we'd have to get a surveyor out, go over your spread. Some acreage is worth more than others, you know. Now, let me see, I took the trouble of making a copy of your original land trans-action record. Now if you'll just allow me—" He looked down the hall toward the kitchen door. "Kitchens are always a warmer spot, a place where you feel most at home, more at ease, don't you think?"

Lucy scarcely knew how to take this remark, except it made her un-easy. The man pushed his way past her and, with out invitation, sat down at the big kitchen table. Reaching into his leather pouch, he took out a sheaf of papers, and began spreading them out.

Marika Johnson stared at the man, looking alarmed. "Lucy—what to do?"

"It's all right. Some business. Perhaps—perhaps you wouldn't mind changing the children's bunks up in the loft? And take Laurence up with you?" The truth was, she didn't want the neighbors in on whatever this man had to say. "But don't go home yet," she added, wondering whether Marika could actually be some help if the man . . . something about him, not quite right . . .

"Ahem," Smith cleared his throat again. "I see by this plat map that you were given 160 acres, is that correct? And these are the boundaries, here to here and then to here?" He traced the property lines with the end of a pencil.

Lucy was not sure about the lines. She'd never even seen a plat map before.

"Hmm, look here," Smith continued, "what can you tell me about this apparent gap in the property line here? Unclaimed land? Looks like about one-eighth of a section, north west corner." He pointed to a blank spot on the plat map.

"I'm afraid I don't know," Lucy replied. She felt helpless before this man who seemed to know so much. She nodded again, hoping he was right, that he was honest.

He tapped on the section along the river. "And here. I can tell you right now that all that land is probably worth—oh, let's say, not more than fifty cents an acre. Flooded it still is, too badly flooded. Always will be prone to flooding, I suspect. And this over here—where the road cuts through the south section of your spread—looks like about another fifteen acres or so. Has it been cleared ? Worth a great deal less, if not."

"Some of it—that is, I think we—I think we intended—"

Smith looked impatient. "Look here," he said, "I'm going to have to ask one of our surveyors to come up. He'll be able to verify the boundaries, the condition of the land. Then we can better estimate the value. That will be some time early next week—shall we say, Tuesday?"

Lucy heard herself murmuring "well, all right—yes, I suppose."

"All settled then. If I can't come out myself with the chap, I'll send my assistant, good man named Olson."

He quickly stood and made his way back through the house. He didn't even pause at the door, but quickly went to his buggy. As he stepped up into his buggy he called back, "And, oh, ma'am, by the way, there's a fee for the survey. In the event of a sale, we'll deduct the fee from the sale price, otherwise we'll expect the thirty dollars in cash when he comes. Good day to you, then." The buggy then turned sharply onto the main road toward Little Sauk junction.

Thirty dollars! Why, that was more than they had ever fetched in a month, even at harvest time. She'd have to sell both horses—Blaize and Socks, as well as poor old Brownling, the milk cow. Most likely the chickens, all the grain stored in the barn, even her wedding ring—her only jewelry, apart from a pair of silver earrings Bernard had given her as a wedding gift—and oh, yes, those Limoges plates *maman* had given them after the wedding—to pay this man, and that would be just for the survey. And Smith had convinced her that she couldn't even put the place up for sale without the survey.

Next Tuesday. She had until next Tuesday. No charge for the survey if she agreed. But did she want to sell the homestead? Couldn't she manage it alone, with a little help? Jack Johnson and his sons, she'd pay them a little, pay in kind maybe.

On the other hand, once the sowing seasons came, he and his sons would be fully committed to their own farm. She couldn't expect Noel to provide help from his own place, they'd all be too busy. Or his hired man, John Wold. She couldn't afford to hire her own men, not even one, which might be enough. After all, Bernard had managed on his own without another hand except at harvest time. Then all the neighbors worked together, hired a steam threshing rig from over in Elona. It was unfortunate that the children were still too young to be of much help. Not like Agnes's.

Then there was the question of help from the Holbergs. She sat down abruptly in the nearest kitchen chair. How—in what way—could she ask? No, she could not do it.

Before Tuesday came, however, and the Park Rapids surveyor with it, Mary and Noel arrived Sunday afternoon for a visit. "Well, now Josie and Raymond—I'm sure your cousins have some things to show you," Noel said as they all came bustling in through the front door—their big surrey hitched up across the road in the barnyard.

Within minutes the older boys started a wrestling match in the parlor, the girls went up to the loft where Sabine wanted to show off the new rag doll her mamie had made.

"New litter of kittens over in the barn," Lucy called up after them with a hint of enticement. She suspected Noel had something important to discuss, something the children need not overhear.

Once they'd settled themselves around the big kitchen table, Mary was the first to start. "Hear about the Clarks' new general store?" she said, passing around some walnut muffins she'd made. She spoke quickly and, it seemed to Lucy, rather nervously.

"Bigger than the old one?" Lucy asked. "No wait, before you start on those muffins, let me make some coffee." She busied herself for a few moments, filling the big tin coffee pot at the sink pump, emptying in three spoonfuls of grounds into the basket, setting it on a front burner of the range.

She opened the grate and stirred up the fire, which had almost gone out. All this time Mary and Noel remained silent. Yet there was a nervous tenseness about them, an expectancy. She sat back down at the table and waited.

Mary finally ventured, "Say, Lucy, did you hear about doctor Maynard?"

"No use for that man, Mary. He didn't come in time to save Bernard."

"But Lucy, listen. Friday's *Long Prairie Argus* had a story about the trial."

"What trial?"

"The one about the man accused of robbing, then murdering him and trying to make it look like an accident at a railroad crossing, that crossing on the way to Twin Oaks."

"Well," said Lucy bitterly, "that explains some things, but it doesn't bring Bernard back. Whatever the reason—I can't but hold him responsible for what happened."

"He's paid the price."

"Nonetheless—" The sound of coffee boiling in the pot made her get up and take down three mugs from their hooks on the sideboard. As she filled them, she noticed Mary leaning over, whispering something to Noel. What are they up to? Lucy wondered. Obviously this was no ordinary visit. At last it came out.

"*Eh bien, chère belle-soeur*—er, that is, my dear sister-in-law—" he cleared his throat again. Lucy had learned that he—as well as Bernard—fell back on French words when under stress. He began tracing the checkered designs on the tablecloth intently for a moment or two. Then, exchanging another look with Mary, "*Eh bien, assai de bavardage.* Enough chit chat, eh, Marie? Now *chère* Lucy, you are getting along on this place?"

"Well enough," she answered tersely. "More coffee?"
Noel shook his head. "*Non, merci.* We ask—*eh bien*, we ask because we are family. We are concerned."

"Yes, Lucy dear. We worry about you." Her solicitous remarks confirmed Lucy's suspicions about a conspiracy of sorts. When would they get to the point?

"And so we ask ourselves—*excuse-moi* for being so blunt—what if you sold this homestead?"

Now it comes out, thought Lucy. They assumed she'd be helpless on her own. Would force her to sell. "Well, no," she heard herself saying with forced conviction, "no need to sell, this is our—my—home, the children's." She saw Noel and Mary exchange another look, another subtle set of signals.

"*Eh bien*, Lucy," Noel began again slowly, hesitantly. Then, in a rush of words, "Listen. We have a plan. It is one plan excellent. A big step, risky, *peut-être*. But—*le voici*—here it is."

Lucy shook her head. "Don't bother. I know what's best for me." She wondered how much she should tell them about Smith's offer. Was Smith God's agent for consolation? Was Noel?

"At least, please listen, Lucy," Mary pleaded, "don't be so stubborn. You must listen."

"All right, I'll listen," she decided to say, "although I warn you, my mind is already made up—if you call that stubborn, Mary."

"Made up and stubborn for certain," Noel answered with a wry smile, "we know you, do we not? But *le voici*. To make short the point. Do you know the DeLaurier place? Old homestead down the road from Little Sauk to the Narrows."

"Only a few miles from us," Mary added helpfully.

"No," she answered, surprised at this unexpected turn in the conversation, "can't say as I do."

"Well, it's for sale," Mary interjected, "or rather, was for sale. What Noel's trying to say is, when the DeLaurier family put their homestead up for sale last fall, planning to move out west to North Dakota—near Bismark, I think—Noel went over to look at it. He was interested because . . ."

"Because this very homestead is so close to ours, across the road and two farms down toward the Narrows Bridge. Because—would you believe it? What do I discover? They also have twenty acres on my side of the road, rye from long time, border my own rye field, better crop than mine, even. And so, *naturellement*—naturally, what else could I do?"

"Well, I'm going to be blunt as well, Noel. Why buy another farm? You already own I don't know how many acres."

"No, you see," Mary explained. "it was too good an opportunity to miss. Big house, newly remodeled—lots of land. Good neighbors, too—the Skinners, the Sweitzers, the Holbergs—"

The Holbergs. . . neighbors. Those men . . . that man, across her husband's grave . . . Lucy's mind raced with images, strange inexplicable images.

"So we hope our children will eventually settle here, raise their own families nearby."

"I still don't—" Lucy said vaguely as she shook her head.

"*Eh bien,* we have one problem," said Noel. "You see, this place is now empty. There is a long time wait for our children—Josie only thirteen, Raymond only eleven. And Sarah's only six. So—what meantime?"

"Rent it out."

"The problem, precisement—precisely! Too long to rent, Mary not content with strangers in the house, too close, too—maybe, even, not reliable with the property."

Mary drew herself up and took a deep breath. "Which is why we're offering it to you as a tenant."

"To me?" It was out.

"But of course," Noel added. "Here is what we say. We need you and your children in this DeLaurier house until that moment comes when we know what to do with it, when we can pass it on to one of our children. Those fields I can work along with my own fields, take down a few fences even, use my hired hands, sow and harvest all together."

"You know Noel," Mary smiled, "always so practical about things like that."

"But what about this place?" Lucy cried. She was losing patience. "Are you telling me I must sell it?"

Noel hesitated, then said, "well. . . well, yes. Impossible for you to manage alone. Sell, put that money in the bank for—who knows what later. As it happens, I perhaps have a buyer for your place."

Lucy's heart sank. "Is it someone named Smith?" Now her thoughts turned to the possibility of a demonic conspiracy.

"Smith? Do not know the name. No, one of the men looking at the DeLaurier place, name of Lundgren. Very anxious he is to settle here, two brothers already in Gray Eagle." He leaned back in his chair and grinned in self-satisfaction. "Now, is it not a proposition *très bonne*—very good? Do you agree? Yes?"

The back door burst open. "Ma! Saw a wolf out there!" Martin shouted. "Sniffing 'round the barn."

"We put the kittens in a box in the loft," said Raymond. "Safer there."

"Are we going home soon, Mama?" Josie asked hopefully. "I've so much homework for tomorrow."

Lucy was saved from having to answer Noel's question. His proposal had come too suddenly, and, worse still, veiled equally as both divinely and demonically inspired.

She needed time to think about it, although she was certain of one thing—selling the homestead would be selling part of Bernard's life. And now that Elias Smith planned to come back on Tuesday, she had to make a hasty decision. There wasn't much time.

Over the next few sleepless nights, Lucy's mind raced with questions and answers, a debate between staying and leaving, between keeping and selling—she couldn't seem to think clearly. If only Noel were here—if only Bernard were here. Someone . . . dreams and waking moments searched frantically for some sign, some indication of the direction she must take. None came.

At last Tuesday morning came. She waited anxiously, apprehensively, for the sound of Smith's buggy, the buggy which would bring him and the surveyor to go over her land, the land which Bernard had worked for, in a sense died for. It was this last thought which provided the resolution she needed.

The sound of his buggy, a knock on her door. She smoothed back her hair, took off her apron as she left the kitchen and headed down the hall, shaping the needed words in her head. They came readily as she thought about Noel's offer, about Mary's enticements, about the possibility of seeing Mattias Holberg again, and perhaps after that. . .

RIVERS RISING

No! SHE WOULD NOT SELL HER HOMESTEAD to those men. Something about Smith . . . or that smirking man named Cliff. Pushing, forcing her to defend her land's very boundary lines, the number of acres, the well water, the behavior of the river itself. That wasn't the only reason, though. It would be a betrayal of all she had left of Bernard. As for Noel Dubois' offer . . .

"How are you getting on, Lucy?" Noel asked, stopping by on horseback two days later. "John Wold brought over the rye seeds yet?"

Lucy was relieved he came alone, without Mary. It was impossible to face them both just now. She was still unsettled after that emotional encounter with that man Smith and his surveyor. "Your loss, then, missus," he'd shouted, after she'd refused to go ahead with the sale. He'd slammed the front door with a stream of abusive threats.

"As well as could be expected, Noel," Lucy said vaguely, hanging his jacket on the pegs by the door and set a chair. "No, mister Wold's not shown up yet."

"Should have. Seeds have to be in the ground while the spring rain holds. *Eh bien,* I get after him. Come to think of it, didn't I hear the Holbergs offer help?"

"I couldn't ask them. You never know how sincere people are with offers like that." But Lucy knew perfectly well there were other reasons.

"*Probablement* occupied with their own place. Fine young men, Sep has. Too bad they struggle so long, so hard to—to *réussir*—make a go of it. Their homestead acres bad, not much yield these past two, three years. Those brothers ready to move on, out west, Sep tells me. Good, free land out in Montana."

Lucy suspended in mid-air the coffee mug she was filling for Noel. "What did you say?"

"Those Holbergs—been talking about leaving for last year or so."

She abruptly set down the mug on the table. "Oh. I see." It felt as if the floorboards under her feet were giving way.

"*Mais oui.* "Good land out there. Maybe *la bonne fortune*—she smiles on them, oui?" He picked up his mug. "*Eh bien,* only half a cup this morning?"

Lucy tried to recover herself. "Oh, sorry," she said, going back to the stove for the pot, feeling as though she'd just been delivered a shock to the heart for which she'd been totally unprepared. What reason was there now to accept Noel's offer of the DeLaurier House?

As if reading her mind, or part of it at least, "You remember about the DeLaurier place, eh?"

The subject came up too soon. Giving herself a little time, she poured herself a mug of coffee, deliberately set the pot back on the stove, filled the sugar basin from a canister in the cupboard, pulled out a chair, and sat down opposite him. "You want my decision now? "

He looked surprised, embarrassed. After a moment of preoccupation with his coffee mug, dropping in two spoons of sugar, stirring somewhat decisively with the spoon clinking from side to side, he cleared his throat. "*Mon dieu,* Lucy. Always were a woman for being direct."

"Life is short. There's so much to do. Right now Laurence and I need to go gather the eggs in the hen house. Children will be home late, a cleanup day at Prairie Lake schoolhouse."

"*Eh bien.*" Again he cleared his throat. "That is *precisement* what I came to speak about."

"The eggs—or the hens? Or the cleanup day?"

"Lucy, you know *precisement* what I mean. Have you come to a decision yet?"

"About what? The eggs or—"

He set down his mug in annoyance. "Lucy, you know exactly what I mean. *Mon dieu,* you can be so—so—*énervante!*" When Lucy made no comment, he sighed and started again. "You've thought it over? My proposal—the proposal of Mary and myself. About the house."

The moment she'd dreaded. "The old homestead you just bought? What was the name of it?"

"DeLaurier place. Just north of my spread."

"Oh, yes. Well, what about it?"

He sighed, heaved up his shoulders. "*Énervante! Tu sais très bien,* Lucy. We've already explained. It's empty now. Needs a tenant."

Obviously this torrent of French meant he was losing patience. Should she give him an answer? If she turned him down, he'd be hurt and angry. She wasn't ready to give up her homestead. Yet what if she couldn't manage it, the crops failed, stock got sick—or the children? Or herself?

Noel sighed again, impatiently fingering the buttons on his wool shirt. Finally he said, "I must tell you, we may have a good tenant. I need to let Nils Lundgren know very soon, so it's necessary to know first what you want. I am making this offer—*parce que*—because you are—you are *de famille.*" He paused again. "The widow of my brother."

Now it was Noel coming directly to the point. Lucy pushed back her chair, got up stiffly from the table and placed the empty mugs in the dry sink. She arranged and rearranged them, moved the coffee pot off the range.

She walked over to the small kitchen window that faced the east pasture and stood there in silence for a moment, looking out on the faint whiteness of the first blossoming apple trees. Brownling was out grazing with her new calf. Mid-April, the prairie grass already greened to delicate iridescence. The silhouetted black branches of the oaks showed first buds. Down by the river lingered a faint haze of golden willows.

"*Eh bien?*" Noel looked increasingly uncomfortable. "I listen."

She turned away from the window. In a rush of words she blurted, "Noel, I appreciate your offer. So generous. So reassuring that you—and Mary—are concerned with my family—our future. But I'm not ready—not ready, you undersand. Not ready to accept it. No, not just now."

Noel remained silent for a moment. "Ah, *oui*," he finally said slowly. "Ah, *oui*."

She knew he was puzzled, disappointed. What could she say? "I know I owe you a better explanation. My gratitude is—is—is beyond bounds. But it's difficult for me to explain." To explain her inner conflicts—Bernard's death, her guilty feelings about her attraction to Mattias Holberg, to come to terms with the apparent hopelessness of any future relationship in view of his intention to leave for the West—this she could not do. Not to Noel. Hardly to herself.

When he didn't answer, merely kept tracing designs on the table cloth with the handle of his spoon, she realized more words were necessary. "This place, you see, it's part of me. Part of me and Bernard. Part of our children. Just as your place is part of you—all your hard work, your memories."

"Ah, *oui*," he repeated, more thoughtfully. Then, looking up, "*Difficile, oui*. But I think I understand. Yes, that is life here. *Moi, je comprends*. Life on these prairies. I think of my own *patrimoine*—my old home—the *chateau* of my father—" He got up from the table and buttoned up his jacket. "I go now. Next to find Monsieur Lundgren. He needs to move in his family soon. Before the planting season is over. Yes, soon."

What more could she say? She followed him out the back door to where he'd tied his big bay to the porch post. As he stepped up heavily into the saddle, she stammered, "Yes, soon."

For days afterward that decision tormented her. What if . . . what if . . . those words running through her mind over and over again. A thousand possibilities, successes, disappointments, failures.

Jack Johnson arrived early Saturday morning with his teen-aged sons, Tim and James. "Boys go directly out to the barn," he said, standing in the back doorway. "Clean out a couple of stalls while I hitch up that horse of yours, see if'n I can plow the lower field yet. Plantin' already late."

"Don't have the seeds."

"How's that?"

"John Wold was supposed to pick them up at Lano's in Long Prairie. I haven't seen him yet."

Jack looked worried. "Well, best get on to him 'bout that. Can't wait much longer." He shrugged as he went around the house toward the barn.

Turning back to her work in the kitchen—wiping off the bread-board, sprinkling out some flour, emptying a lump of moist dough out of the big mixing bowl, she wondered whether she should send word to Noel, reminding him about the seeds. But after turning down his gener-ous offer, could she now ask for his help?

Kneading the dough, aggressively attacking it, pushing, pulling, hit-ting it down with her fist, she began to realize she was somehow acting out those worries lying repressed within her. Yet there was another feel-ing deep within her body, sensations denied in disbelief. She immedi-ately dismissed it and punched in the dough more vigorously.

It wasn't long before Jack Johnson returned, pausing to take off his muddy boots outside on the back porch. "Can't do it yet," he an-nounced. "Water ain't gone down one bit. 'Fact, come up another cou-ple of yards. Spreading into that little piece of north pasture."

Lucy's heart sank. When Jack earlier predicted the loss of those fifty acres due to flooding, she'd hoped he be wrong. The water had al-ways gone down by planting time. Somehow that odious man, Smith, had guessed it, had denied the land's value as a result. "What about that south piece alongside the road?"

"Dunno 'bout that. Have to take a look at it. Only part of it cleared, as I recall. Your husband always intended—"

"Yes, yes—never had the time, I'm afraid."

"Well, I'll see what I can do 'bout it. Need some help clearin', though. Takes time, takes time—them big old oak trees, mighty resist-ant."

He pulled on his boots. "Got to get back to my place. Lots to do there—won't have no crops myself if'n I don't get busy." As he climbed up into his wagon with Tim and James, he added, "My missus be over day after tomorrow. Sure looks like you need help inside—well as out."

"You look—look *müde*—tired," remarked Jack's wife, Marika, several days later, as she studied Lucy thoughtfully and clucked her tongue.

They were folding laundry together, arranging it in piles on the big bed. Sheets, pillow cases, night dresses, underclothes—it had taken most of the day to wash, peg things to the clothesline, bring it all in late that afternoon. It filled the small bedroom with the fresh smell of sunshine and grass. It seemed a shame to fold it things up and force them down into the dark confines of the cedar chest at the foot of the bed.

"Well, Marika, I do apppreciate your concern," Lucy answered. "Guess it's no surprise I look tired. Or you, either, for that matter. Washing day always is exhausting, and it would've been much worse without your help. Most grateful to you—and to Jack and the boys for all their help." She added another sheet to the chest, pressing it down with unnecessary care, betraying her concern as to how long she could ask for it. "But don't worry, I'll be fine after a good night's rest."

Marika smiled as she held up one of Laurence's little shirts. "Gets bigger, your *kleine junge.* Need to save."

"Of course. I'll pass it on to Mary Dubois."

"She expect again? *Mein Gott!*"

"Their fifth or sixth, I think. Hard to keep up. That shirt probably came from them in the first place. My children are in several generations of hand-me-downs, so to speak." No need to waste money, Mary always argued. As if those Dubois didn't have enough already. She felt a twinge of guilt over her criticism and recognized its basis was jealousy.

Yet, despite Lucy's self-assurance, the next morning Lucy could not get up. She felt the night's rest had never happened, as if one day had passed directly into the next. It was getting late. Hank the Plymouth rooster had been crowing away in the barnyard across the road for a good hour already. Laurence was crying upstairs, wanting to come down from his crib in the loft. Sabine and Martin needed to get ready for school. So much, so many things.

Her body felt like a dead weight pressing against springs of the parlor's horsehair sofa, where she'd been sleeping since Bernard's death. Forcing herself to put her feet on the floorboards, to stand up, she felt a wave of dizziness, of nausea. She reached for the edge of the headboard to steady herself, then rushed toward the kitchen to vomit into the sink. A realization. An unconscious denial all along. A disbelief. Bernard—it must have been only a week before the accident, only a few weeks before he died—yes, Bernard had given her one last gift, one last child.

That night, for the first time since Bernard's death, Lucy slept in the big bed which she and Bernard had shared for the past nine years. The fresh linen sheets, scented with the promise of spring, was comforting. The bed, with its high-carved head and foot, now seemed a kind of sanctuary, a space protected and nourishing the new life growing within her. Outside were the usual night sounds . . . an owl hooting in the big oak tree beside the back porch, a strong west wind off the Dakotas, rustling the prairie grasses, flinging a few twigs against the window pane. Far down by the river marshes she heard the falling cadence of a sora.

Her exhausted body drifted between sleep and waking, dreaming, remembering. The comfort of Bernard's strong arms around her, their talks about choosing children's names to link them with France, with Quebec. The times for spring planting, the harvest, next Christmas.

Yet more than once Bernard's nightmares kept her awake, strangely revealing those anxieties and fears hidden from her. "Lucy . . . do you . . . *tu sais que . . . guerre . . .*" He'd lapse into French, struggling to say something about the war, the struggle between his memories of the siege of Vicksburg and the frustration of forgetting the English words to describe them. The horrors of it, the exploding cannon that wounded him and killed many others. She'd heard some details, not from Bernard, but rather from his brother, Noel. Clearly Bernard's healing was beyond her. The war had left scars not only disfiguring parts of his body, but some lying deep within him, deep within the recesses of his brain. Those regions he struggled to suppress, not only from her, but also from himself.

Was he at peace now? She'd not considered this possibility before. *Requiesecat in pacem.* Strangely, unexpectedly, the thought now comforted her.

Dawn the next morning brought sharp contrast to those fleeting moment of peace and consolation she'd experienced during the night. Although she'd heard the wind pick up and rain begin to fall heavily toward morning, she hadn't anticipated the results. Looking out the small kitchen window while preparing breakfast, Lucy saw the rain had stopped, but broken branches littered the yard.

"Big storm's comin'," announced Martin ominously, his mouth full of oatmeal. "Do we have to go to school today?"

"How do you know, smarty?" retorted Sabine. "Besides, Missus Hamline promised I could help her put up the pictures we drew for geography class."

Lucy glanced out the window again. "Look, a bit of sun coming through. There's Brownling already out in the pasture with her new calf. So hurry up, now, or you'll be late. Just watch out for branches and stuff in the road on your way. Martin, I don't have to tell you to stay out of the puddles!"

"But you just did, Maw. You did just tell me."

"And none of that back talk, either."

Just after they'd left, however, Lucy began to worry. The sky was quickly clouding over with heavy, black clouds. Now, from a dead calm, the wind began to rise, at first strongly from the southwest, then shifting to the northeast. In the distance there were strong, erratic flashes of lighting reaching right down into the trees, followed by deep, rumbling thunder. Laurence began to whimper, wanting her to hold him in the rocking chair in the parlor.

She lifted the chimney off the glass oil lamp on the little table before the window, took the box of matches out of the drawer, and lit the wick. Taking Laurence in her arms, she rocked him back and forth. In the rhythmic motion, she sang to him whatever snatches of childhood songs she could remember. The one *maman* used to sing, the one she and her sister used to sing together with her—"*Sur le pont, d'Avignon . . . L'on y dance, l'on y dance . . .*"

Lucy's mind was scarcely on the remembering, however, or the words. She was thinking of Sabine and Martin, who'd left about an hour ago, heading for school in Prairie Lake. Surely, after the three-mile walk, they were there by now. Surely they were safe, surely their teacher, Missus Hamline, knew, what to do. "*Sur le pont, d'Avignon . . .*"

A tremendous clap of thunder shook the house. The lamp on the table teetered and smashed to the floor, where the smoldering wick ignited some spilled oil. Hardly realizing what she was doing, she snatched up the braided rug before the fireplace and threw it over the flames, then snatched up the dishpan in the kitchen sink, still full of soapy water from the breakfast dishes, and poured it on the rug.

Another clap of thunder shook the house, even closer than before. Laurence screamed in terror and kept crying for his stuffed lion, Leo. Increasingly stronger howls of wind buffeted the house again and again.

No denying that this was a major storm. Martin was right, for once. Looking out the kitchen window, she noticed that the sky had turned yellowish green toward the southwest, surrounded in all directions by black clouds, racing violently through the sky. And the wind had once again shifted, this time from the west.

Lucy knew that storms like this often came in the spring. None, however, had ever seemed like this. She remembered once reading about one in the *Long Prairie Argus*, back about the time Martin was still a baby. That storm struck Elona, nearly wiping out the town. Five people had been killed, crushed under trees, or their houses. The newspaper had called it a tornado. The thought raced through her mind that she and Laurence might be crushed by such a tornado. That the Prairie Lake school house might be blown off its foundations and spun around like a top, the children spinning and spinning in the air until they fell to their deaths, drowned in rivers, in lakes.

Snatching up Laurence, she rushed out the back door and pulled open the flat, double doors to the root cellar below the kitchen. There was no time to check on the horses, Socks and Blaize. She only hoped Jack had turned them out to open pasture as he'd done with the cow and calf.

Trying to stop Laurence's terrified cries, she said, "Come, darling, let's do a little exploring down here in this old cellar. Maybe we'll find some treasure, do you think?"

But Laurence still clung to her neck sobbing, while she tried to pull the doors shut over them. Twice the wind whipped them out of her hands before she could pull them closed. Now they were enveloped in darkness, with only faint stabs of light coming through the cracks in the doorframe. It was hard to see the three or four steps leading down to the earthen floor and she almost fell. The place smelled damp, musty, of rotting apples from last September's harvest. A small hole dug underneath one corner of the kitchen and lined with shelves, there was nowhere to sit except on a wooden box from Lano's in one corner with a few remaining glass jars for putting up jams and jellies. Holding Laurence tightly, she sat down on the box, swaying her body slightly back and forth in nervous apprehension. And waited.

Outside the wind howled with intermittent roars like some wild beast. It rattled the cellar doors, whistled through the cracks, and threatened to burst them open any moment. In her anxiety she forgot about Bernard, the children at school, the flooded acres down along the Sauk. She forgot even about her nausea and swelling belly. She wondered whether the cellar doors would hold, whether the relentless wind might suck them out in an instant and dash them both against the sodden ground, the trees, the house.

Desperately she tried to shift those images into something safer, more comforting. Mattias—Mattias Holberg. The name kept running through her mind, reproducing with it images of a tall, blond bearded man, standing tall and strong, not opposite at her husband's grave site, but now in his own field, amidst rows of golden wheat. *Come*, he was saying, *stand here with me—you will be safe—safe—*

"Oh help me," she cried out against the wind. "Help us!"

Laurence's cries had exhausted him. He pressed his face against Lucy's shoulder as he clung to her neck, breathing in short gasps. She realized she was having difficulty breathing as well. A strange force sucked the breath from her body, a humming, vibrating noise in her ears. Were they about to die?

Her apprehension rose as she heard strange noises above the howling wind—the screech of what must be the wind uprooting a tree, the crash of wood against wood, the chatter of hail stones, the frightened whinny of a horse.

It seemed an eternity before the noise gradually lessened. With a few final bursts of wind-driven rain, the storm seemed to be passing northward, accompanied by ever more distant claps of thunder. Slowly the strange greenish light seeping in through the cellar doors turned to gray, then to pale sunlight. At last the only sounds were Laurence's weak, gasping breath, and the slow, regular dripping of water from tree branches outside.

"It's gone, darling," she said. "Passed over."

Raising his head from her shoulder, he looked puzzled. "Te-sor? No te-sor?"

"No, Laurence. No treasure down here, except finding out we're still alive. That's worth more. Now hold tight to Mama, while I carry you up the stairs." She sighed with relief. She'd been spared, her child as well. Surely there was a reason.

Flinging open the cellar doors and looking around her at the swath of devastation, she uttered a cry of despair. Two big oaks down, a gigantic limb from one of them blocking the back door. The body of their best plow horse, Socks, lying dead not ten feet away. A large section of the cedar-shingle roof blown off, the shakes strewn around and into the pasture. The loft window broken, some stones from the chimney gouged out and nowhere to be seen. The back porch steps ripped off and flung against the pasture fence. The yard around the house so littered with tree branches that it was almost impossible to walk through it.

Still, the sun was shining. The homestead cabin had survived. They had survived.

"Ma!" exclaimed Sabine the next morning, as she, Lucy, and Martin—even Laurence—worked to pile debris in a corner of the yard, "will we ever get this mess cleaned up?"

"Seems hopeless," Martin complained. "No fun sleepin' down in the parlor, either. And Laurence—stay out of the way. You're no help at all!"

"Your uncle said he'd send a couple of men over to fix the roof." Lucy threw another armload of tree branches onto the pile. "Meantime, good thing Mister Johnson had a tarp to put over the hole. Besides, the beddings all wet—that's why it's all spread out over the fence to dry. And what's wrong with the parlor? Nicest room in the house. We'll build a fire in the fireplace tonight, and we'll have a picnic there with toast and cocoa."

Martin mumbled something as he continued to stack rescued shakes in a pile under the kitchen window. Then, pointing over to a the far corner of the yard, "Over there, Laurence—see that one? Bring it here. You can at least do that, can't you?"

"For that matter, young man," Lucy added, "count yourself lucky—you and your sister—that the Prairie Lake school was only slightly damaged, that you got a ride home early last evening in Miss Hamline's buggy."

"Suppose so," he answered grudgingly, then brightened as he added, "Well, least ways no school for a while." He pointed across the yard. "No, Laurence—I said over there!"

At least she could still use that pail jammed up against the fence. At least Brownling and her calf were safely back in the barn along with Blaize. That the barn still stood, with only one window shattered. Hay littered the whole barnyard, even way down the road. Even though the outhouse back of the cabin was untouched, the hen house beside the barn across the road was tipped over, and the chickens scattered. They'd had a hard time just before it got dark last night chasing them down as they ran around the barnyard, out into the fields, and down the road.

How strange, she thought, that the storm badly damaged some places, left others untouched. Was that something like life itself, she wondered, one person taken, another spared? Surely there was some reason for that.

There was no time to contemplate such troublesome thoughts, however, for Jack and his boys, along with another neighbor, were entering the yard in Jack's wagon. "Brought my bucksaw, couple axes," Jack pointed out. "Holberg, here, too. Said he'd be glad to help."

Lucy's heart skipped a beat. Mattias had come, after all. She hadn't had to ask. He'd known to come, he'd known!

"Mornin', ma'am," he said, climbing down out of the wagon. "Thought you might need some help." He looked closely at her, then turned away shyly.

Her words simply would not come. She was relieved when the men busied themselves with unloading the wagon.

"Mattias here'll get busy on them branches, missus. Wood too green for firewood, I 'spect. So's we'll just stack it up longside your chimney, you can use it come next fall, I reckon. Sure was a weird storm, all right."

"Tornado," Mattias offered. "Seen couple of them before. Freakish. Can't ever tell what they'll do—or where. But ma'am—consider how lucky you were. Children, too." He bowed his head slightly toward her. "Only too glad to be of help." After a pause, he added, "My brother Erik wanted to come but I—but I —" He broke off, his face reddened, and he turned away toward the nearest fallen branch.

So, here he was, beside her. She watched him, lifting the heavy logs, powerfully swinging an axe to break them up. It was difficult to focus elsewhere because of his presence, and she couldn't explain it. Each blow of his axe sent a ripple of muscle across his back and shoulders.

Just as the others began to saw through the massive oak branch blocking the back door, John Wold drew up in Noel's buckboard, obviously loaded with wooden boxes, gunny sacks, and a large plow share. "Mornin', ma'am," he said to Lucy, tipping his straw hat. "Brought a few things, compliments of Mister Dubois. Said he thought you'd need these.'"

"Mornin', Wold. Help you unload?" Jack Johnson handed his end of the bucksaw to Tim, and strode over to the wagon.

"Thanks kindly," said Wold. "I'd appreciate a hand."

"Wait, wait, gentlemen," cried Lucy. "You're sure of that? Noel Dubois sent all this?" Embarrassing to be seen accepting such charity.

"Yes'um." Wold proceeded to lift out the first box. "Where'll I set this, ma'am? Looks like can't get in the back door."

"No, wait—" She hesitated, struck by the dilemma. Should she refuse what Noel had sent? Yet what food had she left in the house, how soon could she take Blaize and the wagon down to Thurstrom's general store in Little Sauk for provisions? And for how long would they grant her credit? The bill had been growing since Bernard's death.

There seemed no alternative. She well knew it would take time and effort to clean up the debris, make repairs, get the sowing done. She needed whatever he'd brought, as embarrassing as it was to demonstrate that need before Mattias Holberg.

"Wait, I'll let you in the front way," she found herself saying as she led the way around the corner of the house.

"Finally picked up them rye seeds," Wold said, setting down the box in the front hall and extracting a small cloth sack. "I'll talk to Jack 'bout this. Doin' the sowin' for you, Mister Dubois said?"

"That's right, probably next day or so. Been busy at his own place."

By the time Lucy had unpacked the box on the kitchen table—a smoked ham, crocks of pickles and preserves, a sack of potatoes, and a jug of cider—Wold had gone back around the house and was in an animated argument with Jack.

It seemed to her that Mattias looked her way more than once. It gave her an uncomfortable feeling, that strange conflict of senses, which she could not explain.

"I tell you, it's too late!"

"But now, Jack, Mister Dubois said—"

"No, it's too late to plant them seeds. Besides, couldn't plant 'em even if'n t'weren't."

"What d'ya mean?"

"I mean there ain't no place to plant 'em."

"No place? Why, there's them bottom fifty acres. Mister Dubois said—"

"They're gone. Gone, I tell you. Under water from the river—even more taken away by them rains yesterday. Up into the lower north pasture by now."

His words struck like a knife through Lucy's whole body, piercing the very womb that held her baby, slicing through to her very soul. Gone. One-third of her whole spread. Maybe two-thirds of all her useable land. It wasn't because of John Wold's negligence. Nor lack of Jack's efforts. It was due to water. Simply, water—the weather—the elements, the earth itself.

"Right sorry, ma'am," Mattias offered. "I'd help you if I could, but you see, me and my brother—well, the truth be told, our place not much better off than yours."

And now what could she do? Her choices were few, his announcement disappointing. Had she thought that—Well, she didn't know what she'd thought.

In a kind of daze, with words of thanks spoken almost automatically, she watched the men finish their work and reload Jack's wagon. In one last gesture, Mattias Holberg went over to where Laurence, screaming for help, had gotten entangled in a pile of fallen branches. He pulled him out, brushed him off, and placed him in Lucy's arms.

"Here's your boy," he said, "none the worse for wear, I hope." With that he climbed up into Jack's waiting wagon, gave a half wave and nod in Lucy's direction, and was gone.

Summer 3 Spaces

B Y EARLY JULY, THE RIVER RECEDED enough to reveal ten empty furrows along the south edge of the fifty-acre field. From that edge, Lucy stood looking down upon their emptiness, that rich earth barren, never sown this season because of the flooding.

On an impulse, she picked up a handful of soil and let it sift slowly through her fingers. A fleeting memory of standing beside Bernard's grave, letting the snowflakes fall glittering in the sunlight, down onto his coffin. An instantaneous memory of that one act, that link to a single moment in time, yet linked to timeless emotions impossible to dispel, linked as it was to a tall, blond man standing hatless in the weak sunlight of a March day on the other side of that grave.

"Ma, do'ya think that river's anything like the Amazing River my teacher told us about?" Sabine had come down toward the edge of the field with her, the water lapping at her feet.

Lucy smiled. "You mean the Amazon, in Brazil. We've already talked about it—it's much bigger." It had been some time since her own geography lessons, but she remembered comparing it with the St. Lawrence of Quebec, which seemed as wide and as deep as the sea itself.

"I see Martin down at the bend, fishing. There's Laurence playing around the rocks. I sure hope Martin keeps an eye on him. Think Martin'll catch anything?"

"I hope so." Any food from the land—or the river, for that matter—was precious. She'd bartered enough over the past two months of whatever they could spare to a passing peddler in exchange for soap, to Thurstrom's in exchange for flour and coffee, to the neighbors for hay and corn, to Ridgeview Dry Goods for overalls for the boys. A week ago Blaize needed to be shod at Bertrand's smithy, and she'd paid with a jug of apple cider from the cellar.

All this humiliated her. By far the worst was parting with some of Bernard's clothes, especially the jacket he'd been wearing when he fell, the muffler she'd knitted for him last Christmas. She'd drawn the line at his old Union army uniform. That was carefully folded and put away with camphor deep down at the bottom of the cedar chest at the foot of their bed, along with a photograph taken when he'd first joined the Minnesota Third regiment at Ft. Snelling back in 1862. Bernard sat stiffly in an ornate chair before a draped flag, hands on his knees, looking as eager for battle as if he really understood the war's cause or its purpose.

"Expect we'll have more river trout for supper," she said.

"Oh, not again," wailed Sabine.

"Maybe there's some rhubarb left in the garden." Smiling, Lucy added, "You know, I once read a recipe in the *Long Prairie Argus* for a compote made from roasted rhubarb and maple syrup. And I think there's one last jug of syrup still down in the root cellar. Shall we try it?" Yet she found it difficult to convey any enthusiasm. Her own appetite for fish was not much better than the children's. Each day presented new discomforts as her body prepared for the coming birth.

It occurred to her, in fact, that her increasing belly seemed to keep pace with her increasing anxiety. The approaching winter was not something she could face at the moment. "Come, Sabine, let's go back up to the house. But first, please go down and get Laurence. No telling what he might do when Martin's not paying attention."

Jack's predictions about a meager rye crop proved accurate enough. Once the neighbors, who'd joined together to hire a threshing crew with a steam thresher, brought in the sheaves, the crop fell far short of a good yield. Jack took them down in his big wagon, along with his own harvest, to the central grain market down in Sauk Centre.

"Did best I could, Lucy," he'd said apologetically, handing her an envelope from the bank. "What's here'll maybe buy some new shoes for your two eldest, need 'em to start school next week."

The evening on the day school started in the repaired Prairie Lake schoolhouse, Lucy and her daughter sat talking together in the kitchen. Laurence and Martin were finishing up their chores in the barn. Sabine talked eagerly about their first day of school, how she'd been promoted to fourth grade, Martin to second, how miss Hamline now had an assistant— a girl not much older than herself, and maybe next year she'd be the one.

"Teacher said I was smart enough," she said proudly. "If I work hard enough. But, you know, Ma, seems to me I already work hard enough 'round here. Taking care of those chickens, weeding the garden and all. Not to mention looking after Laurence."

"Yes, dear, we've all worked hard this summer. Worked desperately hard, even Laurence discovers things he can do, like carrying in fire wood—even if only one stick at a time, which he keeps dropping." They both laughed, remembering some of the predicaments he'd gotten into, like once getting locked in the outhouse.

That night Lucy sat in the kitchen, the children in bed, the house hushed, trying to take a hard look at her situation. Her increasing awkwardness, her sleepless nights and the pains periodically shooting through her body made it hard to do anything. Optimistic hopes for the rye crop yield proved false. Brownling's calf? Well, that sale was still a month off.

There was, however, one positive thing. The Holbergs had postponed their move to Montana. When asked, Noel seemed a bit evasive on that point. *Ne pas certain*, he'd say. *Cela depend*—but he never said what it depended upon, only that the brothers had some big, innovative idea about dairy farming out west.

Sitting alone in the kitchen with the lengthening shadows of a late summer's evening, unwilling to light the oil lamp over the table, Lucy's mind was in turmoil. Was she herself ready to face the facts of her own situation? Several times she'd thought about moving into town, even as early as last July. Before that, even, she'd thought about selling this homestead, a possibility she could even now hardly accept. Under the circumstances, however, it was coming to that, perhaps even—although she resisted admitting it—inevitable.

Her mind teemed with possibilities. With the homestead sale money she could rent a small place in Prairie Lake and find a job somewhere. Or perhaps Long Prairie, a bigger town, more possibilities. Perhaps at Reagan's—no, no, unthinkable. She'd never go back there. A shop somewhere. West's general store, Lano's. The bank. Surely women could get jobs. She'd seen a few during infrequent trips to town. Maybe an assistant in a school—if Sabine's miss Hamline had one, why couldn't she do that? She could read, write, teach French.

Noel Dubois's offer last April? Too late now, he already had a tenant. What was he thinking in making that offer in the first place? That she couldn't succeed on her own? Was he right? The sense of shame in that likelihood was overwhelming. Overcome with so many questions, so many emotions, she laid her head on the table and let go with wrenching sobs. It was the first time she had wept since Bernard's death.

Next Friday morning, leading Laurence by the hand as she entered West's general store in Long Prairie, Lucy's nervous anxiety made it difficult to breath. Besides, the crepe festooned widow's bonnet, borrowed again from the Johnsons, sat heavily on her head, its ribbons choking, its musty odor nauseating.

"Yes, miss?" A middle-aged man, bespectacled, reddish hair fringed around a balding crown, looked up from behind a long counter at the back. He wore a black vest over a white shirt, a long white apron from the waist down. "May I help you?"

She'd been in West's several times, usually just before Christmas, and recognized him as the proprietor, Homer West. Apparently he failed to recognize her, which was just as well.

"I've come—I'd like—you see—" She could not get it out.

"Would this handsome young lad like a piece of penny candy?" He smiled engagingly as he reached into a large glass jar and took out a greenish lump, which he offered to Laurence. Laurence looked down and pressed his head into his mother's skirt.

"He's rather shy, sir, but I'm sure he'd like it. Say thank you, darling." But Laurence stepped farther back. She had thought that the boy's physical presence would at least offer some support, but he was no help afterall.

"Now then, what can I do for you, miss? What do you need today? Some staples? Flour, sugar perhaps? Good price on cornmeal today. He took the pencil from behind his ear and held it poised over a notepad."

"No, thank you, no staples." She had to say it, and say it before things went further. "No, I need a job."

West looked shocked. "A—job? Here? In this establishment?"

"Yes, sir. I'm a widow. Moving into town from down near Prairie Lake. Is there something—"

"I'm afraid I can't—you see, there is—well I'd like to offer —" His engaging manner rapidly dissolved as he stumbled over his words.

"I've had good schooling, reckoning, write a good hand."

He came out from behind the counter and stared at her bonnet, her face, her belly. "What could you expect to do, a woman in your condition? Even if I had an opening in my establishment, I'd no sooner hire you than you'd be off giving birth somewhere. A widow? Who'd look after the children? Expect them to run out of control around this establishment, breaking things, stealing candy? Really, madam, I'm surprised that you'd even—"

Lucy did not wait for him to finish. She grabbed Laurence by the hand and headed toward the door, her face felt flushed, her knees weak. Yes, the man was right. How could she?

"Want candy," Laurence wailed, and he started to cry as they headed down the board walk along Main Street toward where Blaize was hitched with the wagon.

"Some other time," she said. "You'll see." Now she was passing by Reagan's Hostelry, where the saloon's stale smells of beer and cigars brought back traumatic memories of her time working out there, before she married Bernard. Bernard had saved her from that place, however much she recognized that love had brought them together. Perhaps Henry Morton, for all his faults, had saved her sister Agnes, although not the way her parents had hoped; the element of love lay in doubt. Agnes never talked about whether she was happy with Henry or not. Anywhere near the subject and her mouth would tense up and the subject abruptly changed.

"Well, well, if it isn't Missus Dubois." Tim Reagan's son, Patrick, who'd taken over the hostelry after his father had been jailed on conspiracy charges connected with his gambling operation, was standing outside on the boardwalk.

"Condolences on your husband's passing. My apologies for not having the opportunity to express them earlier. I see you have your youngster with you. My, my, what a fine young fellow." He patted Laurence on the head, who would have backed away but for his fascination with Reagan's bright red brocaded waistcoat.

"Thank you, mister Reagan," Lucy said, finding it difficult to say more, hoping to move past him as quickly as possible.

"You shopping in town?"

"Yes."

"If there's anything I can do—"

"Thank you, sir. No, nothing." She swept past him, stepping off the boardwalk onto the street, and now, only three yards from her hitched wagon, the notion struck her. The time was now, not then. The man was Patrick Reagan, not Tim Reagan. She was a grown woman, not an eighteen-year-old innocent.

"Laurence, darling," she said. "Get up into the wagon and stay there until I get back. Only a few minutes." She mounted the boardwalk just as Reagan was going back into the saloon. "Wait, sir," she called. "There may be something." When he said nothing, simply looked expectantly at her, she continued. "You see, we may soon move into town."

"Oh, that so?"

"The farm—without my husband—"

"Yes, Missus Dubois, I think I understand. So when might that be?"

"I don't know. It depends—"

"Well, let me know. If you need help—" He gave her a strange look, half friendly, half calculating.

Lucy did not know how to continue. At a loss, she readjusted her bonnet strings, took a step backward. "I—yes, Mister Reagan—I shall let you know. Soon, perhaps." Then she turned quickly back toward the waiting wagon.

She had her step on the wheel spoke and was pulling herself up onto the driving bench when Reagan caught up with her.

"Wait, wait a moment," he said, staring at her swollen belly. "Come back and see me, after the baby's born. It could be—well, it could be that

I may have something. Yes, something most suitable for an attractive young woman like you, with your breeding, your education. Yes, I'll do my best for you, Missus Dubois." He'd laid particular emphasis on the word missus. He offered her a hand up to the bench. "You'll let me know, won't you?" Then he added with a smile, "You know where I'll be, of course."

"How awful, how uncomfortable all that was," she said to herself, to Laurence, to no one else in particular as she whipped up Blaize and headed her wagon south as fast as it was safe to drive, south down the main road between Long Prairie and Sauk Centre. "Don't know how to take him. Courteous enough, but yet—"

Her brief encounter with Patrick Reagan had led to no disappointments, no hopes, no promises, yet it disturbed her greatly. It was just as she passed the road east toward Eagle Lake, the road leading to her sister's farm and mill, that Lucy met Agnes's elder son, Abe Morton. Evidently he was coming into town with a wagonload of bricks from their clay hole down by the river.

"Hello, there, Auntie," he called. "Just leaving? No time for a chat, cup of coffee, and a piece of pie at Matheson's?"

"Afraid not, Abe. Laurence is getting restless and the children almost due home from school. Must get back. By the way, how's your father doing?"

"Up and down, up and down. Doctor says a man of sixty-three got to expect more down than up. Especially him, considering what he's been through and his heart condition and all. Say, I'd like that piece of pie, can't beat old Ma Matheson's, but lots to do myself. These here bricks—see, we've got a new imprint on 'em? MBW for Morton Brick Works. We're turning out more, now we've got that steam engine hitched up to the clay press. Well, after delivery to Lano's hardware, I'm s'posed to go to the big auction outside Farley's livery stable."

"Big auction? For what?"

"Buying, of course. You prob'ly heard my sister Jane's getting hitched. Maybe going out west soon with her better half. They got big plans, you see. She gave me a list a mile long of things she wants. Sure don't know where they'll put 'em all in a covered wagon. Unless they ship 'em by freight. Heard the Northern Line railway's planning to run all the way out to Glendive. How's this for our modern age, eh?"

He laughed, then turned serious. "Trouble is, Paw don't like her intended. Says he's a no good, he and Maw arguing 'bout that. Sure don't know what'll come of it." He paused, picked up the reins. "Well, got to get moving. Hup! Hup!" He pushed off the brake and eased the wagon forward.

"Tell Jane that I—" Lucy called out. But he'd already turned the corner onto Main Street.

Urging Blaize down the road, she considered Abe's unexpected news. So Agnes's foster-daughter was getting married, about to leave home, despite her father's opposition. How would that effect Agnes? An extra strain on the family, more likely, because Agnes depended so much on the girl, now almost a grown woman of eighteen.

Suddenly the thought struck her. Suppose she moved in with Agnes and Henry? Not that she liked him much. But, still, they could join households, resources, regroup the family. Without Jane, Agnes could use her help and Sabine's, Henry's condition being what it was. Say, maybe she could take over Agnes's job in the brickworks office. As for the boys, well, Martin and Tom were the same age, got along well. And now with her own baby coming . . . It seemed a hopeful, a possible solution. She wouldn't dismiss it. Not yet, anyway.

She recalled Abe had mentioned something about an auction. She hadn't thought of that for money, either. Perhaps she could sell some of the furniture. The horsehair sofa—the parlor table—the bed. No, not the bed. Must be something else. With lists forming in her mind, she glanced back at Laurence, now curled up and asleep in his "blankey," the quilt he always carried with him. Pulling hard on Blaize's left rein, she turned the wagon around in the middle of the road and headed for Farley's stable.

"Five dollars, do I hear five-fifty? Five—five—" There was a huge crowd gathered around an assortment of furniture, boxes, tack, bales of straw, lumber, old window frames. Hitching Blaize to the nearest rail, she pressed in as far as she could. How did auctions work? How often? What kind of prices asked? How much could she expect?

"Say, there, little lady," asked a tall, burly man, making a place for her. "You interested in that there sideboard? I'll make a good bid for you—only ask ten percent of what you pay." He smiled as he took her arm.

"No," she said, extracting herself. "Not interested in that piece." She paused. "But can you tell me—how does a person get things here? Put them up for auction? Is there someone to ask?"

"Sure, miss," he said. "See that there man in the top hat, sittin' up on the platform? That's mister Guyer. He's in charge, him and the auctioneer next to him. Big crowd today, lots of bargains. Say, what are you interested in?"

"I'm not sure," she answered lamely.

"Well, ma'am, those Lundgrens—they had plenty of stuff. Couldn't take it all with 'em when they took off for Montana."

Lucy looked at him, puzzled. "The Lundgrens?"

"You know, that family rentin' out the old DeLaurier homestead, down near Little Sauk."

"You say they left for Montana? When was that?"

"Oh, 'bout a month ago, I reckon. Seems their oldest son came into a large spread. Wanted to start up a cattle farm—ranch, believe they call it."

"And left all that furniture?"

"Well, ma'am, kind a hard travelin' across the prairies so loaded down. Best to sell some of it, big pieces 'specially, use the money. Mister Dubois, they left him to take care of it." He paused to survey the crowd. "Don't see him around right now. Expect he's got other things to do, what with the last of the harvestin' and all. Big spread like he's got down around Little Sauk."

In a daze, Lucy pushed her way out of the crowd, the auctioneer's cries ringing in her ears—fine chest—set por-su-lan dishes—five—ten cents—seven dollars—Noel's tenants for the DeLaurier place. Already moved out. The house once again waiting. Empty.

Why hadn't he offered it to her again, once the Lundgrens changed their minds? She wanted to think it was because he wanted her to make up her own mind, wanted to force her to do so, to come to terms with his charity. She would have preferred to think that his motive was to reserve it for her alone, a question of *famille*, as he once said.

Now what was she to do? Did she dare approach Noel? How humiliating that would be. She'd be admitting she'd failed. Worse still, in abandoning the homestead, she'd be betraying Bernard. There was also the possibility Noel would not renew his offer. He had his pride as well. As for Mary—she most likely had mixed feelings. *Had your chance, what do you expect us to do now?* Or, on the other side, *I'm not sure I want you closer to Noel.*

Yet—and yet—the rye yield minimal. The price for the calf unknown. West's rejection. Reagan's insinuating and suggestive words. The stench of beer and cigar smoke. Winter coming. A baby coming. Alone on a snow-bound prairie. Firewood running out. Martin too young to split logs or clear two feet of snow from the lane, the barnyard. Sabine too young to look after a new-born and a three-year-old.

And then, possibly a reason just as critical in her mind but unconsciously suppressed. The Holbergs. Neighbors. Not yet left for the West.

A thousand images, crowding her brain, spinning webs of confusion, doubt, anxiety, helplessness—all at once.

Her road home passed through Little Sauk. She'd always thought the town should have been named Four Corners. At the crossroads, the road went east toward Prairie Lake. Noel's road went west, their homestead only about a quarter of a mile farther on. Hardly aware of the passing miles south, hardly conscious of reining Blaize around deep ruts and holes in the worn road, she suddenly realized they were there. The crossroads. Thurstrum's general store on the left, schoolhouse on the right. The crossroads of decision.

"Whoa, boy," she called as she jerked back the reins and threw the brake lever forward. The wagon rolled to a sudden stop.

"Why stopping, Mama?" asked Laurence, waking up with a start. He stood up and pointed left. "Home that way."

"Sit down, Laurence, or you'll fall out." She hesitated. East—or west? Her hand reached for the brake lever. With a cry to Blaize, she flicked the reins and the wagon turned to the right.

That last quarter of a mile. Her mind in a turmoil, torn between hope and the possibility of Noel's refusal. Now their large house came in sight. Newly refurbished from a humble homestead, two storied, verandahs, around it scattered barns, storage sheds. Noel Dubois, the grand *seigneur*, as Bernard jokingly called him. Not far beyond their house, just down the road, was the DeLaurier house. Should she drive on past and look at it?

No, her courage would not extend that far. Instead, she drove into the lane beside Noel's house and tied Blaize's reins to the hitching post. Taking Laurence in her arms, she mounted the short flight of steps and raised the elaborate brass knocker on the front door.

A few moments later, she and Mary were sitting in the front parlor, Laurence in Lucy's lap, looking around him in awe. "I hope my visit isn't at an awkward time for you," she said.

"Not at all," Mary answered smoothly. "An unexpected pleasure. Baby Guy just nursed, put down for his nap."

"How are you and the children?" She could hear several of them playing upstairs. "And Noel?" Lucy desperately hoped Noel was around, that she would not have to bring up the subject with Mary.

"Quite busy, as you might expect. And yours? I'm sure you all are kept busy, too, especially now that school's started. The days aren't long enough to take care of everything, are they?"

Lucy grew more uncomfortable. She sensed this was Mary's way of getting even with her for letting them down. "We manage, I suppose."

Mary continued with her usual small talk—how the village was growing, the school expanding with two new teachers, the bounty of their rye and wheat crops, a new recipe for cucumber relish. "Laurence, darling, would you like to go upstairs with your cousins?"

At last Lucy's courage gave out. "No, we really must leave." She could not continue, could not bring up the subject she'd come for. She slid Laurence off her lap and rose to leave. "I really must get home. My children must be already home from school."

"Well, sorry you can't stay. I'm sure Noel will regret missing you. Won't you let me give you some of those cucumber pickles? Stay, won't you? I'll just go out to the kitchen and put some in a little crock. Be right back."

Waiting out on the porch, Lucy's frustrated anger rose. After reaching such a hard decision, such an impossible decision, she'd lost this opportunity. There was no turning back now.

Heavy footsteps sounded on the stairs at the other end of the porch. "Ah, Lucy, I see your wagon, your Blaize, and I say to myself, here is *ma belle-soeur* come to pay an unexpected visit. And, would you believe it, also this young *gentilhomme* beside her." He embraced her with one of his warm, bear-like hugs, stroked Laurence's fair hair. "Tell me, *quelles nouvelles*—what news?"

Lucy drew herself up, resolving this time not to miss the opportunity. "You know I'm always direct."

"*Mais oui. Certainment.*"

"That DeLaurier place—the Lundgrens have moved out. It's empty?"

He hesitated. "*Mais oui.*"

"What are your plans?"

He turned away and leaned against the porch railing, looking out over his yard as if searching for something—a rodent, a forgotten child's toy. Finally, facing her, he said slowly, "Tell me—what are *your* plans?"

Less than a week later, Lucy found herself moving through the empty rooms with Noel and Mary, rooms musty through vacancy and darkened by closed shutters. Her impressions were mixed, confused. The one thing she was certain about was that the house had a strong presence about it.

"Something about this house—" she remarked to Mary. "Doesn't it make you feel—well, strange?"

"Why, no, a lot of old houses seem strange at first—maybe it's the smell."

"The last DeLaurier family? How many were there?"

"Why, this homestead was one of the earliest in the county, built about 1850." Mary seemed all too content to rattle on about the house. "That was long before Noel and Bernard acquired their mustering out grants after the war, must be at least two or three generations ago."

"Who built it, then?" Lucy asked. The place intrigued her. She wanted to know more.

"This will interest you, I'm sure," Mary replied, "because it was another French settler, named Pierre DeLaurier. Came from Canada—no relation to me, of course, my family were settlers from Manitoba, the Joinvilles, you know." Mary never lost an opportunity to impress people.

"At first this place was a small, one-room log cabin, almost a shanty, built in haste to settle his homestead claim. Then, in time, the shanty became a cabin, the cabin a house—just like Noel did with ours, Bernard like yours, except Bernard didn't quite get that far, did he? The usual upstairs loft, then a kitchen spur."

"We'd hoped to make an upper floor with separate bedrooms," Lucy added in self-defense. "Never had the money."

"Well old Pierre DeLaurier, now, he had good land, no prairie wilderness tracts, like yours—or your parents."

Another status barb. Lucy bit her lip. "How many acres, then?"

"Oh, the usual 160-acre homestead claim for the county."

They were looking out the kitchen window. "What's over there beyond that low rise to the north? Looks like the trees haven't been cleared."

"The land drops down to river bottom. That's the Sauk River, same river, you know, that runs behind your homestead. People say there are some meadows along the river down there, good for pasturage. I've never ventured that far, even though I was friends with Marianne De-Laurier and often came over for visits."

"Beyond here—west. Where does the road go?"

"To the Narrows, about four miles. It's actually a bridge, where the Sauk River where comes out of a big lake called Osakis. Then there's that other twenty acres. Don't ask me to explain why about twenty acres of the DeLaurier place is on the other side of the road that runs in front of this house. And, as it happens, they're squeezed in between our parcel to the east and the south."

"Why on earth divide up the spread like that?"

"Who knows? Actually it's one of the reasons Noel was interested in buying this place. Now that he's bought this whole property, he'll eventually just incorporate those fields into our own."

"Shouldn't think he has to wait—why not just annex them now?"

"Well, you see, he—we—hope that keeping this place intact will make it more attractive to Raymond later."

"This house, now. It really doesn't look like much of the old house remains, inside or out. Maybe that's why I was confused. Was it re-built, then?"

"Looks like a large part of it was, although I suspect the old log homestead is still intact inside the walls, the inner shell you might say, the heart of the house. Most likely DeLaurier's son faced over the logs with white boards on the outside, re-did the inside with plaster, wall paper. It was Marianne who insisted on the green shutters and the fancy gingerbread work around the eaves."

"How about that big front porch?"

"Her, too. We used to sit out there on a summer's afternoon."

"Wouldn't expect to have much time for that," said Lucy. Let Mary take that remark as she wished.

Despite the constrast between her old log homestead and the De-Laurier house, despite its musty, shut-up feeling, Lucy felt strangely attracted. She couldn't resist imagining her horsehair sofa along the far wall in the parlor, or the carved walnut bed in that spacious front bedroom upstairs. Nice that a big brass bed had been left behind in one bedroom, a large braided rag rug in another. She supposed they'd been sacrificed as too awkward to move across the Dakotas in a prairie schooner, or maybe just left in haste and never made it to the auction.

And that stairway which curved gracefully up to the right of the entrance hall—how the children would love playing on it, sliding down the banister. The wide front hall ended with a heavy paneled door, locked by means of a big, brass key. At the top was a small, fan-shaped window. How different from the old hall, so dark and narrow.

Standing there, she hoped she'd made the right decision. So major, so unsettling, that she experienced a shortness of breath . . . moistness in her palms—a tremor down her spine. Only time would reveal the wisdom of it.

The sound of footsteps above, creaking floorboards, murmured conversation, broke into her train of thought. Noel and Mary were taking measurements, walking from room to room, windows and doors opening, shutting.

"Lucy, you'll need to replace the curtains," Mary called down. "Just look how faded and rotted by the sun they've become, disgusting! And a broken window, too, curtains billowing out, water stains on the floor."

Replace the curtains, Lucy reflected—wasn't her own life being replaced? A new house, a new life—without Bernard. She sat down heavily at the bottom of the curved DeLaurier stairs, overwhelmed. It was the moment for tears.

But no tears came. There came, instead, a moment of revelation. Her new life could be here, in this new space, even if Bernard would not share it. Perhaps she needed no partner to share it. Suppose there was a way to manage on her own, without Noel, with Mattias leaving? Without any man at all? On her own, yes, perhaps on her own.

WHISPERS THROUGH THE HOUSE

OCTOBER CAME, AND WITH IT THE MOVE, the last whispers of lives past, the first whispers of life to come. Lucy stood in the barnyard of the DeLaurier house, struggling with the implications of both.

"*Eh bien*, Lucy, to believe you had so much in that little cabin back there! On this road—how many times we come already, eh?"

Noel, along with his neighbor, Sep Holberg, unloaded the last of her belongings from Noel's big farm wagon in the barnyard of the old DeLaurier place. Sep had used his own wagon for earlier loads, and it was now standing over in one corner of the barnyard, his horse allowed to graze in the nearby pasture. She wondered why Mattias hadn't come with him, or another son. She hoped it wasn't because they were preparing to leave for Montana. October wasn't safe, snows could hit the northern plains anytime now. More than one wagon train was lost that way, her sister's among them, along with the man it's said she married. No, there was more than one reason she hoped Mattias wasn't leaving. Now, idly glancing at the wagon, she also wondered why one side of the Holberg wagon was painted blue, an oddity she'd noticed at Bernard's funeral. Had they run out of paint, or just become tired of the job?

Noel lifted out a small washstand and set it down on the grass. "*Eh bien*, the last piece? Now, Sep, we take a rest, eh? At least one of your big strapping sons should help."

"Agreed, Noel," replied Sep, "but you know darn well it's late harvest time—all three of them needed in the west five acres, since we hired out one of them new fangled steam threshers. Had to finish by end of today. Other folks want it. Got Schweitzer and his oldest boy to help in exchange for usin' the machine for his own wheat. Lot more to do around the place afore—" He broke off to fan himself with his straw hat. "Sure is a warm one today, though. Warm for October, Indian Summer, they call it."

"Good sign or bad?" Noel asked.

"Dunno 'bout that." Sep smoothed back his graying hair and replaced his hat. "Say, what're your plans for that DeLaurier back forty? Thinkin' of lettin' that field go fallow come spring? Maybe a better yield next season."

Both men leaned against the sideboard of the Noel's big wagon, mopping their faces on the backs of their sleeves and exchanging comments about crops, the weather. Noel took out a Mason jar of water from a basket of provisions Mary had packed at sunrise that morning, gulped down several swallows, and offered it to Sep.

"Prob'ly right, there, Sep. Enough land here on this place to bring in a fair crop. Heard from young DeLaurier once, before they moved on, their granary barn usually filled to the rafters."

"Still, timber brings in a fair price these days."

"Sure thing. Plenty of building, railroads needing ties. Good profits to be made there, you know. Heard that from some of those fancy railroad men, up in Long Prairie, over at Reagan's . . ." He glanced guiltily at Lucy as he made a quick decision not to speak further about Reagan's saloon. He knew how she felt about the place.

With a helpless sigh, Lucy looked around at her belongings. They stood scattered all over the barnyard—a group of kitchen chairs here, a wooden crate there. She'd not been able to see much of the outside of the house before. That raw September day a month ago, when she'd come with Noel and Mary to look at the place, to make her decision, darkness had come early because of the storm. Was that storm a bad portent? She'd know soon enough.

What she needed now was how to situate herself in it and try to possess it. Watching Noel and Sep Holberg stretch out on the grass, chatting about one man thing or another, her imagination visualized the area around her. That thing called a map—Sabine had shown her one she was making for her geography class. Lucy had never seen one before. What a marvel to look down on the earth from above and know exactly where you were.

First of all, the barnyard was behind the house, not across the main road as it was for the old homestead, where the road split the spread in two. Here, from the main east-west road, a U-shaped lane looped around the back of the house, through the barnyard, to connect again to the main road. At the south front of the house, a brick walk connected the driving lane to the steps of the front porch. At the northeast corner of the house, just off the back stoop, there was a large, abandoned kitchen garden. To the east of the main barn was a small granary. She and Bernard had never had enough harvest to fill one. She could imagine that granary filled, as the DeLauriers filled it, each grain promising greater riches. Now it stood empty, its door swinging back and forth on rusty hinges.

Shifting her vision slightly, she mapped out the left side of the main barn, where the outhouse stood, attractively faced with white boards and shingled as if to mimic the house. Behind the barn was a fenced-in area in which she recognized raspberry canes, last season's berries dried on their thorny stems, their leaves curled and brown. Beyond stood a big apple orchard with a few apples hanging on stubbornly. Most lay rotting on the ground, their pungent, cidery smell filling the air.

Still, despite the neglect, the waste, it seemed like paradise to her. So much promise of abundance, the large house like an island in its midst. Viewing all that neglect and waste, Lucy wondered whether, when spring came, she'd be capable of bringing the place to rebirth? Right now, however, she must think about the birth of her baby, so close to its time.

Noel had propped the disassembled carved walnut bed up against an old, gnarled oak tree near the front corner of the house. In the middle of its brilliant fall cycle of golden leaves, the tree threw a delicate shade over most of the yard, the furniture, the boxes. In that strange, shimmering golden light, Lucy's mind-map took on an ethereal quality. And in her mind was the nagging thought that it was all unreal, not a part of her present and very real world, with its warmth, its odors, its gentle breeze.

The men stood up, preparing to leave. She was suddenly overwhelmed by the thought of how much she owed them, Noel especially. "I'm so very grateful to you, Noel, and you as well, Mister Holberg. Not to mention Mary's help as well. Such a blessing to have the children looked after these past few days. Especially starting in their new school at Sauk Centre. Frankly, I don't know how I would have managed otherwise."

"With your time so near," commented Noel, "it was the least we— that is, Mary, could do." He recapped the Mason jar of water and placed it and the provision basket tucked into a corner of the wagon. "*Eh bien, mon ami* Sep, we go home, no? Time for noon dinner, Mary promises chicken with dumplings."

"Right with you," said Sep. "But, if you wouldn't mind going a little out of your way to drop me off at my place first? Just couple miles down the road. Too much trouble hitch up my wagon when I'm coming right back. One of my sons can bring me. The missus expecting me." He managed a rueful smile. "Maybe not for chicken and dumplings, though."

"Well, *mon ami*," Noel answered, "least I can do for your help. Was it three loads since yesterday? Have lost count, for sure."

He turned quickly to where Lucy was carrying a kitchen chair to the back porch. "*Non, non* Lucy! *Arrete, arrete, ne pas*—leave those things to us. And you must not stay here alone until we come back. *Allez-y,* let me help you into the wagon." He took her by the elbow. "You come home for dinner with Mary and me, yes? Then we all come back, carry everything inside the house."

Lucy shook her head. "No, but thank you, Noel. I'd prefer to stay here, to get a little more used to the place. It'll take time, you know."

"*Eh bien,*" Noel commented with a shrug and guarded wink to Sep, "I know better than to argue. Here, then," he said, taking the basket of provisions out of the wagon and setting it down at her feet. "Here, take this—not much, only some corn bread, maybe still a ham sandwich." He rocked back on his heels, putting his thumbs into his belt. "*Eh bien*, you know Holberg—he eats like a—dunno what. But whatever, you must eat to keep the strength."

Lucy couldn't help but smile—it was Noel who'd eaten at least five of the sandwiches and most of the cornbread, along with several pieces of Mary's special Bishop's Bread and half a jar of her dill pickles. He'd always been a prodigious eater himself, as his girth announced, although curiously it never seemed to interfere with his great strength.

Once Noel's team pulled out of the barnyard and turned into the lane connecting to the main road, she longed for a place to sit down. Her body ached with fatigue. Intermittent pains shot through her belly, the baby continually making known its eagerness to enter the world.

Yet there was another difficulty, the one in her brain. In addition to sheer fatigue of body, her mind seemed overwhelmed. Her whole life with Bernard was packed away and now surrounding her. In that box were his tools and his old army rifle. Way down in the bottom of the big cedar chest lay his army photograph, enfolded within his Union uniform. Folded next to it was the dark blue, flower-sprigged dress she'd worn at his funeral. She'd never worn it since, but, like the uniform, she could not part with it. They seemed to identify certain roles, certain periods in their lives, which were indelibly interwoven within it.

The old parlor rocking chair beckoned invitingly, and she sank gratefully into it. After an earlier load that same morning, Noel had set it down at the bottom of the earthen ramp leading up into the barn. From inside came the occasional low mooing of a cow, the restless movements of a tethered horse. The livestock had been brought over yesterday, with Noel's hired man John Wold driving the wagon pulled by Blaize. In it were her chickens in wicker cages and some bales of hay. Brownling was tied on behind the wagon, the cow reluctantly being towed with her calf, and the calf continually trying to wander off in the opposite direction. It must have been quite a sight—a traveling barnyard going down the road like that—chickens, squawking and clucking, Brown-ling baulking. It felt good to laugh. Unexpectedly, it released some of the tension and anxiety within her.

And how good it was to rest! For a moment, relief was all that filled her mind. She closed her eyes, pressed her fists to her temples, and rocked back and forth, back and forth. That creaking rhythm of the rockers—like wood sawing or the rocking of a cradle. It reminded her of Laurence's cradle when he was a baby, the cradle which Bernard had made out of red oak, first for Sabine, then for Martin, finally for Laurence. An empty cradle for now, an empty garden. The rhythmic sounds, rocking, whispering something . . .

She woke with a start. "Missus, you haven't touched your dinner yet!" Sep and one of his sons were leaning over her.

The ham sandwich she'd started to unwrap from Mary's linen napkin had slid off her lap onto the ground and was covered with ants. She didn't know how long she'd dozed off. She still felt more exhausted than hungry. "Oh, I'm sorry about the sandwich," she said apologetically.

"Don't fret about that, missus," said Sep. "I'll just throw it over to the chickens, they'll 'preciate it."

Lucy started to lift herself out of the rocking chair, but her body felt so heavy she fell back. "Oh, dear," she said, "don't seem to have the strength after sitting so long."

"Here, allow me, ma'am." It took her a few seconds to realize that he was Erik Holberg, Mattias's brother. He put a strong hand under her elbow and eased her up. "Careful, now, hang onto me for a minute, 'til you feel steady."

"You're very kind, thank you . . . I'm not sure of . . ." In fact, Lucy wasn't sure of anything. The man's touch, his brother's touch—"I'm not sure—" she repeated vaguely, reaching for the back of the chair to steady herself. His blond resemblance to Mattias was uncanny, his voice very similar.

"All right, son," Sep interrupted, "best get back to work. Noel's of-fered me a ride home when we're done."

"I could stay, Pa. Help Missus Dubois more." Slowly he released her arm, but continued to stand close to her, the earthy smell of his jacket strong in her nostrils, the impression of his tallness above her vivid. "Mattias and the others—they're doing well enough without me."

"No, Erik, we'll manage here, eh Sep? Done in an hour or so," Noel pointed out. "So now we begin to place what belongs in the house. Now this house begins to be a real house." He picked up one end of the sofa, and motioned Sep to take the other.

Was she disappointed? Lucy, for the first time, felt a strange confusion. Erik so like his brother. His gentleness, his touch, his concern. Yes, a strange confusion of impressions. She was almost sorry when he headed back toward his team, acutely aware when he turned to look back at her, mouthed words she couldn't make out.

Absently, she started to drag the rocking chair toward the back door. "No, no, Lucy, no, *pas de tout*! You not do that, not at all. I—we men lift , you direct. So—inside, you say where this goes, where that!"

When the house begins to be a real house—Noel's word echoed in her memory all the next week. Yes, it was beginning. Most of the furniture was in place, most of the crates unpacked, Mary's new lace curtains hung in the bedroom windows, some billowing out like miniature sails when a breeze moved through the house. Delighted Martin once described the house as a clipper ship, sailing through seas of prairie grass. Yes, that was fitting. It was a new voyage they were taking in life.

John Wold came over with Sep several times to get the barn in order. Each time Lucy hoped he'd brought Mattias. Once, in fact, she'd caught herself thinking not of Mattias but Erik. Yet there was always a confusion, a conflict in those thoughts she failed to understand. She threw herself into awaiting tasks. There was still much to do. Hay in the loft, the tack sorted out and hung in the tack room. The wagon wheels greased. Plans for the spring garden.

It disturbed Lucy greatly that she was so helpless. Worse, still, it seemed that Wold did more than Noel had asked. Increasingly he spent more time talking to her or simply staring at her. She was in no position to deny his help, and so each time she devised small strategies to avoid him.

Toward the end of the second week in the DeLaurier house, there came a knock at the kitchen door. Lucy gasped. Wold again! And she alone in the house with only Laurence, since Sabine and Martin had just gone off to their new school in Little Sauk. They'd been picked up just at the main road by a passing wagon and saved much of the long walk.

Pretending not to hear it, Lucy went on cleaning the shelves inside the kitchen sideboard in order to unpack the last of the wooden crates. She was eager to set on display along the groove in the upper shelf the four Limoges plates *maman* had given her and Bernard as a wedding present. They were very old, her mother had said, very valuable, but perhaps more valuable to her because they'd come all the way from France. Moreover, they were beautiful with a delicate pattern of vine leaves and pale yellow flowers, some small violets peeping out from behind a few bronze colored leaves, the porcelain so thin you could almost see through it, with a fine gold edge around the outside

"Can't do much in this kitchen until it's set to rights, can we, darling? Let's start with the dishes here from this crate," she remarked half to herself, half to Laurence, who sat on the floor trying to unwrap heavy folds of newspaper. Another knock, more insistent. "Hush, Laurence," she cautioned, putting her finger to her lips. "No noise."

"Look, Mama," he said in a loud voice as he reached into the crate and took out a wad of newspaper. "I can help, see!" He tore off the last fold of newspaper and there was a penetrating crash.

"Oh, dear, now look, one of my Limoges plates—oh Laurence!" He began to cry, and she knelt down to put her arms around him. "It's all right, my darling," she said, trying to sooth him, "It's all right—only one old dish. Here, don't cry now. Mama will find something else for you to help with." Laurence gave another wail of despair.

What's all that caterwauling about, then?" said a stern voice. "You wail like a cat in . . . well, never mind. Boy, stop all that noise this instant,

I say! Do you hear me?" There was a choked gasp from Laurence. "Such a big noise from such a little tyke," the woman added.

From her position kneeling on the floor beside Laurence, Lucy saw a pair of large, black, button-hook boots beside her. Following her gaze upward, she saw a long white apron over a green gingham dress, a black wool shawl criss-crossed tightly over a woman's breast and tucked into a wide leather belt. The woman's face, looking out from a black straw bonnet tied firmly under her chin by a piece of string, looked stern and tanned by the sun. Wisps of iron-gray hair escaped from under the bonnet's brim here and there, giving the woman a wild look. She seemed very tall, and once Lucy got to her feet, the woman towered over her. Impossible to know what to say to the woman, her surprise took any coherent words away. Laurence simply gaped.

"Here, don't touch those broken pieces or you'll cut yourself. Reckon it'd serve you right." The woman pulled Laurence away. "Now hand me something to clean this up with," she commanded Lucy.

Still speechless, Lucy went into the mudroom and came back with a broom and a dustpan.

"You, young man, no more wailing, do you hear? You just sit right over there in that corner and don't move." The woman swept up the broken china in swift, deft movements, then emptied the dustpan with a crash into the rubbish bucket near the back door. She wiped her hands on her apron, turned to Lucy, and leaned back, hands on hips. "Now then," she said in an authoritative voice, "how do. I'm your neighbor two spreads east, name's Skinner, Margaret Louise Skinner—some call me Mother Megs."

She held out her hand. Lucy shook it, wincing a little at the woman's firm grasp. Like a man's, she thought.

"Don't mind if I do." Without being invited, the woman abruptly sat down in one of the kitchen chairs, removed her bonnet, and laid it on the table. Laurence still sat open-mouthed on the floor, apparently forgetting all about the recent crisis with the Limoges plate.

"And your name's Lucy Guyette Dubois. Heard all 'bout you from your sister-in-law, Mary Dubois. Seems like I met your ma and pa—the

Guyettes—some years ago, homestead couple miles south of Little Sauk, before they took off right sudden like, back to Shakopee. Sorry about your husband. So young, too, prime of life. As tragic a story as any. Heard you met him while you were helping Mary with her young'uns when you were working at Reagan's— you and your sister Agnes working out in the saloon. That is, 'til she married that feller name Morton, then all that 'bout him bein' accused of murder."

Lucy gasped again. This woman seemed to know everything. What right had she to push her way in here? Take over the house?

"Yes, Missus Dubois, must have been a right trying time for you. Good that Bernard Dubois came to your rescue, though. Married right off."

How dare this woman? Lucy's anger was rising. It wasn't like that with Bernard. They'd fallen in love. She had other choices. But Bernard—well, he was the one. And it wasn't that he had no other choices, either.

Almost as if reading her mind, the woman continued. "Yes, siree, not hard for a woman to get married these parts. So many men for so few women, men even known to get a mail-order bride. Maybe you and your hubby luckier than most, didn't have to go that route."

Hardly stopping for breath, she pointed to Laurence. "This your youngest? Where your other young'uns? Oh, at school, of course. Hope they're settling in all right down here at Little Sauk. Don't know much about that school. No children of my own, you see. Appreciate a glass of water, if you don't mind. Little bit of a walk down the road from my place, you know. Hot sun for this time of year. Still the likes of Indian Summer."

Lucy quickly filled a glass from the pump beside the kitchen sink and handed it to her. "Who—" she started to ask.

"I thank'ee." The woman drained the glass in a few gulps. "Sure goes down well. You'd better sit down in one of those chairs there—looks like you're nearly due. Now then—"

Up to this point Lucy had not been able to get in a word. What kind of woman was this, anyway? Came in uninvited. Should have left the backdoor locked. Knew everything about her. Rattling on and on. "Why—" she started to say, but sat down as ordered in the nearest chair.

"You're bein' nearly due is why I'm here. Heard that from Mary Dubois. She 'n' I do a bit of mid-wifery round here—me more'n her. She's got so many young'uns of her own, you see. Mary told me to come see you, introduce myself, like. And so, here I am. Mother Megs, some folks call me, or Maggie will do nicely, thank you. Be pleased if you'd call me that, too." She paused to see if there was any more water in the glass." Lucy hurried to refill it. "Now then. Let's get on with this business of birthing."

Lucy hardly knew how to respond. Mother Meg's stern looks matched her manner. Her small, black eyes seemed to pierce right through everything. A large nose dominated her face, and a very firm mouth spat out words in rapid succession. Laurence still sat motionless on the floor, staring at her as if mesmerized.

"Thank you—Maggie," she finally managed, although this didn't seem quite appropriate. "It's good of you to come. I—I haven't been able to meet all the neighbors, yet. You see, I—"

"Well of course, woman," Maggie snapped. "Can't be expected to. All this unpacking, setting to rights. Chaos, dirt, never my thing, but I can say that order is. Now then, let's get back to the business of birthing. Birth—God's business of order, you might say. You'll be needing me soon, looks like."

"No," protested Lucy. "I'll be sending for a doctor, Doctor Wilson in Long Prairie. My son Martin can go in to fetch him when the baby starts coming. He's only seven but can already hitch the horse, drive the wagon. The doctor already knows. Went to see him last month."

"Yes, yes, so you think—and so he thinks. But what if there's no time?" Maggie replied. "Some babies just pop out unexpected like, hardly any labor at all. No guarantee yours won't. No siree. No predicting anything where birthin's concerned. Mary Dubois and me, we know better. Lot of experience around here, me in Iowa before I came here five years ago with my husband, Lemuel, for his claim. Burned out twice, we've been, but still keep on. No sense crying over spilled milk—over blackened embers, I should say—ha, ha. Now about birthing. Not often will women turn to a doctor for that, you know—prefer a woman. And there sure ain't no women doctors around here yet, although I've heard of a few back East."

Lucy felt uneasy. Although she'd had misgivings about trusting a doctor from Long Prairie for this coming birth—the memory of doctor Maynard was still fresh in her mind—and now, to trust this weird woman? A woman she didn't even know? This pregnancy had been difficult. A mid-wife rather than a doctor of medicine? Could she trust this woman for Bernard's last gift?

As if again reading her thoughts, Maggie said: "Now listen, my girl, you've got to trust me. Besides, Mary's too far away, too busy these days. There's Greta Schweitzer next farm down, but she's not so experienced—could come to help, but not take charge. But you can bet your boots, I'll be here for you, soon's you call. You can be certain of that."

"How will I do that?"

"Well, here's what we do 'round here. You can send one of your young'uns, I'm just under a half mile east down the road. Or you can signal."

"Signal? "

"Women 'round here have worked out a pretty good system. Soon's you feel the first pain—the first, mind you, don't wait—you can hang a white sheet out on one of the bushes at the main road—somebody passing, maybe even the next farm over sees it, passes the signal on down the road. Or, you can put a little linseed oil on the stove fire—sends up puffs of black smoke, can see 'em for miles."

She rose to go, tying the string of her bonnet with a determined last tug. "Now don't forget, call me soon's you feel the first pain, and you should know by now how that feels. Well, good morning to you, pleased to have made your acquaintance I'm sure. And as for you, young man, make sure you behave yourself." And she was out the door.

It wasn't but a week later that Lucy had to put Maggie Skinner's signal system to use, although not as easily as she'd been led to believe. The first pain began late one Sunday morning. It was a stormy, rainy, late fall morning, the sky heavy with leaden gray clouds. Intermittent showers drenched the country side, followed by periods of violent wind, which whipped the budding trees into frenzied activity and rattled the windows of the house. Lucy wondered whether the house would stand. She was alone except for Laurence, since Noel and Mary had taken the other two into town for church. They planned to make a full day's family event out of it, eating noon dinner in the Grand Hotel dining room, visiting an aunt of Mary's in Gray Eagle afterward.

The stabbing pain cut through her like a knife, forcing her to double up abruptly on the sofa in the parlor. She couldn't catch her breath and tried desperately to remember what Maggie Skinner had said.

The woman had been right. There was no hope of sending someone to Long Prairie for a doctor, any doctor. The smoke signal with linseed oil? She doubted there was any such oil in the house, and certainly the black smoke wouldn't have gone very far because of the wind and the rain. The white sheet at the road side? Could she get one down to the road? At the moment it seemed impossible. Besides, it was Sunday. There wouldn't be many traveling along that road today.

The pain was lessening, fading away for the moment. She managed to cry out for Laurence. No answer. "Laurence!" she tried again. Where was that boy? The weather was too violent for him to have gone outside to play. "Laurence," she cried, "come here—Mama wants you." He couldn't be of much help. She had little choice. After several more repeated tries, she heard some thumps on the ceiling from the bedroom above, then *ka-bump-ka-bump-bump* on the stairway.

Laurence came slowly through the parlor door pulling a toy wagon by a string. "Yes, Mama?" he said. "You sick, Mama? Leo go for ride. Bad Leo keep falling out of wagon." He pointed to his yellow velvet stuffed lion, even more inseparable since they'd moved. "Leo sick, too. Now Laurence take Leo upstairs. Put Leo to bed. Then Leo get better, won't he, Mama?"

This was a routine Laurence had often acted out over the past two months—the sick lion, the recovery. It didn't take much imagination, Lucy concluded, to realize that Laurence was acting out his father's accident, and trying to resolve the loss by having the animal recover.

She couldn't upset the boy further by implying that she herself was sick, that there was a potential crisis. Perhaps she could make a sort of game out of it. "Well, darling," she said, giving him a hug as he came up to the sofa, "let's pretend Mama is sick like Leo, and that you can make me all better."

"How do that, Mama?" He looked perplexed. "Me put you to bed? Here afghan. Put on you." He picked up the crocheted afghan draped over the back of the sofa and spread it over her feet. "Here, take Leo. Now Leo, give Mama hug." He folded her arms around Leo.

"That's very good, darling. That will certainly help Mama and Leo. But now we need something else, too."

"What, Mama?"

"Can you go upstairs and bring me something out of the big chest at the foot of my bed? The big chest with the shiny brass lock on it, the lock you like to play with? Laurence nodded. "When you get there, open it up and look inside. You can pretend you're looking for pirate treasure." He nodded eagerly. "Now inside you'll find a big white cloth, just like the one you have on your bed."

"A sheet, Mama?" he asked.

"Why, yes," Lucy said, surprised he knew that. "Bring it down here to Mama, as quick as you can."

It seemed to take a long time, but at last Laurence came back downstairs, dragging the sheet and getting it tangled in the stair spindles along the way and caught against the door as he came into the parlor. He struggled to pull it free and, with a look of great satisfaction, handed it to her where she still lay on the sofa.

"Oh, thank you, darling," she said, patting his arm. Another violent pain, worse than the first. As soon as it passed, Lucy forced herself to her feet, holding on to the back of the sofa for support. She could not ask Laurence to take the sheet out to the main road and tie it to a bush, as Mother Megs had instructed. Not in this weather, not something that difficult. She would have to force herself to do it. Wadding the sheet up and tucking it under her arm, she wrapped the afghan loosely around her and instructed Laurence to stay right there on the sofa with Leo until she got back.

As she pushed open the front door she looked and wondered if she could make it. It seemed so far to the main road, and the strong wind had littered the lane with branches and the last of the autumn leaves. There was no choice. She pulled the afghan more closely around her, and, clutching the sheet, headed down the driving lane. Every gust of wind seemed to force her backwards. She drew the afghan up over her head, but, as she did so, dropped the sheet. It seemed ages before she got it free from the branches, soaking wet as it was.

The main road at last. It was deserted, not a wagon or rider in sight. She wondered anxiously if anyone would be out in this weather. If could be hours before anyone came by. Nevertheless, she tied a corner of the sheet to a small buckthorn beside the road. Would it hold? It could be hours—could be too late, if before anyone saw it. Before anyone could go for Mother Megs.

Before—before—the trees around her seemed to spin in circles, the whiteness of the sheet blowing in the wind, wet, the sound of the wind crying out as if for help, the wool afghan binding her feet on the road, she couldn't move. She felt herself falling, tried to catch herself with the nearest branches, but they were too fragile, too slippery.

The sound of wagon wheels on the road, coming closer. They stopped. From where she lay, she could see a horse's legs, then a man's legs.

"Here, missus," a voice said. "Let's get you back into the house." Strong arms lifted her up, trying at the same time to draw the afghan around her body against the wind and rain. "You're in a bad way, I'll get—"

She couldn't make out his words, pain shooting through her body, the wind howling in her ears, the rough earthy scent of the man's jacket as he held her close, each step toward the house increasing her pain. Then being carried upstairs, placed on her bed, the familiar smell of her pillow case, of the quilt as it was tucked in around her. The man's voice was soothing, reassuring. Gradually it faded. She heard it again in the hall talking to Laurence, then a distant door shutting, the front door. Then silence, then darkness, then light, then darkness.

Time seemed to be endless, an eternity of light coming and going from shifting clouds and lightning flashes, an eternity of heavy drumming sounds from rain on the roof above her. intermittent pain. She awoke fully with a start when a clap of thunder sounded directly overhead, shaking the whole house.

As flashes of lightning filled the room, she could see the intricate carving of leaves and flowers, of flying and perching birds on the bed's headboard above her, the big walnut bed which Bernard had ordered for their log house, the bed in which she'd lain with him that first night, the bed in which they'd conceived this child. How long ago that seemed, almost an ageless time suspended in a void. As the pains with increasing frequency tore through her body, she squeezed her eyes shut, clenched her hands, and tried to will away all consciousness.

"Stop your moaning, girl!" Out of the depths of some remote part of her brain she recognized the voice. "Come on now, let me get this folded sheet under you." It was Mother Megs. Lucy had no idea how or when the woman had come. Outside the window it was dark and quiet. The storm had passed, and it must be night. The oil lamp on the bedside table was lit, its wick hissing, its light flickering around the room.

More instructions. She found herself obeying, breathing out, pushing with all her strength. "Push, now," the voice kept saying, and she obeyed, even when the effort made the pain even sharper. Her body was wet with sweat, the bed sheets seemed clammy and restricting, wet with something sticky. Someone pressed a cool cloth to her forehead, touched her cheeks and temples with it. People were talking. There must be someone else in the room with Maggie. Another woman. Who was it? Lucy was sure she'd never heard that voice before. She tried to see the identity of the person with the cool cloth, but she, who ever it was, sat beside the bed slightly behind her head.

"This young'un's 'bout to come out all wrong," she heard Maggie say. "Will you just look at that!" Lucy still could not see who the other woman was—they both were standing behind her raised knees, there was a sheet draped over them.

"Hmmm, well now," said the other woman, "breech birth for certain. Seen a few of them in my time. Do you suppose we should send for a doctor?"

"Yes, send for—doctor, doctor—" Lucy tried to raise herself up from the bed.

"No need, my girl," Maggie's voice was firm. "Now you just lie back down there." She pushed Lucy back onto the pillows. "Know how to manage this. Done one just last week. And that baby girl—and the mother—survived just fine, thank you."

Maggie and the other woman began to talk in hushed voices. There was movement around the room, the sound of a door opening and closing, a firm hand pushing against her belly, searing pain, more voices, more footsteps, a cool cloth on her forehead, someone squeezing her hand, stroking her arm, murmuring words in a language she didn't understand. Whatever they meant, the tone was soothing, reassuring. The words became fainter and fainter. She could hardly hear them. A gray fog in the room, then total darkness.

"Here he is," said the voice. Warmth and softness was placed against her right neck and shoulder. Someone took hold of her left hand and placed it on the bundle, for she seemed to have no strength. A strange little cry, like a door creaking on its hinges. "Little tyke made it into this world with a little help. But now here he is."

"Mother Megs—" Lucy began. "Is he—how—" There was so much she wanted to ask, but it was difficult to speak. An enormous wave of relief swept over her, a sensation beginning in her head and mind and rippled down through her breasts, down her abdomen, and down both legs and into her very toes. Yet it didn't end there, it continued on until it seemed to fill the room. She had never felt such a sensation before. The birthing was over, and she had a son. It was her son. It was Bernard's son.

"Too bad his father can't see him," the other woman remarked. "Great pity, poor babe."

"Well, now, Greta, see what you've gone and done, brought the poor girl close to tears! You go on home now. I'll finish up here, clean up, make her comfortable and look after the baby until Mary Dubois gets here. Shouldn't be too long, now."

Lucy heard doors closing, the sound of a horse and buggy receding down the driving lane beside the house. Maggie came over and sat down beside her, placing a hand firmly on top of her head. "You musn't fret," she said, a softness in her voice Lucy hadn't expected. "Everything's all right now. The baby a fine boy. With a little nursing care, you'll do very well. Breech birth it was. Young master Dubois here insisted on making his entrance into this world upside down. Old wives' tale means he'll face some troubles in life, for sure. Who knows, though? Don't we all? Now the best thing for you both is to rest, try to sleep."

But there were worries. "Where are Sabine and Martin?" she asked, "and little Laurence . . . where—?"

"Don't fret, they're all at the Dubois. Noel will be back here with Mary. Promised that'd be soon."

"But how did you—?"

"Well, now, the Lord was with you there," Maggie said. "Just happened that one of the Holberg boys—not sure which of the two blond ones it was—passed by your house, on his way up to Long Prairie. Suspect he had in mind an evening's tippling with the boys at Reagan's. Whichever one it was, saw the sheet tied to the bush, found you lying in the road. After he carried you back inside, came to fetch me. Had the sense to bring Laurence with him. Little tyke was sure in a fine state. Sent that Holberg boy—Erik or Mattias, not sure which—back to fetch Greta Schweitzer. Good thing, too, as it turned out. Time I got my wagon hitched and arrived here with Laurence, you weren't much better off. Greta got here a few minutes later."

"But Noel and the children?"

Noel and his family brought the children back just about dusk. You didn't hear them? Children came into your room. You'd fainted a couple of times, guess you didn't know. The birthing wasn't going too well just then, so I shoo'd them out. Noel said best to take them all back to his place, get Mary to come. Children could stay with them for a while."

"No, no," Lucy said emphatically. "I want them here. It'll be all right, Sabine and Martin will both help. I don't want to burden the Dubois anymore than I have to."

"Well, you'll have to work that out with Mary. But you know, I'll be dropping in over the next week whenever I can, just to check on things. Wouldn't mind taking the little tyke Laurence home with me for a day or so—taken a real shine to him, bless my soul, provided he doesn't cut loose with my crockery." She laughed good naturedly.

"You said Greta Schweitzer was here, too?"

"Like I said, a good thing. Knew from the looks of you earlier that things might not go too well, that I'd need a little help. You ain't met Greta yet? Farm next down from you toward the Narrows, 'bout half mile. Family moved here last year, from somewhere back east, Ohio, I think, Bavaria before that—if I haven't gotten them confused with another German family over to Gray Eagle."

With deft hands, she changed the bed-clothes, straightened up Lucy's pillow, and firmly tucked in the quilt around her. "Here, let me take this stubborn boy, put him in this cradle. He'll sleep for a while, until he gets hungry. Hmm, beautiful piece of work this cradle. Rocks smooth as silk. There now, young man, let your mama get some rest. I'll just turn this oil lamp down a bit."

The room grew darker, then quiet and empty except for her and her son—Bernard. Yes, she thought, that's what he would be, after his father. No, that didn't seem quite right. He should have a different name, a different life. Mother Megs had saved his life. Wasn't her middle name Louise? A French name, too, another reminder of his father, of France, where Bernard had been born.

And now here is where **Louis Bernard** had been born. In this old DeLaurier house—where other babies were born, generations of babies.

And the Holberg man who'd found her on the road, carried her into the house, went to fetch Maggie, Greta—His gentleness, his concern, his voice—How frustrating not to know which brother it was. She hoped it had been Mattias. Yet in some way she hoped it had been the other one. She could not easily accept the fact that Mattias might have seen her in such a state, in the midst of a painful labor, her hair disheveled, her clothes muddy. So helpless, so dependent.

More and more difficult to think. Lucy's thoughts grew more and more confused into dim fragments. They seemed to cover so much time, space, and emotion. The air around her vibrated with whispered memories, the old house itself seemed alive with them. Still, what comfort it was, thinking about all those families sitting together over supper in the big kitchen downstairs, the women who'd cooked on that iron stove, who'd enjoyed the bounty of gardens and orchards. Spring, summer, autumn, winter. The cycle of life.

She felt herself drifting deeper and deeper toward sleep. She pieced together imagined fragments of conversations taking place in the formal front parlor—dreams unfolding during long winter nights, weddings, loving, christenings, parties, women screaming in childbirth, men tossing in fevered pain, dying. Dying, like her husband, Bernard.

Yet another presence seemed to be within this room. A strong presence, a strength beyond herself, beyond Bernard. And that presence was waging war within her mind, her heart, her very soul.

NIGHT VISITORS

B y November, life at the DeLaurier house had edged into that period between harvest and winter. The crisp air smelled of snow which never fell, the ground hardened under deeper and deeper frosts. Neighboring men—Wold, Holberg, and Schweitzer—had seen to it that firewood was stacked up behind the house to the level of the kitchen windows and would last the winter. Brownling and her calf—never auctioned off, to Sabine's joy—were bedded down for the winter in the spacious DeLaurier barn stalls along with Blaize, and fed with hay and oats from Noel's rich fields.

Still, Lucy sensed an unfamiliar strangeness in the house. An eerie feeling, sounds, whispers, words she could not distinguish. Once she'd reached for a door where there wasn't one, only to find that there had once been a door in that spot, long since boarded up and plastered over. Another time she found herself standing before an upstairs window, surprised it was there, then realizing it was a new addition. No window had ever been there in the original homestead. Sometimes it seemed she'd lived in this house before and betrayed it by leaving. She seemed pressured to make some sort of reconciliation.

Late one night toward the end of November, Lucy sat bold upright in bed, jolted awake by a strange noise. Then it came—the sound of horses and a heavy wagon, rumbling fast down the main road before the house.

"Strange . . . a passing wagon, this time of night?" she muttered, falling back against the pillow, annoyed at the disturbance and waiting for the sound to grow fainter.

It grew louder. Now it sounded as though the wagon was actually turning off the main road and coming down the lane toward the house, jolting headlong over ruts and occasional rocks. Cracking, banging, swearing. Someone was in a desperate hurry to risk that lane in the dark.

What could it mean? An all-out attack on the house by a band of robbers? Fear seized her, fear for the children and for herself. She snatched up her shawl on a chair beside the bed, threw it over her shoulders, glanced at Louis thankfully still asleep in his cradle, and rushed to the front window. Pitch dark, no moon, no riding light on the wagon. She felt her way along the upper hall and headed toward the stairs, afraid to show a light in the house.

The cold stair boards were a shock to her bare feet. A draft came from somewhere—had someone already broken in? Once in the downstairs hall, she put her ear against the parlor door. Still quiet in there, safe to go in, look out that window. She edged cautiously toward it, and stayed well back of the lace curtain. Outside, impenetrable darkness.

From the sounds, the wagon was almost at the house. With a horse snorting and blowing, it came to a sharp halt beside the brick path leading up to the front porch. A man's harsh voice, curse words, an exclamation from someone else, arguing.

Terrified, alone with the children, her nearest neighbors a half mile away in either direction, Lucy was thankful to have regularly bolted both front and back doors each night. Noel and Maggie both warned her about possible break-ins. Local harvests brought money, and not many farmers trusted banks. They felt safer hiding their cash at home. Only last week, Maggie's husband, Lemuel, shot at a man as he tried to get away in a wagon with several other men. Never caught them. Rumor claimed the gang was still around.

But there were still the windows to worry about, and she backed away. Both porch windows—the parlor and the dining room, once a source of delight for all the sunlight flooding into the DeLaurier house, now offered easy access to intruders. She quickly made her way out into the hall and shut the parlor door. It had no lock. Feeling her way in the dark along the wall into the kitchen, she picked up a chair and wedged it under the parlor doorknob.

Yet, surely, if they were thieves, they'd be quiet about it and creep up stealthily. Could this be some sort of all-out attack? The gang Lemuel shot at was bold and ruthless. It occurred to her that Bernard's old rifle might be some protection. She reached up along the wall until she touched the high shelf to the left of the front door and lifted down that old Springfield rifle which Bernard was allowed to take when he mustered out. He used it only occasionally for hunting—last time for the wild turkey at Christmas. She'd packed it away, but now, with talk of thieves in the area, she'd put it up on the shelf by the front door, out of reach of the children.

Did she remember how to use it, though? Was it still loaded? Her last experience was when Bernard had taken her out by the barn, shown her how to charge and fire it, aiming at some old oil cans placed on a fence post. But the explosion was so loud and the kick against her shoulder so painful, she vowed she'd never fire it again.

Outside, heavy footsteps thumped along the porch. She aimed the rifle at the front door, ready to shift her aim toward the parlor if the sound of breaking glass announced a break in. "Please, Lord," she prayed, "let me know how to work this thing."

The front doorknob turned once, then again, rattled. Pounding on one of the panels. Kicking against the bottom, "Open up! Open the door!"

"Who—who's there?" Instantly she regretted those words. They'd given her away.

More insistent pounding. "Know you're home. Now open the door!"

With a pang of recognition, Lucy recognized the voice. Although muffled, it sounded like Henry Morton, her sister's husband. Was it some sort of family emergency? Then why come all the way here, almost fifteen miles, to Little Sauk? Long Prairie would have been closer to their homestead, with doctors, a sheriff.

"Ma! What's going on?" Behind her Martin scrambled down the stairs. She heard Sabine up on the landing trying to calm Laurence. From the bedroom came the sounds of Louis, awake and beginning to whimper.

"Martin," she whispered, "go out to the kitchen and light that oil lamp on the sideboard."

"What's wrong, Ma? What's wrong?" Martin whispered back. "Who's out there?"

Again, loud pounding on the front door combined with more shouting and cursing. "Lucy! Know you're there! Going to let your family in or not?"

So it was Henry. "Go on Martin—go light the lamp and bring it out here. Hurry up, before he breaks the door down!"

After several minutes, "Can't find the matches. Too dark." Some shuffling noises, drawers pulled out, matches striking. Slowly light filled the hall as Martin cautiously emerged, both hands tight around the glass base. The light cast by the lamp exaggerated the fear on his face. "Gee, Ma, why're you pointing that rifle? Gee, is it loaded? Who's out there?"

"Going to let us in or not?" Henry's voice more impatient. "Open up, I said!"

"Lucy—" Outside, Agnes called her name, said something in French. Other voices, someone crying.

So Agnes was with Henry, the others, too. "Wait! Let me get the door open." Sabine had come downstairs and now emerged from the parlor with the poker in her hand. "You can put the poker down, Sabine. It's your Uncle Henry. Don't know what's wrong. Some sort of trouble."

Lucy replaced the rifle on the shelf, slid back the deadbolt at the top of the door, and reached for the big brass key in the lock. "Watch out, Martin. Stop waving that lamp around. You'll set the house afire." She struggled with the key. "Martin, bring the lamp over here so's I can see better."

She tried the key again with both hands, but it wouldn't budge. It had always turned hard, having been bent no telling how long ago by a

DeLaurier impatient with getting in—or out. "Oh, this key!" she exclaimed in frustration, "just doesn't work!" Upstairs Louis's whimpering had given way to persistent wails. Laurence at the upstairs banister kept shouting for his mama. "Key stuck, Henry," Lucy yelled through the door. "You'll have to be patient."

"Patience be damned," Henry shouted as he hurled his weight against the door. The lock gave way and the door burst open with a loud splintering of the frame. His huge form filled the doorway as the cool night air rushed in. The lamp's flickering flame smoked against the glass chimney and illuminated him with a grotesque light against the total darkness beyond. The image was so frightening that Lucy gasped and stepped backwards. She bumped into Sabine, who'd sheltered behind her with the poker.

Striding into the dim, wavering light, the man's large bulk seemed to fill the hall. He had always seemed exceptionally tall and broad shouldered, but now, even in his advanced age, assumed a massive, threatening presence. Worse still, his face was partly hidden because of his full, graying beard and the old black felt hat pulled down low over his forehead.

Immediately behind him cowered Agnes, crying, Jane's arm around her, and behind them, Tom. In the uncertain lamplight they all looked dazed.

"All right, boy," Henry said gruffly, "go back out and get your things out of the wagon. Can't fool around here much longer, late enough already. And you, Agnes, stop your damn blubbering. Doesn't help the situation much." The horsewhip he kept flicking against his boot made short, snapping sounds.

Lucy was stunned, not knowing quite what to say, waiting for some sort of explanation. Henry offered none, but pulled his hat down farther and shifted from one booted foot to the other. The snapping grew more impatient.

"Come on now, boy," he shouted as he looked back out the front door, "what's taking you so long? Haven't got all night!"

Tom struggled in with several bundles of clothes tied up in bed sheets and dropped them on the floor. Henry grunted, flicked his buggy whip one more time, and strode out without another word. He slammed the door behind him with such force that it shook the wall, rattled the front windows, and drew renewed shrieks from Louis upstairs. It also brought an immediate response from Agnes, who, until now, had remained transfixed against the wall with Jane. She now slid to the floor as Jane knelt beside her.

"Ma—Ma, don't!" Jane took her hand. "It's all right. All my fault."

"Agnes—Jane! What's wrong? What's happened? Surely one of you can tell me. Agnes? Tom?" No one seemed ready to say anything. "How can I help if I don't know what's happened?"

"Well, Auntie Lucy," Tom began hesitantly. "Well, Auntie, you see, there was an argument back home."

"An argument? About what?"

"About me," Jane answered. "All my fault. But please, Auntie, it's been so hard on Ma. Couldn't we talk later—"

Lucy realized this probably wasn't a time to demand explanations, but she needed to know something, at least. Why had they come down all the way from their homestead on the river? In the middle of a cold, dark night? This was no ordinary visit, and, from those bundles of clothes Tom brought in, it looked like it was going to be a long one. Perhaps, if she tried to reach Agnes in their language—their language of the heart, rather than the tongue. "Agnes—*cherie*! What has happened, *qu'est ce qu'il y a? Qu'est que t'arrive?*"

This approach, too, was unsuccessful.

"What happen, Mama?" Laurence, wide-eyed, called down from upstairs, his face between the railings. "Baby crying. Wants Mama," and he pointed to the front bedroom.

"Sabine," said Lucy, "please go up and look after Louis. There's enough going on already without all that. Take a candle in a holder. And get Laurence back to bed, put him in your bed for the time being. Tom can sleep in Martin's room."

"Guess so, if he'll have to," complained Martin, stiffening, shaking his head. "Hope he don't snore, anyways."

"Well, a fine mess this is," Lucy muttered. "What have I been landed with? I guess I'll just have to deal with it, somehow, Lord help me." She turned to Martin. "Son, please take that lamp into the kitchen before you go upstairs. Set it on the table. And Tom, why don't you go upstairs now with Martin? You can have the upper bunk. Take your things. And there's a candle on his dresser, matches in the drawer."

She heard the boys clattering up the stairs, movements around in the bedrooms above, some boys' shouts, laughter, running, the whacking noises of a pillow fight. Sabine speaking soothingly to Laurence, Louis's cries diminishing. Comforting sounds, all, providing a kind of antidote to the shock of that night's arrival and a welcome delay, if only momentary, of learning its reason. .

"Let's go out to the kitchen, Agnes, Jane. It's warmer out there. Look, both of you are shivering with cold. Such a long, cold ride. Several hours, at least. Come, come. Leave your shawls on until you warm up."

The kettle on the back of the range held water recently heated for the supper dishes, and Lucy reckoned that some chamomile tea might have a calming effect. Both Lucy and Jane were silent as she took down a tin box from the cupboard near the back door and hurriedly dumped several teaspoons of dried leaves into the teapot. She poured in the hot water and took down three cups and saucers from the top sideboard shelf.

"Now then, we'll let that steep for a moment." She sat down with them around the kitchen table, touched by the anxiety reflected in their faces. Should she wait for them to speak? It was an awkward situation. "Feeling a bit warmer?" she finally asked, pouring out the tea and hoping someone would say something.

"Somewhat better, thank you, Auntie." Jane picked up her cup in both hands, sipped it eagerly.

"Agnes?"

"*Oui*–yes." She continued staring at the tablecloth.

"I know you've had some kind of a shock," Lucy offered. Perhaps it was too difficult, too painful to discuss.

Jane set down her cup decisively in its saucer. "Ma, I'm sure Auntie Lucy is wondering why we're here. Right, Auntie?" Not waiting for Lucy's reply, Jane continued, "You see, there was a big argument with Pa."

"About what?"

"About Daniel."

"Daniel?"

"Daniel Benson. My intended."

"I see. Yes, I knew you were going to marry, your brother Abe mentioned it when I meet him by chance last month." And indeed, she was beginning to see. She recalled what had happened with Agnes. Back then, Papa found out she was pregnant, found out the man was Henry, that it had happened while Agnes was working out at Reagan's. Furious, cursing, went into town to confront him. She and *maman* were afraid he'd do something violent. He claimed that man Morton wasn't good enough for his girl, his girl so innocent, so trusting. "Yes, I think I see, Jane. You're not—you're not—"

Jane blushed, picked up her teacup. "No, Auntie. No, not that way."

"Why, then? Why's Henry objecting?"

Agnes spoke up for the first time. "Lucette, *cherie*, it is, what you say, *compliqué*." She paused, sipping her tea, searching for words.

"Yes, complicated because of who Daniel is," Jane added.

"Well, who is he, then? Abe made him sound like a good catch."

"Don't you remember, Lucy? Way back, Daniel's father got into trouble with the law, tried to dupe my pa—Henry Morton, that is—out of his land. There were several men—connected with Reagan's, somehow."

"Well, what's that got to do with Daniel?"

"The problem is with Pa. You wouldn't expect anyone to object to Daniel, would you?"

Agnes hastily added, "*Oui, un gentilhomme*—such a fine man, twenty-six."

"A carpenter, good job working on the packet boats, running between Long Prairie and Staples," Jane added all in one breath.

"When I met your brother, Abe, he said you were planning to marry this man and go out west, raise cattle or something." Lucy added more hot water to the teapot.

"Still plan to do that. He's saving his money, wants to build up a good herd. But he's also planning to get work as a carpenter. Real need for that in the new settlements, they say."

"Why then all the fuss? How could Henry possibly object?"

"Well, Pa thinks the son will turn out to be like his father."

"That's ridiculous."

"Of course, but you know Pa." She sighed. "And that's the long and short of it."

Lucy was puzzled. "Why are you here, then? Did something happen?"

"Because—because," Agnes said, reaching over to take Jane's hand, "because he wanted to prevent Jane from running off with Daniel."

"Eloping? Now? With winter coming on? Across the Dakotas? Now? That'd be crazy." Lucy's thoughts focused briefly on the Holberg brothers, the risk they were about to take.

"Pa said he wouldn't put it past him. Steal his girl, like the boy's father tried to steal his homestead."

"But don't you think it unlikely that Daniel would come all the way down here, even if he knew where you were?"

"If Daniel comes to the mill, Pa made Abe swear not to tell him."

"All right then. Let's hope while you're here it'll give us all time to work things out." She pushed back her chair. "Now look, I know you're tired and upset. It's been a long, cold ride. What you need is a good night's sleep. Follow me upstairs—I'll make up to the guest room."

"No, Jane, *attende.*" Agnes pulled at her sleeve. "Jane, go up first, take our things. I want to—to finish my tea." She looked directly at Lucy.

Lucy sensed some hidden message there. "Yes, Jane, I'll be up directly. The guest room's just to the left, top of the stairs. No wait!" Lucy took a small oil lamp off the sideboard shelf, lit it. "You'll need this."

As soon as Jane was down the hall and halfway up the stairs, Lucy sat down beside her sister. "Now, Agnes, what is it?"

Agnes hesitated, toyed with the cup, the spoon. Finally, in a rush of words unusual for her, she said, "*Pas seulement* Daniel."

"What else, then? Besides Daniel?"

Again, Agnes seemed reluctant to speak. Finally, with a sigh, "*C'est* Matthew Creighton."

"What? The man you—" She hardly knew how to finish the sentence. The man Agnes had supposedly married, the man who'd rescued her from Eagle Lake all those eight years ago, the man who was Jane and Abe's father."

"*Oui, c'est ça.*" She sighed again, uttered a stream of French Lucy found difficult to uncerstand.

"What's that? What're you saying, Agnes?"

"Henry," she began. "Henry."

"Well, what about him?"

"Henry is afraid Jane has another reason for following Daniel out west." She looked down, staring at the tablecloth. With another sigh, another stream of words, "*Tu sais*, there was never proof that Matthew drowned in that canyon river. His body was never found."

"Never found? It's been years. Why hasn't he turned up, then? Surely he would have tried to find you, his children."

"There were people who drowned on that day. Lost. The first part of the wagon train got across, went on before the snow came. *C'est possible*—possible that he thought we were lost. Possible himself injured, without memory." She shrugged. "*Qui sais?*"

"But Agnes, why would Henry not want Jane to find her father?"

"*Tu sais, tu sais,*" Agnes repeated several times, pushing aside her cup and saucer and getting up from the table, "she would also be finding the man who—the man who—the man who was once my husband."

Yes, now Lucy understood. A complicated matter indeed. She hardly knew how to expand on those words. Instead, she simply said, "Come upstairs to bed."

Little had Lucy realized, in first seeing the brass bed which the Lundgrens had left behind in the spare room, who would be the first to sleep in it—her sister and her niece, in some sort of midnight flight from home.

Sleep did not come easily for Lucy that night. She lay awake for hours, nervous over the security of the house because of the broken lock, full of compassion for Jane, whom she'd come to love. A girl after her own heart, outspoken, capable. And distress at Agnes's distress, over Henry's actions, Henry's anxieties about Matthew Creighton.

Anger, fear, anxiety—it seemed impossible to sleep. The hours passed, as she heard every sound as if magnified. Louis, stirring in his cradle. Sabine occasionally comforting Laurence in the next room. Sometimes Agnes coughing in the guest room.

Tossing and turning, still unable to sleep, Lucy's thoughts went from the broken treaty to present-day ownership of the land. To Henry's land, to Noel Dubois's land, which was not her own, could never be her own. To the Holbergs' land. To the Holberg son's great strength as he lifted her up from the rocking chair in the yard on moving day. To his image in his brother, Mattias. To the fact that, despite their strength and ambition, they could not make a go of their land.

With a start she realized her mind was leading her where she did not want to go, to where she was not yet ready to go. And now here was her poor sister, Agnes, asleep in Lundgren's brass bed in the room next door, perhaps coming down with the croup after being so chilled. Jane separated, perhaps forever deprived of the man she loved and future happiness. Agnes deprived of the man she'd once loved.

Now perhaps she herself was to be pitied. Deprived of her first love, Bernard. There was every indication she would be deprived of the only man who could take his place, Mattias Holberg. What was wrong with the man, anyway? Hadn't he seemed attracted to her? He lived just down the road, had easy access to the DeLaurier House, and perhaps easy access to her heart as well. What kept him so distant? So silent? Hours went by, the old carriage clock on the mantel downstairs chiming them one by one. She dozed off and on fitfully with these repeated unanswerable questions until the sky was silvery gray and house sparrows began their tuneless chirping.

Despite her emotional turmoil, and as if to mock it, the day dawned as one of those glorious early winter days on the central plains when an intensely bright sun shines down from an intensely blue sky and illumines the few golden leaves still clinging to the trees. It was actually warm enough not to have to stoke the kitchen stove except for cooking, thankfully one less chore, for she felt very tired after so little sleep.

"Martin," she said as the children were finishing their breakfast, "suppose you take Tom out to the barn with you and Laurence. Maybe he'll be willing to share some of your chores."

Once the boys headed out to the barn, Sabine helped her mother clean up the kitchen and look after baby Louis upstairs. There was no question of their going off to school today. What a blessing the children were, Lucy thought. After Bernard's death last March, she could never have managed without them, especially Sabine.

There was a knock at the back door, surprising because she hadn't heard anyone drive into the barnyard. Not a good time for visitors, she thought in annoyance, opening the door and then the screen. "Oh, it's you, Maggie," she said with relief. Even if it had been Mattias himself, she could not have faced him.

"Come on in, although I hope you'll excuse things around here. Some visitors arrived late last night, things are still upside down in the kitchen and everywhere else."

"Don't mind, you know I don't. Can I help? Here, let me at least take care of that bread." Maggie set down the basket she was carrying, took off her knitted shawl and fur-lined cap, wrapped a large tea towel around her waist, and proceeded to lay the dough in the kneading trough. "Now then," she said as she began to fold the dough over and over, "who's here? Oh, but before you tell me, here's some of that curd cheese you asked about." She wiped her hands on her apron, went over to the basket she'd set down by the back door, and lifted out a small brown crock with a piece of oiled paper tied over the top. She placed it on the table and resumed her kneading. "Someday, you know, I'll show you how to make it. Now then, what visitors?"

"My brother-in-law, Henry Morton, arrived in a wagon late last night with Agnes, he in some kind of fury, her in a state of shock"

"Your sister?"

"Yes, along with her foster children, Jane and Tom, but not Abe. Henry just dropped them off, along with a few belongings, then drove off into the dead of night as fast as he'd come."

"Where's your sister now?"

"Upstairs, still asleep. With Jane. Hadn't the heart to wake them."

"What was it all about?"

"Not exactly sure. It seemed to be over Jane's intended, a man named Daniel Benson."

"Not the same Benson who was jailed couple of years back? Scheme to take over Henry's land?"

"No, his son. He seems to be all right, from what Jane says. A carpenter. They plan to go out west, find a place in Montana."

"Well, then, why all the fuss?"

"You know Henry Morton. Stubborn, not very sensitive to other people's feelings. It's apparently hard for him to separate father from son."

The back door slammed with a bang. Martin burst into the kitchen, his brother Laurence hovering just outside. "Ma, Ma!" Martin yelled, "Tom hit me!"

"Shush," cautioned Lucy, putting her hand over his mouth. "You'll wake your aunt. I told you to be quiet this morning. And say hello nicely to missus Skinner. Now, what happened? No, no, don't come in here with those dirty boots. Take them off outside like you're supposed to." He angrily pulled them off and threw them out through the open door. "Not like that. All right, now tell me what's all this about."

"Well you see," began Martin, "Tom hit me first, just swung out his arm and hit me with his fist. Look, see, here is where he hit, there's already a lump here and it hurts." He pointed to the side of his head.

"Hmm," she said, running her fingers along his scalp, "I don't see anything. It can't be all that bad. Now Tom," she looked over to where the boy was standing hesitantly in the doorway.

"You got a story to tell there, young man?" Maggie interjected.

"Well, auntie—er, ma'am," he began, looking down at his boots, which were shamefully muddy. Obviously he wished he had taken them off earlier with Martin, and dared not come farther into the kitchen. "You see, ma'am," he continued hesitantly, then with more confidence, "Martin said I didn't know much about farms and such. Was no hand at the kind of thing 'round here—feedin' cattle and such. Then I told him he didn't know much 'bout millin', either." He drew a deep breath. "Then he tried to hit me. So I just couldn't help myself, Auntie Lucy. I just swung out and hit him first."

"Now, Martin," Lucy said, pulling him towards her and holding on to his jacket collar, "and you, Tom. Apologize to each other. Did you hear me, Martin?"

"Yes'm, " mumbled Martin, ducking his head and digging his hands deep into the pockets of his overalls.

"And you, too, Tom. Apologize to Martin for hitting him. We don't do that here." Tom nodded and backed hastily out the door, apparently glad to have escaped more than verbal punishment.

"Best way to handle that little upset," commented Maggie, punching away at the dough. "But I can see you're in for a lot of that, if'n that family intends to stay very long." She took off her apron, pulled on her shawl, hat. "Well, set this dough to rise. I got lots to do at home. I'll be off. Just listen, now, if you need me—"

As Maggie left, Lucy realized the morning was passing quickly. What was happening upstairs? Lucy went up as far as the landing, relieved to hear Sabine and Jane talking together as they were dressing baby Louis. "Try not to wake Auntie, Sabine," she said. "She needs her rest."

I could say the same for myself, Lucy thought, returning to the kitchen to set the loaves of bread to rise in their tins. Thinking over the events of the past ten or so hours, Agnes's dramatic arrival with her children seemed like deja vu. Only two months ago her brother-in-law, Noel, had brought her and her children to this same house. Not quite as dramatically as last night, of course, but still, it was late, dark, and they'd been packed into a big farm wagon rumbling headlong down the road, come in by lamp and candle light, found their way around unfamiliar rooms by candle light, and awakened to unfamiliar sounds.

No time for day-dreaming, she guiltily realized. Upstairs baby Louis was crying. Martin had come back from the barn and was arguing with Tom on the porch about something. *Don't want to,* she heard Martin say, to which Tom answered something she couldn't make out. Then they clumped across the porch and were gone.

As she hurried out into the hall on her way upstairs, with a start she noticed the rifle was not on its rack on the wall. Had she put it back last night? She distinctly remembered doing that. One of the children had taken it—Don't want to—she'd just hear Martin say. What were they talking about? The gun?

Lucy rushed out the door and burst into the barn. Laurence was in Brownling's stall, feeding the calf. "Laurence," she cried, "where's Martin? Tom?"

"Went house, Mama," he said, annoyed to be interrupted in his favorite chore.

"No, they're not there. Think, Laurence! Think! Did you hear them say anything? Say where they were going?"

"Well, said somethin' 'bout huntin'."

Her heart sank. Those two, with the old Springfield. No telling what might happen. It might still be primed, ready to discharge. Martin had seen his father use it only once or twice. But what about Tom? Most likely he and Abe had gone out hunting together. Where would they go here? So far Martin was unfamiliar with the place. And there were acres and acres, woods, fields. They could be anywhere.

She rushed back into the house. "Sabine!" she called. "Come down, help." Sabine came downstairs with Jane, Jane carrying baby Louis.

"We've got to go find the boys. No, Jane, better stay here with your mother and Louis."

She pulled on her shawl as Sabine followed her out the back door. "Sabine, better for you to head out toward those woods on the east side of the pasture."

"What about you, Ma?"

"I'll head down toward the river. That's where your Uncle Noel once mentioned there was game."

She ran up to the top of a little hill behind the granary and, cupping her hands around her mouth, called "Mar-tin! Tom! Maar-tin! Come back here!" She looked as far in every direction as she could. There was no sign of the boys.

Suddenly there was a loud report, a rifle shot off in the distance, someone screaming. She couldn't be sure of the direction. Immediately a flock of ducks flew up down near the river. That's where they were.

Hiking up her skirts, she raced up the rise in the direction of the woods, crawled under a barbed wire fence which contained one of the unused pastures, then forced her way through the tall prairie grass. The grass cut at her hands and face. In places, where it was higher than her head, she couldn't see where she was going. She had only the instinct that, to find her way out, she must keep the sun at her back. Tangled clumps of spiked gayfeather caught at her feet. Now she was at the edge of the woods where the trees a dense combination of fir thickets and large oaks. Some screams erupted ahead of her, and she followed the sound.

Martin was lying prone on the riverbank, Tom standing over him, the rifle in his hand. "Oh no, oh no," Lucy cried as she knelt down beside her son. He lay still, his eyes closed. "Martin, darling—are you— what's happened? Oh, Tom! What've you done?"

Tom seemed unable to speak. He bent over to peer at Martin, then backed away. After waving the rifle in the air, he threw it as far as he could into the woods and fell to his knees, doubled up sobbing. "Didn't mean no harm, no harm. Deer there, tried to shoot it 'fore it got away. Martin—so dumb—just walked into the bullet."

At this Martin stirred a little. "Ma," he moaned, his eyes still closed, "Got me, he did. Tom got me."

"Where, son?" she asked. Frantically she tore open his jacket, looking for blood, and raised his head. Martin moaned again. "Where do you hurt? Tell Mama."

"Oh, everywhere," he whined. "Hurts everywhere. Oh, oh—the pain!" He opened his eyes. "That Tom's the dumb one—so dumb—oh—don't know how—how to shoot," he gasped.

"Can so!" shouted Tom emphatically.

"Oh, is that right?" Martin, propping himself up on his elbow, then sprang to his feet. He rushed over to his cousin and began punching him in the back.

"Thrown it away, I have," said Tom. "Thrown that old gun into the woods. Naa, naa, now you can't have it now neither." He punched Martin back.

Before Lucy could do anything, the two boys fell to the ground, rolling over and over hitting each other. In their scuffle, she noticed that the sleeve of Martin's jacket had a tear along the outer edge. A bullet had gone right through the cloth, missing him in the chest by only a fraction of an inch.

"Boys, boys! Stop that this instant!" She seized Martin by his collar. "Get up now, we're going straight back to the house. First though, mister Tom, you go straight into those bushes and find that rifle, give it back to me at once. We're not leaving here until you do."

She knew she might need it another time, perhaps in a question of life or death. She also knew, however, that it no longer belonged on the shelf by the front door. "And now, mister Dubois," she said as she frog-marched Martin toward the house, Tom following guardedly some distance behind, "tell me exactly what happened down there at the river."

"Well, Ma," Martin replied reluctantly as the three of them pushed their way back through the tall prairie grass, "Tom saw that rifle in the hall last night. This mornin' said he wanted to go huntin'. Said I didn't want to. We had an argument. I went back out to the barn to help Laurence. You know how he messes things up awful bad."

He hesitated, brushed the dirt off his jacket. The words came faster. "Sure don't know how Tom got Pa's rifle down from the shelf. Saw him headin' down toward the river. Followed him. Got down here just as he was 'bout to shoot a big buck coming down to the water, you know there's that big waterin' place? Well, then Tom, he pulls the trigger but that ol' gun didn't fire. Good, I ses to myself, ain't loaded. Then just 'bout the time I came up, that deer ran past me, knocked me down, hard, like, just when Tom tried to fire again. This time that ol' rifle went off. Bullet barely missed both of us, I reckon—I mean missed me—and the deer. But I sure thought he'd got me for sure. Tom, I mean, not the deer."

By the time the noon dinner was over, Lucy felt she could not take much more. It had been a stressful night before, a most trying morning—one of painful memories, of demands, and of crises. Worse still, all these had conspired to remind her of her marriage to Bernard, their life together, his tragic death, her aloneness, and Mattias's distance. And, as if that were not enough, she was now facing responsibility for three more family members and, quite possibly, threatened violence from Jane's intended.

Now, the noonday dinner things washed up, put away, Agnes and Jane upstairs resting, Sabine napping with Louis, the boys playing dominoes in Martin's room—apparently having made up, Lucy had to escape. Was this to be the future pattern of events the DeLaurier house generated?

She walked into the barn, for her a place of retreat when she needed to find some kind of inner peace. The DeLaurier barn was a large, empty space, dark except where shafts of sunlight pushed their way in, a space smelling of the earth and the fields. Today she was glad she'd pulled on Bernard's old canvas coat, something she'd never sold or packed away because it was so useful for farm work. Sometimes, seeing it hanging there on a peg by the back door, she could almost imagine he would soon slip it on, she'd hear him say he'd be back shortly.

Today its warmth was some comfort. The weather was chilly, the sun had passed its peak and, as the clouds increased, the afternoon promised much colder weather for that night. The woody scents of late autumn, of burning leaves and field burn-offs, hung heavily in the air. With Bernard's coat around her, she recalled the nights they had lain together, the seasons they had shared together. Winter, spring, summer, autumn, winter once again. Over and over.

Piled in the far corner of the barn was some fresh hay, thrown down from the loft but not yet pitched into the mangers. She sank into it, taking off the big brown leather work boots she'd slipped on, most likely boots left at the back door by Noel's hired man, John Wold, and tucked her legs under her.

She lay back against the sweet-smelling hay and looked up through the barn rafters, fixing her eyes on a shaft of light coming in through the hay-loading window. It was fascinating to watch the shaft being broken by the aimless fluttering back and forth of barn pigeons, who made their nests up under the eaves.

Yes, she mused, the seasons of the year—surely, were part of a cycle which began long ago in the seasons of the past. With the first DeLaurier family who cleared the land, the family who built this house with the logs they cut. Time would pass on ahead into the future, long after she and her children moved from the DeLaurier house. It did not belong to them. Could not, for it belonged to Noel Dubois. She and her children would not—could not—remain here for long, nor could Agnes and her children. They might leave their whispered lives behind in the house, but they would no longer be a part of its fabric, its shelter.

The shafts of sunlight disappeared. Reluctantly Lucy pulled John Wold's boots back on for the walk through the barnyard and back to the house. Walking through the lengthening shadows of the passing afternoon, she wondered whether the flood of images which came unbidden, even resisted, by her conscious mind, were a means of understanding life. If not, she wondered, could you deny them, or by sheer force of will, change them?

WINTER VOICES

"How long has it been, Ma?" Sabine sounded concerned. "Where's Uncle Henry?"

"Over a week—no, let's see, more than that. We're near the end of November already." Lucy didn't dare reveal her anxiety, not to Sabine and especially not to Agnes. "How was your day at school?"

"Oh, all right, I guess. We're practicing the Christmas program. "Fact, Ma, I've got to go work on my part. Martin, too, if I can get him away from Tom and the checkers board." She paused on her way upstairs. "Jane's looking after Louis?"

"Yes, they're in the kitchen. She's been a real help."

"That's good. Well, call me if you need me."

But Lucy considered she needed more than just help. She needed some answers. There'd been no word from Henry Morton. She'd considered trying to contact him, whether by post through the post office in Thurstrom's general store at Little Sauk, or driving the wagon all the way up to Eagle River. Then, on second thought, considered that might reveal Jane's whereabouts to Daniel, exactly what her foster father was trying to prevent. Yet to wait until he could accept Jane's intended, Daniel Benson—if, indeed, Henry ever could, meant increasing anxiety and tension, not only for Lucy, but for the entire household.

Yes, answers. That's what Lucy needed. She resolved to speak frankly to Agnes. She went into the front parlor, where she'd earlier built a fire in the little iron stove in the corner to try to keep the room warm. Agnes spent most of her time in there, her mental worries no doubt contributing to intermittent chills, fever, and a rasping cough.

Lucy pulled up a chair beside the sofa, where Agnes lay passively bundled in shawls, and took her hand. "Come, now, *cherie*, we need to talk."

"*Pourquoi*, Lucette? What can I say? The situation—she is already explained."

"No, it's more a question of what we can do."

"We wait for Henry to—to—*changer son avis*—change his mind."

"How long do you think that will take? What will change it?"

Agnes shrugged. "That I do not know. Talk, maybe? Talk from Jane?" She broke into a spasm of coughing, then closed her mouth tightly, and passed her hand over her eyes, her forehead. "He will listen?"

"You think Jane could persuade Henry? She's a remarkable girl."

"*Eh bien*, again I do not know. *L'amour*—love is hard for him to give. Love for a child, *l'amour filial*—not so much. But love between a man and a woman—what they call, I think, *l'amour romantique*—no, that is hard. Henry and I, we have over these years come to something, I do not know what *exactement*." She paused. "*Ah oui, l'amour romantique.* My gift from Matthew."

Lucy sensed the subject was still too painful for Agnes to sustain. "Don't you think it's getting rather cold in here? I'll put another piece of wood in the stove."

"Warm—feels good."

"Yes, it warms better than those big old fireplaces. The DeLauriers knew how to keep up-to-date, all right."

"*Ah, oui.* That *famille.* They had what one calls—*la bonne fortune.*"

"Yes, but you know, Agnes, they must have worked very hard for all they had. I can feel it in this house. I see it all around—in the barn, the gardens . . ."

"You feel at home here, *non*?"

"Perhaps." Lucy could not explain, nor indeed herself fully understand her feelings about the DeLaurier house and the way it seemed to speak to her. "Some places have a feeling about them, don't you think?"

"The cabin of Henry—old homestead rebuilt after the fire. Afraid, sometimes. Something there—*une peur ancienne*—old fear." Agnes shivered and drew a shawl more closely around her.

Lucy knew something of the story—how Jake Benson and the men had first threatened Agnes, then burned it down in an attempt to remove Henry's homestead claim. "We'll speak no more of that, Agnes. There's no point in bringing up painful memories."

"Not speak of Henry. No, the pain is here—" She touched her heart, her head. "And for Jane." After a long pause, she added, "Jane. Speak to her."

After putting a few more pieces of wood into the stove and shaking the grate, Lucy went back out to the kitchen. It wasn't going to be easy, speaking to Jane. She seemed increasingly more moody and withdrawn. And now Jane was nowhere to be seen. Louis was alone in the kitchen, asleep in his pen in the corner.

For once, in contrast to the noise and activity throughout the house during the past week, the house seemed empty of life. Lucy sat down in the old rocking chair near the range, soothed by its gentle and rhythmic motion. She allowed her mind to wander where it willed, sometimes to the curled up body of Louis in a corner of his pen, sometimes to Sabine's reports on her geography lessons, sometimes to the pot of rosemary growing in the window sill, emitting its strangely pungent smell of pine.

She longed for those sustaining chats with Maggie, but over the past few weeks Maggie, too, was pre-occupied. Lemuel was recovering from pneumonia, and Maggie, as Mother Megs, the district's mid-wife, had been called out three or four times. Yet what Lucy really missed were those quiet moments of reflection alone, especially in the barn milking Brownling. They went a long way toward helping her sort life out, and having sorted as well as her present perspectives allowed, to come to terms with it.

"This old house getting smaller everyday, I reckon," Maggie Skinner remarked several days later during a rare visit. "Well nigh to bursting at the seams. Here, brought you these supplies from Thurstrom's general store down t' Little Sauk. Just like you ordered. Harald Thurstrom drives a hard bargain now that he's taken over from his mother, Stina. Worse than her, although maybe not as nosey." She pointed to Martin. "Now you and your cousin there—whatever your name is—bring in those sacks of flour and sugar from the back of the wagon. And don't forget that box under the seat, either— some dried beans in it, side of bacon, and a pound of coffee."

Then she stood back on her heels, tucked her thumbs into her belt, and remarked, "Well, here they are. You owe me $9.45. Coffee's my treat. Don't suppose all this stuff'll last long, given all these mouths to feed. Now where's that husband of your sister's? Somebody ought to tell him he can't just dump his family somewhere. No word from Abe, either? Land sakes, what's wrong with 'em? All right, I've got a few minutes to spare today. Here, let me dry those dishes." She reached for a dishtowel.

"What can I do?" Lucy later said to Brownling in the barn during that evening's milking. The regular hissing of the streams of milk into the pail were almost musical, and the cow's placid air reassuring. It felt good to rest her head against Brownling's warm flank, feel the soft warmth of the cow's udder in her hands, for the weather had turned very cold and windy, a smell of snow carried on strong winds from the west "Any idea how to solve this problem of Jane's, Brownling?" But a slight turn of the cow's head was the only answer she got.

Late the next afternoon, the answer did come, although not from Brownling. Lucy was out in the kitchen skimming off risen cream from the milk pans in order to churn it into butter next morning. "That old cow still doing well—but one of these day's she's sure to dry up," she commented to Sabine. "We need to build up a supply of butter and curd cheese while we can. Finished with that homework? How about your brother? Tom's falling behind in his lessons, the longer he stays here and not attending school. Listen—hear those boys there? Sounds like leapfrog, off and on the beds. I'll go up in a minute, soon's I finish the cream."

"Where's Auntie?"

"Don't know—probably in the parlor by the stove."

"She doesn't talk much, does she?"

"I suppose not."

"Why not?"

"Maybe because she has a little trouble with words. They don't always come out quite right, and it embarrasses her. Or maybe because her mind is special. She sometimes sees things differently from the rest of us. She was like that—when we were growing up in Quebec." Best change the subject. "How's that homework coming? Suppertime soon."

"In a minute, Ma. I have to finish this map for Miss Fitch, my teacher at Little Sauk. Can't say I like her as much as Miss Hamline. But she sure knows a lot. Geography first thing tomorrow. Did you know that—" A heavy step on the back porch, an insistent knock on the mud room door. Sabine broke off, startled. "Oh, somebody out there! Who could it be? Shall I go?"

"It's all right," Lucy said, "I'm expecting Noel's hired man, John, with the new barn lanterns." She laid down the flat ladling spoon on the work counter and untied her apron. "He said he'd come by a week or so ago. Sure have needed them, because those old the wicks don't turn up properly, the knobs so rusted out I suspect. Probably date back to the next-to-last DeLauriers."

"Why's Mister Wold coming only just now? He knew you needed them. You know, Ma, I've never liked him much. Always seems to be snooping around, spends a lot of time here in the kitchen with you. I'd have thought he should be out working, doing the things Uncle Noel tells him to do."

The girl's right, Lucy thought. She had a growing sense of uneasiness about the man. What could she do, though? She needed him, and he was being paid by Noel. "Well, guess he's just now been able to pick them up from Little Sauk station. Those lanterns had to be ordered all the way from St. Louis, don't ask me why." A more insistent knock. "Coming, coming, John!"

The door burst open just as she reached it and she was pushed aside as the man strode into the kitchen. "Where are they?" he demanded. "Well—cat got your tongue? Ha, that'd be a new one for you, Lucy. Always ready with words. I've come for 'em. Tell 'em to get ready, and we'll be on our way."

Lucy felt her anger rising. The insult. His sudden rude appearance. His demands. "Henry! Where've you been?" she heard herself say.

He looked at her sharply. "What's that to you?" Then, somewhat mollified, "Family business. Concerns Jane, if you want to know."

"I know about that."

"Oh, you do, do you? Well, expect you're sympathizing with the women. Don't expect you to understand."

Suddenly Tom appeared in the hall doorway. "Heard you down stairs, Pa, came down to see if—" he said hesitantly.

"Well, boy, go get your ma and Jane. You're leaving."

"Where we goin', then?" he asked. "Home?"

He didn't answer, just cleared his throat harshly while tapping his fingers impatiently on the table. "Get a move on, don't just stand there dawdling." Tom turned and ran upstairs.

Henry pulled out a chair with a scraping noise and sat down heavily. "Now what's all this?" he asked, noticing Sabine's open schoolbook and scattered papers on the table. "Hurry up there, Tom! Go fetch 'em!" he shouted in the direction of the hall. Then, to Sabine as he shuffled through her geography book, "Book learning's a fine thing if you've got time. Pushes your sight out from where you are." He paused as if recollecting something, then smiled ruefully in Lucy's direction. "You might say, hindsight is better than foresight, eh, Lucy?"

What exactly did he mean by that? Could be any number of things. His marriage to Agnes, for example. She also remembered something Agnes had once told her. Way back in Pennsylvania, before settling in Minnesota, Henry intended to become a schoolteacher. Something happened, however, and he couldn't. He still had a few books around, though. How ironic it was that, in fact, he had been a teacher after all. He'd taught Agnes to read and write. He'd taught her courage and self-sufficiency. At least that was one redeeming quality about the man.

But now Henry was in a questionable mood—rude, demanding, even threatening. He'd burst in and taken over her household. Had he been drinking? Had something happened back at the brick works? No, it was about Jane, he'd said. Seizing an excuse, she ventured, "Let's go upstairs, Sabine. We'll help your aunt get ready to leave."

After several trips up and down the stairs, they all gathered in the kitchen before loading into Henry's big farm wagon. "Dress up warmly, Agnes," Lucy cautioned. "Getting colder by the minute, and most likely dark before you get home. Henry, have you got rugs in the wagon?"

"Pa—about Daniel—" Jane caught him by the arm.

"Best wait 'til you're home to talk about that, Jane. Best wait," Agnes cautioned.

"No, Ma," she insisted. "We need to talk about it now, Pa—about Daniel!"

Jane, ever the outspoken one, Lucy thought. Yet it occurred to her that something else was prompting the girl. That she not only wanted to have it out with her foster father, once and for all. By insisting on doing it here, she might be counting on her support. She and Jane had had long talks over the past week. She felt she knew the girl's mind much better and her sympathy for her had increased. Jane loved Daniel deeply and was determined to make a go of it, however uncertain the immediate future out west might be. Sometimes it was like hearing herself—her hopes, dreams, her love for Bernard. In fact, it was almost like having another daughter, one more like herself, while so often Sabine reminded her of Bernard. Daniel—Bernard—she could only hope that Jane would never experience the same sense of loss.

Yet there was something else, too. Jane spoke of her father, Matthew Creighton, something she'd never done before. It was almost as if she hoped, that by going out to Montana with Daniel to the place where she'd last seen him, she'd find him. It was hard for Lucy to dispel that hope, even harder for her to point out the hardships of trekking west, the length of time it would take before they could grow out of the poverty it imposed.

"You haven't any more to say about the matter I haven't heard already," announced Henry decisively.

"No, there is, Pa. We need to talk." Jane repeated.

"Well, then, let's have it out," said Henry gruffly. "Might as well sit down. But make it quick. Don't want to get caught in that snowstorm on the way back. Front moving in, mighty fast. Lucy, how 'bout some coffee? All right, I'll tell you why I object to that boy," he continued, once Lucy handed him what he wanted.

"You think that because he's Jake Benson's son it makes a difference?" asked Jane, jumping right in with what she considered the heart of the problem.

"You're damn right. It's in the blood."

"But, Pa—"

"Only have to look at him to know that. Eyes too close together, for one thing."

"But, Pa—"

"Seen it all. He'd no sooner take off, pocket your money, than he'd leave you. On to somebody else, another woman, most likely."

"Now see here, Henry." Lucy could stand no more. "That's so unfair, so prejudiced, not to mention ignorant. I'd have given you more credit. How much do you know about the man?" She hesitated, then blurted out before she could catch herself, "And, for that matter, who are you to talk about abandonment? It seems to me—"

He set down his coffee mug abruptly and stared at her. Just as he opened his mouth to protest, Jane interrupted.

"You don't know him, Pa. Never took the trouble. Got a good job, lots of promise. A skilled carpenter. Hasn't seen his father in years. Never goes to Reagan's."

"Told you that?"

"Of course. I've seen his work, too."

"What would you know 'bout that? He was going to take you away. Hare-brained scheme to go out west."

"Good opportunities out there. Everybody says so."

"Take you away. From home." He paused, looked down at the table, stirred his coffee. "From us."

"Well, if that's it—" Lucy sighed. "You can't hang on to your children forever."

"No, that's not it. That's not it all." Henry drew himself up. "Not by a damsite. Now you're forcing me to come out with it. Don't say you blame me. Jane, girl, you'd better sit down, 'cause I've got some bad news. Fact of the matter is, he's taken off without you, Jane. Left his rented room in Long Prairie, bought a wagon team. Heard that from Bertrand, my old friend the blacksmith. Left town, plumb gone, lock, stock, and barrel."

"Gone? Left? Moved out?" Lucy and Agnes together, while Jane turned pale and stared at Henry in disbelief.

"Impossible," she insisted. "You're making that up."

"No," Henry said. "Folks 'round Long Prairie saw him leave this morning. Wagon piled high, leading his other horse behind the wagon. Heading down toward Sauk Centre. Sure enough from there West—without you." He shook his head. "Started out after him, I did, wanted to confront him."

"To confront him?" Lucy asked hesitantly.

"Yes, damn it. For leading Jane on like that." He paused, shook his head again. "Then I figured, well, what was the use? So then I figured, well, damn it, good riddance, he's not after Jane any more, safe to bring 'em all home."

"I can't—can't believe—that," Jane was close to tears. "Daniel'd never do anything like that. Leave me without a word." She fell back into her chair. "We were going to get married just after Christmas. Stay here until the spring thaw, then go out to Montana together. He'd already applied for the homestead grant at the government office in St. Cloud."

Henry looked a little mollified, touched, in fact, by Jane's emotional response. "Maybe better you know what kind of man he is, before you got married. Good advice for anybody." He glanced at Agnes.

For a few moments, no one said anything. The only sounds were Jane's stifled sobs and the wind picking up outside the kitchen windows. Finally, Lucy left the table and took down Bernard's heavy canvas jacket from the pegs by the back door. "Here, Tom, you'll need this for the cold ride home. Martin, rake out some coals from the parlor stove into this bucket. It'll keep their feet warm—for the first few miles, anyway."

As they prepared to leave, Henry muttered, looking out the kitchen window rather than at Jane, "You know, girl, there's a couple of other fine men around—Long Prairie, Prairie Lake—why, even here in Little Sauk. Maybe—" He broke off as they filed out to the wagon.

It took a while after that episode for Lucy to settle down to the business of preparing a quick supper, getting the children ready for bed, stoking the kitchen range, damping down the parlor stove, checking the doors and windows. One more trip out to the barn with a lantern to check on the stock. She'd missed the evening's milking and hoped Brownling would be all right until morning early. Drying up, anyway, with the calf nearly a heifer. Already snowflakes whirled and danced in the yellow lantern light cast before her. Winter had definitely come.

She was in her nightdress, brushing and braiding her hair. Louis, just nursed and content, was already asleep in his cradle beside her bed. Her bed looked very inviting tonight, and she laid back the quilt, smoothed the sheets.

So Henry had left with his family. The house now seemed empty, eerily quiet. Only the vague, indistinct whispers of past DeLauriers floated here and there from room to room. Had there been arguments about suitors, marriages, tears over loss? Even though Henry and his family had gone and would probably just be pulling into their own barnyard by now, they'd left behind anxiety and worry. Worry over Jane, compassion over her disappointment. The girl had just experienced a shocking betrayal by the man she loved. Her soul would bear those wounds for some time to come. Perhaps a life time.

In a sense, Lucy reflected, Bernard, too, had betrayed her by dying like that and leaving her. One could not always prevent accidents nor stop death when it came. When it did come, it could leave a person's heart empty, the mind fragmented like shards of glass, like that glass oil lamp which had once stood in the window of the old homestead parlor and was shattered by the tornado. It could never give out its light again.

Blowing out the wick in the new oil lamp on the table beside her bed, she lay down and reached to pull up the bedclothes around her. She might need another quilt before morning. She hoped the children would be all right. Perhaps she should—

The sound of glass breaking. For an instant she attributed it to her imagination, a carry-over from the image of the oil lamp she'd just created, but immediately realized the sound was real and coming from the guestroom. The storm—a strong gust of wind had broken the window. She must hang a quilt or a sheet or something over it, lest the snow blow in. Jumping up, throwing back the quilts, she walked out into the hall in her bare feet and opened the guestroom door. It was true, a strong wind was causing the curtains to billow inward. Now she realized that she could not reach the window because of broken glass on the floor. Turning to go back for her slippers, she heard the indistinct sounds just below, under the window.

Someone must be about to break into the house through that window, although that didn't seem to make sense. What should she do? The rifle! John Wold had reloaded it for her after Tom shot at Martin. For safekeeping, she now kept it under her bed. Creeping quietly back out into the hall to retrieve the rifle, she realized she couldn't lock the guestroom door behind her. It locked only from the inside. She'd have to aim the gun at the window and wait for the intruder to come through it.

But what about the door downstairs? She drew a sharp intake of breath—the front door! After Henry burst it open that time, it wouldn't lock. What if there were more than one person out there? The gang, still roving the area. She couldn't be in both places at once. Her knees felt weak, and her hands trembled so much it was hard to cock the gun, to hold it steady. And the children, oh, the children. She'd never felt so helpless before, so vulnerable.

For what seemed an eternity, she waited. No further sounds, except the wind outside. Where was he? Or them? Were they playing some sort of game, waiting for her to confront them, then easily overpower her? Obviously they didn't know about the front door. But why not break through the front windows? Force the back door? Nothing made sense.

Walking carefully over the broken glass, she edged closer to the broken window. Was that a voice she heard? Strange, though. No sound of a horse, a wagon. It seemed as if someone had crept up stealthily, silently, right up to the side of the house.

Now cautiously brushing away a billowing curtain, her heart pounding violently, she peered down from a corner of the casement. It was dark, but a half-moon shot in and out of snow clouds, just enough to reveal momentary glimpses of the yard below the window.

A man stood there, looking up at her. She jumped back, nearly dropping the rifle. As soon as he saw her, he stepped back into the shadows of a spruce tree at the edge of the lane. This was even more terrifying. What was she to do?

She couldn't be sure there was only one person down there. At least she had the rifle and a good vantage point from which to aim. She waited. After a few moments, the figure she'd seen stepped out of the shadows. A voice saying something—she couldn't be sure. She didn't believe in ghosts, but yet there was something so strange about this. A fleeting thought—someone from the past—a long dead DeLaurier—wanting to get in. Nonsense, nonsense. She couldn't let the house take possession of her like this.

Courage seemed to come, she wasn't sure how or why. Coming directly up to the window, she pointed the gun down directly at the figure below. "Who are you? What do you want?"

"Jane."

"What did you say?"

"Jane. I want to speak with her. I thought she'd be in that room. Didn't mean to break the window. Stone bigger'n I thought."

"She's not here," Lucy heard herself say, although she was hardly aware of putting rational words together, given her uncertainly about the situation. "And how did you know she'd be in this room?"

"Did some carpentry work in that house for mister Dubois, a while back. Thought that room'd be the most likely."

"She's not here, I said."

"Where, then?"

"Gone."

"Gone?"

"Back to her father's place." Now why did she say that? It would put the girl at risk, Henry's anger at a more dangerous level.

"Oh. I see. Just wanted to tell her something. Guess I'll have to write, then. On my way, left my team and wagon out there in the road. Didn't want to disturb anybody."

"You certainly did. You're very lucky I didn't take a shot at you. And it's very cold, standing here in the broken window." She laid particular emphasis on the word.

"Sorry, ma'am." He retreated to the lane, calling back, "Tell her—" The rest was lost.

Quickly she attached a spare quilt over the open window and heard the man call to his team, heard the sound of his wagon grow fainter in the direction of the Narrows, not toward Little Sauk as she would have expected, had he been heading down to Sauk Centre, as Henry implied. It was clear now that Daniel Benson had come to find Jane, most likely intending to take her West with him. He'd missed her by only four hours. "A great pity," she sighed. "Yes, a pity."

The winds of that November night tore off a section of DeLaurier house shingles. Next morning, her heart heavy with a sense loss hard to explain, Lucy went up to inspect the damage by way of the pull-down ladder in the upstairs hall, intrigued by the collection of trunks, boxes, old, broken furniture scattered around between the joists. Was there anything of value? Even so, it'd be Noel's, not hers. Covered with years of dust, cobwebs, she had no desire to investigate, at least not yet. Leave that for the spring.

By mid-week Noel and John Wold arrived for repairs, Noel concerned about damage to the house from snow drifting in and melting through the rafters. When a third man with them climbed out of Noel's wagon, Noel explained, "Mattias Holberg's one of the best roofers around." He laughed as he added, "Or will be, if he gets any more experience. Sure has been a windy season, not to mention that tornado last spring."

"Yes, ma'am," John said, helping Mattias unload several bundles from the rear of the wagon, "no time to lose, winter's upon us. Got those cedar shakes just in time, picked them up at the lumber yard in Long Prairie late yesterday."

"Hard to tell how much damage is up there from that last windstorm." Noel looked up at the roof, as he walked back and forth. "Seems to be mainly in front. We'll soon find out. John, you keep the ladder steady while Mattias takes up the first shoulder-load of shakes."

"If you don't mind, sir," said Mattias, "best you go up first to pull off the old shingles. Then I'll come up—the new ones are tricky to put on, 'cause they need matching."

"What're you going to be doing meantime, then?"
Lucy detected something in Wold's question. Suspicion—or jealousy, perhaps. She wondered why, she'd certainly never given the man any encouragement. Mattias didn't reply but looked embarrassed. "Come inside," she offered. "Might as well keep warm."

"Thank you, ma'am." He hesitated, glanced at Wold. "That'd be fine."

Once inside, however, Lucy noticed he seemed uncomfortable. Offering him a cup of coffee, she said helpfully, "Everyone fine at your house?"

"Yes, ma'am."

"Your brothers well? Your mother?"

"Yes, ma'am."

"More snow expected soon?"

"Reckon so."

Lucy was at a loss. What had gotten into the man? "Wouldn't you like to take off your jacket? That range keeps the kitchen nice and warm."

He seemed to debate this question for a moment. Finally he said, "Thanks, don't mind if I do." His face seemed flushed and he avoided looking in her direction.

As Lucy helped him slip off his heavy canvas work jacket, she felt him trembling. It occurred to her that he'd contrived a way to be alone with her. Having done that, he now didn't know how to take advantage of it. She wanted to help him, but wasn't sure how to draw him out. The situation produced in her a strange feeling. She was disturbed to notice her hand shook as she refilled his coffee mug. "Tell me, Mister Holberg, are you and your brothers still planning to head west?"

"It's Mattias, ma'am. Missus Dubois."

"Well, my name as you know is Lucy. Now tell me, what your plans are? Are you planning to go into roofing? Here? Or out there? Noel tells me it'd be a good business, with all the building going everywhere."

"I 'spect so, ma'am." He drained his second cup of coffee. Still holding the empty cup, and in a rush of words, "Say, I was wondering if—"

"*Eh bien*, Mattias," said Noel, stamping his feet while coming through the back door, "John's up there on the roof ready for you. *Vite, vite!* We're running short of time. *Mon dieu*, gets dark early, these winter days."

Mattias, his face now reflecting resentment and frustration, pulled on his jacket and went out the door without looking back.

Noel followed him a ways, calling after him, "When you two have finished up on the roof, take the wagon. John'll drop you off, then head back home to my place. I need to check some of the fencing along those fields across the road—don't worry, I'll walk on home from there." Without further invitation, he poured himself a mug of coffee from the big pot on the stove and sat down at the table. Lucy was a little taken back, but, after all, it was his house

"*Mon dieu*, more damage than I expected up there. Good thing we take care of it now. But that's not what I came in to tell you." He looked around. "Where are the children?"

"Sabine and Martin, of course, aren't back from school at Little Sauk yet. Laurence is upstairs playing, Louis asleep. You can see I've fixed up a pen for him over there in the corner, so I can keep an eye on him while I work." She smiled. "As you know, a woman spends an awful lot of time in her kitchen. The hub of the house, so to speak."

"*Donc, c'est bien*—that's fine, then. I mean, 'bout the children."

"You wanted to talk about them?"

"*Mais non, pas exactement.* Not directly. No, although it may concern them. *Éventuellement, tu sais.*"

"What, then?" He looked serious, far from that good-natured aura of well-being usually surrounding him. And that unusual amount of French—what did it mean?

Noel joined his hands together as he leaned forward across the table toward her. "The bank," he began. "You have been to Long Prairie lately?"

"Why yes, a couple of weeks ago. Just before Agnes came. I had to do some shopping at West's, at the dry goods' store. A new kettle from Lano's hardware."

She recalled painfully her earlier encounters with Patrick Reagan, with Homer West, in her first—and last—attempt to seek employment in Long Prairie. By necessity coming into West's for some other things, Homer West recognized her immediately. *Ah, missus Dubois, if I'm not mistaken. You are well?* He stared at her belly. *The birth went without mishap? Little one thriving? Now what can I do for you this fine winter morning? No trouble with drifts across the road, I trust.* Then he had the nerve to suggest she buy this or that. And when she unpacked the paper-wrapped parcel after arriving home, she discovered he'd put in some stick candy for the children.

"You went by the bank then?" Noel persisted.

"No—o," she answered slowly, her anxiety rising. "Had a little cash on hand, left over from last time. Why, is something wrong?"

Noel fidgeted, looked embarrassed. "*Eh bien*, there is a problem. He took a deep breath. "*Oui, et quel problème!*" That money you received from the sale of your old homestead, you remember?"

"Yes?"

"Bof! You see, it has been used up."

"What do you mean, used up? There was quite a bit left last time I checked. Just under fifty dollars, I believe. Here, I've got the receipt somewhere." She started to look in the sideboard drawer.

"It is no more. There has been a lien placed on it."

"What?" She turned toward him, shutting the drawer. "What does that mean? That word lien?"

"*Cela veut dire*—it means there was a mistake in your property lines. It means, Lucy, *ma belle-soeur*, that you and Bernard did not own some thirty or so acres beyond the line of where you'd cleared—or rather, Bernard cleared." He coughed. "The county surveyor, Perkins—he saw me in town. Knew you were staying on my property, called me in to his office. He pulled out a big book, a ledger, all the records in it, plat maps." He paused. "You have seen one of your homestead?"

Lucy remembered Smith's visit, his attempt to persuade her to sell the homestead. He'd raised some doubts about the property lines then on the map he'd brought. She hadn't believed him, convinced he was merely trying to force her into selling. "No," she answered vaguely, her mind going desperately over the details of that painful visit.

"So I look at that map. I read the records. *Difficile*, you know—that handwriting. But, *mon dieu*, it was clear. Perkins was right. Now comes the problem—*très compliqué*. Because you did not own that land, you could not sell it. And because you have already sold it, you must return the money—the value of it—to mister Goddard, the man who purchased that land from you. And now he must purchase it from the county."

"The county? The county owned it all along?" She was stunned. "How is that possible?"

"*Eh bien,* some mix-up of records, or records not there—who knows what. Ah, *la bureaucratie*—so possible to mix up."

Lucy began to take agitated steps back and forth between the table and the back door.

"Now Lucy, *calme-toi,*" Noel hastened to say, "*calme-toi!*" He, too, rose and began to keep pace with her back and forth across the room. "Listen, it may not be as bad as all that. You know, you are here. You and the children. The roof—he is now sound. The firewood—still stacked up behind the house. Food—well, if not enough, I provide."

"But—but I can't—"

"Now Lucy—" He put his arms around her, held her in one of his warm, bear-like embraces. "Now, now, *cherie, calme-toi,*" he said, stroking her hair, "it will work out. You'll see." Then, almost immediately, he released her. "No, it is right not to worry. We are—we are, you know, *de famille.* That is right."

Yet, through all her shock and disappointment over Noel's news, there was another feeling, another sensation, one she knew instinctively to resist.

Noel stepped away, headed for the door. "You know *c'est la vie,* life—she is not always fair, *n'est-ce pas?*" Just before it closed behind him, he said, "I must go walk those rye fields across the road. Those DeLaurier acres—they did not do well this harvest, as you know. One must look why. Some other crop, maybe? I hear that wheat, now—" and he was gone.

Noel's news, Noel's visit, left Lucy highly agitated. She paced around the whole downstairs, through the kitchen, the hall, the parlor, and back again. What could a woman in her situation hope for? Nothing.

After thinking about this for a day or so, she came to the conclusion that there was something she could do. She would swallow her pride and confront her situation straight on. Confront Patrick Reagan. And so, on a cold, snowy Friday morning at the beginning of December, she gathered up her courage. As soon as Sabine and Martin had left for school, she hitched Blaize to the wagon, and, bundling up Laurence and the baby, headed first for Noel's house near Little Sauk.

"Well, I don't know," Mary said doubtfully. "I surely don't mind looking after Laurence and Louis. Their cousins will be glad to see them. But you're going all the way into Long Prairie? Today?"

"Not good, *pas de question*," Noel warned. "Some snow drifts across the road after that last snow. Especially the first four miles main road up to Long Prairie. You'll never make it."

Lucy hesitated. "Well—what about your box sled? Wouldn't that be better? Couldn't I borrow it?"

"Lucy, be sensible," Mary insisted. "Don't go. Stay here, we'll have some tea." She looked out the parlor window. "And just look at those dark clouds over there. More snow for sure."

"No, I must go. There's something I have to do. Something urgent." She didn't expect them to understand, no use explaining.

"Ah, Marie," Noel sighed. He spoke aside to her in French. Although Lucy couldn't make it all out, it clearly implied he found her stubborn, headstrong, and unwilling to listen to reason.

After more discussion and protests from Mary, Noel reluctantly agreed to hitch Blaize to the big box sled. "*Eh bien*, don't know if this old horse can manage—bit heavier than the beast is used to."

Mary rushed out to the barn, loaded down with Noel's fur coat and mittens. "Here," she said, "as long as you're going to go against all good sense, at least put these on and pull that hood up over your shawl. It's already ten degrees below freezing!"

It took Blaize some effort to get through the first mile or so, but with considerable urging from Lucy he pulled the sled along, its long wooden runners occasionally slowed by slight drifts across the road, but gliding easily over portions where the snow was smooth and hard-packed from earlier traffic. A smooth stretch. Lucy was elated as they picked up speed, there was only another mile or so to go, around the next two curves.

A sudden jolt, a sharp whinny from Blaize as he stumbled, his forelegs going down into a gully in the road concealed by a large snow-drift. Lucy was propelled headfirst off the driving bench and the reins

slipped through her mittened hands. There was a terrible stinging coldness against her face, then darkness.

"Ma'am, ma'am!" A voice shouting something. "Are you all right,
miss?" Someone lifting her up. A face surrounded by a black-brimmed
hat was looking down at her. A face she didn't recognize—no—yes, something about it . . .

Nothing seemed to work—her lips, her arms, her legs. The stranger
had turned her body so that she was sitting propped up against a tree
trunk. "You all right?" he repeated. "Nasty spill there. Anything broke?"
She still couldn't speak, so shook her head. "Well and good, then," he
said. "Where you headed?" She pointed up the road. "North, toward
Long Prairie? Dunno 'bout that, ma'am. Worse farther on, just came
from there. More snow headin' this way from the east. See, nobody
comin' from that direction or down from the north either, for that matter."

Lucy shook her head. She was regaining some feeling in her face,
her hands. She tried to get up from the snow bank in which her legs
were still buried. "Must—must go, have to make it to—must see—"

"No ma'am," the stranger said, pulling her up by the arms out of
the snow bank and helping her to her feet. "Easy, now, don't try to move
too fast just yet. Say, don't I know you—aren't you ..."

Then it dawned on her. The man was Smith, the man who'd tried
to force her to sell the homestead. Out of the few people coming along
this road—why him? With great effort she tried to think of what to do—
she'd made the man angry, in a sense cheated him. What if he recognized her—worse, left her here to freeze to death? She pulled Noel's fur
hood farther around her face, hoping it would cover most of it, nestled
her chin down into the coat collar. "Oh, oh," she pretended to moan,
"my—my sister, Lucy Dubois—down the road there—she's—"

"So—that woman was your sister, was she?" He let go of her arm.
"Well, you can tell that woman from me, she sure missed a sweet deal. And
for all that, I hope she regrets it." He turned back to his buggy. "I'll just be
on my way, then, 'fore the weather hits again. Worse farther on down."

"But, sir," Lucy called after him. "Can't you at least help me get the sled turned around?"

Either he didn't hear her, or pretended not to, and drove on. Lucy saw Blaize wandering over by the fence, apparently the harness had broken loose somewhere. Now what was she going to do? She felt shaken, frozen in every bone in her body. If she ever longed for help, if she ever felt prepared to accept it, it was now.

Pulling up part of an old, rotted fence post from the side of the road, where the original fence had broken down, she used it to dug away as much snow as possible from the runners. She had little feeling in her fingers as she tried to hitch Blaize back up to the sled. Some of the harness had snapped in the impact, but there were several loose pieces she managed to tie together. With great difficulty, she slowly climbed back up into the sled and then, by urging the horse forward and backwards, she finally got the sled turned around and onto the smoother, snow-packed portion of the road.

As Blaize moved forward, more cautiously this time, Lucy realized her whole body felt strange. Worse still were the stabbing pains in her fingers. She didn't know how long she'd lain in the snowdrift. Since it was nearly dark, it must have been for some time. Smith's words echoed in her head—worse farther on . . . worse farther on . . .

Feeling chilled to the bone, her body aching all over, she stopped to pick up her children and the wagon at Noel and Mary's. Noel insisted she keep the box sled for the remainder of the trip home.

"Road west maybe a little better, but why risk it? And so late already."

Only after they'd reached home, after she'd sent Sabine with Laurence and baby Louis to warm by the kitchen stove, only after she and Martin had unhitched Blaize from the borrowed box sled—it was only then, when she'd begun filling Blaize's pail with mash and she kept dropping it, that she realized her hands were turning blue with frostbite. Moreover, Smith's words kept echoing in her head, round and round—*worse farther on.*

That man, Smith. He could have been responsible for her death. Yet wasn't it her own decision to go, against all reason, against all those warnings from Noel and Mary? Fortunately she hadn't taken the children. They might have died, too. The thought, the guilt, was hard to bear. Painful, too, were the sensations in her frostbitten hands as she tried to revive them by applying warm, moist towels back in the kitchen. Aches all through her body, especially her head. Yes, that man, Smith. Vengeful, mean. Would have left her to die.

Smith. What if it had been someone else who'd found her? She imagined an alternative sequence. The box sled gliding down the road, swaying rhythmically over the snow to the horse's movements. Suddenly a jolt, a wrenching sound. Reins slipping helpless through her hands. Blaize whinnying in terror. The feeling of intense cold, the burning sensation against her face a contradiction. Blaize broken free, galloping across the snow-covered fields, his leather straps snagging against thorn bushes, fences, farther and farther away, until he disappeared.

Now it seemed that she was looking down on herself, lying there in the snow bank, Noel's overturned box sled beside her, the steel runners sharp, gleaming like knives. A voice. "Lucy—Lucy!" That voice—so familiar. She tried to look at his face. She couldn't open her eyes. "Are you hurt?" Still she could not respond. Then he lifted her head and kissed her, first on the forehead, then on the mouth.

He lifted her up in his strong arms and began carrying her through deep drifts of snow, the rough wool of his jacket sleeve against her cheek. "I will take you home, now," the voice said, "home where you belong. When you awake, you will know that."

Awakenings 7

"Ma!" exclaimed Sabine. She and Lucy were folding sheets off the line running from the back porch to the big elm tree at the edge of the barnyard. "Ma, did you know there are whole continents, one called Africa, and—and—all kinds of strange things—deserts and jungles, with lions and tigers, and—" She talked on excitedly about the day's geography lesson. For reasons unknown to Lucy, that was her daughter's favorite subject. And yet those images took shape and place in her own imagination and created an expansion of her own, constrained world which often served as both comfort and escape.

Despite the enervating late April breeze, flapping and billowing the clothesline into glorious promises of an early spring, Lucy found it hard to concentrate on what Sabine was saying. In fact, it was difficult to concentrate on much of anything.

Christmas and the remains of winter had passed as if in a dream, leaving only fragmented memories. That painful encounter with Smith on the road to Long Prairie, abandoning her in the snow bank to die, frozen to death for all he cared. The man's voice . . . the other man's voice. Christmas with Noel and Mary, their house filled with an elaborate Christmas tree laden with glass ornaments imported from Germany, the odors of roasting turkey, spiced apples, yeasty breads. Elaborate gifts, which they could never match. Guilt, a sense of helplessness. Her own house full of whispers and the imagined odors of past celebrations, yet irrelevant as to the present.

One of Sabine's geography words repeated itself over and over again in her mind. Continents. That meant whole spaces in the world, spaces far away. She unpegged the next sheet and handed two corners to Sabine. The two corners of the world. The third and fourth beyond her grasp.

"And Miss Fitch told the class about those things called pyramids in—in e-jep I think, with kings buried deep inside them. All dark, with poison arrows ready to fly into you if you try to steal the treasure. And she said . . ."

But Lucy's mind wandered again, burial places. It occurred to her that she was, in a sense, buried in her own place. She recalled again that wonderful vision, had recalled it many times. Thrown out of the box sled into a snow bank, lying unconscious, until a man's voice—familiar but yet so distant—wanting to bring her home. Home! Yet if it were Mattias Holberg's voice, the man himself was as distant as—as if he were on another continent. She knew the brothers hadn't left for Montana yet. But that was all she knew.

"No, no, Sabine, hold up the corners of that sheet like this." The voice faded, the vision vanished.

"I did, Ma," her daughter retorted, "you just weren't paying attention. And I'm trying to teach you something. You ought to listen."

More important than Egypt or the pyramids at the moment, however, was Lucy's assessment of the family situation. That caught her attention. That's what she listened to, most of the day, a good share of sleepless nights.

"Watch out, Ma! That sheet's still fastened to the line. You can't take it off until you take off the peg! Aren't you paying attention at all?"

The continents . . . Lucy's own continent the DeLaurier place. A miniature continent, confining, isolating. No, not a continent, more like a tomb inside one of Sabine's pyramids, trapped within its three sides. The DeLaurier place was at one corner, Long Prairie the second, Noel's place third. No, not just three corners. Four. The four corners of Little Sauk's roads. The old homestead with its compelling memories of Bernard, of a happier time, now most recently causing that financial loss which would further confine her. The restitution of money paid for land not hers. That small remaining sum for the original sale of the homestead had been her last hope for independence.

Little Sauk, yes, Little Sauk. Not a crossing of two roads continuing on in four directions. Rather, it was more like four roads confronting each other at dead ends.

"Ma—this sheet won't—" Sabine let go the end of a sheet while trying to describe a pyramid, and the wind whipped it beyond reach.

"Watch out for that end," Lucy admonished sharply, "it's trailing on the ground! You should be more careful! Get your mind out of that geography book!" Immediately she felt remorseful, aware that she'd spoken harshly. "I'm sorry, dear," she added. "You're always such a help. Now please take that basket upstairs and put the linens in the chest."

In the quiet moments which followed, sitting alone on the back porch steps, Lucy thought about what Sabine had been saying. Many years ago, still a school girl in the lycée at Ste-Anne's, she had known about such things, her imagination nourished like Sabine's, her desires quickened for worlds beyond the banks of the St. Laurence, for worlds touched by those ever flowing waters. How strange, how unforeseen her family's immigration to this prairie world which she could never have imagined, her life with Bernard, her life now without Bernard, her life both with and without Mattias.

Those pyramids . . . she tried to visualize them now. They seemed somehow connected with the thought of going beyond Little Sauk, to faraway places, beyond the restricting world to which she seemed to have been confined. Those pyramids . . . surely they rose high out of the sand, everything a burnished gold color, even the sky, the pyramids so high they dwarfed the few palm trees found only in a distant oasis. The desert air would be oppressive with heat, heat radiating in great waves over the land. Yet there was no life about them. They symbolized death. Monuments to the dead, containing within them bodies once alive, objects once useful, plants once growing.

Surely the old DeLaurier place was not like that. It was full of life, the gardens and fields full of verdant promises, a green island in the midst of prairie, a continent surrounded by ocean waves of prairie grass, an oasis in a desert. Where, then, was the contradiction? She found it difficult to describe those feelings often descending upon her, waves of restlessness leaving her feeling hollow and empty, a yearning which couldn't be satisfied. A yearning for something else.

In such a mood bordering on frustration, it was difficult not to think about the man named Homer West. She'd first seen him while working out at Reagan's with Agnes, before she'd married Bernard. After Bernard's death, when she'd gone to West seeking employment, he'd humiliated her. Yet she'd been forced to go back to his store for one thing or another and each time he'd seemed more cordial. Moreover, each time she found something she hadn't asked for in her wrapped package—candy for the children, a scented candle, a small bottle of lavender water. She'd returned all but the candy. The last time he'd said, in his strangled kind of voice, *Please, Missus Dubois, if there's anything I can do for you, just let me know. Just anything.* The look on his face while saying that made her uncomfortable.

Unfortunately the only other store carrying his stock of merchandise was way down in Sauk Centre, too far to consider, unless she took the new train, a short line recently laid between Sauk Centre and Long Prairie. But that was too difficult, too impractical, too expensive. A pity that Thurstrom's at Little Sauk was so limited, especially since miss Stina's son had taken over. Harald Thurstrom seemed interested only in stocking farm implements and running the small post office. That Homer West—how should she respond?

Several days later Lucy was setting out onions in her kitchen garden. Hearing a buggy pulling into the barnyard, she was shocked to see Homer West already getting out of his buggy. There was no way to avoid him.

"Mornin', Missus Dubois. My, my, what a fine morning to be working out here, fine for a fine-looking lady, if I may say so." Laughing at his own joke, he happened to notice Noel and John over in a nearby field repairing some fence posts. They saw him and Noel tipped his straw hat slightly. Noel often expressed his dislike of the man, but was always polite in his courtly, French way. "Well, well," West continued, somewhat disconcerted, "see you've got some help this morning. Just stopped by, see if you needed anything—came out to make a delivery near Little Sauk, not far from your place."

"No, not today, thank you. And I'm too busy at the moment to work out a list."

"I'll be happy to wait, must be something you need. And your credit's always good with me." He smiled engagingly.

Lucy was growing increasingly uncomfortable. At a loss, she waved in Noel's direction. "It's possible, though, that Mister Dubois needs some things. I'll just call him over."

"Well, I really must be getting back to the store," Homer West said uneasily. "I'm sure he'll be up to Long Prairie one of these days soon." He remounted the buggy. "Say, wanted to ask you—Memorial Day picnic coming up at Faith Church on Third Street. There'll be lots of food, fireworks." He paused to check the horse, already getting restless. "Just wanted to ask if you'd do me the honor of being my guest?" He paused, adding, "You and your children, of course."

Lucy had to think up an excuse quickly. She knew no one from that church, she'd have to rely exclusively on him. For sure it'd be a subject for local gossip, no telling what the local column of the *Long Prairie Argus* might do with the sight of the two of them together at a church picnic, even if surrounded by her children.

She bent down to put in a few more onions, packing them in firmly. "No, thank you," she finally said. "I've already made plans with the children for that day."

"Oh, too bad," West replied, obviously taken back and disappointed. "Some other time, then." He released the buggy brake, snapped his whip, and drove out of the barnyard, turning to wave as he rounded the house.

During the next few weeks Lucy mulled over this brief encounter with the man. Each time it left her with more unsettled emotions. It was clear she needed to talk to someone who could help her sort things out. Noel wouldn't do, certainly not her sister-in-law, Mary. Mary was so practical, her imagination so limited, and her tongue so sharp.

Then there were Agnes and Jane, of course. She'd only seen them briefly over the past year, Agnes last September, both once just before Christmas, when good weather held and she'd taken the children all the way up to their place at Eagle Lake. They'd spent the day together, Martin and Tom hunting wild turkeys down by the river, Abe and his father, Henry, turning out an urgent shipment of bricks. And she, along with Jane and Agnes, baked for the coming holiday, full of talk, memories, laughter, tears.

How unfortunate such good times did not last. Just last month she'd met Agnes and Jane shopping in Long Prairie. Jane seemed very distressed, so they stopped in Matheson's for tea, and a chance talk. There had been no word yet from Daniel Benson. Henry felt justified in his suspicions about the man, and never overlooked a chance to say so. Loss—missed opportunities—*Speak for yourself, Lucy,* she said to herself. *Speak for yourself.*

Yes, Lucy definitely needed someone to talk to about her own affairs. Maggie Skinner. Leaving Sabine in charge at home one Sunday afternoon, Lucy put the riding pad on Blaize and rode east to Maggie's place, a mile down the main road.

She found Maggie hoeing her kitchen garden, a large plot surrounded by a white picket fence to keep out rabbits and raccoons. Lucy admired the neat rows of green onions and lettuce, the line of stakes where tomato plants in another month would be knee high, the border of thyme, rosemary, and savory just inside the gate. The bush beans promising to provide them in two more months with enough beans for canning. Although Maggie often complained about the fact that her husband, Lemuel, left the kitchen garden to her—woman's work, he claimed, just an extension of the kitchen where she really belonged—she was proud of it, bestowing much loving care upon it from March to October, then enjoying the fruits of her labor for all next winter and early spring.

"Afternoon, Lucy." Lemuel was also outside, nailing up a few loose boards on the side of their chicken coup. He paused to take off his straw hat and mop his forehead with a red bandanna, pulled out of his back overalls pocket. "Fine day for workin', sure the good Lord don't mind if we take advantage of the weather to work on a Sunday. With all that rain we've had, things pilin' up, weeds a-growin'. Just ask Maggie on her knees down there. All's you can see is her sunbonnet, bobbin' up and down."

Maggie got up and brushed the dirt off her apron. "Enough for now," she remarked decisively, "don't know which is worse, them weeds or that hot sun." She shut the white picket gate behind her, untied her bonnet, and fanned her face with it. "Come on in for some lemonade, sure will be good to sit a spell and cool off a bit. Too warm for April. All that's hard on the knees, sure I'm about to get that rheumatism my poor old ma had so bad."

Waving a hand toward Blaize, she called, "Lem, look after Lucy's horse for her, will you? Let him drink first, then let him go into the barn, or else tie him up under that shade tree over there. Now then, Lucy, let's go on in and talk. I'm sure you're here for a reason, were never much for idle gossip—not like some I know. But come on in, let's sit while we can."

Maggie's kitchen was always a comforting place, flooded with sunshine from the big windows Lemuel had put in along the south wall. Unlike the DeLaurier house, built squarely on the north side of Little Sauk road with the kitchen in the back spur facing north, the Skinner farmhouse was on a small hill some distance from the main road and faced southwest, with the big kitchen windows opening to the south and east. That, combined with Maggie's attention to waxed and polished floor boards and the big, glass-domed cupboard filled with pretty blue and white china, always conveyed a sense of order and well-being. How like Maggie herself, Lucy thought: definitive, orderly, matter-of-fact, outspoken. Strange how one's home reflected the person.

What about the DeLaurier house? It seemed that house said very little about her—such a confused, mish-mash of add-ons, reconstructions, furniture—so much not hers to begin with. Only the high-carved walnut bed was worth anything, or the Limoges plates which had been a wedding present from her mother. The bed spoke of her past. The plates? Well—surely the promise of something beautiful and valuable in the future, she hoped.

"Here, wet your whistle." Maggie poured out two glasses of lemonade as they sat down. "Well, now, tell me why you're here? Every thing all right at home? Children fine, no accidents lately? Laurence behaving himself? Baby teething well, no fussing? Good, fine and dandy. Say, I'll bet you're here because of that Rachael Olson. Sure don't know how that woman comes by so much gossip. Never know what you're going to read in her country correspondent letter to the *Argus* every Friday. Sometimes interestin', usually not. Wouldn't be surprised if we read next week 'bout your bein' a visitor here at my place. Sure can't imagine how that woman knows so much. Must have eyes and ears everywhere. Ha, ha, fit and proper job, too. Seems I heard somewhere or other that *Argus* was the name of some old god—somethin' like that—with a hundred eyes." She stopped to take a breath and smiled broadly at her own joke.

"Rachael? You'd better watch out for Harald Thurstrom, too," said Lucy, seizing a welcome opportunity to break into Maggie's relentless chatter. "He hears all the latest down at his store, probably reads all the mail, now he's post master. Ought to be a law."

"Prob'ly is, though he's not one to pay attention. All right, enough chit chat. What's really on your mind?"

"Homer West."

"No! That Homer West? Never suspected you were interested in that druggist, as he calls himself. Sure wouldn't trust him with any of my medicine. Be poisoned sure's you're born."

"Be that as it may, I've had to give him some thought," Lucy hesitantly answered. "You know my situation, it—it—well, it hasn't gotten any better, especially with the children growing and becoming more demanding."

"Well, you know what they say. Children don't grow more demanding. Their demands just change. Say, that reminds me, I guess you knew your sister-in-law Mary expectin' again, come fall. Lost count what number this time." She paused to drain her glass of lemonade. "My, oh my, we've got off the point, haven't we? What was it we were talkin' about? Can't quite remember. Oh, Noel's big family. Good thing he's doin' so well. Did you know—Oh, wait a minute. Got off the point again. Now, let me see—talkin' 'bout somebody in Long Prairie—somebody . . . no, wait. Glass empty, here, let me give you some more lemonade."

Lucy pushed her glass forward. "Homer West."

"Oh, yes. Homer West, of course. Can't say as I care much for him. Suspicious look about him. Homer West, you said?"

"Yes."

"What about him?

"Should I marry him? That is, if he asks me?" she might as well come right out with it.

Maggie looked surprised. "Him? Well, guess he's not so bad lookin' if you squint your eyes, hold your breath. Hair all oiled down like that with some kind of smelly oil, big nose pushing out over a bushy mustache. Maybe a bit old for you, although you wouldn't know it. Hides it well—has a good barber, spends a parcel of money I'll bet on those dapper clothes of his."

Although Maggie's description of the man seemed a bit harsh, she had to admit there was some truth in it. "Mind you," Lucy went on, "I'm not saying I'm going to, he hasn't even asked me yet. But what if he did? I could move into town, life would be easier. Just think what that would mean. We'd have a nice, big red brick house in town, with a porch all around and a flower garden, carriage house in back. Maybe a big house like that right close to the town square, where all the best houses are."

"I suppose you'll be tellin' me next you'd join the Ladies' Circle, heard tell they just formed one in Long Prairie, Little Sauk'll be next, don't doubt. Ladies get together to exchange all the latest sewing patterns and the like, crocheting now all the rage. I can just see you sitting together with old Missus Bidwell, makin' lace doilies." Maggie chuckled, then slapped her knee as the image took hold and she burst into robust laughter. "What about that for a life, eh?"

Lucy felt the blood rush to her face. "Stop, Maggie!" She had, in fact, considered how wonderful it would be just to sit in one's parlor, talk about things like that, do fine handiwork, read books, learn things about the world. Those pyramids, for example, sure sounded interesting. Bernard had left some books, but reading Voltaire, Descartes, Rousseau—and in French—didn't much attract her. As for social contact—she'd had so little. Life always seemed too busy for such luxuries. "You can stop that, Maggie," she repeated. "I've no interest in any of that," knowing full well that it was only partly true. If it meant some kind of security, well then, she'd stomach it.

"Lucy, girl, listen to me." Maggie grew more serious. "I can't really tell you what to do. You must find your own way. And you will find your own way, I'm sure. Just have faith—and courage. And keep that—for the man you really love."

Keep that for the man you really love . . . As she rode back home to the DeLaurier place later that afternoon, Lucy thought over Maggie's last words. Maggie sharp black eyes seemed to see through everything, her quick, practical mind grasped problems even before they were fully explained. Yet there was disappointment in the fact that this afternoon Maggie hadn't really offered any realistic suggestions about what to do regarding Homer West, or even Mattias, for that matter.

Stopping by the Little Sauk general store later that month, summer already underway, she hoped to buy some new lids for canning jars. At least Harald Thurstrom was sure to have that sort of thing in stock. Entering the store, she was surprised to see Thurstrom step out from behind the postal wicket with a letter in his hand. "Look, Missus Dubois," he said. "Just came from your brother. Real big letter this time, not his usual postcard."

Lucy was annoyed. Over the past two years her elder brother, Georgie, had sent a few postcards from various places, their scanty news known by Thurstrom even before she read it. Now, as he held out the letter, Lucy noticed the envelope partially opened.

Lucy couldn't read the smeared postmark and wondered where George was now. He and her other brother, Alphie, had moved away with her parents some eight or so years ago. Later she'd heard both brothers were about to head out west for advertised free land in North Dakota, or maybe pan for gold in the Black Hills. They claimed they were going to make a fortune, they'd send for the rest of the family, they'd acquire untold riches.

Desperate to read the letter, she resisted the urge because Thurstrom was sure to ask about it. On the other hand, she couldn't wait until she got home. Pushing it down into the bottom of her basket, she said quickly, "I need a dozen mason jar lids."

"That all?" he asked, obviously disappointed.

He opened a drawer in one of the cabinets lining the back wall, counted out twelve. "How about—"

"That's all I need today, thank you." Once he'd wrapped them in brown paper, she paid him without further comment and dropped the package into her basket. "Good day to you, then, sir." He followed her to the door, obviously hoping she'd change her mind.

Outside, Blaize moved restlessly, tied to the store's hitching rail, his movements limited to the length of the reins. Lucy quickly mounted the driving seat, tore open the envelope. She couldn't wait any longer, although the horse's movements made it difficult to read. "Whoa, there," she said several times, "don't worry, we'll head back soon." Impatiently she unfolded the pages and spread them out over her knees.

The letter was dated some time back, the first of May, nearly a month ago. Surprisingly, it was from Shakopee. Yes, she thought, taking another look at the envelope, the postmark did say Shakopee! How strange, that's where the family had immigrated first from Quebec because of an uncle of her father's. A year or so later they acquired homestead parcels in Todd County, and took the government wagon trail along the Mississippi River and eventually west to Long Prairie. That must have been in 1865, the same time as Henry Morton. In fact, she vaguely remembered seeing him one night, as they camped in an old barn along the trail. Had it really been eleven years since then?

Now what had happened to Georgie's dream of free acres, gold? Why had he ended up back in Shakopee? It could only be disappointing to her, to everyone else, that he hadn't made it rich, that he was back right where the family started. Her instantaneous dream of a solution was dashed to the ground.

Still, she needed to know his news. "Dear Big Sis," he began, followed by a conventional greeting and expression of hope that she and the children were in good health. That's not saying very much, she thought. The news which followed, however, caused a sharp intake of breath:

> *You will be pleased to learn that our little brother, Al, is now engaged to miss Jeanne-Marie Drouville. Her folks own a big flour mill in town came from Quebec too several years ago. They I mean Al not her folks are to be married end June in St. Marys church. Did I tell you that I am bilding a hous, nerely across the street from this church, on 4th street? Oh yes, maybe I forget that pece of news, have not written much lately I guess. Also the job I have now at Mr. Stadthauser's drygoods store sure has helped save some money, at leest enuff to help get started on the house Bought the lot a cupple weeks ago for $25.00, guess I already said it was on Fourth St got a few lads at work to help me dig the fowndation, storm cellar first a few tornadoes through these parts every spring then us boys will start the frame. Got a relly good frend here name of Alfred, Fred for short, Mr Stadthausers son, pears be a good carpenter & will help with the house and all. Maybe bild nother house for ma & pa for when oncle Paul moves way wich he plans to do soon.*

The news took her by surprise, so full it was of unexpected information. Alphie getting engaged—almost still a boy, couldn't be more than
nineteen, Georgie twenty-one, apparently settling down, still hadn't
learned to spell. She turned to the second page:

> *Well, Sis, enuff for now. You know I werent never much
> for writing, specshly in english. Pease reply soon, want to here
> what the familys doing these days.*
> *Ever, your devoted brother, George Guyette*
> *P.S. Al sends his kind regards. Write care of p.o. Just down
> the street from Mrs Smiths bording house, lots of men here,
> coming and going. Good thing he's livin with Stadthauser fam-
> ily, helps round the house. Dont worry they take good care
> of him only let him see his intended miss Drouville Sunday
> afternoons.*
> *GG*

Lucy folded up her brother's letter carefully and tucked it into her
basket of jar lids. She urged Blaize forward, wondered why the horse
wasn't moving, realized she'd forgotten to untie the reins from the hitching rail. Hardly aware of what she was doing, she climbed back onto the
wagon, turned Blaize into the main road. Blaize needed no urging. He
knew where he was heading and started off with a gallop toward the De-
Laurier barn.

Lucy was so engrossed in Georgie's news that she was hardly aware
of the passing landscape. Over and over again, she repeated its phrases,
thought about their implications. A good job. Georgie getting married.
Only a boy. This Drouville girl—what was she like? She wished Georgie
had said more about her, other than that she also was from a French
Canadian family and spoke the same language.

She came back with a start to where she was: sitting on a wagon seat,
the reins in her gloved hands, the wagon jolting and bouncing. The dusty
Little Sauk road stretched ahead of her, rolling hills of yellow-green hay

along both sides of the road, waiting to be cut and baled, the distant blue flash of a lake through trees.

The letter. The engagement. The job. The new house. A house for her parents, who'd been living all these years with her father's brother in town somewhere. She'd had little idea of what it must have been like for them, never having been able to make the long and difficult journey by wagon. Yet it was probably not a bad thing they'd sold their homestead just south of Little Sauk when they did. Poor papa had never been successful, the land poor with so much wooded and marshy. It destroyed his health to keep on trying. A skilled woodcarver, cabinet maker. He should never have become a farmer. The offer of a free homestead tempted him, then trapped him.

She missed them terribly, especially knowing they had never seen her children—their grandchildren. Nor, indeed, Agnes's children. How strange to recall they had immigrated as a family, hoping to create a family nucleus around their homesteads. Instead, the family had been forced apart by one circumstance after another. At least, she thought, there might be some consolation in the fact that her brothers might reconnect the family back in Shakopee.

Lucy sighed. The time for thinking was over. Now to think about the noon dinner for the workmen working in the south fields. Collect Laurence and Louis from Maggie's. Sterilize the mason jars, start canning Maggie's green beans. Yes, summer left little time for thinking. Thinking of alternatives. Of the men, intruding into her life. Of the choices she must make, or face the choices they might make.

Yes, that was by far the worst of her thoughts. Her main direction now had to be, must be, to reveal her thoughts to Mattias before it was too late, before he made his own decision to leave for Montana. Before Noel forced her into further entrapped commitments and confused emotional conflict. Before Homer West forced his attractive enticement of security upon her.

Coming back from a visit with Agnes one afternoon in early July, thinking once again about George's letter—a letter which she'd by now nearly memorized, she was only a quarter of a mile down the road from the DeLaurier place when she saw Homer West's buggy just ahead of her.

An unexpected, unidentified sensation. Of course, she'd given him some thought from time to time, occasionally found him in her dreams, sometimes in situations which she could not possibly account for, situations which caused her to wake up, her face flushed, her heart racing. A conflict of emotions—whether to meet or avoid him. In one way, she hoped he wouldn't notice her wagon on the road behind him. She slowed down, held her breath as he drew up even with the lane leading to the house. Suppose he stopped and turned in?

West's buggy stopped. Now he saw her and waved, waited. What should she do? The children were over at their Aunt Mary's house until after supper, when Noel planned to bring them home once he got back to Little Sauk on the six-o'clock train up from Sauk Centre. He'd gone down to place an order for some big farm equipment from a company in Chicago. It sounded so important. He'd described it as a big thing, the latest model of a steam threshing machine, "revolutionize my methods," he'd said. Just like him.

No, this time she was trapped. *How'll I deal with the man?* she wondered. Maybe she could persuade him not to come in, to leave. Still, there was an element of apprehension in the knowledge of his decisive, persistent manner. Now he was waiting at the head of the lane, no way to avoid him.

"Afternoon, Missus Dubois," he said, raising his fashionably tall hat as he sat in his buggy. "Such a fine day, thought I'm come out to see how you and the children were faring. Last time Noel Dubois was in town, said one of your children was poorly. I've made up something for him—I've a diploma in pharmacy, you know."

She forced a smile, trying to make it look cordial. "Good afternoon, mister West. It's nice of you to drive out all this way to ask about Laurence."

"If you must know, it's not only for that I came out."

"Oh?"

"Yes ma'am, thought I'd just come out to see you as well, ask if there was something you might be needing from town. In fact, I brought a few things from the store the children might enjoy." He motioned toward a brown paper-wrapped package on the seat beside him, then began to edge his buggy down the lane, clearly expecting to be invited into the yard, into the house.

Despite her reluctance to encourage him, she could not do otherwise but motion for him to follow her down the short, u-shaped lane to the house. He stopped at the porch. "I'll just unhitch my horse, let her graze in your front yard," he said, "won't bother bringing the buggy all the way 'round back, if you don't mind. She won't go far without the buggy."

Lucy feared he might try to follow her on foot around the corner of the house to the barnyard behind. Should she take time to unhitch the wagon? Would he follow her into the barn? She wasn't sure of his intentions, only her own suspicions. No, better invite him into the front parlor. She wished she hadn't removed the old rifle from its shelf by the front door and hidden it under her bed. Now, leaving Blaize still hitched, she walked back to the brick path leading to the front porch.

West stood waiting by the front door. Bowing slightly, he held the door open for her, then followed her in. Not waiting for an invitation, he hung his top hat on the stand near the door, then glanced here and there, as if taking stock of the house and its contents.

The front parlor was not used very much, especially in the summer, and smelled musty. Still, she had to keep this visit as formal, as distant as she could. "Please, won't you sit down, Mister West?" she said, motioning toward the horsehair sofa. She took the rocking chair by the window.

"Homer, please. None of that Mister West." He folded his fingers nervously around the small package he'd brought in with him. After some hesitation he jumped to his feet and held it towards her. "I brought some gifts for the children, which I hope you'll accept—just some candy, a bag of marbles for the boys. They aren't home this afternoon?"

"Why, thank you, sir, that's very kind of you, I'm sure. No, the children are at my sister-in-law's."

"There for the day, then?"

Without thinking, she answered, "Yes, Mary took Louis for the day, and the older ones go there directly from school." She instantly regretted conveying this information, which could only render her more vulnerable. Accepting the package, she said, "Really, sir, you need not have bothered." She set the package down at her feet. She couldn't refuse it, yet didn't want to give him the pleasure of watching her open it.

After a few moments of embarrassed silence—West clearly expecting her to respond in some way, Lucy wondering how she could get him to leave, she got up to light the oil lamp on the small table by her chair. The room was growing darker, it was already late afternoon and beginning to cloud up. As she sat down again in the rocking chair, she carefully tucked her skirts around her ankles.

West cleared his throat. "Yes, storm coming up. Could use the rain." He picked a piece of fluff off the knee of his trousers, cleared his throat again. "Fall's coming, winter won't be far off, I'm thinking."

"Yes," said Lucy.

"Looks like winter's likely to be a bad one this year. Lots of rose hips. I keep my eye on such things. Use them for syrup, you know. Good for the grippe and the like."

"Really?"

"In fact, can't keep up with the prescriptions. My business is doing very well these days. Folks coming in from all over the area, even as far as Staples."

"As far as that?"

"Not too many good pharmacists around here, you know. Doctors, neither. Too bad we lost my good friend, Doctor Giles—you know, Dr. Giles Maynard."

"Yes. A loss." Lucy shivered. A loss in more ways than one. In her opinion, the man had been responsible for Bernard's death.

"Now folks 'round here have to go all the way down to Sauk Centre—Dr. Johns, up above the drug store on the corner of Main Street. Druggist a good friend of mine, knows Dr. Johns well."

"Doubt if I'll ever have need of him."

"You never know. He's the only good doctor around, these days."

"What about that new woman doctor in Long Prairie—Josephine Mellgren? I see she's been advertising in the *Long Prairie Argus*, practice just off Second Street."

"Wouldn't count her. Don't think much of her, or any female doctor for that matter," he answered. He cleared his throat again. "You're a long way from Sauk Centre here, Missus Dubois, even from Long Prairie."

"I manage," said Lucy.

"Well, but do you really manage? What I mean is, there isn't much reason to live so far out from everything. I mean, wouldn't it be better to live closer to things?"

"What things?" asked Lucy.

"Why, anything," he said. "Now see here, ma'am—Lucy, if I may call you that. You're known around these parts as a fairly smart woman."

"Oh?" she said coolly.

"Well then—er—can't you see what I'm driving at?"

"No," said Lucy, actually beginning to enjoy his discomfort.

"Well, what I'm driving at is this. I've been admiring you for a long time. A smart woman like you, ma'am—Lucy. You could be a great help to a man in my business, if you know what I mean."

"Does that mean you're offering me a job?"

"Job be damned," said West. "Yes, plague take it. I mean, what I mean is that, no, not right away at least. And maybe not the kind of job you're thinking of." He edged forward on the sofa, their knees almost touching "I mean a more important job, with me, a kind of partnership, like, as you might call it." He jumped up from the sofa, leaned over and rested his hand on the lamp table.

Lucy's nervousness increased. As he now stood directly in front of her, she used the leverage of her hands to move back away from him and up against the chair back as hard as she could. "I don't really know what you mean," she said, lamely.

West reached down and covered her hand where it rested in her lap with his, then seized both hands. "Why, I'm certain you do," he said. "Oh, Miss Lucy, I'm sure you're lonely out here, a young, pretty widow like you. I can offer you so much. How long has it been since you been with a man, a real man?" He pulled her up from the chair and drew her body close to his. Beads of sweat stood out on his forehead. He was breathing heavily.

Lucy now knew why he had come all the way out here. What should she do? What could she do? Yes, it had been a long time since she'd been with a man—a real man as he put it, almost—no, at this point she felt confused, couldn't remember how long, exactly. How often she'd longed to feel Bernard's presence in bed next to hers, how often had she reached out only to touch an empty space. Empty, like the hollowness in her heart.

Her brain didn't seem to be working. It was hard to breathe, she felt dizzy, her legs weak. West now held her firmly in his embrace and trying to force her to sit on the sofa beside him. He pushed her head back and kissed her on the mouth.

"Such beautiful hair," he said. "Rich, the color of saffron—of red-gold elixir, of—" He did not finish, but with a sudden movement pulled out the comb which held her hair in place. As it tumbled around her shoulders, he began stroking it, running it through his fingers, buried his face in it, his warm breath against her neck, her ears.

His efforts awakened an erotic response in her. Such urges were so long dormant that against her will she began to feel great pleasure in its awakening.

"Oh, Lucy, Lucy," said West. "I've wanted you ever since I first laid eyes on you. I used to watch you at Reagan's, swearing that you'd never be anybody else's but mine. Bernard got you first." He turned her shoulders toward him, brushed back her hair, and kissed her again and again.

Lucy felt herself yielding. Yes, it had been a long time since she'd experienced these sensations, the comfort of a man's real embrace and not one merely in her imagination. It was bringing out forceful desires and inexplicable urges. Oh, Bernard—Bernard—*mon amour*—

There seemed to be no movement of time, only a suspension of moments, hours, and seasons. Homer—The room spun around her. In that suspension of reality and heightening of sensations, she was aware only of the closeness of the man's strong body and the perfume of some tonic he wore. A strange odor which reminded her of green palm leaves, the exotic pyramids of Egypt.

"Let's go upstairs," he said. "There's no one home but us. Here, let me take off those shoes, let me see those pretty bare feet." She dropped back onto the sofa, helpless, as he knelt down and unlaced her shoes, pulled off her long stockings. He lowered his head, kissed her toes. A stab of pleasure pierced her body. Cupping his hand around the top of the lamp's glass chimney, he leaned over and blew it out. Then he pulled Lucy to her feet and, still holding her closely with one arm, opened the parlor door with the other and drew her out into the hall to the bottom of the stairs.

She stopped, startled. The hall should have been darkened like the rest of the house. It was strangely light. With a shock, Lucy realized her front door stood wide open. Someone was standing there motionless, a tall figure silhouetted against the pale sky. His unexpected presence caused her to break away from West's embrace and West to draw back farther into the shadows of the hall.

"Oh, evening ma'am, Missus Dubois, and—and, uh, sir," the man said hesitantly, "sorry to startle you. Didn't much mean to intrude. Found your door partly open, ma'am, and was just about to knock." He still stood framed in the doorway against the light, one hand resting on the doorframe. He took a step back and then glanced down at her bare feet. His shoulders hunched up in embarrassment as he said, "Guess I'll be on my way, then. Just wanted to—" He started to turn away.

Although his back was against the light, she recognized his voice. It was Mattias Holberg. How much had he heard, standing there in the doorway? What had he seen? She bent her knees slightly so that her skirt would cover her feet, tried to push back her hair from her shoulders. Not much she could do about her loosened hair. "No, wait," she said, "no need to go." She had to keep him there until she could get rid of Homer West. "Mister West here was just leaving. He was kind enough to bring some things for the children from his pharmacy. Wanted to save me a trip into Long Prairie." She came out to where the man stood awkward and hesitant at the porch railing. Then, turning to speak back into the hall, she said in a loud voice, "So nice of you to come out all this way to Little Sauk, Mister West. When Noel brings the children home—and he'll be here any minute now—they'll be delighted with what you brought."

West's face, as he emerged from the house, was red and distorted. In fact, his whole body seemed to radiate angry frustration. Although his appearance frightened Lucy, it also provided her with an element of satisfaction. She had won the struggle, not only over him but also over herself. She stared at him fixedly and said in her firmest voice, "And you needn't come out all this way again, sir. We'll be able to manage well enough all our needs in the future."

She hoped West would fully understand the hint. But what if his anger and frustration led to greater determination—what if he came back, planned some sort of revenge?

"Found this mare wandering down the road, Mister West," Mattias offered as he untied the horse from the porch railing and led him over to West's buggy. "Grazing along the grass as she went. Figured she belonged to somebody visiting here, so brought her up to the house. Must've come loose from where she was tied up in the first place, seems to me. Here, I'll help you hitch her up."

As soon as this was done, West seized the horse's reins with a rough jerk, placed one foot on the buggy's iron footrest, and urged the horse forward even before he'd fully seated himself. Without turning his head, he called back grudgingly, "My thanks to you, sir, I truly am—" The rest was lost as West applied his whip to the horse and rapidly pulled out into the main road.

Returning to the porch, the man looked down at the floorboards, shifted his feet a little, then said to Lucy, "Didn't expect to find your door open, though. Didn't mean to intrude."

"That's quite all right, Mister Holberg—Mattias," Lucy replied. "This door must not have latched properly, we've always had trouble with it. You did us a great favor, really. It would have been most unfortunate if Mister West hadn't been able to find his horse and get back to Long Prairie just now."

Hopefully he would not pick up the double meaning of her words. It wasn't certain whether he'd seen them embracing in the hall, or even whether he suspected the reason for West's visit. "But now that you're here, can I give you something to take home to your brothers, ma and pa? Made some apple pies this morning."

"No thank you, ma'am," he said, as he turned back toward the main road. "Can't stay. Almost dark. Bit of a walk home."

Lucy realized he was nervous and embarrassed about *something. He was in too much of a hurry to leave. And he had not called her Lucy. Did he think she and West were courting? Of all people to suspect that. What would he think of her? If only she could explain. And yet, if he hadn't come by, just at that moment what could have happened? What a dilemma!*

The worse was yet to come. Several days later Maggie came by to drop off her copy of Friday's edition of the *Argus*. "Here, take a look at this, will you! See what Rachael Olson's latest "Echoes from Little Sauk" says. The nerve of that woman." She handed Lucy the newspaper, folded to the country correspondents' page.

Hear our Green Prairie pharmacist isn't able to keep his mind on prescriptions these days. Watch out, all you gals down Little Sauk way.

Lucy's reaction was mixed anger and embarrassment. The so-called news meant that she dared not go near West's store any more. Ever.

Her heart sank each time she heard wheels in the lane leading to the house. She'd rush to the parlor window to see whether it might be Homer West. Noel knew of West's determined interest in her and joked about it whenever he saw her. *So he can't resist you, eh?* he'd say, or shall I start looking for a new tenant at the DeLaurier place? If she didn't know better, she might have thought Noel jealous.

No, he was jealous. She was becoming increasingly aware of that, his subtle advances. Worse still, was the feeling that she'd almost been seduced. Why had she let herself go like that? Was she so weak? If only in thought, she'd unfaithful to Bernard's memory. She couldn't forgive herself for her lack of resistance.

It was even becoming a problem to go to Thurstroms's, no telling whom she might meet, what gossip she'd hear about herself. Today, though, there was no choice—a few staples she absolutely had to buy and she hoped Thurstrom had them in stock. There might also be another letter from George. Drawing up to the store, she was disconcerted to see the Holberg team and wagon alongside. She recognized it for its distinctive blue color on one side. Depending upon which Holberg was in the store, things might be awkward. She wasn't sure she could face Mattias after that last encounter. It would be hard to bear his low opinion of her, or for him to think she had no interest in him. Perhaps it was better not to go into the store and risk such a meeting. She didn't know how he might respond.

However, just as she was about to turn Blaize around and return home, Hans Holberg emerged, carrying several large parcels. Mornin', ma'am," he said abruptly. Not waiting for a reply, he quickly turned away and occupied himself with loading the parcels into the back of his wagon.

Lucy mumbled something. Although the man seemed cool and distant, at the same time she was relieved there was no need for further conversation. It seemed safe to go inside. Slipping the handle of her shopping basket over her arm, she climbed down from the wagon and entered the store. It was dimly lit inside as usual. Harald Thurstrom was busy chatting with Rachael Olsen, the dangerous—in Lucy's mind— country correspondent. Two women whom Lucy didn't know were looking over a display of yard goods. Several men sat on stools at the end of the front counter where Thurstrom kept the big Chicago and St. Louis mail order catalogues. Lucy couldn't quite make out who they were, the Clarks, maybe, looked like Will from the side.

"Well, well, Missus Dubois," boomed Thurstrom. "Ain't seen you in a coon's age, two, three weeks maybe." He emerged from the little barred cage which formed the post office. "Just beginning to wonder if you was all right."

At the sound of her name, one of the men sitting at the front counter turned toward her. Even with his back to the light, she realized it was not George Clark but Mattias. Was he staring at her? He closed the catalogue he'd been looking at.

Just then Thurstrom took her by the arm and led her back to the postal cage. "Come now," he boomed out, "got a package for you, don't know what, but think it's from some where down there, maybe Shakopee. A photograph, maybe? Look, see, studio's name stamped in the corner."

What bad timing! His nosey manner annoyed her, this time more than usual. Why was it that Thurstrom seemed bent on making his own world larger by incorporating everybody else's business into it? And at the wrong times?

He handed Lucy the package, and he stood there impatiently, waiting for her to open it. She had no choice but to slip off the string and tear open the heavy brown paper. A single large sepia photograph was enclosed inside a stiff cardboard folder, edged in gold. It showed a young woman wearing a ruffled dress, low on her shoulders, a cameo on a dark ribbon around her neck, a fan in her hand, thick black hair drawn back from her face and piled elegantly high on her head. She was sitting primly in a velvet-covered chair, the dress falling in heavy folds around her feet. Standing stiffly beside her was a man with a big, bushy mustache, dressed in formal clothes, a brocade vest, high collar and cravat, a silver-headed cane in his hand. It took a moment to recognize her brother, Alfie. Their wedding picture. Seeing it moved her more than she might have expected, yet she had no intention of satisfying Thurstrom's curiosity further. Quickly she wrapped the paper loosely back around the cardboard folder and tucked it under her arm.

Her thoughts went to Mattias, sitting at the catalogue counter and looking as though he wanted to speak to her. This would be an opportunity, perhaps her only one, to try to clear up whatever wrong impressions he might have. She dropped the photograph into her shopping basket and looked back toward the front of the store. Yes, he was still there. Seeing her looking in his direction, he reached down for his canvas bag and slung the strap over his shoulder. Turning at the same time, he pushed back the stool and started to get up.

"Ah, Mattias," called Thurstrom. "I see you're ready to place that order, yes? Stay there, I'll just get my book from the back."

Although disconcerted at the interruption, Lucy was all the more determined to set things right. She'd go over to Mattias now, while he was waiting for Thurstrom to return with his order book.

"Oh, Lucy, a word with you before you go." Rachael Olsen blocked her way. Lucy tried to push past, but Rachael, insistent, seized the handle of her shopping basket. "What's this I hear about you and Homer West? My, my, you've been busy, haven't you?" she said mockingly.

"Just a rumor."

"No, no, it must be true, on best authority!" Rachael protested, her voice growing louder and more insistent. "Come on now, 'fess up. When can we expect the wedding?" She let go of the basket handle and seized Lucy's arm. "Must find out the truth, I've got to have some interesting news for my readers, you know."

"Excuse me, I can't talk now," said Lucy, breaking away. "Someone's waiting to speak with me, he's just—"

But the stool at the catalogue counter was empty, knocked over. Mattias Holberg was gone. Outside came the sound of wagon wheels crunching on gravel, then receding. In a moment distance swallowed them up.

LETTERS FROM THE RIVER

8

Another letter from Georgie. Lucy had stopped by Thurstrom's for some lamp oil, and Harald Thurstrom was all eagerness, waving an envelope with a Shakopee postmark. "Your brother again, missus. What news this time?" As if he didn't already know.

She sat down on one of the catalogue stools to read it. The usual formal greeting, a word or two about Al's wedding, his hope she'd gotten the photograph, his own job at Stadthauser's. He'd been promoted to principal drayman, was completing the house he and his friend Fred Stadthauser were building on Fourth Street. The remainder was of more interest:

> *Tell you what I'd like to do is build a house for Ma and Pa, what do you think, seems that the lot next door is coming up for sale soon, according to my boss Mr Stadthauser. He knows all the goings on round these here parts. Wouldunt that be something, them living here close in town since I know you dont live to cloose and have a lot of worries. Town here growing like crazy, new gran-arys, flower mills Jacob Ries Bottling works pays good hoping that for pa. Hastings and Dakota Railway the H & D, we call her the Hell and Damnation RR now runs through all the way through Shakopee to the Dakota. Fact is that's how I ended up here in Shakopee no need to travul all the way by wagon like the old days.*

Then Georgie closed with his full name in elegant flourishes.

After reading the letter, she thought of Georgie's situation often enough over the next few weeks. He was successful. He was independent. He was able to provide for their parents. And where was she?

It was a day when she and Martin were working out in the barn, cleaning out the stalls after sending Brownling to the east pasture and putting Blaize in the stock pen. The barn seemed a different place under those conditions—no time for envious thoughts about Georgie's situation. No time for mental escapes, romantic fantasies. The work was back-breaking in the late summer heat, the dust dry and choking.

"Be careful," Lucy called to Sabine as she noticed her daughter heading down toward the river. She carried a picnic basket over one arm and Louis on the other hip. Laurence trailed along behind carrying a fishing pole and picking wildflowers.

"Don't worry, Ma. I'll just let them cool off in that shallow place and play in the sand. Laurence says he's going to catch a lot of fish."

"Ma," Martin said, "watch out. I'm going up to the loft and pitch down some more hay." With that he scrambled up the steep ladder and worked up in the loft for a few moments. As the hay started to drift down, Lucy forked the accumulated piles farther down toward the end of the barn and into the stalls. Within about a quarter of an hour, "Only one more bale up here, Ma. Guess no more 'til harvest."

"This'll have to do then." She wondered whether they'd make it. "And now don't forget to clean the floor by the tack room."

"All right. Wait, I'll go out to the trough and bring back a bucket of water." No sooner had he disappeared out the door, than he burst back in. "Ma, someone's coming down the lane—nice lookin' horse and buggy." He stood looking out the barn door. "Say, it's stopped down there by the walk to the front porch."

A sinking feeling struck Lucy in the back of her spine. A nice looking horse and buggy—it could only be—"Hush, Martin," she whispered. "Let's wait and see. Come back in, don't let him see us." She cautiously peered around the edge of the door. The buggy was empty, but she recognized it. Homer West was probably at this moment crossing the front porch and about to knock on the front door. "Stay back, Martin," Lucy whispered. "Keep out of sight."

Unable to wait longer, Martin took a cautious look. "Say, now that man's standing beside the buggy and looking around."

"Martin! Get down—stay inside the door!"

Martin lay flat on the barn floor and inched up toward the doorway. "He's getting back in the buggy—now headin' towards us. Hey, now stoppin' at the back porch."

"Missus Dubois, are you home?" The man knocked loudly on the back door. "Missus Dubois—Lucy? Lucy? Hello there? You must be around, I see your wagon in the yard."

She drew back even farther into the shadow of the barn.

"Look, Ma," Martin whispered, "he's coming over here!"

"Quick, Martin, up into the loft! No noise, quick!" Martin ran for the loft ladder back of the harness room and scrambled up with Lucy just behind him. She dared not risk another encounter.

When they reached the top, without another word between them, they ran across the boards until they reached the last remaining loose bale of hay, then rolled over it until they tumbled down into the narrow space between the pile and the wall. "Stay well down, Martin," she hissed. "Let's hope—"

"Lucy! I know you're here somewhere." His voice came from the entrance to the barn.

"I've something for you." Now his voice came from near the bottom of the loft ladder. "Are you up there? I need to talk to you."

"Ma—what's he want to talk to you about?"

"Shhh," hissed Lucy, covering his mouth.

"Lucy, dear?" West called again, apparently starting to walk away from the ladder. Lucy breathed a sigh of relief. Where was he now? How maddening as well as frightening to be a fugitive in her own barn.

After what seemed an eternity, she heard the creak of the buggy frame as West mounted the step and sat heavily on the seat. He seemed to be muttering to himself, and gave an angry snap of his whip. A rattle of wheels, growing more distant. With a sigh of relief, she followed Martin shakily down the loft ladder.

"I'm going to do some weeding in the garden," she said. "Now where'd I put my yellow sunbonnet? Could have sworn I hung it here on the harness rack. Not here—oh well, must have left it somewhere. Must be getting more absent-minded."

That was, in fact, a growing concern. Misplacing things, forgetting things. As summer's days folded one into the other, life seemed to depend more and more upon habit, routine, rather than rational thought.

And now, in the days that followed at the close of summer, her second summer in the DeLaurier House, the barn more frequently served as a refuge. It was, after all, a real refuge. That desert oasis Sabine had described in her geography book was its original concept, but the one Lucy developed provided an oasis of a different sort. The dark coolness of the barn, its quietude, even its pungent odors of cattle and fresh hay were hers.

That incident with Homer West still distressed her, diminished her. She relived its details over and over. She could not control each time a heightening of emotions—her face flushed, body quickened, spine tingling. The man's warm strength, his scent of palm trees, exotic and enticing. It was impossible to erase them from memory. And now that last near encounter in the barn—

Again, that strange conflux of sensations as she visualized Mattias, hair the color of ripe wheat, eyes of a strange intensity, the strength in his shoulders, the skill of his hands, the accidental brush of his woolen sleeve against her face that day, when he carried Sabine over to the Holberg's wagon after the funeral. His gentleness as he took Sabine in his arms. The strength of his arms as he lifted her up from the road on that stormy day when she was in labor with Louis's birth. At least, in her mind it was Mattias, not his brother Erik. No one had ever clarified which brother.

Lucy now realized Homer West was dangerous in the sense that she could not trust herself around him. She suspected she might be betrayed both by her senses and the enticement of security, a security paradoxically granting her freedom from the threat of drudgery and poverty. She also realized that she must come to some understanding with Mattias before it was too late. Could she do it through his brother, Erik? He seemed so sympathetic. Yet what were Erik's real feelings toward her? That was a part of her dilemma for which she was not prepared. Nor was she yet prepared to deal with Noel's interest in her, which seemed to go beyond any ordinary family relationship. In a way he was holding her hostage through the DeLaurier House and her financial dependence upon him. It was not right. It was not fair. It was not to be solved easily.

Now, with summer drawing to a close, the promise of her second harvest before her, there were other times when Lucy simply sat for long periods of time staring out the parlor window. She'd not seen her sister, Agnes, much over the summer. They were busy up there—the farm, the sawmill, the brickyard. Besides, it was painful to witness Jane's disappointment over Daniel Benson's apparent abandonment of her and listen to Henry's continued berating of the man and his father. For Lucy, either staring out the parlor window or engineering her other escape, that desert oasis—the close earthiness of the barn—that site seemed safe enough.

"What's the matter, Ma," Sabine asked one morning at breakfast, concern in her face.

"Nothing, dear. Why do you ask? Hurry up, finish your bread and jam so you can get on to your chores before school."

"Well, you look so . . . so peaked, like."

So Sabine had noticed. Lucy glanced in the mirror hanging over the washstand just inside the back door. It was true, she did look a little peaked. The dark circles under her eyes made them look sunken, her nose longer. Her hair looked dry and sun-streaked, only carelessly pinned back into a knot, strands escaping here and there. How could anyone be attracted to her?

No wonder she'd gotten into such a state. There'd been too much work during the day, too little sleep during the night. She would toss and turn, thinking of Bernard, of Agnes, Homer, Mattias, Noel. Her own situation. When sleep finally did come, it was restless and filled with nightmares. Mornings woke her with renewed exhaustion.

The nightmares repeated themselves over and over again, with only the details varying. She was on a train, going she wasn't sure where. She had a large, heavy suitcase which she couldn't lift up to the net rack above her seat. In some versions it was more than one. *Please help me*, she'd call out, *I can't reach the rack.* No one seemed willing to help. Finally she managed to reach the suitcase down on the floor and grab its handles. But in trying to swing the suitcase up onto the net, the lock flew open and the contents spilled out. At the same moment she was aware that the train was pulling out of the station.

To her horror, she saw there was still another even bigger suitcase left behind on the platform. It seemed the children were also on the platform, although one of them appeared to be missing—she couldn't tell which one. The catches on the window were so rusted shut she couldn't open it. She pounded on the glass, trying to shout something but nothing came out. At that point she woke up crying, *Stop, stop!* Her body was drenched in cold sweat, the bed clothes thrown about in disarray. Louis was whimpering at having been awakened. Grown too big for his cradle, he now slept in her bed.

What could this nightmare mean? Her mother used to believe in dreams. She'd tell about an old woman she knew named Madame Lesage who could reveal a person's deepest thoughts, tell a person's worst fears. Village girls used to go to her with their dreams to find out whom they were going to marry, or whether a woman was carrying a boy or girl, whether they'd be rich or not. What was the secret of her own dreams? Lucy searched for clues, but found none.

The end of her search came suddenly, unexpectedly. One evening after supper she was mending Martin's stocking under the kitchen oil lamp. The rush of impressions, of connections, was so powerful that she cried out and dropped the stocking and darning egg into her lap.

"What's wrong, Ma?" Martin sat next to her, struggling with his homework. "You look so—so funny. Did you stick yourself?"

"No, just a sudden thought. I need to find something. Keep on with your work and don't leave 'til I come back to check it."

She lit the lamp on the parlor table and opened the drawer of the little writing desk. Taking out Georgie's last letter from its envelope, she unfolded it, moved closer to the lamp, and began to read it through for the hundredth time. This time, however, certain words caught her eye:

Hastings and Dakota Railway the H & D we call her the Hell and Damnation RR now runs through all the way through Shakopee to the Dakotas. Fact is that's how I ended up here in Shakopee no need to travul all the way by wagon like the old days . . .

And then, what he'd said about the houses:

save some money, at leest enuff to help get started on the house. Bought the lot a cupple weeks ago for $25.00, guess I already said it was on 4th Street, got a few lads at work to help me dig the fowndation, storm cellar first (a few tornadoes through these parts every spring), then us boys will start the frame. Tell you what I'd like to do is build a house for Ma and Pa . . .

Carefully she folded up the letter, replaced it in the drawer, and sat down in the rocking chair. There was a connection. There must be a connection. Something, deep down in the recesses of her mind. The signals she'd hoped for with regard to selling the old homestead. They came. Not all at once. No, now they were coming in a series. One connection, a second connection, a third. Georgie's letter one connection, the train, two houses.

She stood up abruptly, the rocking chair continuing in motion for a second or two. "Of course, of course," she exclaimed aloud. "Two houses. The train. We could leave this DeLaurier house, leave these problems here. We could go to Shakopee. I could find work there. We could manage."

"What's that, Ma?" Martin called from the kitchen.

"Nothing," she answered. "Just reading your Uncle Georgie's letter. Keep on with your home work."

Yet as Lucy considered this decision over the next day or so, nothing hardly described it. Her mental list of things to do was confused and fragmented, the steps out of order, surely many omitted. Even by train it would be difficult. Packing, furniture to go by wagon. The stock auctioned off. Train fare? Louis only sixteen months old. Martin and Sabine—another new school, new friends. Agnes and her family—a hopeless distance away. She'd probably never see them again. Then, the tenancy of the DeLaurier place.

Yes, indeed, the tenancy. Noel and Mary's eldest son, Raymond, only thirteen, and long before he could carry out Noel's plan to invest him with the DeLaurier place. New tenants until then? She thought of the garden she'd planted, the fields she'd helped harvest, chickens she'd raised, canning jars and crocks filling cellar shelves. True, in a sense, none of these things were really hers. Nevertheless, they had extracted a large part of her life, a part she could never recover. Could she start all over again somewhere else? Would it be better—or worse?

Suddenly a wave of realization hit her so forcefully that she gasped in surprise. What of Mattias? Of course he was one of the problems facing her. Yet to break off that fragile relationship, if indeed it was a relationship, just as her attraction to him had grown into something possessive and compelling . . . Why didn't he give her a stronger signal? Well, she couldn't wait. She'd go to Mattias and have it out, however improper that might be. Surely it was improper to fall in love with him in the first place. Yes or no? she'd say. What are you waiting for?

Early that evening, leaving Laurence and the baby with Sabine, Lucy walked the mile down to the Holbergs', nervous about her mission, uncertain what she could say. It wasn't something she'd planned to do, but matters seemed to have come to a head, and their urgency gave her a kind of strengthened resolve. Sep was sitting on the porch as she came up.

"Evening, Sep. Came over to see how you were. While back you son said you were ailing. Brought you this apple pie. We sure had a good yield of fruit this year, how about you?"

"Oh, fair enough, Missus Lucy," he answered. "Fruit flies pretty bad, though, took half our Macintoshes. Mighty nice of you to come over, though. As for me, well, feelin' a mite better. Just a minute, I'll call Karin." There was no answer. "Well, must've gone down the road to see Greta. They always seem to have a pack of things to talk about. Sit a spell? Wouldn't mind your company."

"Thanks, Sep." They chatted for a few minutes about the crops, the weather. She took a deep breath. "Your sons around? Thought they'd enjoy the pie, too."

"Nope, Erik was here while ago. Went into Little Sauk to see 'bout some business at the bank. Big trip out West 'fore comin' up all too soon."

"Out west?"

"Yes, guess they'll be leavin' 'fore long. Don't know what Karin and I'll do, though, prob'ly sell out, join them 'em."

"Them?" Lucy's hands went suddenly icy cold.

"Well, you know my son Hans—once he makes up his mind. Got great plans, ideas. All started after he met a man at Reagan's not long ago. Big spreads just for the asking in Montana, he said. Hans got a notion 'bout dairy farmin', thinks that's the better place than these parts."

"What about Erik? Mattias?"

"Erik? I guess he's pretty well made up his mind to go out with Hans. Matt? Well, him, too. Been mopin' round here somethin' awful these past few weeks. Somethin' eatin' on him, dunno what. Seems to me it started with somethin' he read in the *Argus*."

"Something he read?" She knew what it was.

"Don't read that paper myself, 'cept maybe bushel prices for wheat."

The icy feeling of her hands was painful, her heart pounded in her head. "They're leaving—when?"

"Soon, I reckon. Lot to take care of—government papers, arrange to join a wagon train goin' soon—'fore winter sets in. Them mountains, you know."

"Yes, plans for—for—travel—always—always—hard." The words came out automatically. She hardly knew what she was saying.

"Say, you're not thinkin' of leavin' Little Sauk, are you? Rumor goin' round, can't recall where I heard that from.

"That's still—still more or less uncertain," she stammered.

"Uncertain? Depend on something?"

He'd hit the mark. "I'm—I'm not sure." She forced herself to her feet and laid the apple pie on the porch railing, her hands still icy cold, the coldness seeming to pass through her entire body.

"Well, I'll pass the word on to Karin. She'll be mighty sorry to see you leave. We all will. Need any help, let me know."

"There's one thing—" she had a chance, one last chance. "Would you please tell Mattias to come over to see me? I need his opinion about something connected with the place." Her mind raced desperately after more words. "About—it's about those roofing shingles he put on a while back."

Sep looked puzzled. "I see. Well, I'll try to do that, Miss Lucy," he answered. "Memory ain't what it used to be, but I'll try remember tell him soon's he comes home tonight."

But the next day Mattias did not come, nor the next. He had obviously made his decision.

That Saturday, leaving Sabine once again in charge of the younger children, Lucy hoisted Louis up onto her back and walked the mile down the road to Maggie Skinner's place. Maggie didn't believe in dreams or portends or such like, although she set great store by the Farmers' Almanack. Usually she insisted in seeing things in a very, no-nonsense sort of way. That was what Lucy needed just now.

"Well, well, if it isn't the youngest young'n," Maggie exclaimed as she reached over to take Louis from Lucy. "Here, set you down, young man. Come in, come in—just made a pot of coffee. Hey, there, keep out of that pile of kindling wood, no, not that cupboard door, neither! Here's some big spoons to play with. Can't take your eyes off'n them littl'uns a minute, can you? Well, let's you and me have some coffee then." She motioned Lucy toward the opposite chair at the kitchen table, filled two blue enamel mugs. "Can tell somethin's on your mind. Somethin' not in the *Farmer's Almanack*, I reckon," she laughed.

Lucy was uncertain how to begin, how much to say. She played with Louis and his spoons for a few minutes, giving herself time. "You're right, Maggie, something on my mind." Then, all in one breath, "I must leave here—no, I mean—I must stay."

"Well, girl, that's the darndest dilemma I ever heard of. Can't do both."

"Hard to explain. There's so much to think about, so many things."

"What kind of things? Name just one."

"Men, marriage. Dependency."

"Marriage? What about it? Thought you'd resolved Bernard was the best and the last. Not still thinkin' 'bout that Homer West, are you?"

"Well, I—" Lucy already regretted the direction this conversation was taking. "I need—can't manage—too dependent on Noel—want—"

"Looks to me like you're pretty darn independent as it is," Maggie snapped. "You really want to lose that?" Then, in a gentler tone, "True enough, I reckon, true enough. It's hard for a woman on her own, little'ns and all." She stopped, extracted the tablecloth from where Louis was trying to pull himself up, stood him on his feet, and pointed him in the direction of the cat, asleep in a basket by the stove.

"There, Pushkin might keep him occupied for a time. Now then, what were we talking about? Oh, yes. Your Bernard. Well, Lucy, with all due respects to your Bernard, did you have someone in mind? Someone 'round here?" She suddenly got up. "No, Louis, don't pull the cat's tail. She don't like that." She sat him back down with the spoons.

"I think—" Lucy began hesitantly.

"Let's see, now," Maggie interrupted. "Who's 'round here? There's Homer West," ticking him off on her fingers. "Well off you might say, established in Long Prairie, easier life for you—he such a bad choice? Been out to see you a few more times, has he? What 'bout one of those lads down t' Holberg place? Still trouble tellin' 'em apart, 'cept for Hans. Nice lads, broad-shouldered, strong, decent, hard working—blond boys not bad looking, though I think—" She smiled, ticking off two more fingers, then a third. "Yes, think I'd prefer Hans if'n I was you."

Lucy's heart began to race. How much should she tell Maggie about that incident with Mister West, with Mattias later at Thurstrom's? Her conversation with Sep Holberg and the knowledge that the brothers were planning to move West?

"And I hear," Maggie rattled on, "that the widower Clark's lookin' for a wife—Rachael Olsen's ear for gossip useful, for once. Hmm, you'd have a step-son nearly your own age, might be a problem. Then there's Noel's hired hand, John Wold. Maybe 'bout your age. Seems to spend a lot more time over at your place than he needs to, must have his eye on you. Hard workin', good handyman, useful around a farm, you sure could do worse. How many does that make, now?" She held up one hand. "Lookin' like five already. Then that son of Georgie Hart's, who's helpin' his father build the new flourmill in Little Sauk? Bit young for you, maybe, but his father's mill will sure pay off eventually, bring in a pot of money. And, as you get older, difference in age don't matter. 'Course you'd have a real bitch for a mother-in-law."

Lucy had no answer to this distressing catalogue. Were she to single out any one name on the list, it might lead to confessions she wasn't ready to reveal, was hardly sure of herself. Then there was that deep secret within her heart, the secret she would never reveal to Maggie. The secret that was Noel Dubois.

"'Course, you know darn well, don't you, that you can't have marriage and independence both at the same time. Marry any one of them fellers, and you know dang well how it'll be."

Lucy caught her breath. Leave it to Maggie to hit home with a truth so obvious, so forceful, that she wondered why it had never struck her before. With a sigh of frustration, she answered, "Well, Maggie. Guess I'll have to think about that, won't I?" She handed Louis another spoon to play with. "So, what about that recipe for corn chowder you promised me?"

After a few more minutes of gossip about this and that, mostly placed on Rachael Olson's reporting, Lucy gathered up Louis and headed back toward the DeLaurier place.

She walked down the dusty road, this time allowing Louis to toddle on his own through the plume-like prairie grasses and brilliant black-eyed-susans along the edge. He still walked a little unsteadily, but she was continually surprised to see how fast he was growing, how independent he seemed.

She was disappointed once again in Maggie. She hadn't offered any real insights into Lucy's situation, merely provided a list of tentative options, then concluding with annihilating all of them. Maggie was no Madame Lesage, there was no preordained plan for Lucy's future. That plan, however uncomfortable, however brutally difficult, must derive from Lucy's herself.

Keeping an eye on Louis wandering along the roadside, her thoughts turned for the hundreth time to Shakopee as Georgie described it. Shakopee—a big town, places to work, make a living. After all, hadn't they all begun life in this new country there? As for her own children—maybe Martin could enroll in one of those academies she'd heard about. He'd be able to go on to the big city and study to become a doctor, or an engineer. And Sabine—even more opportunities for her.

She and Louis reached the lane turning off toward the DeLaurier house. With a cry of delight, and shouting "Home, Mama—there home," Louis ran ahead of her down the lane toward it, dropping his little bouquet of wild flowers. He'd been born there. It was his only home. The thought did not escape her. Yet the thought of Georgie's new home in Shakopee, the opportunities it offered, the ease of getting there by train—these were beginning to awaken a new debate within her deepest consciousness.

For the next few weeks, the debate seemed to revolve endlessly in Lucy's mind. In one version, the positive reasons won her over; in another version they lost. How selfish she was in even considering such a plan! Who would truly benefit? The realization that she was, after all, considering only an escape, stung sharply as a serpent. She needed to talk to Noel and Mary. Would they agree? They might not, for the tenancy of the DeLaurier place was at stake.

Late the next afternoon, she resolved to confront them. If she timed it right, she could also pick up Sabine and Martin from Little Sauk school, which had just started again after summer vacation. Putting Laurence and Louis in the back of the wagon, hitching up Blaize, she headed east down the road.

The end of summer had definitely come. Row upon row of ripened wheat and rye covered the hills in golden waves, broken only by occasional mounds of bleached gray rocks or dark green stands of trees. A few maples already showed brilliant orange splashes in their upper branches. There was the smell of smoke in the air from the burn-off in fields where grain had already been harvested. Their nakedness revealed islands of gray and pinkish rocks, growing higher each spring as rock-picking cleared the ground of what the winter's frost had heaved up and what threatened to shatter the first plough share to break the ground.

The sun felt hot on her back. Lucy reached down beside her on the wagon bench for her old straw hat—she couldn't seem to find her one sunbonnet, and jammed the hat down over her hair. It was so beautiful here she wondered how she could consider leaving. It had been her home, her real home where she had set down roots, watched the children grow and the fields change season after season. What did it matter which house she lived in and with whom? Perhaps she didn't need another husband. The land was important. If she could only accept the fact that, after all, the DeLaurier *place* was just a *house*, not the whole of all this *place* surrounding her.

Mary invited her in for some tea. "Our peaches are ripe," she said, "and I've just made some cobbler. Come up here on the porch, we'll have a chat. The children are out of school, but they're across the field, playing baseball—practicing hard for the big game next Saturday against

Grey Eagle. Looks like they're having fun. And say, did you see Josie's pitch? She plays as well as the boys. And look, your Martin seems to be doing well at the bat." She pulled over a wicker chair, saying, "Come, sit here in the sunshine—it'll do you good, you look a little pale to me. Feeling poorly lately?" She grabbed Laurence by the collar. "No wait, sweetie, don't go over there yet—I've got something for you."

She went into the house, shortly returning with a small tin box. "Here, sweetie, take these cookies over there to share with the others. Off you go now, but be careful as you cross the road!" She turned to Lucy. "So much more going and coming these days on the road between Long Prairie and Sauk Center, don't you think? Let's just have our tea out here on the porch, shall we? Such beautiful weather, too early for Indian Summer."

"Yes, it has been nice," Lucy commented vaguely, cradling Louis on her lap. She dreaded raising the subject she'd come for.

"And your little Louis—my, how he's growing. They do grow like weeds, don't they? You can put him down on the porch floor. Don't think he'll crawl off. Railing's all around."

"Walking already."

"Is that so? My, he *is* growing." She placed a pillow behind her back. "So hard to get comfortable these days. Due just before Christmas, you know. They say birthing gets easier. Not true in my case." She motioned toward the back of the house. "I expect Noel is sure to come over from the barn, once he sees your wagon in the yard. There now, let me move this little table a bit closer to your porch chair. Excuse me for a moment, while I bring out the tea things."

When she returned, they chatted for a few moments about nothing in particular—the last Dubois baby, asleep upstairs in his bassinet, the weather, Raymond's accident with the harrow when he cut his arm on one of the blades, the Clarks' cow giving birth to a two-headed calf, or the new woman doctor, Josephine Mellgren up in Long Prairie. After a few moments, Lucy grew impatient. This kind of chatter was really not what she needed. Her mind wandered as Mary's remarks droned on

In a way she was relieved when Noel arrived and settled himself in one of the wicker porch chairs, his great bulk threatening to challenge its delicate structure. "Just arrived, Lucy?" he asked, taking the cup of tea Mary handed him. "Tell me, how are things down DeLaurier way? John and the boys getting ready to harvest the upper fields. They look good. A fine year, *merci à dieu.*"

"I'm glad for your sake," Lucy answered. "Then there's been no problem with the yield?" She'd try to bring the subject around to where she needed.

"*Mais non.* To change that rye for wheat, a good move. More farmers changing now—this county becoming more—how you say it—more prosperous."

The subject still hadn't come around to where she'd intended. She'd just have to raise the issue now, while the children were occupied with the baseball game, Louis now content to play with a doll one of the Dubois girls had left on the porch. "I must tell you, both of you. I do have a problem of my own."

"Well, of course, Lucy," said Mary. "If we can help—" She looked distractedly across the road toward the baseball field and shielded her eyes against the sun. "Oh, look, they seem to be finishing the game—be back over here soon."

Lucy realized she'd have to be quick about it. She rested her elbows on the arms of the big wicker chair and leaned forward, struggling to find the words to begin. "You know I've been so grateful for your help—for the DeLaurier place and all your support." What to say next? "But I've come—come to the conclusion that I can't continue this way, dependent upon you." Noel looked at her in surprise. "You see, I must make a difficult decision."

"No, no, Lucy, not at all. You are our only family here now," Mary protested.

"That may be true. But I'm compelled now to make a choice. You must realize that there are very few choices open to me. There is probably only one chance of marriage for me now, and you know with whom. At least that's what everybody seems to think, thanks to the *Argus.*"

Mary giggled. "Of course. Nothing secret anymore."

Noel looked more serious. "You will take it?"

"It would mean selling myself for security." Maggie's point had penetrated her thoughts, ever since their visit.

"*Mais non—*" Noel interrupted.

"Yes, that would be true. I'm not sure I could love the man. I doubt if he loves me. He's said things—about his business, his ambitions. No, there's someone else—" She broke off suddenly, shocked that she'd allowed herself to go in that direction. "Anyway, who would want me, at my age, and with four mouths to feed?" She forced a wry smile. "But I have to tell you that living here as I do, dependent mostly upon your generosity and charity, is also becoming more and more difficult."

"*Pourquoi*—why difficult?" was Noel's concerned response as he raised his hand in protest. "No question of obligation, you know."

Did he really mean that? Lucy doubted it. After this past year and a half, surely they both were growing weary of her dependence.

"We want you here," he said. "Unthinkable to leave—"

"You mean you're thinking of leaving?" Mary had a strange look on her face. "Why, Lucy! Such a big decision."

Lucy couldn't quite read the look, a strange mixture of concern and relief. In some ways it confirmed Lucy's sense that Mary had somehow become jealous of her, that she was suspicious of Noel's relationship. More than once Lucy had seen her eyeing the two of them together, thinking, calculating, her suspicions fed each time Noel expressed a desire to help. The realization was unnerving, for it generated further conflict deep within her.

"Do you really mean it?" Mary continued.

"Yes." She could think of nothing else to say.

"But for where? When?"

"You are not happy with the DeLaurier place?" Noel asked. "Something wrong there, not fix something? Something I could do?" Mary threw him a glance.

"No, it's not the DeLaurier place—well, yes, it is in a sense. But to come to the point, there's the possibility I could join my brother in Shakopee."

"That place, *par bleu!*" exclaimed Noel in surprise. "Your little brother Georgie is not in the north of Dakota, not digging gold in Montana? Not a millionaire yet? Why Shakopee, of all places in the world? That boy Georgie—he had the whole States of United America before him. You know, Shakopee, *mon dieu*, that is the veritable place we left from to claim this homestead, way back 'bout 1865 I think, *n'est-ce pas*, Marie? *Aussi le même temps que* Morton, *n'est-ce pas?*" Inevitably, the memories, the emotion of the moment brought on a torrent of French. "*Tu te souviens, eh?* You remember? And your family, Lucy, the Guyettes. Big, big community of people there from Quebec, France. Why, I dunno—big church maybe, river traffic."

"Well, whatever his reasons, Georgie has resettled there, along with Alphie. They now call themselves George and Al. He's doing so well that he is building his own house, and going to build one next door for our parents."

"But, Lucy," Noel commented thoughtfully, "*certainment* it is true. You and the children could all live with them in those two houses, but what then?" Thinking ahead as usual, he added, "You would not be so happy like that, all *bondé* together, and still—" He stopped, replaced his empty plate on the tea tray.

Had he intended to say *dependent?* That shattering word? Surely he realized now that depending upon him for support was, in fact, a major part of her problem. In a complex way, it was also tied in with Mary's concern about the relationship between Lucy and her husband.

"But Lucy, what about the children?" Predictable that Mary's reaction would also involve the children.

"How will you get there?" Noel looked even more doubtful. "Still a long way. It'll take over a month."

"And in a wagon—alone—with the children!"

"Things have changed. George tells me there's a train. The Hastings and Dakota line goes through Shakopee—in fact, all the way out to the Dakotas, now. Special fares, even."

"You'd go by train—with the children?" Noel looked thoughtful. "I see," he said simply.

Mary walked over to the porch railing and looked anxiously across the road. "We're out here on the porch, children," she called. "Treats for you here."

Lucy knew it was time to leave. She'd said what she'd come to say. Noel and Mary had made their preliminary responses. No doubt more questions would be asked, objections raised. But at the moment she felt shaken and drained, unable to enter into further discussion of matters both painful and difficult. Some of them touched the innermost secret of her heart. She must be more self-protective.

That secret admitted and recognized. Her attraction to Noel began soon after her arrival at the DeLaurier house. She hadn't recognized it at first, but gradually, through dependence upon him and his comforting of her, she—perhaps even he—sensed a subtle relationship growing between them. Perhaps this was the unconscious reason she was hesitant with regard to Mattias, an unconscious pulling back. Perhaps, too, her feelings for Noel had also colored her feelings toward Homer West, a willingness to consider marrying him out of guilt, a way to end whatever might ensue between herself and Noel, a way to save herself—and Noel's marriage to Mary.

With the noisy band of cousins now climbing up the porch steps, Lucy rose to go. She scooped up Louis, picked up her hat from the back of the chair. "Come, children," she said. "We're leaving—it's getting late. Get into the wagon. And, Martin, don't forget your lunch pail like the last time."

"Wait," said Mary. "I'll pack up this left-over peach cobbler for you. Be right back. And you, Raymond, you and Josie take Sarah and Rosalie in to wash up." She steered them through the door. "Now, Lucy, before you go, we'll talk about the move. When I come back with the cobbler, I'll bring a pad and pencil. We'll work out what you need to do first, make a list. Oh, so many things to think about!"

After she'd gone into the house, Noel remained silent for a moment, an awkward silence implying any number of unspoken issues and concerns. Finally, in a shrug which indicated an end to further discussion, he said: "*Mais certes*, you will learn, *ma chère*, that independence, she will come with a high price."

September 9 Storm

S UMMER TRANSITIONED INTO FALL as the first tamarack leaves grew pale to yellow to brilliant gold. Although nearly time to leave the De-Laurier place and Little Sauk, Lucy found it difficult to get past the first thing on Mary's list. For her, the first thing was that initial decision to leave. Certainly, it had not come without pain, remorse, and regret. She now began to realize how much she'd become a part of the house, the house a part of her. On windy nights she imagined the house spoke to her, whispering its secrets as she lay in the high, carved bed. Even more disturbing—that bed was losing its ties with the old log homestead, with Bernard.

Mary was busy organizing the move. Indeed, her efforts fed Lucy's conviction that Mary was anxious for her to leave. There were two possibilities. Either Mary feared that Lucy would become so situated in the DeLaurier house that she would not give it up when time came for one of her children to take over. Or she was jealous and suspected a relationship between Lucy and her husband.

The latter possibility led Lucy to examine and re-examine her own feelings toward Noel. She had to admit an attraction. He'd been the mainstay in her survival. She was dependent upon him for nearly everything, as were her children. He was warm, caring, practical, and physically attractive. Some aspects about him reminded her of Bernard. The innermost secret of her heart—yes, it had been lurking there for some time.

Yes, she must leave the DeLaurier place, his house, his land. She could never be sure that continued dependence upon him might break down that moral barrier veiling the truth. Sooner or later he might demand a payment she could not refuse.

This year the autumn storms came early. The corn had already been harvested, but farmers struggled to get the last of the remaining wheat and rye in while still dry, not always successful. A heavy rain flooded some of the low-lying fields, including those DeLaurier acres along the Sauk River bottomland. Fortunately Noel and his threshing crews managed to save most of the wheat on her side of the farm and all of the rye in those higher acres across the road.

"Told you," Maggie said to Lucy one morning as they were sharing a pot of tea in Maggie's kitchen. "Told you what The *Farmers Almanack* predicted for this year, 1877, way back in January when it first came out. Folks who write that book read signs—don't know how, but anyway Lemuel swears by it. Never failed him yet, he says."

Lucy couldn't help smiling. "But Maggie, how could those *Almanack* predictors possibly have known? What signs did they use? Just guessing, most likely."

"They know," Maggie insisted. "They have their ways."

But after several more storms in close succession, Lucy began to wonder about the truth of the *Almanack*'s predictions. On the last night of September, thunder and lightning, combined with heavy, sultry air, made it difficult to sleep. During the worst of the storm, Louis climbed out of his crib and slipped into her bed for reassurance, but even asleep he moved fitfully, occasionally crying out from some frightening dream. Lying next to him, sometimes holding him in her arms, Lucy could hear the boys moving restlessly around in their room, Martin trying to comfort Laurence.

Memory was a strange thing. At the end of this year's harvest, the second at the DeLaurier place, Lucy lay there in the big walnut bed this night with baby Louis in her arms. The storm was breaking all around her, reminding her of the big storm the night Louis was born, the night she'd first held him in her arms. Of how one of the Holberg men had summoned Maggie. How Maggie and Greta Schweitzer had saved her and Louis.

She also, like Sabine, who constantly asked for a photograph of her father, wanted to remember what Bernard looked like, his image fast fading as in that old army portrait which she'd finally taken out of the chest and given to Sabine. Bernard in an army uniform—it had never seemed right— foreign, alien and strange—not in character at all. If only there'd been a wedding picture, like Alphie and Jeanne-Marie's. She tried to remember some of the things he'd said, sounds becoming more indistinct like words spoken during a rainstorm. This night, like all nights, were difficult for her. And she was always apprehensive that they might bring, once again, those nightmares about the train. The train that was to take them away.

On this stormy night, one thought after another filled her racing mind, one association leading to another and yet another until her head ached. The house seemed to be saying something to her through the wind. She imagined hearing once again the sound of Bernard's voice as he asked Martin about the day at school, as he expressed hope about the new crops, as he read stories aloud to her out of Friday's weekly *Argus*.

Slowly it dawned on her that it wasn't Bernard's voice she was hearing. Not imagined, the voice was real and coming from beyond the bedroom door. There were other voices, no longer only Martin's.

Sitting up in bed, she noticed a light under her door. "Sabine?" She'd probably lit a candle and was about to bring Laurence into her room. Not the first time, he'd always been afraid of storms. It might have been that experience in the old homestead's root cellar, the time the tornado hit and they'd huddled there together for what seemed hours, listening to the cabin being torn apart.

But something wasn't right about the light under her door. Now wide awake, she realized there was also a strange flickering light on the ceiling. Throwing back the bed covers, she rushed to the front window and saw the sky glowing red. A fire! One of the buildings in back of the house! How did it happen? The storm—a lightning strike—

"Louis, darling, wake up!" she shouted as she tried to shake him awake. But he'd fallen into a deep sleep and merely rolled over on his side. She snatched him up, quilt and all, and rushed out of the room barefoot and in her nightdress.

"Sabine, Martin!" she shouted as she threw open the doors of the two back bedrooms. Sabine and Laurence were jumping up and down on Sabine's bed before the open window.

"Ma! Mama!" she cried, "a fire—a fire! See, out there!" It was the granary barn, directly behind the house, not more than ten yards to the right of the main barn. "Look, Ma, there's men down there, pointing up here, shouting."

How could that be? The granary barn! Only yesterday Noel's crew had finished loading in the wheat crop, anxious to get it done before the storm. Now the barn was filled with a whole year's worth of work and profit, and going up in flames! And who were those men, their words muffled by the roar of the flames?

"Missus! Missus Dubois!" seeing her at the bedroom window, one of the men cupped his hands around his mouth. "Fire spreading, quick—get the children out! Fast as you can! Not the back way, too close to the fire. Take them out the front door!"

By this time the flames were shooting up into the sky, the wind sending sparks and embers directly toward the house, some falling through the open window of Sabine's room and already smouldering on the rag rug. She started to stamp them out, then drew her bare foot back in pain. Still holding Louis in one arm, who by this time was awake and staring out at the roaring fire with wide eyes, she snatched a pillow off the bed with her other arm and swatted at the flames licking their way across the rug. Throwing the pillow down, clasping Louis in both arms, she cried, "The window, Sabine! Shut it, shut it, we've got to keep the sparks out!"

"Stuck, Ma." Sabine struggled for a moment, with Martin's help finally banged it down on the sill.

"Now, children," Lucy cried, "out! We must get out of here, fast as we can." It wasn't easy to disguise the panic in her voice. "Here, Sabine, grab that quilt off the bed, put it around Laurence, take his hand. Martin, stop, no time to put those overalls on."

"But Ma," he protested, "can't go out there in my nightshirt! I'll be half naked!"

"Never mind—no one'll notice."

At this point she saw a brownish stain began to creep across one corner of the ceiling, and, to her horror, realized the roof had caught fire. "Come on now, quick, down the stairs, out the front door, the fire's spreading!"

They almost fell down the stairs in their haste and, once in the hall, Lucy threw herself against the front door. Louis in her arms gave a cry of pain from the impact. She turned the knob. The door refused to open. Only then did she remember she'd locked and bolted it as usual before going to bed. It was dark in the hall, only a little light coming in from the open door into kitchen, a nasty, flickering red light.

Frantically, Lucy felt for the bolts, drew the top one back. As she reached for the lower bolt, her hand hit the key in the lock and it fell out onto the floor. "Oh, Martin," she cried, "got to find that key, get down on the floor, the key, the key—see if you can feel for it."

"Can't find it, Ma, too dark," Martin shouted above the roar of the flames, groping frantically around the floor on his hands and knees. "No light, can't see, must've slid under somethin'."

"Oh—Mama—want Leo! Want Leo!" Laurence screamed.

"The back door, then, we'll go out through the kitchen," she shouted. Suddenly she stopped and Sabine, carrying Laurence, bumped into her, and the three of them fell to the floor. They got to their feet, Lucy crying, "Oh no, we can't use the back door because it's the same key for that lock. Now the fire's spreading through the roof—" The strong, acrid odor of smoke was beginning to drift down into the hallway. "Try not to breathe it," she gasped, "cover your faces with your clothes, the quilt."

This time there was no disguising the panic in her voice. And in that flood of panic and helplessness, what with Louis's terrified shrieks, Laurence's whining, and Martin's shouting about the key, she couldn't think straight. Her only thoughts were how ironic it was. They were now fatally locked in by the very efforts she'd taken to protect them against intruders, replacing the lock after Henry Morton had broken through the door when he'd arrived last November with Agnes and her children. It had made her feel safe, all that security. Now it meant their death.

In one last desperate gesture, she gathered them in her arms and knelt down on the floor. She covered little Louis with her body, pulled the quilt over them all, and waited for the fire to engulf the house and them together. "What was that prayer? What are the words? *Notre Seigneur*—" she began haltingly.

The sound of a hard object hitting the window of the parlor, of smashing glass, someone coming through the room. The parlor door into the hall burst open, the tall figure of a man silhouetted against the opening, his face hidden in darkness.

"Thought there was trouble here, all right, when you didn't come out. Tried both doors, wouldn't budge." One of the Holberg brothers. "Come out quick now, missus," he said. "Follow me!" He tried to open the front door from the inside.

"Key lost—door locked," stammered Lucy.

"Have to force it." He threw his weight against it, but it wouldn't give. "Through the window, then." He seized her arm and pushed her ahead of him into the parlor. When she turned to look at him, she saw it was not Mattias, but Erik.

"Watch out for that glass 'round the edge of the window, ma'am," he said. "And pieces here on the floor inside—might cut your feet. Wait, I'll go outside to the porch first, you pass the littl'uns out to me."

Lucy handed Louis through the window first, still wrapped in the quilt, and Erik held him in one arm as he took Laurence in the other. Once outside, "Here, lad," he said, "you hold this baby while I help the others. Don't drop him, now!" Next came Sabine over the windowsill, and finally Martin.

Lucy was grateful to feel the man's strong arm steady her as she climbed out onto the porch. Her body seemed to have lost its strength.

"Everybody out? Got to get back to the fire," he called out as he leapt over the railing onto the ground, not bothering with the steps at the far end. "You stay here with the children, ma'am, a ways off from the house—go under those trees down by the road." With that he disappeared around the corner of the house.

From last night's storm the grass was cold and wet under her bare feet. Carrying Louis, she led the others to the clump of trees alongside the lane. Lucy began to shiver, concerned that the children were barefooted, too, and dressed like her only in their nightclothes. She spread the quilt out on the ground. "Here, Sabine, you take Louis. Martin, you're in charge. I've got to go help. Stay right here, all of you. You'll keep warmer if you huddle together under this other quilt. And Sabine, make sure Laurence doesn't wander off. Keep him out of the way."

"Oh, Ma! Look at that!" Martin pointed to the sparks flying up behind the house high into the sky, an ominous red glow reflected against the clouds.

Sabine was beginning to cry. "The house—our house—going to go up any minute—do something, oh, do something quick! Why can't they stop it, Ma?"

Yes, she had to do something, and quick. Willing the strength she seemed to have lost, she ran toward the house. Even before she rounded the corner of the front porch, Martin was at her side.

"Got to help, Ma," he shouted above the noise. "Let me—I can do it."

"But the others—no, go back," Lucy protested, grabbing the flannel sleeve of his nightshirt and trying to restrain him. He was trembling from cold and excitement. "You must go back, stay with—"

"No, it's all right Ma," Martin insisted. "Sabine's there. Remember. You're teaching me how to drive the wagon. So if I can drive the wagon, I can sure help put out a fire!" And he was off and in the midst of the men.

By then the granary barn was totally engulfed in flames. Figures were swatting at the fire with gunnysacks, running back and forth between the barn and the watering trough near the stock barn to wet them down. She recognized not only the three Holberg brothers but also another neighbor, George Clark. That seemed to be his teenaged son with him. She couldn't remember his name, although she recognized him from when he'd helped out with the harvesters.

Following their example, Lucy picked a sack off the pile, immersed one in the trough, then ran with the dripping cloth over to a small blaze running down a line of straw, spilled from a wagon as it had entered the barn earlier the day before. She hit the flames with the wet sack again and again until only a black line of ashes remained. But now there was another line of flame starting closer to the barn.

Now where was Martin? It was difficult to see much in all the confusion. There he was helping pass buckets of water from the windmill pump to the barn. It seemed to be doing little good. The men worked frantically. Despite the earlier rain, neither the roof nor the barn timbers were wet enough to resist the flames as they gained strength.

One of the figures rushed over toward her. "Here, ma'am," the man said, breathing hard from his efforts, "you shouldn't be out here, doing that." He tried to snatch the gunnysack from her hand while forcibly pushing her back.

In the light from the growing fire, Lucy saw it was Mattias. She hesitated, not knowing what to say, heard herself protesting, "No, no, you need all the help—"

Mattias grabbed her wrist and twisted her hand up against his chest and held it there. "Let go, Lucy. Leave that to us. Here, give me that—let go, will you!" Struggling to get free, she fell backwards and brought Mattias down with her. She felt his denim shirt wet with sweat, his heart pounding. "Let go, I said. You'll get burned. That sack's already smouldering." As they rolled on the ground, he pried open her fingers and snatched the sack away and threw it some distance. "Shouldn't be out here at all—get up—get back! See, that grass is on fire just behind your head, it'll catch your hair!" He pulled her to her feet and out of the way. "Now go, Lucy—too dangerous!"

"No," said Lucy emphatically. "Let me help!"

Mattias shook his head. "Don't understand you," he shouted above the noise, "but if you gotta do something, take this horse blanket, heavier but works better. And do like this, see. Hit the flames with it, make sure it's soaked through. Then drag it a ways to spread the embers, then beat 'em out. Like this." Quickly plunging the blanket into the horse trough, he handed it to her. "Make sure you keep it wet," he said, as he turned to join the men working on the granary, then shouted back, "and remember to keep ahead of that patch on the ground there—and watch out for your bare feet!"

Lucy concentrated on attacking the flames and embers around her with the horse blanket. Yet there were thoughts she couldn't suppress, fragmented thoughts interspersed with attention to the flames, fear for Martin, concern for Sabine, Laurence, and the baby out in the cold at the front of the house. How strange to encounter Mattias like this, before she'd had a chance to explain about Homer West. That he should suddenly call her by her first name. That he should have such strength in his hands. That she would feel the weight of his body against hers as they rolled on the ground away from the flames, feel his sweat-stained shirt and the beating of his heart. That he would mention her bare feet.

And, for all that, what had Mattias meant? That time with Homer West in the hallway, that time she'd tried to cover her bare feet with Mattias standing there, after Homer West had removed her shoes and stockings. He might have guessed the nature of West's visit, and now was trying to warn her about any future relationship. If so, the man was deeper, more perceptive than she'd realized.

Ridiculous to puzzle over all this now—another flame flickering along the grass edge, and there—and there! She whacked at a small blaze licking up from the steps to the back porch and threatening to move quickly toward the back door. The house! She had to save the house. Noel Dubois's house—and yet—and yet—

The men were shouting. "Get back, boy, back out of the way—roof timbers 'bout to crash!" In horror Lucy watched as Martin just stood there in the granary doorway, apparently frozen with fear.

"Martin! Martin!" she screamed. Before she could reach him, one of the men rushed at him, knocking him to the ground. Together they slithered away from the flames, their clothes already catching fire. Someone threw a bucket of water on them, and another, and another. Seconds later Martin was up and filling another bucket at the trough, then rejoining the line of men.

During Lucy's moment of distraction, flames had already gained on the back door. In the process of rushing back to the trough to soak her blanket, she saw Erik Holberg pointing to an upstairs window, his mouthed words indistinct.

To her horror, she saw Laurence standing there. "Mama! Ma, help me!" he screamed, pounding on the glass.

"Laurence!" Lucy shouted above the roar of the flames. "Get back, get out of the house!" But the boy just stood there. "Laurence! Come down—go out by the parlor window—the way we came out." Laurence refused to move.

George Clark came over, his face and hands blackened with smoke. "Get out, boy!" he shouted, "do as your ma says." But Laurence was still hypnotized by the flames. "Guess I'll just have to go in after him. I've got to get him out quick, looks like the house'll go up any minute. See, up there on the roof—goin' like—"

But Lucy didn't wait for him to finish. She was already around the corner of the house, across the porch. She climbed through the parlor window, trying to avoid the jagged points of glass still in the frame, the shards on the floor. A sharp pain in the ball of her foot, but she couldn't stop now. Running up the hall stairway, she could hardly see because of the smoke which stung her eyes and her lungs hurt each time she tried to breathe. Bunching up the front of her nightdress with one hand, and holding it against her nose and mouth, she felt her way along the upstairs hall to the boys' room. Laurence stood outlined against the flames at the window, fascinated by the fire.

"Laurence!" she cried. "Mama told you to stay outside with Sabine and Louis. What do you mean going back into the house like that?"

"Martin there!" He pointed down to the men below. "Leo."

She picked Laurence up and rushed down the stairs, slipping, falling, pulling herself up, half carrying and half dragging Laurence. She didn't stop until she was outside in the middle of the lane beside the house. Only then did she notice blood all over her right foot and soaked up into the edges of her nightdress. She also realized that Laurence was holding his arms tightly around Leo, his yellow velvet lion.

"I told you to stay down here," she repeated angrily, anger merely masking relief.

"Not want Leo burn all up."

"But you might have—don't you realize—" But of course the boy didn't. She hugged him and sat him down with Sabine on the quilt under the clump of trees near the road.

"Couldn't stop him, Ma," Sabine said. She was rocking Louis in his arms and had pulled the quilt around them both for warmth. Louis was sobbing in exhausted gasps. "Laurence wouldn't listen to me—just took off like a jack rabbit, into the house. I couldn't go in after him and leave Louis all alone, could I?"

"No, of course not," Lucy said. "It's all right, just keep him here out of trouble. I've got to go back and help. The fire's gaining."

By the time she returned, however, the granary was beyond help, now only a heap of glowing embers and blackened beams. The Clarks, along with Martin, had turned their attention to one corner of the house roof and the back steps and porch. "Just 'bout got it stopped in time," shouted George Clark. "Will and I, we tried to save them steps, porch, too. Weren't nothin' we could do, though."

"Least we saved the barn, ma'am," Will added. "Not that there storage shed, though."

The steps and half the back porch were gone, the screen door frame door fallen away and door itself blackened. Long, spidery smoke stains climbed up the white walls of the house as far as the second-storey bedroom windows. The northeast corner of the roof was blackened around a gaping hole. The glass in Sabine's window had shattered from the heat. Had Laurence been at that window and not the other, he might have been hit with flying shards of glass. All for the sake of Leo. Over by the granary remains, Lucy saw the Holbergs kicking at remaining scattered embers, pouring buckets of water over clumps of dried grass and dampening down a portion of the rail fence along the pasture.

It was now dawn, and rain returned with a fine drizzle. Too late to be of any use, for, along with damaging the whole back section of the house and part of the roof, the fire had consumed the entire granary barn and a nearby shed. A few black timbers rose up from the still smoking ruins of the granary.

To Lucy they looked like skeletons. They reminded her of the blackened bones of cattle she'd once seen burned alive in an uncle's barn, back in Quebec. She shuddered. Her eyes stung from the smoke, her foot had stopped bleeding but now throbbed with pain. Her arms ached from her efforts with wet gunnysacks and heavy horse blankets. In fact, her whole body ached, and she leaned against a side of the trough for support. Yet, the house had been saved, the children were safe. How was that to be weighed against the fact that not only the granary building was lost, but also a whole harvest of grain.

"Well, ma'am," Erik Holberg said as he came up, carrying a pile of sodden gunnysacks, "you're sure a sight for sore eyes—if'n I may be so bold as to say so."

Mattias came up behind him. "Did real well," he said, shyly, his eyes seemingly fixed on her feet.

With a shock, Lucy realized she was standing before these men in her nightdress. Not only that. It was blood-stained around the hem, blackened with soot in several places, singed by flames all up the sleeves, and the whole upper part wet and transparent—whether from sweat or water from the sacks, she didn't know, but most certainly clinging to her body. She might as well be standing there naked. Much of her hair had escaped from the thick, single braid she usually wore at night and hung in damp, ash-encrusted clumps around her face. "Oh, my," she said, pushing strands of it back and trying to pluck her wet gown away from her body, "I must look a sight!"

Hans looked embarrassed and lowered his eyes for a second. Then he said, "I guess we're all a sight for sore eyes, ma'am. The Clarks are over there with your boy trying to wash up under the pump at the watering trough, we need the same. Truth be said, though, we did save your main barn, house, too. And your boy kept the buckets moving as fast as any, good as any man here." He paused. "You, too, ma'am—you're a real fighter, if I may be so bold."

"I owe you so much, you boys. Can't thank you enough for all you've done. And the Clarks."

"Well, George saw the fire first," Erik explained. "Said he'd gotten up in the night to check on one of his cherry trees, struck by lightning. Knew your place'd been hit too, but wasn't sure whether the barn or not—barn's most likely place, why they put them new rods on 'em nowadays. Anyway, he and his older boy, Will, saddled up a couple of horses. Will rode over to our place quick as he could, took Hans ridin' double. Our pa still a mite under the weather, sluggish liver, so we left him. Then Matt and me, we hitched up the wagon, brought as many sacks, horse blankets, as we could find." He looked down at the few he was holding. "Not many left we can still use."

"How about Noel Dubois?" She was surprised she hadn't thought about him earlier, despite the fact he'd been so much on her mind. Now she had to be concerned about his reaction to what would be a large financial loss for him. That, combined with her departure, which might mean more than simply finding a new tenant for the DeLaurier place.

"Didn't have time to go for mister Dubois, ma'am," Erik said. "Wasn't time to fetch him and his hands from their place over t' Little Sauk."

"He'll know soon enough, I guess," commented George Clark, with a wry smile. "Come ridin' over here 'fore long, I reckon."

"I'm most grateful," Lucy hurriedly said. "Mister Dubois—and I—owe you so much. But I think I owe you some breakfast, too. So won't you come into the kitchen when you're ready?"

First, though, she had to bring in the children. Out in front on the grass Sabine was asleep, wrapped up in the quilt with Louis, Laurence curled up beside her, still clutching Leo. "It's all over, dear," she said, gently shaking Sabine's shoulder."

"Fire?" asked Sabine sleepily.

"It's out, we can go back in. Here, I'll take the baby. We'll have to use the back door—front one still won't open, remember?" She tried to smile as she added, "At least the fire took care of the back door. But be careful. And upstairs, Sabine, don't go into your room until we clean up the glass, fix the ceiling in the boys' room. You can use the guest room—that'll be some kind of a treat, I think, won't it?"

Making their way over the remains of the back porch, climbing up through the half-open back door into the kitchen, Lucy concluded that, in a way, she was glad Noel had not been fetched. How could she excuse the damage to his property, the loss of his crops? How to repay a debt already beyond her ability to pay?

Down in the kitchen, after she'd cleaned up a little, re-braided her hair and pinned it up, changed into a brown-and-white gingham dress, tied a fresh apron around her waist, she set about making breakfast for the men. Her foot throbbed, and she was conscious of the fact that it was still bleeding through the strip of cloth she'd wrapped around it as well as her stocking. She hoped the men wouldn't notice the stains, or the fact that she was limping.

"Well, Ma," Sabine said, coming into the kitchen to help, "got Louis back to bed. He fussed but finally settled down. Laurence would only go back to bed if I let him sleep in the big brass bed. Got Martin washed up—he was a mess, hair partly burned off in one spot. Sure looks funny. And that night shirt—chucked it in the stove."

That Sabine would have taken charge like that—Martin fighting the fire alongside the men—not the first time they'd had to grow into roles beyond their short childhood, must continue to do so—

Men started coming into the kitchen, accompanied by the acrid odor of smoke. "Ready for us, ma'am?" Erik Holberg asked.

"Yes, oh, yes," she answered. "Please sit down. Breakfast ready in a minute." She was grateful her line of thought had been interrupted. She doubted she could have sustained it.

She continued beating up eggs in the big blue bowl to scramble in the iron skillet, instructing Sabine to lay the table. Martin was at the sink pump filling the big tin coffee pot. After Lucy had cut off thick slices of bacon and laid them in another frying pan, she was struck by the silence in the room apart from the sizzling of the fat. Clearly, the men were exhausted, in no mood for talk, content for the moment just to sit around the big kitchen table and wait.

After several rounds of eggs, bacon, oven-toasted bread and butter, and two or three cups of coffee, they gradually began to revive, and talk returned. "Must think about gettin' back to the farm, ma'am," said Hans, munching the last slice of bacon. "Must be past mornin' milkin' time, I reckon."

"Sure was a long night, all right," George Clark commented, finishing his third cup of coffee and second plate of bacon and eggs. "Glad we got the horse and cow out of the barn, couldn't be sure it wouldn't go up, too. And young Will, here, had the sense to put 'em in the stock pen. Otherwise that horse would've bolted, for sure. Wouldn't look forward to chasing all over this here country looking for 'em."

"For sure, lucky this time," said Erik, "although not certain but what you didn't lose a few chickens, ma'am. Yes siree, lucky in the long run. But, truth is, it could've happened to any farm. Lightning will strike any barn, unless you put up rods on the roof. Good thing Noel Dubois put 'em up there on his place down at Little Sauk, this barn, too, though he forgot about that darn granary. That feller sure believes in new fangled things, he does. Can't say as I agree with all of 'em, though." He gulped down the last of his coffee. "Even then, I seen barns where it didn't work, burned down anyways."

Hans got up from the table and tested his jacket, which he'd spread out near the stove to dry. "Hmmm, still a wee bit damp, but it'll have to do. Yes, now about lightnin' rods. Thought 'bout puttin' up 'nother barn, can't be too careful," he said. "But now, Erik and me, along with Matt—we're thinkin' 'bout leavin'."

"Didn't say I'd go along with you yet, did I?" Mattias interrupted.

"Well, all right, then. Maybe Matt's not sure yet 'bout the idea, thinkin' about buildin', roofin', carpentry. Anyways, we're addin' more milk cows so's to increase our dairy herd. Pa's acres—well ain't much there make a livin' off."

"You say, dairy herds?" Clark asked. "Heard some talk up at Reagan's 'bout dairy cattle. They say this land 'round here, 'specially pasturage long the rivers, if'n you could clear it, would make for good herds. Well, be that as it may, I ain't got time for that. I'm for stickin' with rye, done real well some harvests, 'though have to admit, not this one. Storms, rain, come too soon. Heard wheat'd do better. Dubois thinks so, anyways."

"Best be goin', men," said Erik. "We thank you for the fine breakfast, ma'am. Feelin' quite restored."

With some confusion over recovering smoke and water-stained jackets, hats, and gloves, they all went out through what was left of the back door and porch. Lucy followed them out as far as the barnyard. She suspected this might be her last chance to speak to Mattias, and she needed to clear up matters between them. It was probably too late, but she also knew that leaving Little Sauk without that release, without that closure, would be something she'd find difficult to live with, whatever direction her life in Shakopee might take. Perhaps it was her imagination, her wishful thinking, that he'd looked at her pointedly several times over breakfast, requested another cup of coffee when his mug was still half full.

Although the air was still heavy with smoke, the scene was somehow not as depressing as it earlier seemed. The drizzle of rain had let up, the sun now fully risen above the horizon in a blue sky totally devoid of clouds. Its warming rays drew up moisture and produced a soft mist lying in wisps, caught within the lower undulations of newly threshed fields and hovering over the pond just beyond the stock barn.

The morning had that special kind of radiant beauty which always stirred her. She couldn't explain why, other than a general wonderment over the whole miracle of creation. The granary was lost and everything in it, but life would go on. Here was another dawn, next spring the fields would be sown, cattle would graze in the fresh new grass. Cattle—cows—the thought triggered something Hans had said. Perhaps that would provide the excuse she needed to speak to Mattias.

"Wait, Mister Holberg," she called, running after the Holbergs's blue-sided wagon just as it was about to drive out of the yard. "Wait!" The three looked back expectantly as Erik stopped the team. "There's something I'd like to talk to you about, something you mentioned just now." Mattias stood up.

"No, not you Matt," said Hans, pulling his brother back down to the seat. "Your turn to do the barn chores, remember? I'll go. Most likely it's me she wants to talk to."

There was a low-voiced conversation between them which Lucy couldn't catch. Hans Holberg got out of the wagon and motioned his brothers to drive on.

"Yes ma'am?" he said, as he came up. "Can I do somethin' else for you?"

Lucy hesitated, disconcerted. And, yes—disappointed. She'd expected Mattias, not Hans. It occurred to her that, if she invited Hans in for another cup of coffee, it would give her time to think of something to say, some excuse. "Do come into the warm kitchen," she said, "there's still some coffee left in the pot."

"Sure, willin' to do that if'n it don't take too long." He seemed pleased. "We've got a pile of work to do back at the farm today, bushels of wheat to take down to the mill 'fore old man Hart gets too busy to grind our yield."

"It won't take too long," Lucy said. "And I'll drive you back in the wagon."

"Won't be necessary," Hans replied. "Can always walk back to the farm. Less'n a mile. Besides, you got a lot to do this mornin', looks like."

Back in the kitchen, Lucy helped him off with his damp jacket and poured out more coffee. Then, sitting down at the table across from him, she was at a loss as to how to begin. "Tell me," she finally managed, "you must be feeling very tired. All that effort."

"No, ma'am. Used to hard work."

"Do you think anything can be saved from the granary?"

"No, ma'am. Expect not."

"How much loss, do you reckon?"

"Can't tell, ma'am. Up to mister Dubois."

"You said he'd put up lightning rods?"

"Only on the stock barn."

"You're thinking of doing the same?"

"Yes, ma'am."

"You're thinking of dairy farming?"

"Yes, ma'am." He paused. "Out west, maybe."

This is getting nowhere Lucy thought. She might as well, end it. "Well, Mister Holberg, sometime I'd like to know more about that, but, like you said, you don't have the time this morning."

He looked at her, interested. "More 'bout lightning rods?"

She wasn't sure how the idea came into her head. "No, tell me more about—about—"

"About them dairy herds?" Hans asked in amazement. "Why on earth would you want to know about cows and such?"

"It sounded interesting." She didn't quite know how to follow this up. With her last chance to talk with Mattias gone, did it matter?

Well, I'll be blessed if I know why you'd be interested, but here goes, anyway." He gulped down half a mug of coffee as if to prepare himself. "It's like this. Been goin' to meetin's of that Agricultural Society. Told us lot a things they picked up at the Dairy Fair last year. Learned all sorts of things."

"Do they advise people about business—about managing dairy farms?" What else could she ask about? "Making more money?"

"Lot of experts. They say to diversify—hope that's the word, not much for big words, you know—diversify your crops, keeps one crop from exhaustin' your soil year after year. Some feller talked about that vampire wheat, although not sure what a vampire is."

"Someone who sucks blood."

"That a fact?" He scratched his head. "Well, in this case, not sure 'bout that. Sucks up all the best soil, maybe. Besides, bushels o' wheat too subject to monopolies those big fellahs create and high railroad tariffs. Lost near three cents a bushel last year myself, down from eighty-nine cents, then had to pay more freight charges down to that big granary in Shakopee on top of that."

"Shakopee, you said?" Strange he mentioned that place. "Why Shakopee?"

"Too risky puttin' near all your wheat in one bushel," he said, laughing at his own joke. "That's to say in one granery." He caught himself, looked embarrassed. "But you're not interested in all these numbers, are you? Probably talkin' over your head, borin' you."

"No," she answered, a little annoyed at his put down, even if she didn't fully understand what he was talking about. What else could she ask to make him think she was interested? Shakopee—the railroad. "Do you think the new railroads part of all that?"

"Have to be. They say that's the future. Railroad can take butter and cheese to the markets, even into the Twin Cities. Even got cars refrigerated—if'n that's the right word—I'm told, loaded up with blocks of ice, keep the butter from melting, mold off the cheese."

"But where would all that ice come from?"

"A person can saw blocks out of the lakes in winter, store 'em in sawdust underground. Be surprised how long they keep. Ice here, you know, five—six feet deep in middle of winter." By now he'd finished his coffee and seemed anxious to leave. "Don't know too much about how it's managed, but somebody'll have to do that, make sure all that's when and where it should be."

"Could you make a lot of money?"

"Reckon so, ma'am, providin' you had the know-how." He got up, drew on his jacket. "Now, if'n you'll excuse me, ma'am, really got to get goin'. Sure would like to stay on, keep talkin' to you, but can't let my brothers do all the work, 'specially with our pa ailin'." He headed out the door, stopping to pick up a pair of work gloves he'd left. "These here gloves still a mess, set 'em in the sun later, maybe they'll dry out. He slipped them on, strode through the barnyard, and disappeared around the corner of the house.

Later that morning, Sabine and Martin left for school, not without protest. They could not, however, afford to miss a day, not with tests coming up and the prospect of a new school in Shakopee, where they might have to meet different standards. The house quiet, Louis and Laurence still asleep, the windows all open to air out the acrid smell, Lucy sat on the front porch to try to collect herself. The stresses of the morning left her in a dazed state, not ready yet to think about the next items on Mary's list.

The DeLaurier house had nearly been lost. Yet she had decided to leave it before that. If she could imagine such a thing, it was almost as if the house were taking its revenge, a live thing, a vengeful thing. She was no longer listening to its whispers. She was rejecting its links to the past, rejecting its comforts of the present. Such thoughts distressed her. More, perhaps, the question of Mattias.

The thought of Mattias brought back fragments of her earlier conversation with Hans Holberg. Frustrating as it was and certainly not the one she'd hoped for, she considered that she'd carried if off well. Whatever he thought of it afterward—or her—well, she couldn't do much about that, nor did she especially care.

She did care, however, about what Noel was going to say. Just at that moment she saw him turn his horse down the lane toward the house. He'd already gotten word of the fire and come to inspect the damage.

"*Mon dieu,*" he said, tying his big bay to the front porch post, "*quelle catastrophe*—catastrophy. The whole granary lost, Clark says. Came by my house just now, although I knew there was a fire. Did not know where. Now, *malheureusement*, I know. Yes, by God, I know." He came up the porch steps and stood before her, his massive form dominating the space.

Suddenly, as if by way of an afterthought, he added, "You are well, Lucy? Your children—they were not hurt?"

"No, I'm thankful for that. It could have been much worse." She shuddered, remembering Laurence trapped upstairs. All of them trapped in the hallway before that, unable to open the doors. "Only my foot—cut on broken glass. One of the men had to break this parlor window to get us out."

"Ah, that is good. Maybe not so about the window. Well, I must go around back and look things over."

Lucy walked around with him as he made a mental checklist. "*Eh bien*, bedroom window up there, roof damage—means the ceiling in the bedroom. Will go up to measure, order glass from Lano's Hardware. That will take a while. Third window from him, *n'est-ce pas?*"

Lucy knew he was thinking of the window broken last November by Daniel Benson. He'd complained about it, while commending Henry Morton for saving his foster daughter, Jane, from, as he claimed, such a man.

Now he examined the remains of the granary, kicking over the metal blade of a scythe here, a charred timber there. "*Eh bien, eh bien*," he kept repeating. Finally he commented, "Wheat crop still the best source of income for the DeLaurier property. Rye not worth seeding next spring."

Wheat or rye? Lucy could not easily dismiss her earlier conversation with Hans Holberg. "Noel," she began, "are you sure about the wheat crop being the best? I mean, what about something else? I'm told by mister Clark about your progressive ideas. Is that right?"

"*Eh bien*, like to think so, anyway." He laughed. "Already paid off, *n'est-ce pas?*"

"What about other crops—other ventures?"

"*Mais non*—no, perhaps—who knows?"

Lucy felt she must somehow try to make up for his loss, make up for her own relinquishment of the tenancy. At first she hesitated. Finally, while he seemed preoccupied with pacing off the length of the original building, she asked, "Well, what do you think about dairy farming? Have you ever considered it yourself?"

He looked taken back, stopped pacing. "What do you say? Dairy farming? *Eh bien*, to farm for milk? Bof! Crazy idea, *bien sur*. Consider how. One cannot just add a diary cow here, a diary cow there, another hired hand here—there. *Non, non, impossible, pas de tout pratique.* As for what cows give—*eh bien*, cannot just arrive at the station, put maybe only five, ten pounds of butter on a train. Would not pay at all, better to take them to the local stores, or maybe sell from a wagon Saturday's market up in Long Prairie. *Non, non, ma belle soeur,* not *practique* at all, never will be. Believe me, I know. You think I am successful, yes?"

"Of course." What else could she say?

"It is because I know the land—this land," and he gestured toward the fields behind the house. "Yes, to farm with dairy cows—no." He paused, looked at her strangely. "But why do you ask? It is not—" he broke off, his face reddening as he reconsidered what he intended to say. "It is not what I would expect, not at all, Not at all would I expect you to say that to me. Not you, Lucette. Not after—not after this—this disaster."

He seemed rather cool after that, saying little else before he re-mounted and disappeared down the lane. It left her with an uneasy feeling. She had touched a nerve somewhere, challenged him somehow, shown ingratitude. Now, more than ever, she needed to start working down Mary's list of preparations toward departure.

Autumn Changes

WHAT, LUCY? YOU'RE GRATEFUL for the granary fire? Whatever put that crazy idea into your head?" Maggie came over several days later with a basket of apples and two jars of peach jam. "Say, do you mind if we move off this here porch into your kitchen? Your stove stoked up? This wind's got a biting chill to it. It doesn't like my old bones. Besides, that stench of smoke and ashes from the fire still hanging around out here. Can't stay but a minute or two longer, but might as well be comfortable."

Once they were settled around the kitchen table, Lucy added, "I only said I was grateful in a way. It's helped my resolve to leave."

"Sure can't figure that one out."

"It's too complicated to explain. I hardly have all the answers myself."

Maggie took off her black straw bonnet, scratched her head, replaced the bonnet, and firmly tied the bonnet's dangling strings under her chin. "Long as I've known you, you sure've always come up with a puzzle or two out of that deep mind of yours. But you know, right sorry I'll be—Lem and me both—to see you leave." She quickly ducked her chin into the bonnet strings to hide her emotions. Then, looking up, she added, "But, well, guess if you've a mind to do somethin', reckon you'll do it."

In a surge of emotion, she reached out to touch Lucy's hand, thought better of it, abruptly pushed back her chair, and abruptly made her way toward the back door. "Maybe you'll return that basket? The empty jars? Later?"

Lucy couldn't confess to Maggie all the reasons for her decision. First, there now confirmation that the Holberg brothers—all of them—

intended to leave soon for a homestead in Montana. Unfortunately mister Clark had mentioned over breakfast her own intention of leaving Little Sauk, and she had noticed its impact upon Mattias. No telling what the consequences of that remark might be as far as Mattias was concerned.

Then, there was Noel Dubois, her brother-in-law. Their meeting in the aftermath of the fire resulted in harsh words and a change in Noel's attitude toward her. Lucy recognized that it went deeper than that. He felt betrayed by her resentment at being dependent upon him. But could she have continued that relationship, as illicit as it would inevitably become? She wasn't sure. Certainly Homer West's persistent attentions were another reason she felt compelled to leave. No, these thought could not be shared with Maggie.

And there was yet another dilemma. Her sister Agnes's increasing ill health worried her, for she'd never fully recovered from her bout with the croup, which resulted in recurring bronchitis and other problems. Lucy's frequent visits up to Eagle River served to remind her of their important link with the past, through both culture and language. Once in Shakopee—how could this continue?

Maggie had no sooner left when Mary arrived in the Dubois buggy and made herself at home in the front parlor. "Just met Maggie down the road," she announced. "She looked a bit down in the dumps. What'd you talk about?"

"A lot of things. My leaving, mostly."

"Well, that's mainly why I came over, to see how you're getting along. Made your way down my list, yet?"

"Not quite. So much still to do. There's my sister, Agnes, for example. She's not well. This isn't a good time to leave her."

Mary thought for a moment. "Now don't worry about her. Don't you remember that original discussion—out on the porch—the peach cobbler? I might be able to bring her down on the train for a visit later, once you get settled. No doubt it will do her good to see your parents again, her brothers. And I do hope you'll be settled soon. I'm sure you're making the right decision."

It was not difficult to recognize what lay behind Mary's eagerness to see her leave. She wanted Lucy out of the DeLaurier house, possibly to bring the place under her control. She maintained a suspicion about Noel's relationship to her, and, convinced that she could not persuade her in the direction of Homer West, now wanted Lucy far away. Yet there was no point in confronting Mary, or revealing her true feelings. So she nodded, and said simply, "Of course, I can't thank you enough for that offer."

"I know it'll take some time to make arrangements with Henry and all the rest. Jane, you know, is quite reasonable. But of course I'll leave most of that to Noel ."

"Are you quite sure about bringing Agnes? It's a lot to ask—too much, in fact."

"No, no, I agreed and that's that. No, you go ahead and make your plans, we'll manage. Do you plan to leave within the next week or two?"

"I'm not sure."

"What's keeping you then?"

What was keeping her? "I'm still uncertain about one or two things."

"Well you know, Lucy, winter's coming. Can't travel much once the weather turns bad. Best make up your mind right soon. There's so much to do. That list I made out, you know—"

"Yes, Mary, I know. I'll try." She wished the matter were simpler, as simple as Mary implied. Yet Lucy suspected Mary's mind was more complicated than that, more deeply into contrivances and plots than would appear. She had, after all, facilitated Lucy's decision to leave every step of the way.

It seemed endless, Mary's list. Nevertheless, over the next few days Lucy ticked them off one by one. Room by room she went through the house, sorting and packing, bestowing the late garden and orchard produce on Maggie, the root cellar contents on the Schweizers. John Wold and mister Schweizer made plans to take the stock and chickens into the Long Prairie farmer's market for auction on Saturday. Most of that money would go to Noel, but she hoped he'd allow her enough at least for the train tickets.

Two days before she was to leave, Mattias Holberg drove his blue-sided wagon into the barnyard. His appearance caught Lucy by surprise—an emotional confrontation she'd not expected nor was prepared for. She stopped gathering in the last of the tomatoes and put down her basket as he climbed down off the wagon and walked decisively over to the kitchen garden.

"Heard you've made up your mind, Lucy," he said with a set look on his face. "Sure looks like you have."

"Well, yes—I mean no, I—" She suddenly felt light-headed.

"Worked everything out, have you?"

"Well, yes, I—" she was totally confused and sat down beside the basket of tomatoes on the newly replaced back steps.

"Sure of that, now?"

"As you can see—" What else could she say?

"Looks like you've got things packed up."

"More or less." She pretended to examine a half-green tomato.

"Stock, chickens sold?"

"Not yet. Yes. John Wold's going to see to that."

"Tickets bought, and all that?"

"Noel took care of it." She dropped the green tomato back into the basket.

"I see." He toyed nervously with a button on his denim jacket, looked down at the ground, then questionably back up at Lucy. "Well, then, I guess your mind's made up?" shifting his feet a little.

Something prevented her from giving a direct answer. "I believe Noel's already looking for another tenant."

"Reckon so, reckon so. Crossed your bridge." He paused. "Well then, just thought I'd come to say good bye. He paused again and reached into his shirt pocket. "Wanted to give you this." With a shrug, he handed her a small box, then quickly backed away. "Goin' away present."

Lucy laid the box on the step between her and the basket of tomatoes. Was this the moment to confront him, the moment she'd hoped for? "Why, I—what can I—" she began, but Mattias interruped her.

"Also I wanted to let you know 'bout my brothers. You know they've been plannin' to head out West. Well, now they're all set, maybe next week or so when the next wagon train for Montana comes through Little Sauk."

Lucy tried desperately to find the right words. "You—what are your plans, then?"

He looked at her steadily for a full minute. "That depends."

What *should* she say? *What does it depend on?* Hesitating, she picked up another half-green tomato and stared at the worm hole eaten partially through it.

"Well, you said you're leavin'." He traced a square in the dirt with the toe of his boot, then, "Truth be told, I'm leavin' too. I plan to go with them, looks like lots of opportunities out there for me, too." He paused. "Not much here."

So, Lucy thought, with a strange, sinking feeling, he's made his decision.

"They—we, that is, we wanted to know if we can buy your stock— milk cow and that horse of yours? Be a good idea, take 'em out west, give us a start toward the ranch."

Lucy's emotions were in a turmoil. If she'd felt trapped before by staying dependent upon Noel Dubois, she now felt trapped by leaving. In a daze, she reached over and slid the small box into her apron pocket. "Horse and cow? Best talk to Noel about it."

"Right, then, I'll do just that." He mounted his wagon, headed out of the yard down the lane. Turning back, he said, "Wish you a good trip, ma'am." And he was gone.

"Oh, what have I done?" Lucy cried as she got to her feet and watched his wagon round the corner of the house. She stared at the empty lane, heard the sound grow fainter, just as she'd heard at Thurstroms that awful day when Rachael Olson's careless words changed everything. She stared without seeing, aware only of the silence which followed his departure.

Yet what had she expected? The box—Half-unwilling to look, she opened it to find, wrapped in thin paper, a simple silver ring with raised wires in twisted knots around its circumference. There was nothing engraved inside. Such a gift—how had he been able to afford it? Why had he given it to her, what had he intended? Now she would never know.

Another sign, another message in that series of signs. Just like the sign of the granary fire warned her about Noel, this last meeting with Mattias Holberg only reconfirmed her decision to leave Little Sauk and the DeLaurier place. Although she felt an emptiness no words could describe, she was struck by the symbolism of Mattias's ring. Those twisted wire knots, coming full circle, intertwined. One event leading to the resolution of another. The fire, which clarified her relationship with Noel, which in turn clarified her decision to leave. Mattias's ring, his last words —all serving to release her.

Her one fear now was that Homer West would suddenly reappear. What if Rachael Olson had put something in the *Argus* about her leaving for Shakopee, as Sep Holberg had suggested? It would mean she could expect Homer's buggy drawn like a magnet to her doorstep, her house, her barn—that is, Noel's house and barn. He had a disturbing way about him, a way disturbing to her vulnerable senses, and she didn't trust herself. It would be especially difficult with Bernard's memory so recently awakened in the process of packing the belongings they'd shared, his army uniform, his photograph.

And yet—and yet . . . She could not entirely dismiss her troubled feelings about Noel. Everything Mary had done over the past few weeks seemed to confirm the fact that she was jealous, suspicious.

By the beginning of the next week, Lucy had reached the end of Mary's list. The last day came, a day which she'd been both looking forward to and dreading, a day which generated confused and contradictory feelings. She thought again of the first day she'd come with Noel and Mary to look at the house. The DeLauriers had moved on but left their stamp on the house, the gardens, and the fields. They would always remain a part of this place. Would she and her children? Would the next tenants feel as she did?

That evening Maggie and Lem drove over to say goodbye. Lucy hesitated inviting them inside, because most of the boxes, chests, and furniture had been packed and sent to the Little Sauk station to be shipped as freight. That is, all the furniture except the big brass bed in the guestroom, which Lucy felt belonged to the house.

She and the children, in fact, would have to sleep on pallets on the floor that last night. Mary had urged them to spend the night in Little Sauk—more comfortable, closer to the station, easier on the children, she argued. When Lucy refused, Mary insisted they at least have their noon dinner in Little Sauk before catching the train at two o'clock. Noel would come for them in the big surrey in the morning.

Her last night in the DeLaurier house. It had to be in that house, an important and significant closure, marking the end of one life and opening the way toward another.

"Do you mind sitting here on the porch steps?" she now asked Maggie. "A bit cool for September but—"

"Oh we won't stay long," replied Maggie, "right, Lem? "Just came to bring you some vittals for the trip tomorrow. First off, though, in this box some baked beans and Boston brown bread for your breakfast in the mornin'—jug of coffee maybe you can warm up if there's any wood left for the range. Now this basket's for the train. You'll be needin' what's in here." She handed Lucy a good-sized basket, covered with square of green oilcloth. "Don't know as you'll be able to get anything fit to eat on the way—most likely cost too much in the first place. Is it two or three changes you'll have?"

"Two—we change in Sauk Centre, again in Minneapolis. About eight hours altogether if the trains are on time. At least that's what the stationmaster said when Noel bought the tickets. Leaving here at two, arriving Shakopee around ten o'clock tomorrow night, about an hour's wait in Minneapolis."

"My, my, long trip for sure. And two changes—and alone, with all those little'uns, lot of baggage. You'll need those vittals, I reckon. And here—have you got that little wallet, Lem? Here's something by way of a going-away present. Folks 'round here—the Clarks, Holbergs—that is only Sep and Karin, all three boys now taken off west like so many folks 'round here—Schweitzers, other folks don't even know, all got together for a Social Hop, collected a bit of spending money for you. Not much, but it'll help on the trip, getting settled. And I guess for once you can thank Rachael of spreading the word around."

Lucy was touched. There was a few moments' strained silence. Finally Maggie said in a different tone, "Sure don't know what you're thinkin', leavin' this place like you are."

"Well, you know the reasons."

"Yes, but still don't make sense." She glanced sharply at Lucy. "Anyways, sure I don't know all of 'em, though I can guess."

"Now Maggie, old girl," Lem put in. "Situation's hard enough for Lucy as it is." He got up from the porch step. "We'd best be goin'—I'm sure she's still got some things to do, a long day ahead of her tomorrow."

Maggie started to say something but thought better of it. As they all came together down the brick walk toward the wagon, she turned to embrace Lucy. Neither woman said anything, but remained with arms tightly around one another for several long moments. Lem handed Maggie up to the bench, climbed up beside her, then whipped the horse up to a trot which took the turn onto the Little Sauk road dangerously fast.

That night, after the children had been bedded down—Sabine, Laurence, and Louis on the bare mattress of the brass bed in the guestroom, Martin on a quilt pallet beside them, Lucy walked through the house. A bright harvest moon shone through the big windows, creating shafts of silvery light across the empty rooms—parlor, dining room, kitchen, her big bedroom upstairs, the empty bedroom where Laurence, clutching his beloved Leo, had stood frozen with terror against the window while the granary fire raged outside.

Looking out the kitchen window, she saw the barnyard was illumined with light, creating sharp contrasts between light and shadow. The ruined granary was only a silhouette of jagged timbers, the barn with its huge door open, beyond it a black hole concealing the empty stalls which had held Brownling and Blaise, now on their way to Montana with Mattias.

For a while, she sat alone on the front porch railing, thinking of Maggie's last visit, her concerns, her generous provisions, her mothering. She scarcely remembered her own mother, the *maman* who'd brought her from Quebec. She'd see her soon in Shakopee. What would their relationship be like? Lucy felt she was not at all the same person she'd been when her parents abandoned their homestead near Little Sauk, over nine years ago. She worried about what kind of adjustment they'd have to make. So much had happened. It would even be difficult to talk, her own French now all but evaporated.

At last she could no longer ignore the chill in the air and went inside. She did not bother to change into her nightdress as she stretched out, still fully dressed, on the quilt pallet. Sleep did not come for a long time. It wasn't so much the discomfort of the hard floor keeping her awake. It was the overwhelming assault to the senses. The bright silver radiance of moonlight flooding through the curtainless bedroom windows. The lingering odor of dinners she'd cooked in the kitchen—beef roasts, greens with bacon, apple pies; the fruity steam of boiling jam, the yeasty smell of bread rising. The lingering acrid odor of burnt timbers and ashes. It was the wind, whispering in the corners of vacant rooms, recalling their memories. It was the haunting call of a wolf, up on the ridge by the riverbank. Yes, she'd made her decision, she'd put Mary Dubois' *First Things* behind her, it remained to put those memories behind her. What would be the *Next Things, the Last Things?*

Just when the first days of October were transforming themselves into the full brilliance of autumn, Noel pulled up alongside the Little Sauk train station and helped the children and Lucy down from his big surrey. Lucy carried Louis, hoping he wouldn't ruin her dress. He was already intent upon pulling off its beaded trim. It was her only proper widow's dress, beaded all around the edge of the jacket and hem with little jet beads, the jacket over a blouse of ecru-colored lace frilled around the neck.

Mary had insisted on paying for it at the fashionable dress shop in Sauk Centre and wear it out of respect for Bernard's memory. Otherwise, she'd said, what would people think? The new black widow's bonnet, with its gray feather plume and tight band under chin, was another of Mary's coercions. Such confinements, those corset stays and tight-fitting sleeves. She could feel them now, digging into her ribs and constraining her arms, worse with the pressure of Louis's weight against her as she carried him onto the train platform.

She sighed, thinking of the journey before her, that last meeting with Mattias behind her. She could not bring herself to wear his gift, the silver ring, but kept it inside its little box, buried deep in her bag. Yes, it was going to be a difficult journey. Who'd made this decision? There had been so many turning points, so many issues. She wasn't sure.

Mary had also worked on the children's appearance. "Let me look at you, now," Lucy said, as she lined up Sabine, Martin, and Laurence on the platform. Yes, they seemed reasonably tidy. Mary had insisted on outfitting them in such a way as to not embarrass their Uncle George when he met them at Shakopee station. Lucy took a handkerchief out of her black velvet reticule, spit on it, and, under Louis's noisy protest, wiped off a black speck from his forehead. She leaned over to button the top button on Martin's grown-up looking tweed jacket, to straighten Sabine's blue velvet tam and brush up the red pom-pom.

"Please, Ma," cried Sabine, "stop your fussing!" She stepped over to the edge of the platform and peered north up the tracks. "Listen! Hear that? Don't you hear the train coming?" She caught her tam just as it blew off and narrowly missed falling onto the tracks.

"*Eh bien,* two-o-clock train from Stillings to Sauk Centre due in a few minutes," said Noel, consulting his pocket watch. "That whistle— must be for the crossing up near Beaver."
Lucy nervously observed that there were still some crates and a trunk or two to unload from the wagon, driven up a half-hour earlier by John Wold. He and the stationmaster were stacking it along the platform where the baggage car normally stopped. What if some of it got lost? Had she packed everything? Broken? Misplaced? So much to think about.

John Wold seemed to glance her way frequently. Just as the last crate was put in place, he hesitantly stepped over and handed her a small bouquet of field daisies. "To say good bye," he said, obviously embarrassed. "You look mighty nice, ma'am, if I may say so. Sorry you're leavin'." He looked agitated—for John, at least, and was about to say something else when interrupted by the stationmaster wanting him to sign some papers.

Despite all her resolutions to the contrary, Lucy was becoming more and more distraught. The crates. The baggage. The children. The tickets. Telegram to George informing him of their arrival time. The moment she'd been half-dreading had actually arrived. A hundred more questions. Everything packed in the carpetbags they'd need right away? The tickets? Laurence's Leo in Sabine's beg? Maggie's food basket? She looked at Noel, carrying Laurence in his arms, calming him in a fatherly way just as he had done at Bernard's funeral. A moment of remorse, of indecision. But it was too late for indecisions, though never too late for remorse.

"No, no, Martin, stay back from the edge of the platform," she called, trying to focus on this present critical moment. "And Sabine, you too! Louis, stop squirming like that—you'll make me drop you in front of the train! Do you want that?" He let out a scream.

They were actually going, actually going, actually . . . She repeated this to herself, unconsciously mimicking the rhythm of the approaching wheels. The future held a mixture of excitement and anxiety, about equal in proportion, she figured. Agnes was still a major concern, but she would see her again soon when Mary brought her later by train. Perhaps this very same train by the very same route.

"*Écoute*, Lucy," Noel said, patting her arm reassuringly as he set Laurence down, "I will arrange for Agnes's journey, talk to Henry. Bof! He cannot refuse. Mary and Josie will come with her. It will be an adventure for them. But, Lucy—" a slight hesitation in his lowered voice, a seriousness—"but you will return, come back here for a visit, *n'est-ce pas?*"

At that moment the locomotive rumbled past and the two cars—one for baggage, the other for passengers—slowed to a stop along the platform. Noel raised his voice above the noise. "*Eh bien*—all will be well, have no fear. My fear is," he laughed, "that I won't be able to cope with the other children while Mary and Josie are gone with Agnes!"

"All aboard," the conductor shouted, "all aboo-aard!" and waved to the engineer leaning out of the locomotive cab. Sabine, Martin, and Laurence helped up the steps ahead of her, Lucy entered the long car and started down the aisle to find some seats. With a jerk and a grinding of the cars against each other, the train lurched slowly forward. Holding Louis tight, Lucy fell off balance into the seat nearest her.

As the train pulled out of the station, Lucy experienced a wave of emotion. She was reliving her nightmare—this long , narrow car, the racks up above. But where she'd seen a heavy suitcase, there were now only their small carpetbags. The windows were not locked shut but open, a fresh breeze blowing in the dusty smell of new-mown wheat, the pungent smoke from burn-off fires, the heavy coal smoke from the engine.

As for her destination—well, surely this was not a dream, surely the train would stop where and when her ticket said it would. To reassure herself, she opened her reticule and took out the long piece of heavy paper, folded into three sections. Yes, there it was, the place and time stamped on each one.

"Lucy, Lucy!" Noel was shouting, running along on the platform beside the train, trying to keep up with its increasing speed. Lucy set Louis down on the window seat, beside her and leaned out. "*Eh bien*, remember—don't talk to strangers, don't lose your tickets and when—" he was now having to run to keep up, "you are—remember, *chère* Lucy, do not—and when you have—" His words were lost in the clanging of the bell and blasts of smoke from the engine. Noel fell behind as the train's speed outstripped him, his voice lost. She leaned farther out the window, looking back and straining to catch his last few words.

But the train went around a curve as it entered a wood and she lost sight of him, the platform, the station. Within the next few seconds, Little Sauk and her familiar world was gone.

In her exhaustion, she dozed off several times before reaching the station at Sauk Centre, the children too preoccupied with looking out the window to notice. With the help of an older couple, she managed to make the change at Sauk Centre without losing children or bags, only forgetting John Wold's bouquet of daisies. Maggie's food basket proved a god-send, just as she'd predicted. It was nearly empty by the time the train pulled into Central station in Minneapolis. Lucy felt a great sense of relief to have that second part of the journey over. Now only a few more hours and they'd be in Shakopee.

How overwhelming the size, the noise, the confusion. "How are we going to find the connection to Shakopee," Lucy asked Sabine in alarm.

"It's not like the station at Little Sauk, is it Mama?" Sabine looked apprehensive.

"Are we lost?" Laurence wailed.

Lucy wasn't sure. The train station in Minneapolis was a shock. Since leaving Little Sauk, they'd been traveling for almost six hours, the train delayed at several points because of repairs to the tracks. "The man said we've got a wait between trains, then at least two more hours to Shakopee."

"Then it'll be so late when we get there," Martin wailed. "I'm ready for bed already. I just wanna get there! And I'm hungry. Now!"

"Do you see it anywhere?" Lucy asked Sabine. "That connection to Shakopee, the Hastings and Dakota line?" She hoped George's name for it—*Hell and Damnation*—had been just a joke. "Count the bags, Martin, make sure they're all here."

"Think so, Mama, 'cept the food basket's empty."

Lucy strained to hear the announcements. Where was that conductor? She had no idea where to catch the connecting H and D train to Shakopee. *Blah blah blah* from a megaphone back near the front of the station, *aark, orm, eeve, blah blah.* "Why can't they speak more clearly? Why aren't there more signs up? How do they expect us to read those small blackboards on easels, sprawled chalk marks? Look like chicken scratches." Her reticule kept slipping off her arm and she impatiently pulled it up each time. "Come, hurry, stay close to me, children! No time to spare. Now which track?"

"But look, Mama—there's all those platforms, tracks on both sides," Sabine said in distress. "All those trains!"

"I'll have to find out. Oh, Louis, you're getting heavier and heavier." She carried him in one arm, her reticule in the other. "If you get lost in this station, I'll never ever find you again. "Martin—Sabine—pick up those things. Sabine, hang on to Laurence. We have to hurry—and stay close to me—don't let me out of your sight!"

The noise blared up, just as another announcement came. A band playing somewhere. She caught the words *Shakopee* and *track*, the rest lost in when puffs of steam erupted from a nearby engine. Nearly running, she headed down the platform toward the waiting room, glancing back to see if the children were still following. Laurence was missing. "Come, we've got to go back, find your brother," she said in exasperation. "Hurry, look for him!"

Another five minutes of jostling past crowds, shouting his name, and there he was, just about where they'd first gotten off the Sauk Centre train. "Look, Mama," he shouted, pointing up to the great glass dome which covered the station. "How can those windows stay upsidedown like that?"

A mixture of relief and annoyance. "Come along! Told you to stay with us, didn't I? We can't miss that train—it's the last one tonight." She clutched struggling Louis tightly with one arm with the handles of her reticule slid over it, and, seizing Laurence by his jacket collar with her free hand, dragged him along the platform. Surely, down there by the waiting room and all those shops there'd be someone who could help.

Desperate, she stopped a passing man in uniform. "H and D, ma'am," he said, "Shakopee? Over there, track six. But you'll have to hurry," he shouted above the noise, waving his arm in the direction of the other side of the station. "It's just about to leave, near an hour late or you'd have missed it for sure. Luck's on your side, I guess."

And so they ran and ran, bumping into people, Martin dropping a bag and rushing back to pick it up, Louis threatening to break loose from her grasp, a flood of people rushing, brushing, pulling against her. Laurence needed constant reassurance that his Leo hadn't been left behind, was still tucked away in Sabine's bag. At last they reached the right platform, the conductor already waving his flag. If he hadn't quickly lifted the children up one by one onto the car's steps, steadied Lucy by a hand under her elbow, they would never have made it.

Lucy collapsed into the nearest empty seat, gasping for breath, her heart pounding wildly, hardly aware when Louis wriggled out of her arms and crawled over to the window by the empty seat beside her. Fortunately he'd not cried from being frightened at all the noise and confusion. Now he seemed fascinated by the metal hinges on the window and was getting up on his knees to look out at all the bright lights around the station.

It was nearly eleven o'clock by the time they got off the train and stood huddled together on the Shakopee station platform, watching the red lantern on the tail end of the last H and D car disappear in the distance with several whistle blasts from the engine ahead. The small station, like the Little Sauk station, stood as a single platform between two tracks. Tonight it was lit by a single kerosene lantern hanging from a bracket at the far end of the building. The building itself was empty. Even the windows of the stationmaster's office and telegraph room were dark. The town seemed very quiet and almost totally dark, with only few street lamps lit along the main street. Lucy saw that both tracks ran along the town's main street. They hadn't been there before when she'd left as a girl. Now the town looked new and strange, hardly recognizable.

Loud noises just down the street interrupted her thoughts. A gun shot, men shouting, laughter, a piano playing a tune she recognized. Dark figures streamed in and out of light coming from the swinging doors of a saloon. Lucy drew the children back into the shadows of the station, tried the door of the waiting room. It was locked. "Come along," she said. "Bring everything back over here. I see some benches along the platform on the other side of the station—we'll wait there for your uncle."

"Uncle George coming?" Sabine asked anxiously. "Where is he? Do you think he got Uncle Noel's telegram?"

"I don't know, certainly hope so. We'll just wait here a bit."

"What if he don't show up?" Martin asked. "I can go down to that place down there that's all lit up—where the music is—ask."

"No, Martin, you wait right here."

A young couple had gotten off the train several cars down. They were waiting, too, pacing slowly up and down the platform. "Do you know how far Fourth Street is?" Lucy asked hopefully.

"Sorry, missus," the man answered. "Strangers here in town ourselves." They strolled down to the end of the platform, came back. There was the clip-clop of a horse approaching, buggy wheels grinding on the brick pavement.

"Look, Ma," Martin cried. "There he is!"

The buggy pulled up. "Well, Lottie, finally made it. "Trip all right? Climb in, here, I'll get that bag."

"Sir," Lucy said as she rushed up to the man, "can you give us a ride to my brother's house? Just over on 4th Street? It's so late, and the children—"

The man looked at them and the pile of bags. "No," he said, scratching his head, "no, sorry ma'am. Can't fit all of you in this here buggy. Sorry—sure your brother'll be along soon, though. But if not, there's that saloon just down the street, hostelry above it. Can't speak for the Meyer's Hotel, next street over down by the river—heard they were full up, though. Big group of flour mill people in town, some sort of convention. Good night to you, then."

A saloon—hostelry above. No, she could not—would not take the children there. It looked as though they'd have to walk through the darkened streets, try to find George's house—but what number was it? Had he ever mentioned that? Maybe look for a house with another house being built along side of it. But was it to the east or west on Fourth Street? She thought it must be east, but she wasn't sure. There'd be a dividing street through the town somewhere, every town had one. Where would that be? Did the street numbers start down at the river or here on this main street at the station?

If only she could remember what the town looked like, how the streets were laid out, but her family had moved away nearly twelve years ago. The town had surely changed with the railroad and all, and besides, it was dark. Hopeless to try to find Goerge's house, but what alternative did they have? With that saloon just down the street, guns, drunken men, no telling what might happen if it were anything like the one she'd known in Long Prairie. Besides, the autumn night was growing colder, they couldn't sleep out on those benches, even if it were safe.

Come along, children," she said resolutely, trying to keep her lips from trembling. Her worst fear was being realized. George had not come. They were alone in a strange place in the middle of the night. "Come, now, pick up the bags, and keep close to me. We can't stay here —we're going to try to find uncle's house."

Louis lay a dead weight against her shoulder, asleep, as she walked down to the far end of the station, turned left across the tracks, and headed what she assumed was south, toward the next numbered street. Now that they'd left the main street, a few lights in upstairs windows provided some means of seeing where they walked, aided by a full moon sliding in and out of a cloud bank. The same moon which had so illumined the DeLaurier the night before.

The children followed closely, Sabine at her elbow, Laurence just behind, hanging on to her skirt. They said nothing, but Lucy knew they were not only exhausted but also afraid. She felt guilty. How could she have brought them to this?

They came to the next street. In the uncertain light, Lucy was relieved to see a street sign—they were on Oak, about to cross Second Second Street. Two more blocks to go—then would come the decision whether to turn east or west down Fourth.

"Can't go no more, Mama," Laurence cried. He broke away and sat down on the curb. "Want Leo," he sobbed, "want my Leo."

Lucy sat down beside him, shifting Louis to her other arm. "We'll just take a little rest for a bit," she said. "And we'll soon be there, you'll see. Uncle George—your Mamie will be so glad to see you—they'll have some hot cocoa for us, something to eat, maybe some of your Mamie's brioches. See, Martin isn't complaining, and he's carrying all those bags. Oh look, there's a cookie or two left in the basket."

"No, don't want cookies, want Leo," he cried, past consolation.

"Just a few streets more," she coaxed, as she pulled him up, still protesting. Together the group headed again down the street. "Just a little ways now, I know you can be very brave—see, look at Sabine and Martin."

They reached Third and Oak. A few lights remained in an upstairs window or two, but for the most part everyone seemed to have gone to bed. It was even more was difficult to see and to negotiate the uneven pavement. It had been a long day. Exhausted herself, Lucy now recognized the foolishness of trying to find George's house. Why hadn't she tried that hotel? If it was full, maybe they could have slept in the lobby. Or even that saloon hostelry—surely that place would have been all right, at least for one night. Then she could have sent someone to fetch George and his wagon next morning.

Suddenly Martin pressed up against her. "Ma, Ma," he gasped, "someone's followin' us!" Lucy looked back over her shoulder, but it was too dark to see anything. "Saw somethin' back there, shadow of somethin' near that last house we passed."

"Oh, Ma . . ." Sabine said when she heard this. She put her arm around her mother's waist, just as Lucy turned her head to look back, and Lucy could feel her trembling.

"Hear that?" Martin said, "sounds like footsteps. "

At first Lucy saw only the pale glistening of the brick street behind them as the moon emerged from behind its cloud bank. Then a momentary glint of something shiny moving along the edge of the street about half a block behind them. Now it glinted, now in shadow. She stopped, the reflection disappeared. The sound of footsteps stopped. She recalled those figures coming in and out of the saloon down the street from the station, the noisy brawling, the gun shot. What if they'd seen her and the children leave the station and were following them?

A prickling sensation decended down into the base of her spine. Louis's heavy weight made it even more difficult to breathe and she felt the palms of her hands grow moist.

"Come my darlings," she said, trying to keep her voice steady, "keep walking. We can go a little faster, can't we? It's only a little way now, we're almost there." They'd passed Third Street, were now almost to the next crossing at Fourth Street. But which way then? East?

A dog barking behind them, the person—or persons—following them must have disturbed it. "A little faster now, I know you're tired, but we're almost there." She could not run carrying Louis, dared not look back, dared not stop.

At last, the next cross street. She had to stop then to decide whether to turn right or left. She strained her ears to listen. What was that? Were those footsteps behind them?

There was a sound, not of footsteps, but something else. From where she stood with the children huddled close to her at the corner, Lucy looked west on Fourth Street toward the sound and saw what looked like a light several streets down. In fact, it looked as though the light was not from a house, but moving in a strange, irregular way toward them. Now the sound was clearer, the clip-clop of a horse, heavy wheels rumbling on brick pavement.

"Quick," she said, "if we stand out in the middle of the street, he'll have to stop."

"No, Ma," Sabine and Martin in chorus. "Most likely run us down! No, wait!" They ran back to the curb.

For Lucy, there was no choice. The wagon coming fast toward them was the only help they could hope for. If a stranger, no telling what, but with whoever that was behind following them, no telling what either. She handed Louis over to Sabine and ran out into the middle of the street. "Stop, oh stop!" she screamed, waving her hands, "stop, please stop!"

A sharp whinny as the driver of the wagon jerked back on the reins, sparks flying off the iron wheel rims as they responded to the brake and were dragged reluctantly along the brick pavement, obscenities coming from the driver as he strained to pull the wagon to a stop. The lantern attached to a post by the seat swung wildly, casting an unsteady combination of light and shadow along the pavement, along the fronts of the nearby houses, on Lucy standing in the middle of the street.

"Lord save us, damn fool woman—what are you doing there!" shouted the driver, as he tightened the reins to keep the team steady. "Well, I'll be damned. Trying to get yourself killed out there in the middle of the street, Lucy?"

"Georgie!" she cried.

11
COLD WINDS

ONCE YOUR STUFF GETS HERE—freight always takes longer—we'll move in your beds," Lucy's brother Georgie offered the next morning over breakfast. "I'm sure those pallets on the dining room floor aren't very comfortable for Sabine and Martin and—what's the little one's name? Oh, yes, Laurence. Rest of those crates and things we'll just have to leave stored out in the shed." Then, half apologetic, "You and the baby slept well last night in my room?"

"Off and on," said Lucy in an icy tone. "Louis is still asleep. Your bed seemed a bit small for both of us, but we'll manage. Where'd you sleep?"

"Parlor sofa, as good a place as any. Ma and Pa have always had the big front bedroom, ever since they moved in from Uncle Paul's. Couldn't very well double up there."

"Of course not. But I was a bit surprised Alphie and Jeanne-Marie are still here. Met her coming out of the other back bedroom when I got up this morning."

"Sure do have a house full, I guess, now that you're here. Hoped to have the new house next door finished by the time you got here, but some set-backs. Oh, I know what you're going to say, Ma, but first, how about some more coffee?"

"And what's happening to that house next door you promised?"

"Georges, Georges—*la maison*—" *Maman* came around with the coffee pot, shaking her head. "*Tu sais très bien que . . .*"

George extended his empty cup. "I, know, I know. Should've spent more time on your house. But, listen Ma—I've been telling you, you've got to speak English these days—you can do it. Sounds kind of weird, but at least you usually get your ideas across. Think of your grandchildren—want them to grow up foreigners?"

His mother grumbled, started again. She clearly resented having to make the effort, but George's last remark seemed to have struck home. "*Tu sais*—you know our Lucy was in the act of arriving," she said, wagging her finger at George and diverting the subject of language back to the question of house construction. Her mouth set decisively, she leaned over to fill the breadbasket with more brioches out of the oven and passed it around the table. "Please to serve youself. *Merci à dieu*—thanks be to God—brioche dough put to rise last night—otherwise a breakfast very poor. Jeanne-Marie, please, the crock has need of more butter."

Lucy's father nodded at his wife's remarks but said nothing. Although last night he seemed pleased to see Lucy and his grandchildren, this morning he sat moodily in one corner of the dining room. The kitchen was too small for anything but two stools at the counter and a bench by the back door.

"Doin' my best on that house, Ma, last four months—Fred, too," George said, slathering his brioche with butter. "And you know, still more to do on this one, as well—porch off the back, another room over the kitchen. We're waiting for some more lumber, other stuff." Then, between mouthfuls, "Besides all that, Fred's pa is expanding Stadthauser's dry goods store. Told you that already. We've been working on your house next door as much as we can, evenings too."

"That why you didn't meet the train last night?" snapped Lucy, certainly not in the best frame of mind this morning. "How could you do that to us? Why, no telling what might have happened." She was exhausted from the effort of the long trip, angry at George. It would be some time before she could forget that long and difficult walk carrying Louis through the darkened streets, the fear they were being followed, the sickening feeling of being helpless and lost, and in the presence of some unknown threat.

"Well, I'll tell you how it was. More coffee in the pot? Oh, thanks, Jeanne. Yes, really good, those brioches of Ma's—nobody else comes close, eh Ma? Your coffee sure needs improvement, though, Jeanne. Well, Lucy, here's the story. You see, yesterday I took the afternoon off to try to get a little more done on the house for Ma and Pa next door, speed things up a bit. Fred, too. Lost a little pay, but don't matter. Things a bit crowded around here, eh Jeanne?" His sister-in-law looked embarrassed and busied herself with clearing off the empty plates. "Knew the H and Damn train from Minneapolis was due 'round ten o'clock or so. Supper here, then went down to the livery stable at First and Pine to borrow Stadthauser's delivery wagon to go to the station, meet your train. Another brioche, Ma?" He cut it in half, spread butter on both halves, chewed on several bites. "Well, as I was saying, picked up that wagon from the stable, reckoned we'd need a big one, what with all those young'uns and baggage."

"But when we arrived at the station last night, you weren't there."

"Know that, and I'm mighty sorry."

"We waited and waited."

"Know that."

"Didn't you get Noel's telegram?"

"Yes, but—"

"Well then, why didn't—?"

"Listen," George interrupted. "Here's how it was. Got to the station plenty early, 'bout nine-thirty or so. Station master just closing up the place. 'What's happening, sir,' I ses. 'Last train cancelled,' he ses. 'Why's that?' I asked. 'Dunno, son,' he ses. 'Telegraph message just came in from the Minneapolis station master. Most likely engine trouble. No more trains tonight, so might as well call it a day and head on home.' Well, that was that. So I figured you'd be stuck in Minneapolis, find a hotel or someplace for the night. So I took Stadthauser's delivery wagon back to the stable, walked home."

"Settled down for the night," Ma added. "*Mon dieu*, just put back the baguettes and cheese we'd kept out for you and *les enfants*, threw away the hot milk. Ah, such waste. Just then—"

"Well, just then, like Ma says, heard a train whistle—wind blowing this direction, otherwise can't hardly hear 'em. So I ses to myself, *mon dieu*, there's that blasted train after all. I put my boots back on, threw on a jacket, raced all the way back down to First and Pine. Fortunately the fellow at the stable lives upstairs over the office, but I did have to wake him up He wasn't too happy 'bout that. 'Quick,' I ses to Bill, 'hitch up that delivery wagon again. Got to get over to the station.' Problem was, I couldn't tell whether that train whistle was when the train was coming in or leaving."

"Leaving," said Lucy firmly, recalling her sinking feeling at seeing the train disappear in the distance, leaving her and the children stranded on the platform.

"Well, anyways, got there quick as I could—place empty, dark as pitch—well, nearly anyway. Figured you'd missed the train, be staying in Minneapolis over night. So I headed back down First Street to the stable. Right then I figured Bill wouldn't be too happy me waking him up a second time." He paused, reached for another knife-full of butter.

"'So,' ses I to myself, 'best thing to do is take the team and wagon home, bring 'em back to the stable come morning.' Streets pretty dark by then, thought I'd better light the wagon lantern. Came up Pine Street, then headed east on Fourth. Almost to Oak when damned if I didn't see you standing out there in the middle of the street, screaming, waving your arms like a crazy woman—got an awful fright, I did. Stopped that big wagon just in the nick of time, lucky for you. Damn good thing that wagon had rachet brakes. Those dray horses, you know—lots of power, stubborn once they get moving."

He rose from the table. "And, say, speaking of moving, got to go." He went out to the kitchen and put on a jacket hanging by the back door. "Should get that team and wagon back 'for it's missed. Out there now, tied up in our backyard. Frost last night, hope they're all right, prob'ly hungrier than the dickens. On second thought, better take 'em directly to Stadthauser's, not the stable. Mister S most likely have me delivering first thing this morning, always cusses me out if I'm the least bit late. Be back 'round supper time, Ma. See to getting Lucy settled, maybe Jeanne can help unpack." He added ironically, "That is, if her and mister brother Alphie have no other plans for today?"

Jeanne made a wry face. "You know we've got to go to the land office, soon's he gets up, has some breakfast." She glanced at the empty bread-basket. "That is, if George left any." She sent a dark look after him as he disappeared out the back door. Just then, Alphie came down stairs.

"Oh, hello, sis," he said, obviously just up. "Glad you're here. Say, Jeanne, how about some breakfast?"

And this from the brother she'd not seen in at least ten years. With only a quick embrace and a mumbled word or two, she said, "Here, *maman*, let me help you with those dishes. Then I'd best get upstairs and look after Louis."

The situation was not at all what Lucy expected. Tension in the air, conflicts within the family. All so cramped in this small house. She regretted not waiting to leave the DeLaurier place until George had finished the house next door. If only she'd known. If only she'd waited. Yes, another reason, too. Another chance to see Mattias, to straighten things out with him. If that had happened, there might have been no reason to leave. Her mind formed—she could not control it—that scene might have been like, what it might have been like afterwards. What might have been—But yet, weren't there other pressing reasons why she had to leave when she did? "No, no, let me dry, *maman*," she said, taking the towel off the rack.

Over the next few days, Lucy herself had much to see to. For one thing, Sabine and Martin had to be enrolled in school. They'd already missed nearly a month. Wednesday morning, she left her mother in charge of Laurence and the baby and with Martin and Sabine walked the five blocks to Union School to see the principal.

Principal Mullen was very matter of fact. "I'm certain your boy—your daughter, too—will have a difficult time catching up, missus—er—Duboyce—"

"It's pronounced doo-bwa, sir," she said, "a French name.".

"Well then," his tone sounded annoyed, "they may find us ahead of their old school in—where did you say? Ah yes, I see it here on the form. Little Sauk."

Martin and Sabine stood in front of his desk, shuffling their feet, looking helplessly at their mother. "I must tell you that Union School is one of the best—one of the most progressive schools in Shakopee, in fact, the whole Twin Cities area. This whole section of town burned down in our great fire of January 1870. Destroyed the old log school. We were fortunate in being able to rebuild a more progressive facility."

"What do you mean by progressive?" Lucy felt she was being insulted in a back-handed sort of way. "We had a good school in Little Sauk."

The principal grew defensive. "Well, I mean—being progressive, we enjoy the facilities of a gymnasium, sports field, a shop, a science laboratory, teach several modern languages like French and German."

"My children will catch up, mister Mullen, I'll make sure of that. They already know some French. Martin will certainly like the opportunity for more sports, I expect Sabine will excel in science."

"Unlikely," he said firmly.

Although Lucy had no other choice for Martin, something about mister Mullen prompted her to find an alternative for Sabine. That same afternoon she and Sabine went around to St. Gertrude's Convent and Academy, about the same distance but in the opposite direction.

"Of course, we would love to enroll your daughter," said Sister Elizabeth across her desk. "She will be very welcome here—I can see she is very alert, will be a most satisfactory student. What is her religious education?"

"What do you mean?"

The sister looked shocked. "Of course I mean, does she know her catechism? She's ten, you say? When was her first communion?"

Lucy was dumbstruck. There had been little opportunity for that, only an occasional visit from Father Mundt, the odd mass on special feast days. "I'm afraid—I'm afraid," she stammered, "sister, I'm afraid I must leave that to you."

There was a long silence, Sister Elizabeth gazing first out the window, then at the crucifix on the wall, tapping her pencil on her desk the whole while, fingering the crucifix on a chain around her neck. "I see."

"But my daughter would receive here the same education as at a boy's school? Math, science?"

"We attempt to do that," Sister answered evasively. "Along with the strictest religious education. For the sake of her soul, you understand."

Lucy asked about the fees. They were high, but she calculated that, with the social hop money Maggie had raised, it might just be possible. It might be worth it. "I shall bring Sabine tomorrow," she said.

The first day Sabine started school at St. Gertrude's, Lucy and Jeanne were clearing up the breakfast things, in and out of the dining room, the kitchen. *Maman* was doing something upstairs with Louis and Laurence. Lucy could hear them moving around, her mother insisting on speaking French to the toddler despite George's warning. "How exciting," Lucy remarked to Jeanne over the dishes. "Buying your own farm. How big is it? What'll your crops be?"

"Oh, about eighty acres, I guess. As for farming—don't know yet, depends on what the county agent recommends. Corn a big thing around here, but with my father's connection to the steam flour mill in town, maybe wheat's the best. These days, you know, you've got to be scientific about things, what works best with the land you've got."

"Too bad Pa didn't realize that."

Both women remained silent for a while, thoughts running deep. Lucy contemplated the reasons precipating her move to Shakopee, what alternatives might have been like if she'd remained at the DeLaurier place, what it might have taken to get her off Dubois charity, what life might have been like otherwise.

"Say, Jeanne," she said, as they made the beds together, "Alphie said you were from a French Canadian family."

"That's right, my father was born in Montreal."

"But you don't seem—you don't seem—"

Jeanne laughed. "Don't seem from there? Well, to tell you the truth, my mother was from Iowa. They met somewhere in Muscatine, came up river to settle here. And by the way, if I may be frank, neither do you seem—whatever you meant." She rolled up the last quilt pallet. "Come on, then, maybe there's some coffee left in the kitchen."

Lucy thought it prudent to change the subject. "How come my brother Alphie wants to take up farming and not milling? I heard through Noel about all sorts of new developments in flouring—man with a French name—La Croix, I think. Something about purifying the middlings, increasing the value—almost doubled the price for a barrel, according to Noel Dubois—my brother-in-law. He's pretty much advanced in things like that. We also get a lot of that kind of information in the *Argus*, the local newspaper. Wouldn't Alphie be better off going into your father's business? Surely more money there."

"His decision. Besides, my two older brothers have their eyes on the business—the Drouville Steam Four Mill, you know." She sat down on one of the counter stools, toyed with a spoon. "I sure hope Alphie gets the property matter straightened out soon. My father offered to loan him the money for the down-payment, but there's been some kind of family disagreement about that. Of course, we're anxious to have our own place—it's so crowded here—our baby coming."

"A baby? When?"

"End of December."

"That's less than three months from now."

"I know."

"Oh," said Lucy, "I hadn't noticed. Then you were already—"

Jeanne didn't answer but quickly began replacing the washed and dried breakfast dishes in the sideboard cupboard.

That night, Louis sleeping in her arms in George's room, Sabine and Martin still on quilts on the floor, Laurence in a make-shift bed which George had made out of a packing crate and put in the upstairs hall, Lucy's mind was in a turmoil. She had to do something about the overcrowding in this house, the tensions it caused—but what? She wasn't a carpenter, couldn't help on the house next door, yet completing it was the solution to their problem.

The real problem, however, was not what Lucy supposed. Next evening the house was quiet. Only she and George were still up, George preparing to go to bed on the parlor sofa, now relinquished by Laurence for the packing crate upstairs.

"Just like to finish this beer," he said. "Been a long day. Mister S. had a lot of big deliveries—heavy furniture, you wouldn't believe some of it. Still, Fred and I did manage to put in a couple of hours next door, Pa's some help, but you know—"

"Speaking of Pa," said Lucy, "you once mentioned—your first letter last spring I think, that there were a lot of places in town where someone could get work. Something about a new bottling factory, I think. Or how about the Drouvilles's flourmill? Any possibility Pa could get work there? He's not so old, not even sixty yet. Fit, as far as I can tell, although those last few crops in Little Sauk took their toll. He desperately needs something to do to make him feel useful."

"Pa and I have talked about that since Uncle Paul left. And of course, Ma would sure like to get him out from under her feet. Problem is, Pa, you know—he's worried about language. Self-conscious. Doesn't want to embarrass himself. People still insist on calling him a foreigner, not a settler."

"He's a skilled cabinet maker, though. Surely that counts for something—all the new houses going up around here—don't they have cabinets? Crown moldings? And, as for language—why, one hears so many languages on the streets, in the stores these days—all the new settlers—hardly foreigners—flooding in since the territories opened up."

"A paying job for Pa—well, that'll take time to work out, him being so resistant and all," George replied. "Our problem seems to be more immediate."

"What do you mean?"

George stopped to drain the last few swallows of beer. "Sis, I've got to ask you something. Promise you won't mention this to anybody."

"Depends on what it is."

"No, really, it's something we just have to keep between us."

"I see. All right."

"It's like this, won't beat around the bush. How much money do you have?"

"Do I have?" she was taken aback.

"Yes, I mean don't you still have that money you got for your old homestead? Pa once mentioned something about your stashing it away in the Long Prairie bank."

"That's true, I did put it there for safe keeping—never knew what might come up. In fact, kind of thought to invest in a place in town, that is, until Noel came up with the DeLaurier place."

"Can you get it out? I need to borrow it."

"What? Borrow it?"

"I've totally run out of money—had to borrow from Fred, his father, the bank downtown, and—Lord help me—Alphie's father-in-law. You'd think he would have offered something, with him and Jeanne living here these past five months—but no, that blankety-blank cheapskate insisted it was only a loan."

"But I thought you were doing well . . . your letters . . ."

"Didn't you ever think, sis, 'bout all this property, cost of building? Supporting Ma and Pa? Guess everybody just took it for granted. Truth is, that's one of the reasons we haven't been able to finish the house next door—can't afford more lumber, had to cancel my order for the kitchen stove. It's coming to the point where I don't know whether I can meet the payments at the end of the month. You see, I was counting on your coming, having something you could contribute. Otherwise—"

Lucy was shocked. What could she say? "I'm sorry George. You know you'd be welcome to it—all of it, if I had it."

"What do you mean, if you had it?"

"That's just it, I don't. I had to dip into those savings over the past two years, didn't want to be a total burden on Noel. Then I discovered I didn't own the whole homestead property and had to pay the county back for a large tract I sold." George looked shocked. "I still have about $10.00 in cash left after Sabine's school fees. You're welcome to that."

"Then we're in a fix, a real fix. If we don't do something soon, the bank will do what they call a foreclosure. I'm at my wit's end, I can tell you, don't know what more to do—was so hoping that you could—" He buried his face in his hands. "And now to bring you in into all this mess—" His shoulders heaved as he tried to stifle his sobs.

"George, George," she said, "*cher* Georges, *frère, mon cher frère—*" She stopped, a sickening feeling of shock, of disappointment. She'd heard of Poor Farms, the county here would have them. She'd once considered that's where she and the children would have to go. They were for destitute people with no place to live, the *Argus* published an account of monthly disbursements—cords of wood, sacks of flour, medical payments, coffins.

Taking a deep breath, trying to hide her true feelings, she forced herself to say, "George, don't worry—I'll give you the cash for the bank tomorrow. Maybe it'll hold them off for a while. We'll work through it. Everything will be all right." She recognized the hollowness of her words for she had little idea what to start working through it meant.

One immediate thing she could do, however, was to withdraw Sabine from St.Gertrude's and enroll her with Martin in the public school. That would be some saving, although Sabine would be heartbroken—she loved the school and had formed a strong attachment to Sister Elizabeth. Before she did that, however, there was another possibility.

The next morning, as soon as the household had settled into its new routine with the children off to school, Alphie to consult with Mister Drouville at his flourmill, and George to Stadthauser's department store, Lucy left Jeanne and *maman* in charge of Laurence and the baby and headed for downtown Shakopee. She was wearing her best dress, the widow outfit and bonnet, the black velvet reticule, finery on the outside, trembling on the inside. Best not to think about anything in particular, best keep her eyes on the brick sidewalk ahead of her, avoid catching her heel in a hole, count off the streets with determined steps until she reached First Street.

Main and First streets joined at the train station where they'd arrived that night and appeared to be the center of town. How different it seemed from that night, even more different from when her family had first come to Shakopee when she was a mere girl. The new train tracks came right down through the middle of First Street, leaving a wide boulevard on each side, fronted by stores and businesses at least for another three or four blocks in both directions. A steady stream of horses, wagons, and buggies passed by on each side of the tracks, a confusion of movement and fragmented talk, the acrid odor of dirt, smoke, and animals.

Uncertain, already regretting her decision, Lucy stopped a woman hurrying by. The woman carried a parasol, even though the November sun hardly warranted it, and a number of parcels tied together with twine. "Pardon me, ma'am," said Lucy, trying to keep pace with the woman, "can you tell me where Stadhauser's Department Store is?"

"Must be new in town," the woman snapped back, obviously annoyed. "Other side of the street—big windows in front, red sign." She folded the parasol up with a snap and stepped up into a waiting buggy.

Hesitating in front of Stadhauser's big front windows, Lucy looked at their display. Behind the glass were two dresses, one a blue chiffon with white silk embroidery around each of the ruffles which cascaded down from the tightly drawn-in waist; the other a wine-colored satin with enormous puffed sleeves extending out from the low-cut bodice. Large round hats with drooping feathers, long elbow-length gloves. Lucy could not remember ever seeing such beautiful things, not even during her rare visits to the dry goods store in Long Prairie or the one time with Mary in Sauk Centre. The other window displayed winter coats, hats, fur muffs. On one metal stand was a long black woolen cloak lined with gray fur, the hood thrown back showing green silk, a matching green silk reticule and black, fur-lined gloves laid out beneath it. She shivered, realizing that she'd left her old knitted shawl at George's and the days were growing ever colder.

A man bumped into her as she stood gazing through the glass. He mumbled an apology, bowed a little, tipped his hat, then turned around to stare at her after he'd passed by. Lucy felt uncomfortable, shivered again. Picking up her courage, enticed by the promise of warmth inside, she entered the store.

Behind the first counter was a woman selling gloves. "Genuine imported French suede," she was saying to a customer, "and just look at this white top-stitching down the seams—a true mark of quality. What did you say? Oh, madam, I assure you, these are the very latest fashion." She looked so professional, standing behind her counter in a tight-fitting black dress with a white collar, a silver watch on a chain around her neck.

Lucy pretended to examine some sample pairs lying on the counter. She wondered whether she could ever dress like that, learn to talk like that, enough to convince customers to buy, to spend. She doubted it. What was she thinking, coming here in the first place? She turned to leave.

"So sorry to keep you waiting, madam." The woman behind the counter had finished with her customer. "May I help you?" Her voice was smooth, polite. "What kind of gloves may I show you, madam? Everyday?"

"I—no, I didn't come in to buy anything."

"Well, then—" The woman's manner changed immediately.

"No, I came to see the manager."

She drew back farther behind the counter. "Mister Stadthauser? I'm afraid he's—" she glanced nervously toward the glassed-in office at an upper level at the back of the store, from where an older man in a dark suit, short, gray beard but bald was watching them. She followed his gaze to Lucy, then said, "Just a moment, I'll see if he's in." They talked behind the glass, the man gesturing several times toward Lucy. After a few minutes the woman returned and made a point of regaining her position behind the glove counter. "Mister Stadthauser will see you now," she said crisply.

"Well then, what is it, miss—or missus? A widow, I take it?" he asked, inviting her to sit down in front of his big mahogany desk while he leaned back in a matching office chair. Filing cabinets lined one wall, a small table with basket trays full of papers stood against the other. His office windows looked out over the whole store, its two aisles flanked by glass-fronted counters and shelves piled high with goods. Here and there iron stands displayed ready-made dresses, men's suits, hats. Lucy was overwhelmed by the displays, the thought of such wealth.

"What can I help you with today? You wanted to see me?" Stadthauser was becoming impatient.

"Yes, sir," Lucy replied, drawing up her shoulders. "I am seeking employment."

"Employment? What did you have in mind?"

"Well, sales perhaps. Something—"

"What kind of experience have you had?"

"Experience?"

"Come, come, ma'am. I mean experience with sales, with pricing, wrapping, shipping . . . surely you're familiar with merchandising?"

"I—I'm willing to learn," she said lamely, beginning to recognize this was a horrible mistake.

"That's good," Stadhauser commented, nodding. "I like people who are willing to learn. Now tell me a little about yourself." He leaned back in the chair, took a cigar from the silver humidor on his desk, and started to light it. Glancing at Lucy, he put the cigar back in the box.

Lucy's mouth was dry, her hands moist. What did a person say in a situation like this? The story of her life? Why she came to Shakopee? Her desperation? "I have just arrived in town, sir," she stammered, "just arrived from Little Sauk up north, near Sauk Centre, you know. I came to be with my family. I wanted to—"

"Who's your family here in Shakopee?" he interrupted.

"I'm sure you know them—know my brother. His name's George."

He struck a match, lit the cigar, took a few puffs, tilted his chair back. A wave of nausea struck her, the smell of the crowded bar room at Reagan's flooded back. "No—no, can't say as I do. George who?"

"George Guyette."

"Guyette, you said?"

"I thought, sir, that because he works for you, that you would be willing to hire me. Please, sir, I do need the job—and I can learn. I like learning. I seem to be always learning."

Stadthauser laid his cigar in an ashtray, and stood up, pushing his office chair back behind him. "Guyette's sister, are you? Well, I'm sorry, but we don't hire members of the same family—store policy, you know. Yes, I am truly sorry, thought you might make a worthy addition to our sales staff, and we are expanding."

"But sir—" she started to protest. Wasn't his own son Fred an employee? How unfair. But what could she say? She was crushed. It had seemed so hopeful. Stadhauser held the glass door open for her. "If you're looking for a position," he said, a rather different tone to his voice, "you might try my friend Pat O'Grady down the street. Might have a place—an attractive woman like you—hmm. Tell Pat I sent you. Two blocks down, number 150 on First Street."

Number 140, 142, 144, 146. Not all the businesses were numbered, some with half numbers for offices on the second floor. If George's desperate words from the night before were not still so fresh in her mind, she would have stopped right there. She would have walked straight up the next cross street to Fourth and then just two blocks over to George's house. But, thinking of George and the difficulty he was in—they were all in—she could not give up. The buildings had run out of numbers. But where was number 150?

"Looking for something?" A large, bearded man in a plaid coat and fur hat blocked her way. She drew back in amazement—it was Noel! A wave of relief swept over her—he'd come to help, he'd gather her in a big strong hug, tell her everything would be all right. "Maybe I can help, you there, pretty little lady," he added with a wink. It was not Noel.

"I'm looking for Number 150," she managed to stammer, bitterly disappointed.

The man burst into laughter. "Right here, right here," he repeated, slapping his thigh. "You've come to the right place, all right. Ha, ha, ha. Just go right on in, little lady." He held open one of the swinging doors.

With a shock Lucy realized that number 150 was a saloon, the same saloon she'd seen and heard that night from the station—the gunshot, the drunken brawl, the piano. Again, memories of Reagan's in Long Prairie. No, she couldn't go in. Stadthauser had played a cruel joke on her. And that awful man holding open the door—he'd assumed she was one of the bar girls.

At this point a middle-aged woman emerged from the saloon's swinging doors. "Can you hear me back there, Sam?" she called back into the saloon. "Weather gettin' colder, time to replace these swingin' doors with the full ones. Did you hear what I said?" Some kind of response from inside. "Oh, excuse me, miss, almost stepped into you," she said in a throaty voice. "Can I help you? Sure and you're lookin' for somethin'?"

"Well I was—I was—" The woman's appearance was unexpected, not like the fancy-dressed women she'd known at Reagan's. This woman wore a plain brown dress with a waiter's towel tucked around her waist, and her dark hair was drawn tightly back into a knot, tied with a green satin ribbon. "Here, best step back on the sidewalk, let that wagon pass. And you, Tom," she said to the bearded man whom Lucy had mistaken for Noel, "you can go on home—that is, if you remember where it is. Been inside long enough, it's not even noon yet. Now then, my girl, what were you about to say?"

"Well, nothing, just—"

"You're lookin' for me, I'll wager."

"No—yes. No, it was someone named Pat O'Grady."

The woman laughed. "Allow me to introduce myself, then. Name's Pat O'Grady—Christened Patricia O'Grady back in the old country—Ireland, in case you couldn't guess. And this establishment here, O'Grady's, don't you see that sign up over the front? My saloon—or hostelry lounge, as some would have it. Surely a colleen like you wasn't about to come in for a snort, was you?" She leaned back on her heels and laughed again, a loud hoarse laugh.

"No—yes—I mean—" Lucy was taken aback, totally confused. Pat O'Grady was a woman—the proprietor of a saloon. She'd never heard of such a thing before. It didn't seem right, let alone proper. Yet there was something about this woman she liked. So different from Maggie, and yet something of the same about her. Before she quite realized it, she heard herself saying, "Well, Mister Stadthauser said—he sent me down here—he said that I—"

"Should ask me for a job? That old coot—an eye for pretty women, that he sure has all right. Well, here, we can't very well discuss this out on the street. Why don't you come inside? My office upstairs in the back is quieter. I prefer to separate my management side from the other activities going on here of an evenin', if you catch my drift."

"I don't think—"

"You don't think workin' here would suit you, you mean?"

"Well, I used to work in a place like this—long time ago, before—before—"

Pat O'Grady smiled, nodded. "I think I know what you're tryin' to tell me. Come on, let's go upstairs."

As if in a kind of trance, Lucy found herself walking back through the saloon, climbing the steep, narrow staircase up to Patsy O'Grady's office, obeying the woman's invitation to sit, to put her feet up on the fender of the little stove in the corner. "Now then, colleen, make yourself comfortable while I pour us a good cup of tea." She took off the towel apron, draped it over a chair. "Been helpin' Samuel downstairs behind the bar—doesn't always wash out those glasses properly." She offered Lucy a cup of tea from a pot kept warm on the stove. "Now then, people I like call me Patsy. Somethin' tells me that name's for you, too. What about yourself? Sure and it's an interestin' look you have about you."

Lucy began telling Patsy O'Grady all about her job many years ago at Reagan's, about Bernard's death, Little Sauk, her children, George's house on Fourth Street. Then she came to herself and the DeLaurier place. What was she doing, telling all this to a complete stranger? "Please excuse me," she said, "I really must go."

"Are you certain I can't help you?"

"No, quite certain, but I do thank you for the tea," Lucy said. "I hope you understand missus O'Grady—"

"Just Patsy will do. Ah, yes, and good tea, it is—imported 'specially from Ireland, make me own arrangements for that." Then she added, as if on the spur of the moment, "You know, I might have somethin' here—"

"I hope you understand—my family—those times when I was a young girl working out in Long Prairie—my sister and I—she was—"

"My girl," Patsy broke in, "believe me—I've been there. Some good days I've had, some terrible days, a few tales'd make your hair stand on end. Sure and I understand." She walked Lucy back out to the street. "Well, my girl, if you're ever downtown again and would like a spot of tea—good Irish tea, that is, you know where to find me."

Discouraged from her day's experience, unsettled by rude and upsetting encounters, especially with the man whom she mistook for Noel, Lucy nevertheless resolved to try again. Surely there were other businesses in Shakopee, surely more opportunities. She discussed it alone with George that evening after supper, both of them making the excuse that they needed to go next door to check on the progress of the house.

"Can't think why old Mister S. would say that about family members," George remarked, joining Lucy as she sat down on the half-completed stairway. "Never came up before. Maybe he thinks you'll find out something confidential about the business he doesn't want people to know, pass it on to me. But, say, Lucy, that sure is a funny one, sending you down to Pat's saloon, like that." He snickered.

"Sorry, I can't appreciate the humor of it," Lucy said dryly. "Be serious, now, and tell me where else I can try."

And so the next morning she walked Sabine to St. Gertrude's and asked for an interview with the Mother Superior. Surely Sister Elizabeth would understand and intervene. She'd been so gracious before.

Mother Martha responded gently but to the point. "Regrettably, my child, we do not hire lay women as teachers here at the school. The nuns take care of teaching for all grades, except that Father Benedict comes in twice a week for catechism. Of course," she added, pausing to straighten the ink caddy and smooth down the edge of the starched white collar of her habit, "of course, my child, there is also the matter of your own religious education, which Sister Elizabeth has informed me about.

Even as a—ahem—lay helper in the kitchen, elsewhere in the convent and school. I'm afraid we could not—"

"I see," said Lucy. She should have foreseen this. "Is there no other way I can pay for Sabine's school fees, then?"

"No, I am sorry to say. We have little enough money as it is—every day we pray that the Lord will provide, and every day in his gracious goodness he does so. But only just enough to keep our doors open one more day. I am truly sorry. Sabine is such a bright girl, she would do well here. But—"

The next morning Lucy braved a second trip downtown. Finding the Meyer House Hotel was not difficult. It was a large, four-storey building fronting on the river. Mister Heinz, the manager, was willing to see her.

They sat in his small office behind the main desk, frequently interrupted by the desk clerk over a dispute about a bill or by the housekeeper about some of the rooms. After the last brief discussion with the latter, who asked Heinz to step out into the hall to discuss what she claimed was a very serious matter, he leaned back, put his fingertips together, and looked out the window. Then he said, "Well, missus, it seems we do have an opening here. I'm not sure, though. This job isn't the easiest, I don't know—"

"What is it? I assure you, sir, I'm accustomed to hard work. A farm is—"

"That very well may be true. Whatever the case, my housekeeper informs me that we're constantly running out of clean linens. Seems that last convention of flourmill men put us behind, in fact some things went missing. What is there about those conventions? Good business, but always something of a problem. Now to come back to the question of the job. Yes, a demanding one. Twenty-five rooms, change of sheets, towels, every day for most of them, depending upon how many rooms we rent out at any one time, how many for longer stays. Linen tablecloths in the dining room, aprons. And now my housekeeper has just informed me that our present laundress has given notice."

"A laundress?" She was shocked. She imagined that her own experience at home over the washtubs in the backyard would not be enough. She would not know how to begin with all those demands. Mountains of dirty laundry. Rivers of water to pump, to heat.

On the other hand, what else was there? A fleeting thought of her humiliating interview with Mister Stadhauser, the leering men on the street, Patsy's saloon, Mother Martha. "Mister Heinz, sir, what will be—how long—do you have—" She broke off, instead heard herself say in a small voice, "When can I start?"

The confrontations were not yet over. "But, Pa," Lucy argued that evening as they finished their supper, "women do work—we work all the time inside the home, why not outside?"

"Not right," he insisted. "Place in the home, the children. Always been, always should be." He'd become very angry when she told him about the hotel and insisted the job wasn't necessary—wasn't proper. It shamed him, he said. *Maman* started to say something, but changed her mind and abruptly went out to the kitchen, followed by Alphie and Jeanne, who did not want to get involved.

George looked uncomfortable and gave her silent signals. They couldn't reveal the urgency of the family's financial situation, nor could Lucy explain why she had to find a job. Moreover, for George to openly support Lucy's acceptance of the Meyer House position would be an admission of his own failure. Their father's objection was no doubt partly based on his own feelings of inadequacy, his own embarrassment about not working.

It was a relief when George proposed an immediate solution to the tension in the air: "Come on, Pa," he said, "let's let the women clear up here. If we take a lantern over to the other house, we might be able to get a few more licks in before bedtime."

The Meyer House position proved more of a challenge than Lucy expected. The steam rose up from the small, walled-in courtyard on the west end of the hotel where she was heating up water for the three great tubs standing on a low trestle table along one wall. An eye had to be kept on the fire in the pot-bellied stove in the corner, wood constantly fed into it to keep it going. The kettle was heavy, and once the water came to a boil it had to be carried over to the tubs. These were the rinsing tubs. Before that, an armload of dirty sheets, towels, aprons had to be put through the washing machine.

Lucy had never seen a washing machine before—she'd always washed her clothes with a washboard standing against the side of the tub, rubbing them on the corrugated surface, applying a bar of strong lye soap. The hotel's machine—the latest invention, Mister Heinz bragged— was a large wooden box on rockers with a handle attached on one end. "We at the Meyer House pride ourselves on keeping up with the times. Women don't need to go down to the river, beat the clothes on the rocks like they used to." He smiled, but Lucy failed to see the humor of this image. "Look," he demonstrated, "you simply open this lid in the top, fill the box with hot water and soap, put in as much dirty linen as will fill about half, close the lid, then rock the box—see, like a child's rocking horse." The linens sloshed back and forth inside. "And then you take the things out, rinse them in those tubs, crank the handle of that wringer over there as you feed the rinsed things through."

It took only one day for Lucy to realize how back-breaking the job was. The number of buckets of water required seemed endless. Water had to be pumped from the pump in the courtyard—it was connected to a pipe which ran down to the river, so water coming up-hill required more effort and some initial priming. The many kettles of boiling water carried from the stove to the tubs sometimes sloshed out and burned her hands and arms. At the end of the washing process came the hanging up. Ropes snaked back and forth through the courtyard on a good day. When it rained, they were strung around inside a storage shed.

But at least it was a job. By the end of the week, she'd earned $5.00, enough to stop by Shanessy's general store on the way home to Fourth Street and fill two baskets with groceries. They would enjoy a feast that night.

"What's the matter, Lucy?" Alphie looked at his sister's half-eaten supper. "Don't you like my Jeanne's cooking? Such a good side of pork you brought home, thought Ma braised it just right. And those sweet potatoes—what a treat."

"It was good, just more food than I needed, thanks." Too tired to eat, she hoped this excuse would be enough.

The approaching winter did not help, for it created some unforeseen problems. Getting no response from the pump in the hotel laundry courtyard early one morning in order to begin the day's process, Lucy went in to see Mister Heinz. "Oh—the pump," he said. "Well, that happens every time the river begins to freeze up. Pipe can't take in water, you see. I'll get a couple of men out there with pick-axes. If they can't free the ice around the in-take, then they'll have to bring you up some slabs of ice. You can break those up enough to melt in the kettle for hot water, can't you?"

The linens froze on the clotheslines, had to be taken down stiff as boards, thawed out enough to fold. It was while attempting to do this one Saturday morning in the storage shed—fortunately Heinz had provided a small wood stove in there—that Lucy felt someone unpegging the other corner of a sheet.

"Remember when we used to do this back at the DeLaurier place, Ma? Talked about continents, Egypt—by the way, I know how to spell it now." Sabine laughed, raised herself up on her toes to look over the line.

"Why, Sabine—what are you doing here? You should be home, helping Mamie and Jeanne. They've got their hands full with Laurence and the baby, and her expecting so soon."

"Came to help you, Ma. Mister Heinz said it was all right. Knew you had too much work—he was very nice about it. Said I could help on Saturdays, he'd pay me something. And you know," she handed two corners of the sheet over to her mother, "you know, Mother Superior at St. Gertrude's said she'd give me fifty cents a week for helping clean up the class rooms after school. Just think, Ma—that's almost enough to pay the fees!"

That her daughter Sabine would sense the critical nature of their situation, that she'd be enterprising enough to find ways to help—Lucy experienced a mixture of remorse and pride, so intense that tears started. "Well, my dear," she said, "watch out you don't drag those corners across this dirty floor. And since you're here, tell me more about your lessons."

"Just like old times, eh, Ma?"

It was not like old times, but it seemed reassuring in its own way. Now if Mary and Josie could bring Agnes for a visit, perhaps even leaving Agnes to stay over Christmas, that would seem in another small way to justify the move to Shakopee.

But unfortunately the freezing weather also slowed progress on the house. "Do you think you could have it ready by Christmas?" she asked George that evening over supper.

"Why the rush, sis?"

"We may have some visitors."

"Visitors—Here? *Mon Dieu,*" her mother cried, throwing up her hands.

"What would you say if I tell you it may be Agnes?"

Her mother burst into tears, covered her face with her apron. She'd not seen her for ten years. The thought was too much.

"Well, I dunno, sis," was George's response. "Still some work to be done and haven't ordered the kitchen stove yet, because—because—" Lucy knew he couldn't reveal it was for lack of money. "Promise you, though, Pa, Fred, and I'll do our best. So cold, though, fingers'll get frostbitten if we work too long at a time."

That night, lying in the bedroom which had been George's, Louis already asleep, Lucy experienced a strange feeling. George's house was full of people, would soon hold more. There was a constant sense of activity in it, of noise, talk, odors of food. But as yet there seemed to be no whispers, no murmurs from generations of life, no whispers of past joys and sorrows, nor hints of those yet to come.

REVELATIONS

MA *FILLE*—AGNES? COMING?" Lucy's mother had already asked that question many times, sounding even more anxious as the first week of December drew toward a close.

"Don't know, *maman*," Lucy sighed. How many times had she said that? "We're still waiting to hear from Noel and Mary. But it should be any time now."

She recognized her words were beginning to sound hollow, beneath them concerns about how difficult it was going to be to fit Agnes into an already over-crowded house, especially if Josie came with her. And especially, in that case, how humiliating to reveal their circumstances, both financial and otherwise. Lucy Dubois—a laundress?

"But you know, *maman*," she continued, forcing a brighter tone, "how wonderful to have the family together again. Think of how long we've been apart? Think of those earlier time times at Christmas—the singing, your *tortière* Christmas Eve?"

"*Ah, oui. Le Noël—c'est ça, le bon temps!*" Her mother smiled and began humming an old French Christmas carol as she began washing the supper dishes.

Yet in her heart, Lucy knew the *good times* could never be the same again, but it could at least *be* again. She needed to find out what was happening from Noel in Little Sauk. "George," she asked her brother over breakfast next morning, "how do I send a telegram?"

Two days later, Noel's reply was delivered by a boy on a bicycle. It lay unopened on the kitchen counter, waiting for her return from work. Without bothering to take off her shawl, Lucy tore open the yellow envelope. With rising excitement, she read:

BABY DUE MARY UNABLE TRAVEL STOP AGNES ILL STOP WILL ADVISE LATER. STOP BAD NEWS JANE STOP NOEL DUBOIS

What did Noel mean by bad news about Jane? What had happened? And Agnes ill? So many questions. Her excitement was dashed into anxiety.

Maman's immediate reaction to the news about Agnes was to be expected. She would go back to Eagle River to care for her. "*Ma fille, ma pauvre fille,*" she kept repeating.

"No, *maman,*" Lucy insisted, "you simply can't make that long trip by yourself. And have you forgotten, Jeanne's due within the next few weeks? With me working, we need you here."

Dropping her gaze once again to the dishpan, her mother nodded, half in recognition, half in defeat, and muttered, "*Ah, oui, ah, oui.*"

"There's really only one solution. I'll try to get time off work. I'll go on the train and bring Agnes back. My employer, you know—he's been so kind—surely he can find someone to take my place for the next two weeks or so."

"*Oui, c'est ça.*" She paused, dish cloth in hand. "*Mais deux semaines? Tellement longtemps?*"

Apparently Mr. Heinz also considered that a long time. "Two weeks off?" he asked incredulously, when Lucy went in to his office the next morning. "*Two* weeks?"

"But sir," she said, "it will take that long to arrange for the trip, the many train changes there and back, and getting my sister ready. She's been ill, I really don't know what condition she's in to travel."

"Well, let me think about it. I'll see what I can do."

Another day went by before Heinz came out to the hotel's laundry court to see her. It had been a long day, rain mixed with snow, making every part of the process more difficult. She used every excuse to go into the storage shed to warm her hands by the small wood stove. She was standing there when he entered the shed, a small envelope in his hand.

"Missus Dubois," he began, clearing his throat, "I have talked to mister Meyer about your request. We are all sympathy, of course. Your situation touches our hearts. But he feels—we feel, that it is not in our establishment's best interests to grant your request. Therefore," he extended the envelope, "we feel we must let you go. It proved impossible to find someone to replace you for the time you requested. Regrettably, our only option is to let you go as of today and take on a permanent employee."

Lucy was devastated. "But, sir," she began. "I could make the trip in less time if necessary, I could—"

"No," he replied firmly. "With the Christmas season nearly upon us, the crush of holiday travelers expected, we cannot risk deficiencies—to so speak—in your duties. I'm very sorry, you must believe me. Both mister Meyer and I extend our deepest concern over your situation. In view of that, please accept this, your wages for this week and one extra week in addition." With that he left the shed, adding in the doorway, "And our best wishes for the holiday season."

Lucy hardly remembered the cold walk home, the supper *maman* had prepared, the children's news of their day. Life seem to exist around her in a kind of fog.

Later that night, when the house was dark and quiet, she came down to speak to George. He was asleep on the parlor sofa.

"Eh . . . what is it? Don't you know it's the middle of the night? I've got an early start tomorrow morning, so do you."

"No, I don't. Not tomorrow, or the day after. At least not at Meyer's hotel." She related what Heinz had said in the laundry shed.

"Well, think of it this way. It means you can just go ahead and make that trip to Little Sauk anyway. Bring back Agnes—I agree she should be here, especially now with Christmas coming up. Didn't you say he gave you some extra money? Well, just take that for the trip. We'll manage—somehow." He shrugged. "Now, let me get some sleep, if you don't mind."

The next day, pretending to go to work, Lucy walked downtown with George as far as the station. "So, you plan to leave day after tomorrow? Good, just get your ticket, send off a telegram to Noel again, telling him what time your train gets into Little Sauk. As you said, you're going there first, then get him to take you up to Long Prairie and Eagle River to the Morton place. I've got to get over to Stadthauser's right now, but you can manage, can't you?"

As Lucy stepped up to the telegraph office window, the operator looked up from his desk. "Oh, missus Dubois, isn't it? Say, another telegram just came in over the wire for you . . . it's, well it's news that— " He broke off, looking evasive, and abstractly began to shuffle some papers on the desk. "In fact, I've just given it to the boy to deliver. Let me see if he's left on his bicycle yet." He glanced out the platform window. "No, there he is. If you hurry, you'll just catch him."

Lucy rushed up as the boy was wheeling his bicycle out of the rack by the baggage door. "I'll save you a trip—that telegram for missus Dubois?"

Although there was a cold wind outside the station, Lucy could not wait but sat down on one of the platform benches to tear open the yellow envelope. It was from Noel, probably with news of Jane. She'd been apprehensive about that. Had Jane gone off with Daniel after all?

But Noel's message was not about Jane. It was about Agnes:

REGRET TO INFORM YOU AGNES DIED FIRE SATURDAY NIGHT STOP FUNERAL TOMORROW ST HUBERT STOP HENRY STROKE STOP CONDOLENCES STOP NOEL DUBOIS

How could this be possible? It could not be true. In disbelief, she read Noel's words over a second, a third time. "Agnes dead—

burned to death—a horrible death," she found herself mumbling aloud. "Henry, a stroke. The family—Abe and Tom—I desperately need to get there. Can't believe it—fire—burned to death—not Agnes—not my sister who's been through so much."

Lucy tried to breathe but breath did not seem to come. She leaned against a corner of the building for support. The telegram was still grasped in her hand as she looked at the words again, but not really seeing them. "Burned to death—such a horrible death, the horrible granary fire—almost burned to death with my children—DeLaurier house—the flames."

As she crumpled the telegram into her fist, she said, "Got to tell George, to find him, what to do? In a daze, she found herself walking back toward the station window and rapped on it. "What to do?" she repeated several times, dizzy and lightheaded, steadying herself against the window ledge.

In a few moments the window slid opened. Leaning out, the telegraph operator asked in concern, "Are you all right, ma'am? You've gone white as a sheet. Sorry for the bad news, I knew, you see—took the message myself. Shall I get someone to take you home?"

"No—thank you. I— But in a brief rational moment, recognized this man could do nothing. "No, my brother," she started to say, then pushed the crumpled telegram deep down into her pocket and began walking stiffly down the street toward Stadthauser's.

The same saleswoman was behind the glove counter and recognized her. "I'm sorry, madam," she said, "we don't—"

"My brother—where's my brother?" she demanded.

"Your brother?"

"George Guyette."

"Oh, he's gone on a delivery, all the way out to Bethany. My, don't you look all in. Can I get you a glass of water?"

Lucy did not answer, but dazedly walked out of the store and continued walking unseeingly down First Street, unaware of where she was until her senses recognized the familiar odor of beer, whisky.

Unconscious of what she was doing, as if drawn in by an invisible hand, she entered O'Grady's saloon, slowly climbed the stairs to Patsy's office, knocked on the door.

"Yes? Come in."

Patsy was warming her feet on the fender. "Do you," Lucy began, "do you have—do—have—cup—tea?" and fell to the floor.

It took a moment for Lucy to realize where she was—in Shakopee, on Fourth Street, upstairs in George's old room. Jeanne was applying a wet compress to her forehead. It must have been the cold shock which woke her. "Just lie still, now, Lucy," Jeanne insisted. "You rest, your mother's making something for you in the kitchen."

"Does she know?"

"George told her. He brought you home in mister Stadhauser's wagon, the telegram we found in your pocket."

"How did he—"

"Well, according to George, somebody at O'Grady's saloon was sent down to Stadhauser's to tell them you'd fainted in the owner's office. You—in a *saloon*? What on earth were you doing *there*? George's first reaction was, *really, Lucy—after Reagan's—how could you?* Anyway, it was lucky George had just come back from a delivery somewhere and still had the wagon back of the store."

Lucy tried to sit up in bed, but the room swam around her and an overwhelming weakness forced her back against the pillow. "I should go talk to *maman*, she'll be grieving—Papa, too. How did they take the news?"

"What can you expect? They took it very hard. Mind you, from what I gather, Agnes has always been on the outside, so to speak. But you know—knew—her best, were closer." She dipped the compress again in a basin of cold water.

Lucy brushed the compress away. "Have to go downstairs, see *maman*. What time is it?" From the lengthening shadows in the room, it looked like late afternoon. Almost a whole day had gone by since she'd left early that morning. Why had she left? Hard to remember.

To go to work at Meyer's? No, something about a ticket to Little Sauk. The train. Yes, that was it. And then the boy handed her the telegram about Agnes. Agnes was dead. Died in a fire—burned to death—the granary—burned in a fire. Buried in the earth. *People ought not to be allowed to die in winter*—where'd she heard that? Opening the frozen earth—so difficult—yes that old caretaker at Bernard's funeral, Prairie Lake cemetery—he'd said that. With a shock Lucy realized Agnes and Bernard were both gone, each lying in their own parcel of frozen earth. The rational part of her brain recognized that shock had distorted her mind. Getting back—finding reality—"How late is it?" she asked, hoping to grasp something specific.

"After four. Your children just came home. Your mother's given them something to eat, good thing 'cause it's kept her busy. That must be her coming up the stairs now with a tray, so I'll go down to look after the children."

Her mother had been crying, her face contorted and her eyes red. She started to say something but checked herself. Suddenly sitting down on edge of the bed beside Lucy, and in one quick motion, she brought her apron up to her face and sobbed into it. Lucy tried to comfort her as she held her frail body in her arms. Together they swayed back and forth in their grief. For the first time, Lucy felt enormous compassion for her mother, a closeness through the common loss bringing them together.

"*Trop tard, trop tard,*" her mother moaned over and over again.

"*Oui, c'est trop tard,*" Lucy grasped for the right words. *Oui, maman,* if only Agnes had been able to come earlier, if only—if only—

After her mother had gone back down stairs, Lucy tried to eat the toast on the tray, to sip the *café au lait*. It was no use. She pushed the tray over to the edge of the bed and let her head fall back against the pillow.

Struggling to repress the terrible events of the day, the nightmares she'd just experienced while lying here this long afternoon. The man in her nightmare looked familiar—could it have been Noel? Yet the man hadn't seemed quite like Noel. He'd tried to force her to do something out of character for Noel—at least, the Noel she knew. No, not quite true. Noel had forced her to sell the log homestead, to move into the DeLaurier house. Strange that the man was not Homer West, that would have made more sense. Besides, she could never have imagined Homer West wearing a denim work shirt like the man in the nightmare, although Mattias wore one. Yet the man was not Mattias.

She must stop thinking about it, brooding over it. All her mind's strength had to be directed to the household around her. She had lost her job at the hotel. What little money remained would go toward a few more months at St.Gertrude's for Sabine. Maybe there'd be enough for some sort of Christmas for the children. Each Christmas since Bernard's death was painful for them—for her, too.

"Well, Lucy," George remarked the next morning over breakfast, "Christmas will sure be a sad affair this year. Can't imagine anybody's in the mood to celebrate. That's really too bad, 'cause do you realize this is first time in many years that we're all together as a family? Now isn't that—"

A sharp look from Lucy made him change the subject. "Say, now that Al and Jeanne are about to move out to their new place, maybe they'll let me cut down a fir tree for the parlor. Been out there, quite a large stand of woods behind the house. That all right with you, Al?"

His brother nodded, his mouth full of toast. "Look for a good one," he mumbled. "Cut one for me, too."

"And you, Ma? Know you don't like the idea of a tree, some German pagan custom, but, well, think of the children. They'll have fun decorating it. And Lord knows, we need a little cheer around here."

The birth of Jeanne's baby on Christmas Eve did provide some distraction from the somber mood pervading the house. The persistent cries of a new-born coming from Al and Jeanne's room upstairs left Lucy and her mother little space for other concerns.

"He reminds me of my own," Lucy commented, taking the baby in her arms. "Louis as well was born in a house not his own. I hope this little one fares better, that his rooms would be his and whisper to him alone." Jeanne looked at her puzzled. "It's a little secret I have," Lucy explained, unwilling to say more.

"We'll leave for our own home just after New Year's," Jeanne said. "You like the baby's name—Noel?"

"Of course, it seems so right, the French word for Christmas." But still, it disturbed her, that ironic connection with the DeLaurier house and Noel Dubois.

The New Year brought its own mood, with Al and his family gone. "How empty, how silent the house now seems," Lucy remarked to Sabine. "Don't you think so?"

"Guess so, but it's sure nice to have Al's room. I do miss the baby, though. He was so sweet, almost like another baby brother. Say, Ma, when do you think Uncle George's going to get the other house done? Then the boys can have their own room."

"He's working on it, he and your grandpa. Too cold to do much, though. George's thinking about getting a woodstove set up in what'll be the parlor—that way they can do more on the inside finishing work." She could not tell Sabine about the other reason for the delay, the financial reason.

The reason for the delay. Lucy was torn between urgencies. She desperately wanted to return to Little Sauk, if only to assess the situation and to visit Agnes's grave and Bernard's. A thousand questions. What was happening to Agnes's children, Jane especially? Noel hadn't communicated since the last telegram. She needed to see Noel, although her real relationship to him was still uncertain. And what about Henry—a stroke? The cause of the fire? In the back of her mind there was grief over a different matter, a grief over another loss.

Her dilemma. She also needed to be here. Her own children—without Al and his wife, Jeanne, could her mother manage? They might need to hire some help, but what about money? Her last wages from the hotel were spent. There was no choice but to find another job.

The Meyer House? No, too humiliating to go back to mister Heinz. Besides, they would already have hired a new laundress. As well, now in the depth of winter, that job would be even more difficult. She doubted she could bring herself day after day melting blocks of ice for the washing, filling the machine time after time in the freezing courtyard, thawing out stiffly frozen sheets in order to iron them with that heavy flat iron which had to be constantly heated on the wood stove. She was at her wit's end.

Next day, wearing two shawls against the cold, borrowing a pair of George's gloves, Lucy kept to the center of the streets where the two feet of snow had been cleared. She was determined to see mister Ries at the bottling factory, appeal to Jeanne's father, mister Drouville, at the flourmill, inquire at several of the general stores along First Street.

After several hours of disappointment, and with frozen feet and fingers numb with cold, she was at a loss. No one seemed to be hiring during the winter—business slow, they all said. Or they never hired women, or they never hired anyone without experience. How did one acquire experience, then? How did a woman stop being a woman?

Passing by the station at 1st and Oak Streets, shivering with cold—the shawls little protection in this sub-zero weather, she was tempted to go into the waiting room to warm herself. They'd have a wood stove going in there. She got as far as the door. The memory of Noel's telegrams brought such a rush of feeling, such a sense of helpless despair, that, pulling the shawls more closely around her, she turned away and trudged through the snow back up Oak Street toward George's house.

Once there, Lucy took off her layers of shawls and headed toward the warm kitchen, chilled to the bone as she was from her fruitless search and long walk. She was stopped by a timid knock at the door.

"Note for you, ma'am." It was the station messenger boy. Another telegram—Lucy's knees almost gave way. "I'm supposed to wait for a response, please ma'am," he said.

"A response?" She was confused, not the usual way to send one. "I don't understand."

"If you'd be kind enough, ma'am," he said, blowing on his mittened fingers, "it's cold out here. Could I please come inside?" Lucy motioned him into the hallway, where he helpfully added, "Wait here 'til you read it?"

With relief Lucy realized it wasn't a telegram but a folded piece of white paper, sealed with a blob of green wax. Breaking the wax, she read,

Come to see me tomorrow morning at ten o'clock. Tea will be ready.

Although unsigned, it could only have come from one person. "Do you know who wrote this?" she asked the boy.

"Yes'm," he said.

"Well, you can go back to that person with my compliments but say that I'm unable to accept the invitation." She made him repeat this to make sure he got it right. He hesitated going out the door, made slow work of righting his bicycle, brushing off the snow. She knew she should give him something and managed to find a five-cent piece in her reticule, for which he seemed grateful. Yes, a lot of money for him as well.

Patsy's invitation. She could not accept. All night she tossed and turned, making Louis fretful and restless. Why did Patsy send it? What did she want? Did she want anything at all, or was it to be only a social visit? Even if only social—impossible to go down to that saloon again, face Patsy O'Grady again. But—what if Patsy could help her? She had many contacts in town, could give advice, recommendations. What other choices did she have? None at the moment, and she could wait no longer.

Despite all misgivings, Lucy next morning found herself in Patsy's office upstairs at O'Grady's and Patsy, although surprised to see her, soon got through the initial pleasantries. No sooner had she poured out tea than she opened a notebook on her lap and drew out a pencil from behind her ear.

"I've a good idea of your situation," she said. "You're shocked? Let me say that, although I'm strictly a business woman, I can usually see a human side. Come, come, no need to look so uncomfortable. We're going to talk strictly business, you understand. Tea's cold? Let me warm yours up a bit."

Lucy didn't feel much like talking. It had required real force of will to accept Patsy's invitation, to come down here and turn in at number 150, confront the stale stench of alcohol and tobacco, walk past that smirking bartender washing glasses, climb the stairs, knock on Patsy's door. Difficult enough to face Patsy, who obviously guessed more about Lucy than Lucy had told her. Patsy's sources of information were spread all over town, and the men who came into the saloon gossiped.

"Now then, to business, Lucy Dubois. You're a very attractive woman, in the prime of life. I need someone like you in the saloon. Two of my best girls just left, went out west with a couple of customers. My place needs—"

With a clatter Lucy set down her cup. "No, Patsy, I—you know I can't, if that's what—" She reached for her shawl.

"Now wait just a dang minute, there. Don't be so hasty. I've more to say."

Lucy hesitated. There was something about Patsy that held a person.

"Hear me out and know my terms. Then you can decide." She glanced at her notebook. "All right. First, as I said, I need a good-looking woman who can add a bit of class to this place. And you have class, my girl —I could tell the first minute I saw you. Good figure, too. Then later— well I need help with the books. Arithmetic? Write a good hand?"

"Well—those, yes, I suppose so. But I don't know about cards, about—" She was about to add that she didn't know much about men either, having made such a disaster of her relationship to all men since Bernard, but decided against it.

"I don't expect you to do much except just be friendly to the men, move around, talk to them. You probably already know from experience how lonely some of them are—away from home, from family—that is, if they have any. New country for some of them, and I like the fact that you know another language. Your family from Quebec, I gather. Still speak French?"

"Well, I—"

"Good. Yes, language, class. Big asset, in my opinion, and for my establishment. None of my other girls have it."

"But what if—"

"If what? Things get rough? Of course they will. What'll you do if a fight breaks out? Somebody wants to get real friendly? Wants to go upstairs?"

"You know I can't—"

"That'll be up to you. Most likely, men will try. You have a sensual quality about you, if that's the right word. Noticed that right off. I'm sure you miss it, don't you—come now, be honest with yourself."

Lucy was taken back. Patsy's frankness frightened her, as she recalled for an instant her uncontrolled urges that afternoon with Homer West, the sensations when Mattias seized her wrist and she fell against his body as they rolled on the ground together during the granary fire, her hand against his chest, sensing the beating of his heart. She felt a flush rise to her cheeks.

"Well, my girl, I see I've hit home. Now here's my second point." She ticked off another item in the notebook. "I can pay you $20.00 a week, Monday through Saturday. Come in about three o'clock in the afternoon—that'll give me a little time teach you about the books. Least ways until abut four—that's when most of my customers drift in. We close at midnight."

The discussion was going too fast. She needed to slow it down, to work up resistance. "No, I simply couldn't manage that. My children—when would I see them? How could I possibly explain—"

"Look, now, can't expect a saloon to keep regular day-time hours, can you? Lose my business quicker than a cat's wink. But, I'll tell you what. Say, four days—Wednesday through Saturday. Saturday night's the biggest, payday you know. That'd be $12.00 a week."

Lucy drew a sharp breath—why, $12.00 for only four days! That was more than George made working the whole week. "Still wouldn't see enough of the children," she heard herself whining. "Only at breakfast maybe. And how would I get home so late at night?" She remembered that frightening walk from the station the night of their arrival in Shakopee, the moving shadows. "And I haven't the right clothes—"

"Sure and if that's your worry, I'll have Jason, my bouncer take you in my buggy up to your brother's house once we close. As for dresses—" She opened an armoire standing against the wall behind Lucy. "Take your pick." It was crammed with satins, velvets, feather trims, sparkling sequins. Patsy pulled out a green velvet, knee-length dress, trimmed with silver braid and tassels. "Think this would suit you just fine—bring out the color of your reddish-gold hair."

Lucy caught her breath. There had been nothing like that at Reagan's. She was reminded of the window displays at Stadthauser's, especially the wine-colored dress with the low-cut bodice. She thought of her dreary widow's dress, the heavy bonnet. "I—Patsy, I—" she finally forced out. "I still don't think—"

"Well, colleen, you just go ahead and think about it." Patsy closed her notebook decisively. "Sure and you'll let me know. Soon."

During the cold walk home, Lucy did think about it. Working out at O'Grady's was the last thing she wanted to do, even on the business side of things. The idea revolted her to the point of nausea. How could she possibly bring herself to that? Although being laundress at the Meyer House Hotel was cruel and back-breaking work, it was at least something her family could know about. Surely there were other jobs available, surely something would turn up.

By the time she reached George's house, however, reality won out. Nothing was likely to turn up, and more money had to be found immediately. It was already well into February. To make matters worse, George had hinted he was thinking of marrying—a girl whom he'd met at Stadhauser's named Emma Kautz.. *Can't get married* he said, *not until I finish the house next door. Can't do that until we put more into it.* Can't you find—can't you do— Can't—can't—cannot— That was the way things seemed to be, ever since she'd arrived in Shakopee.

That evening at dinner, sitting around the small dining table, Lucy broke the news. "You'll be happy to know I've found a new job." *Maman* stopped in the doorway between dining room and kitchen, Papa pushed his plate away.

"*Toi? Pas necessaire* ," he said decisively.

"No, Pa," George broke in. "It's only temporary. Until we get the house finished." He looked meaningfully at Lucy, knowing he dare not mention where it was. "Yes, Lucy's got a new job," he explained, "a dang good one, too. But too bad only it's only evenings. Only job available, you see."

Their mother raised her eyebrows a little, but said nothing, merely grumbled about having more work at home.

"Because of me, Ma?" Sabine asked. "All because of the Academy fees?"

"No, dear, there are other reasons. But come on, finish your dinner, get busy—both you and Martin—on your homework."

Yes, there are other reasons, Lucy thought to herself as she helped her mother clear the table. True, Sabine's school fees were an issue. It was too late to change schools and enroll her at Union with the boys. In fact, hadn't she already convinced herself that keeping Sabine at St. Gertrude's was a major factor in her decision to begin work at O'Grady's the following Thursday night? And yet was her daughter's education and moral upbringing to be made possible by money from a saloon? Lucy quickly forced that notion from her mind, the irony too painful, the duplicity of it initiated by dilemmas not of her own choosing.

It was relatively quiet that first night. Earlier, after Patsy had spent several hours instructing Lucy on bookkeeping, she and one of the bar girls named Lillian had helped Lucy pin up her hair into a roll, topped with a yellow feather curling down from a small clasp.

"Just as I thought," Patsy remarked as she tightly laced the corset, "beautiful figure. Wouldn't have guessed you'd had four children. Now hold in your breath while I lace up the back of this dress." Lucy could hardly breathe from the torturous pressure.

"Suits you beautifully—except we need to have the waist taken in a bit, the top let out. Sure, and you'll be a hit tonight, right, Lillian?" Lillian gave Lucy a guarded look, her jealousy obvious. "Now let me give you some instructions about how to handle the men, the drinks, that is, unless, you remember all that from before."

"No, I never did that kind of thing at Reagan's—mainly the kitchen, the rooms."

"Well, then, let's go downstairs and we'll go through the routines. Lillian, you keep your eye on Lucy, see she doesn't get into trouble her first few nights, give her a hand when you can. I'll instruct Jason to do the same. Sam's behind the bar tonight? Good. He'll understand that when a man buys Lucy a drink, he gets the drink, she gets watered down cold tea in a whisky glass."

"But that's dishonest! The man's paying for more."

Patsy sighed. "That's business, colleen. You sure wouldn't want to be drinking the real thing all evening, would you?"

The evening seemed to go on forever. The tightly-laced dress, those high-heeled shoes were excruciatingly uncomfortable. The loud laughter, the endless tinkling of the piano. She'd never been musical and it grated on her. The strong smell of tobacco, cigars, whisky. Even the tea drinks began to nauseate her. Worst, however, were the advances of some of the men, grabbing her around the waist, fondling her breasts, making lewd remarks.

Toward the end of the evening, however, snatches of conversation between two men over near the bar caught her ear. Here and there a word in French, a few place names she recognized. She was curious enough to try to coax one of them into conversation. After all, wasn't that part of her job?

Uncertain how to begin, she went up to them and greeted them in French. "*Bon soir, m'sieu,*" she said hesitantly.

They looked up in surprise, spoke in undertones to each other for a moment. Then one of them said something about joining a group of men for poker, and she was left alone with the other.

"Say, miss," the man said, "that sure sounds familiar. You a Frenchie? I'd order us a drink, but I've had my limit for one night."

Lucy noticed that Sam behind the bar was making signals of some sort but she pretended not to notice. There was something about this man she liked. He was tall and slender, with light brown hair streaked with blonde, and the paleness of his complexion suggested he'd not been working in the fields. This and his mustache contrasted with very dark eyes, overshadowed by delicately arched eyebrows. Something about him reminded her of Bernard, a kind of aristocratic air about him and delicacy about his hands and gestures. Had his appearance not been in sharp contrast to Mattias, such thoughts about attraction would have been intolerable.

This time, at least, she was determined to ignore Sam and the rules. She drew the man over to an empty table and invited him to sit down. "I can't stay long," she said, looking around nervously, "but it would give me some pleasure talking to you. *Je m'appelle* Lucy."

"Name's Petitjean. Claude Petitjean." He looked uncomfortable, toyed with an empty glass someone had left on the table.

"Please, Claude, speak French if you like."

"Trying to get away from that."

"Oh? I thought . . . well, where do you come from, then?"

"Came down from Quebec last summer, on my way to Faribault." He paused, explained half in English, half in French, how he was taking up a job in a woolen mill. "Trying to get away from that old life," he said.

"Tell me more about the old life," Lucy urged. "You may be wanting to forget it, but I'm not. It's something too precious to lose. Tell me more about Quebec."

"*Eh bien*—you don't want to hear about that, do you? Well, *peut-être*—maybe—"

Eh bien—he'd used Noel's favorite expression. A wave of emotion came over her, the room seemed to grow dim. So many thoughts, confusion. She needed this man, his associations with her past. She couldn't let him go.

Lillian came up to the table. "My, my, I see you're getting along just fine. Here, I'll take over for you, I can tell this fine-looking gentleman wants another drink." She forced herself onto the man's lap. "Come on then, you can tell *me* all about it." She hissed to Lucy, "Don't you see that lonely man with the cigar over there? Go over and keep him company, you'll know how I'm sure."

By the time Jason had driven her home in Patsy's buggy that night, Lucy was too exhausted to think. It had started with columns of figures in Patsy's account books, jumbled sums, red figures and black figures. It had degraded into uncomfortable personal situations, saturated with the smell of whisky.

Was tomorrow night only Thursday? She'd try to get some sleep, get the children off school in the morning, help *maman* with the house, and walk back down to the saloon in the early afternoon to work on Patsy's books before starting the evening all over again.

Thursday and Friday nights passed in a kind of blurr. Another dress, other men, cold watered tea. The fact that it was already developing into a routine was some consolation. Saturday night, however, brought more customers into O'Grady's, who grew more raucous as the evening wore on. The man from Quebec had not appeared Thursday or Friday night, to Lucy's disappointment. Tonight Patsy had dressed her in a wine-colored silk, made something like the one she'd seen in Stadhauser's window, except that the neckline was lower, the length shorter, and the sleeves made of black net—like the black net stockings Patsy insisted she wear. Tonight she had a fake emerald broach in her hair, with small side curls hanging down over one shoulder. Lucy was torn between the pleasure of wearing such things and the realization of what they meant. They meant a selling of herself.

About ten o'clock she was delighted to see Petitjean standing at the bar. Tonight he was alone, and seemed to be looking for someone. "*Bon soir, m'sieu,*" she said, going over to him. Lillian was signaling something—Lucy should slip her arm through his, touch his body. She could not bring herself to do it. Instead she simply smiled.

"Good evening to you, *mam'selle,*" he said, and turned away in embarrassment, seemingly intent on finishing the mug of beer in front of him. Lucy was aware that Sam, the bartender, was looking at her in a meaningful way. What was she supposed to do, torn as she was between genuinely wanting to speak with the man and yet carrying out what her job demanded?

Finally Sam provided a solution. "See your glass is empty, sir," he said. "I'm sure the pretty lady there will be happy to join you in another, but you know, she doesn't drink beer, prefers whisky."

The man hesitated. "Why yes . . . I guess so. What will you have then miss . . . miss? I regret, I've forgotten your name."

"Lucy."

"Ah, Lucette, perhaps?" She gasped in surprise. That he would recognize her French name, her name from the past . . .

Sam set two glasses of whisky before them on the bar. "Well then," said Petitjean, "*à votre santé*—to your health!" and he took a deep swallow before putting the glass back down.

Lucy raised her glass, smiled, and thirsty for the cool tea, took a large swallow. It choked and stung like fire all the way down. Sam had tricked her and given her the real thing. .

"Well, miss," said Petitjean, "let's have another toast—to Quebec this time." He raised his glass, took several more swallows. "*Eh bien,* you want to hear of Quebec? Well, things bad, taxes high."

"Did you live on a farm?"

"Big, big farm, near Ste-Anne-de-Bellevue, maple trees but my brothers fished on St. Laurence."

"Why, that's near where my family were. Do you think we could have met?"

"*Peut-être, mam'selle.* But we have met now—and so let's drink to that." He took another few swallows, his glass almost empty. "Come, come, *mam'selle* Lucy, you must drink to that also."

She took a tiny sip but deceptively held the glass longer to her lips.

"Yes, we may have met—another life," he laughed, "in old Quebec." He took another swallow, and his whole manner seemed to be changing, his words slurred. "*Eh bien—à Quebec, n'est-ce pas?* "Ah, *cherie*, you do not drink to Quebec? To the trees? The fish in the river?" He held the glass up to her mouth, pressed it against her lips. "Want to know— *mam'selle*—"

"My name's Lucy—Lucette—"

"*Eh bien*, Lucette—go over—standing at a bar—no place for a *mam'selle*. Let's go over to that table—by stairs." His speech was becoming more halting, his face flushed.

Lucy realized the whisky was affecting him and herself as well, despite her caution. As she turned away from the bar, the high heel of her shoe caught in the rail. The man ran his hand down her leg to free it, then put his arm around her bare shoulders to steady her, his fingers touching her breast. "Watch out," he said. "Here, help—you. Go over, sit down—talk, talk 'bout old Quebec—*oui, parlons-nous*—" Now his arm tightened around her waist as he pressed her body against his thigh.

The images of her erotic dream came back. The smell of drink was strong about him, yet there was something else. A scent which reminded her of something greenish, like the outdoors, like water, like rivers, like leaves blowing in the hot summer wind. Something like Homer's scent, but more—much more . . .

"Steady there, thas it, lil' way now, miss—miss—*mam'selle* Lucette—Lucy—Lucy—"

Again, "Lucy!" this time louder, an insistent voice not from Petitjean, but from the other side of the saloon. It was difficult to see, the room so full of smoke, something wrong with her eyes, the man holding her so close, hard to breathe, dizzy, hard to see, hard to find the man calling her name.

There was a gasp, then the room seemed strangely quiet, the piano stopped playing. A few murmurs, lowered voices. Someone, not Petitjean, saying her name—

A man emerged from the crowd and came toward her. A dark coat, a face hidden in the shadow of a hat, a voice so familiar—Yet her mind so confused, the room spinning, changing from small to large to distant to small, the voices in waves, loud, soft, loud.

The figure was coming into focus. A strange feeling, a prickly creeping down her spine, her spine held against Petitjean's thigh.

"Lucy!"

Petitjean held her against his body more firmly, stepping backward and bracing himself against the stair railing. "*Non, non*— what d'ya mean, coming at her like thish? No, sir, you shall not harm one hair of *mam'selle's* head!"

"Let go of her! Let go—" the voice insisted. A strong hand seized her wrist, a force pulling her away from Petitjean. "Lucy—come away— come back—"

Lucy knew instinctively it was a critical moment. She knew she had to answer, she had to go with him. Yet she could not find the words or the strength. Words had not come earlier with Mattias, they would not come now. She buried her face in Petitjean's shoulder.

There was a gasp in the room, a sudden violent movement, Jason rushing past her, a loud crash, gun shots. Still in Petitjean's arms, she fell back against the stairway. All around her men were shouting. A warm wetness began to soak through her dress.

"Cover that man up—rug over there'll do." Patsy's voice. "Here, you, Jason, and you over there, carry her upstairs to my office.

Somebody bring the sheriff. Rest of you men—just settle down, enjoy the rest of the evenin'. Sam, drinks on the house."

Lucy had the vague feeling she was now up in Patsy's office with its distinct odor of leather-bound books and tea, she sensed it was Jason who was laying her down on that little chaise lounge jammed into a corner by the window.

"All right, now Jason," she heard Patsy say, "go . . . downstairs . . . send . . . sheriff . . . talk . . ." Most of her words seem unconnected.

Lucy felt weak and dazed. The combination of drink and shock made everything seem unreal. She was hardly aware of Patsy and Abbey's efforts to remove her dress, her shoes, the net stockings. Her hair had fallen down over her shoulders, partly over her eyes, she couldn't seem to raise her hand to brush it away. She heard only bits and pieces of the talk around her.

"Have to cut through the dress—blood soaked—pity, can't use it anymore—point blank —careful, now, can't tell whether the bullet got her, too—hand me that towel—get some hot water—kitchen—tea—shock—well, the Lord be thanked for that—"

Patsy was raising her head, "Here now, some strong tea—lots of sugar. No, try to drink it down, more—more—that's it. Oh, thanks, Abbey. Now let's try to get her dressed back into her own clothes."

"Must get home—late—children—*maman*—" the rest mumbled, incoherent.

"No, Lucy, my girl." Lucy felt Patsy restraining her. "You're stayin' right here for the night. Jason'll bring you home come mornin', if you're feelin' up to it. Now you just lie back there, try to rest. You've had a nasty shock. Sure, and haven't we all? Rest now, I'll be right here."

Next morning Lucy awoke to the sound of water being poured into a kettle on the stove, the rattle of a blind rolling up. "Ah, good girl," said Patsy. "First thing—a cup of tea, then a little breakfast—just toast to start with, maybe."

"Why am I here? What happened?" In between waking and sleeping, Lucy had tried to sort out the events of the night. Always they seemed just outside the edge of comprehension, muddled and confused, dim faces, voices as if speaking down a long tube.

"Sure now, and it's for sure how lucky you are," said Patsy as she poured out a cup of her strong, Irish tea. "Someone—somethin' lookin' out for you, I'd say. Here, drink this down. Tell me what you remember. No, better let me go over it. You cried out a couple of times in your sleep last night—bits of talk, a couple of names."

"What names?"

"Couldn't tell exactly. Your ma, for certain. Other words—took 'em to be French—don't parley that myself. You seemed to be worried about somethin', afraid somethin' was going to be taken away."

"I don't remember."

"Just as well, too. But as to what happened last night, I'd better tell you. Just as you were gettin' cozy like with that Frenchie named Petitjean, a man came into the saloon, a stranger, never seen him before. But he must have recognized you. Saw you with Petitjean, probably thought you were headin' upstairs. Whatever. Anyway, he went crazy, pulled out a gun. Don't know whether he was aimin' at you or the other fellow. About that time Jason saw what was happenin', so's he and another man jumped the stranger, knocked him to the floor just as the gun went off. Couple of other shots, too—not sure where they came from. Some men get trigger-happy, you know, 'specially Saturday nights."

"Shots? I felt—"

"You felt blood, all right, but thank the good Lord it wasn't yours. It came from the man holding you. So unfortunate for that Petitjean, his getting between you and the bullet. No way that crazed man could have missed, shot point blank. Yes, poor Petitjean took it." She smiled faintly, shook her head. "Fortunate for you, though."

"Oh! Petitjean? Oh, no!" The news brought an instantaneous image of a boy with sunstreaked hair walking through the woods on a farm in Quebec, the scent of new-mown hay, leaves burning in autumn, sound of his words speaking in a way she remembered, the strength of his arms around her. Petitjean—the man from—"

"That's the tragedy of it, I'm afraid. Two men dead."

"Two?"

"Why yes, that other man got hit, too, just as he went down. Bodies taken off by the sheriff and his deputy last night to the town morgue—just behind the jail."

"The other man shot?" Her heart felt as though it had seized up, shriveled into a knot. She hadn't been able to see the man clearly, his voice sounded so distant, so distorted, but yet it seemed to her that it was the one person she wanted to see, the one man who she wanted to take her away from this place. And now he was dead.

"Yes, don't know who was responsible for shootin' the stranger, doesn't matter. Did it to keep the man from shooting anybody else. But as to the man—sheriff said he needs to ask you a few questions. Whoever he was, he apparently knew you, knew your name, came lookin' for you for some reason. I'm afraid, colleen, you'll have to go down and identify him, once you feel up to it."

"No," said Lucy. "I can't do it." She dreaded what she would see, could not face it.

"Sure and you'll have to—only one around here seems to know him. Don't worry, I'll go with you, send word to your brother. That old coot Stadthauser'll have to let him off work Now you just rest. I'll come back soon's I take care of some business. Then we'll go in my buggy, soon's Jake brings it around from the livery stable."

"You sure do look pale, sis," George said later, coming into the sheriff's office and seeing Lucy and Patsy sitting on a bench along the wall. "Heard what happened—it's all over town. Wondered why you didn't come home last night."

"And well she should look pale," Patsy countered. "She's been through a lot. So have we all."

"All right, now, folks," Sheriff Johnson said, "got to get through this thing. Won't be easy on you, miss, but we have to have a positive identification, notify next of kin, and so forth. So come along, we can go out the back way through the jail. Not a pretty sight, I warn you, man shot up pretty bad."

There were several bodies laid out on wooden trestle tables, covered with white sheets, a peculiar, sickening odor in the room. Lucy shivered.

"Apologize for the cold, the smell," Johnson said, "have to keep it this way, blocks of ice during the summer. You can imagine—"

"Never mind, Floyd," said Patsy. "Let's get on with it." She was supporting Lucy on one side, George stood close on the other. "Now which is the one? You already know about Petitjean."

"He had some friends here who've already been in to identify him," the sheriff said. They've taken his body away for burial. So we've only got two guests—you might say—in here at the moment."

"This one? Steady, now, hold onto me." Patsy drew back the sheet partly, revealing the bluish-white face of an old, gray-bearded man. Lucy shook her head.

"Well, then, must be this other feller here." The sheriff uncovered the head and neck of the other corpse.

Lucy cried out. The man's face had been partly blown away, bright hair darkened with cacked blood and dirt, the mouth distorted to a sneering, teeth-filled grimace. She instantly turned away, sagging down on Patsy's arm, falling but for George's catching her.

"You know him? Can you give us his name, then?"

It took a moment to be able to speak, to shape words refusing to be shaped, the name refusing to be named. "Yes," she gasped. "Yes—I know—him."

"His name, then? Where's he from?" the sheriff asked, taking out a pad and pencil from his jacket pocket.

"Mattias," she gasped.

"That all?"

"Little—" All she could say as George eased her down onto a chair.

"Mattias Little, you said?" The sheriff began to write it down.

"No—no—Hol—Holberg—" She forced it out, her tongue refusing, her stomach heaving.

"Where does he live? Kin there?"

"Don't know—Montana—somewhere." The shock, that thought—she burst into tears.

"There, there, colleen. A nasty shock." Patsy knelt down and put her arms around her. "I can guess, I can guess. Been there."

"Well," the sheriff said, replacing his pad and pencil, "that's all we needed to know. The deceased left nothing at Meyer's Hotel last night, didn't check in. According to the hotel manager, he just asked for a miss Lucy Dubois, told you were working at Pat's Saloon."

"Yes, news gets around this town fast," George commented with a wry smile.

"Well, then the man immediately left. Said he'd check in and sign the register later. So now ladies, mister Guyette, if you'll kindly step back into my office, sign a few papers, I'll let you be on your way and we can take care of the burying."

"The burying?" George asked.

"Guess we'll have to send his body up by train to—but where, then?"

"Where, Lucy?" George asked.

She shook her head, at a loss. Suddenly it occurred to her. "Prairie Lake," she whispered, scarcely audible.

"Oh, yes. Todd county is it? Sheriff in Long Prairie'll take care of things at his end."

Entering the sheriff's office in a daze and supported by Patsy, Lucy signed her name, answered a few more questions. She hardly knew what she was saying, signing. It was like a dream, a horrible nightmare. It could not be true.

"Oh, one more thing, before you leave," said the sheriff. "The only thing in his pockets was a return ticket to Minneapolis. By law we have to send any effects up with the body if we discover any. Any relatives can claim them there. Least ways, I assume you're not a relative, miss?"

Lucy shook her head. The question had a cruelty about it, a piercing cruelty.

"This girl's had enough for one day, Sheriff," Patsy said. "George, I assume you have to get back to work. I'll take this girl back home in my buggy. Your mother there? Somebody home?"

"Most likely."

"Well, then."

As they rode up Oak Street, Patsy driving at a very slow pace for it was raining heavily, Patsy turned to Lucy. "That man—you loved him?"

"Yes."

"A nasty shock. No one—not even old Patsy here, can understand how you feel."

"No one," Lucy repeated mechanically.

"What's this I hear about your leavin'? Wouldn't surprise me. Wouldn't expect you to stay on with me, sure and I wouldn't blame you."

"There's something I—"

"Of course, of course. Work there not exactly—what you might say—"

It was hard for Lucy to enter into any kind of rational conversation, but she knew she had to be frank, and this was probably the only occasion she'd have. "It has nothing to do with you, the saloon," she began. "No, nothing. Another tragedy. Back home. My sister—she was supposed to come here. But she—she died." Forest Lake cemetery penetrated her thoughts, the cold spring of Bernard's funeral, another cold spring with an open grave.

"Oh, I'm so sorry to hear that. A great shock, I'm sure. Another one. You're mother taking it hard, I suspect."

"Yes." For a moment she was able to force the shock of Mattias' murder aside, but only for a moment. All the issues came together again, and she leaned her head against Patsy's shoulder.

"Ah, colleen—poor girl, poor girl." They were turning down 4th Street. Only a few more blocks before George's house. "Now look, Lucy. Here's what I suggest." She slowed the horse to avoid a passing wagon. "Yes, let me see, now. I owe you some wages, right?" Not waiting for Lucy to answer, she said, "It's clear you've got to make that trip up to—up to—"

"My sister—her family—near Long Prairie."

"Well, fine and dandy then. I'll see to it you get a train ticket. You get yourself up there, and when you take care of things, make your way back, then we'll talk. I've got a few ideas about—"

Lucy looked at her in surprise. "About me?"

"Yes, couple of notions comin' to me. We'll talk."

"It'd be hard for me to get away, Patsy. You're so generous, understanding. But you see, my mother—not able to cope much with all this. My sister's death—" she did not feel she could mention what else—"and, of course, looking after my children."

"That all that's botherin' you? So—so." Patsy thought a moment. "Look here, then. You know, colleen, I live with an elderly aunt who might just be willin' to help, always lookin' for something to do, on occasion helps out house keepin', nursin'. Aunt Maureen Flynn's her name. I'll send her over tomorrow so they can get acquainted while you take care of all the things you have to do to get ready to leave."

"Would she be willing, do you think?'

"She's a real character—bit like me, I guess." She smiled, glanced at Lucy. "They probably won't get along, but it will be interestin'— French and Irish—like -like -chalk and cheese. One of them has to be the cheese, the other one—most likely Aunt Maureen—the chalk."

As she drew up in front of George's house, she pulled back on the reins and put her arm around Lucy's shoulders. "And then, colleen, next thing is to get you on that train."

Lucy wondered for what purpose she was going. He was no longer there . . . No longer anywhere but in the darkness of a cold grave. He was lost to her . . . his words silenced forever . . . in that deathly last grimace . . .

PASSING LANDSCAPES

O NLY AFTER SHE CHANGED TRAINS in Minneapolis and Sauk Centre, only after she was seated in the last train heading toward Little Sauk, was Lucy able to force her thoughts back again to the past week. And inevitably, enclosed and uninterrupted as they were within the confines of the red velvet seat, they wandered back and forth over the past four months and the years before that.

Sometimes she dozed off from the rhythmic swaying of the train and the sound of wheels clicking over the tracks. That rhythm seemed bent on mixing up events and reconfiguring them.

Sometimes it was Bernard she saw, coming toward her at O'-Grady's, shocked to see her there. She tried to explain, but he refused to listen and only shook his head before walking out into the dark street. When she tried to follow him, it was Patsy who held her back.

At other times in her dream-like state, it was not Bernard coming into O'Grady's but Homer West. He shouted that he wanted her and was going to take her back to Little Sauk with him. She screamed for help and rushed past him upstairs to Patsy's office and then Patsy came out with a gun and shot him. The shock shook her awake with a cry causing people seated around her to stare.

While awake, looking out the train window yet not seeing the passing landscapes, she thought of Mattias. He never seemed to be part of her dreaming, never a part of the images from O'Grady's. As if she were deliberately denying the incident, that he'd never been there, never been shot, that she'd never witnessed the nauseating disfigurement of his body. She blamed Homer West for much of that, for turning Mattias away, for—for—

But where, really, was the blame? Rachael Olson's gossip? Hans for intervening after the granary fire? Maggie for ambiguous advice or none at all? Noel Dubois's implicit attentions? For Mattias's death she knew she must accept the brutal truth. She herself was to blame for a chain of circumstances beginning and ending with her alone.

It was not going to be easy, her visit to Little Sauk. Agnes was gone, her family thrown into turmoil. Something had happened to Jane, to Henry. What help could she provide for Abe and young Tom? She would have to face Mattias's parents and find something to say. She hoped beyond hope that they were already out west with Hans and Erik.

These anxieties seemed to stifle her, blurring the landscape out the train window. To close her eyes was no help, for it only brought out of the depths of her memory the image of Mattias on the slab in the morgue. She forced her eyes open, forced them to focus on the passing woods, on water glistening with melting chunks of ice as it rushed beneath the trestle bridge.

It was a good thing the sharp whistle of the train announced the final curve before Little Sauk's station. Looking out at that curve, she realized it was the last familiar thing she'd seen when leaving with the children last October. Now it was the first thing she saw, and with it came a rush of overwhelming memories.

The train slowed, puffing and blowing, metal wheels screeching against the rails. Lucy stood up, steadying herself against the seat back, straightened her bonnet, her shawl, and took down the small carpetbag from the rack. And there was Noel, waving, walking along the platform outside her window, just as before. The train jerked to a stop in a loud explosion of steam.

"Tell me all the news," Lucy said eagerly as Noel helped her into his buggy and pulled the thick woolen blanket up over her knees.

"Still cold, but spring, she comes! *Eh bien*, don't know where to begin," he laughed, then turned more serious. "You will want to know first about Agnes, *n'est-ce pas?*"

"Yes, it was such a shock. You promised more details." The buggy pulled out of the station and soon they were heading the half-mile or so down the road to Noel's farm.

"It was not easy to say," he replied solemnly. "Telegrams—they do not talk."

"I understand. Words are never easy, never enough." The thought evoked a flood of emotion. The thought of Mattias, the difference words might have made.

"There was a story about the fire in the *Argus*. Mary saved it for you to read."

"But Henry—surely you've talked to him?"

Noel shook his head. "*Pas possible.* The fire—all that—had a stroke. Talking difficult. He is still in hospital."

"What about Jane? You said in your telegram there was some bad news."

"Some, yes. Do not know much more."

"Please—what do you know? We're almost at your door—you'd better tell me quick—maybe something you didn't want your children to hear?"

"*Exactement*—you have hit it. *Eh bien*—well then, it was at Reagan's only a week ago that I found out more." He sent a sidelong glance her way, then continued, knowing how she felt about the place.

"More? But you said in your telegram last December—"

"Last December was the first, *bien sûr*. Met Abe Morton just after Christmas in Long Prairie. Had to go to Lano's hardware, he was there for something or other. Said Jane acting strange and not talking much. He thought it had to do with that Daniel Benson."

"But then?"

"At Reagan's last week there was a trapper, name of Cyrus Ives. Just came back from Montana, wanted to clear up some property settlement in Long Prairie. Well, you know how we—men, I mean, get talking over beer and so on." Another sidelong glance.

"Noel—please come to the point!"

"The point is—*voilà*—that Jane has probably run off to be with Benson."

"What? Run off?

"This Ives, he said he met Jane in some town or other, at a hotel near the railway station, Alexandria, maybe. He saw her eating alone in the café, asked if he could join her, thinking—well, bof! Maybe I don't have to tell you, *mon dieu*."

They'd arrived in his barnyard, stopped before the barn entrance. "*Eh bien*, to make a story of length a story of no length, Ives said that the woman explained she was going to join her fiancé in Montana. Place called Glendive, I think it was."

The news disturbed Lucy. Jane, going off like that, alone, unprotected. "Did she say Daniel knew she was coming? Would meet her?"

"*Je ne sais pas.*" He shrugged. "Let us hope so." He stepped down out of the buggy, came around to Lucy's side, and threw back the lap robe. "Come inside. Mary waits." Then, with a furtive glance back at the house, he took her hand and kissed it as he helped her down from the buggy.

Lucy experienced a strange emotion. What did it mean? Was he asking forgiveness? And for what? But there was no time to consider his motives, for, once inside, Mary was full of her usual small talk, the activities of the children, all the local gossip.

"Oh, we heard about the shooting at O'Grady's in Shakopee, an item appeared in the *Argus*," she exclaimed, "I'll get it out for you. But do tell us more!"

Lucy was alarmed. "Did it mention any names?"

"No, only that a man was shot molesting one of the bar girls. Not surprised, given what goes on in those places. The morals of those girls. Just said the murder was under investigation, I think that's the term. An event so far away—not of much local interest. But you were there? It must have made big news in Shakopee."

Under investigation—what did that mean? Were the details still to come out? Would she be mentioned? It was a disturbing thought.

Sharing Josie's room that night, she was glad to retire early. In more ways than one it had been a difficult journey, worse even than the one to Shakopee with its struggle to keep the children and the baggage together, with its uncertainties about the future. So much had happened. It seemed that her whole world, from Agnes's house at Eagle River to the DeLaurier house in Little Sauk, had broken apart. The pieces could never be put back together again, for either they were missing or did not fit.

"Once we have finished breakfast," Noel announced next morning, "I take you in the buggy to see Abe and Tom Morton at their mill and brick works on Eagle River. That buggy—good against the cold, with those isinglass curtains. A fine one, *mon dieu*, but big cost. Then, on the way, I will tell you more what you want to know, although you have read the *Argus* piece, there is not much more. As for the other matter—Jane. Not much more, either. First, though, some business in Long Prairie." He looked apologetic. " I hope you will not mind, it will not take long."

Turning down Maple Street in Long Prairie, Noel drew up in front of the new county court house. "Jon Geske's law office is up on the second floor," he said. "Law practice growing, like the town."

"You're going to see a lawyer?"

"You cannot wait out here in the cold."

Geske ushered them in while inviting them to sit down. His office was spacious, lined with books, and included a sofa as well as chairs around a polished mahogany table. "I'm only glad to be of service regarding this matter, missus Dubois. As you may know, I've had a little experience with early settlers here, including your family." He paused, looking somewhat apologetic. "If I could be so bold as to remind you about Henry Morton's—er, ahem—arrest and so forth. I'm happy to say we got that cleared up."

"Why I come to you, sir," Noel explained.

"So now, Missus Dubois, strange, isn't it, how things come around? How this business brings you here?"

Lucy was mystified. "What business, sir?"

"I have not told her yet."

"No? You've no idea, then, why you are here, Missus Dubois?"

Lucy was indignant. All this going—what were they talking about? "No, I don't, sir." She tried to sound polite.

"I see. Well, here is the case. You are, ma'am, much involved because it concerns that most unfortunate event at O'Grady's place in Shakopee."

"The body of the man shot was shipped here, Lucy," Noel assuming a gentle tone to his voice, one Lucy had never heard before. "Shipped here by train, along with his personal effects." He took her hand. "Ah, *ma cherie*, this is going to upset you."

"Mattias—" she whispered, withdrawing her hand and lowering her head. That all too familiar feeling of grief, of guilt swept over her like a black, stifling cloud.

"Mattias, you said? No, Missus Dubois. The victim was not Mattias Holberg."

Lucy's head snapped up, and she stared in disbelief first at Geske, then at Noel. "What? Not—you—what did you say?"

"Not Mattias Holberg, *merci à dieu*. No, Lucy, you were mistaken in your identity down there."

"Not surprising," Geske added, "given the—er—the unfortunate condition of the body. Perhaps, also, due to what must have been your emotional state at the time."

Then she knew. That image in her dream. She knew it was Homer West. They did not have to tell her. She could not speak, only hold tightly to the arms of the chair, hold on to this moment of truth, of reality, before it could escape and turn out to be only false hope clouding her understanding. "Homer West. Homer West. Not Mattias," she murmured over and over again.

"Yes, yes indeed, Missus Dubois, you are correct. You see, there was some confusion about his personal effects. It was only after the train bearing his coffin arrived at the station in Long Prairie, and matters attended to by our county coroner, that the Shakopee sheriff discovered the deceased's effects, a small leather valise."

"He did not take it to the hotel?" Noel asked.

"No, that does seem surprising, I agree. The hotel manager said he appeared to be in a hurry, didn't bother to check in and sign the register, asked about you, Missus Dubois, then rushed off when told where you might be. Never came back, of course."

Geske paused, looked hesitantly at Lucy, then continued. "Only later did the hotel manager remember the deceased's saying he'd left his bag at the station and would check in later. Once the Shakopee sheriff recovered the valise, he found it locked and had to break it open. For some reason no key was found on the body. Possibly lost somehow. In any event, there was enough in it to verify identity, an identity which failed, I might add, to correspond to what the sheriff in Shakopee had been led to believe. No, the man was not Holberg." He coughed slightly, obviously uncertain how to word what he needed to say.

"That valise—she comes here? *Mon dieu*, so much later?"

"That's correct. The sheriff's only recourse was to send it up, sealed, by a later train. Then it was kept in the Long Prairie sheriff's until such time as we could make a positive identification at our end, so to speak."

"*Comment est-ce*—how is that to be done?" asked Noel. "Is that why you asked us here today?"

"Yes, Noel, and I'm grateful for your bringing Missus Dubois." There was knock on the door. "Must be Sheriff Griffin now." Geske got up from behind his desk. "I've asked him to meet with us about ten o'-clock this morning, when I knew you'd be here."

He and Griffin shook hands. "Just on time, thanks for coming Clyde. You've brought it?"

"Here it is, all right to put it down here?"

"Table's fine."

Griffin set the valise on the table and with his pocketknife cut the cord holding it together, then threw back the lid. Lucy found herself trembling, uncertain whether it was knowing the truth, or the prospect of going through Homer West's personal effects. Both were a shock. She sensed her emotional reserves were rapidly draining away.

"Let's see, now," said Sheriff Griffin, "been through these effects before, but just wanted to make sure they belonged to him, that he was the man. Please tell me, Missus Dubois, if you recognize anything. You are most likely one of the few witnesses we can ask."

"Why do you ask that?" What had people known about their relationship? Rachael Olson's gossip column had given out enough hints.

"Now, what do we have here?" Griffin began. "On top of this pile, a couple of shirts—good quality, too. Consistent with his usual haberdashery. Next, long johns, socks, undershirts, flannel nightshirt." He laid them out one by one beside the valise. "His pocketbook, about a hundred dollars in bills." He flipped though them. "Whew, lot of cash for a fellow to carry around. No wonder he kept it locked up in the valise. Wonder what he was planning. Now we come to the big puzzle." He held up a woman's yellow sunbonnet. "Now, folks, the cash I could understand, but this?"

If Lucy had been upset to see Homer West's personal things laid out, she was even more so now. "That—that—" she stammered, "it's mine."

"Yours, Lucy? How'd he come by that?" Noel shook his head, puzzled.

"He took it—once—came out to the house. I'd hung it by the barn door."

"Well, if that don't beat all," exclaimed Griffin.

"Not unusual," Geske offered. "Sometimes a man will take something of a woman's, a sort of fetish, if you will. If he can't possess her, he'll at least have something of hers, so to speak." He glanced at Lucy. "I hope you'll forgive all this, ma'am."

"I see," said Griffin, rubbing his chin. "Well, I can tell you one thing. If we had any doubts about this stuff being West's, that bonnet provides a strong piece of evidence, wouldn't you say, Geske?"

"You said there was something else in the pocketbook besides money?"

"Yes, this small photograph of a little girl."

"*Mon dieu*, he had a child?"

"No telling who she is," Griffin said. "Recognize her, Missus Dubois?"

Lucy took the faded piece of cardboard and looked at it. A small, sad face, a girl of about six, long light-colored curls hanging down over an elaborate lace collar. "No, it's a surprise to me. He never mentioned her."

"Never mentioned any family, kin, that you know of?" Geske asked.

"No, sir. I was always under the impression he'd never married."

"*Cela—c'est possible—*" Noel began. "Possible to search?"

"Don't know," Geske answered. "The name West's common enough. It may take some time. But I'll do my best. You know, we've got government census records now, although it'll sure be like looking for a needle in a haystack. We start here, then broaden out the search to neighboring territories."

"Mean time, then?" Noel pointed to the pile of clothing. "A will, surely the man had a will in there?"

Geske smiled. "Come, now, Noel. A man doesn't usually carry his will around with him. Even if he has one. And it strikes me that West wouldn't be the sort of man to have a will in the first place. A man like him in the prime of life?"

"*Eh bien,* if he did have one, where might it be?"

"Who knows? Any number of places. In a safe at his establishment. A dresser drawer. Under a rug. Filed at the county records office. With another lawyer in town—although there's only two others in Long Prairie. If with one outside of town, say, Sauk Centre, St. Cloud—then it may be difficult to trace. We could advertise in local papers. That'd take a lot of time."

"Must be done, though," added Griffin. "Not a law man, myself, but I do know you've got to find out whether he was intestate or not."

"Quite, right, Clyde," Geske said. "I'll work on it."

"So what meantime?" Noel was growing impatient, Lucy could see. He wasn't much of a man to tolerate unanswered questions. "What about the man's things? The cash?"

Geske looked at the sheriff. "Clyde? Up to you."

"Well, usually we turn over personal effects to next of kin. In this case, though—don't seem to be any. At least until that little girl's whereabouts gets known. Looks like an old photograph—could be anybody, a grown woman by now, maybe even dead."

Lucy kept turning the photograph over and over in her hand. Never mentioned a child, she thought, never mentioned one. So much she didn't know about the man, had never wanted to know.

"Next of kin most generally means a spouse. I'm going to come right to the point, Missus Dubois, and I hope you'll forgive me for being blunt. As a lawyer, that's my job. Tell me, did Homer West ever mention marriage to you? Ever propose?"

Lucy felt the blood rush to her face and she lowered her head. How could she answer him? "That's difficult to say, sir."

"Why difficult? Did he or didn't he?"

"*Eh bien, écoute*, Lucy," Noel began eagerly, "don't you remember that bit in the *Argus*, just before you left? That nosey gossip, Rachael Olson? Mary keeps track. Wasn't that a clear indication of his intentions? That you were going to celebrate a wedding soon?"

"That only constitutes heresay," said Geske. "Wouldn't stand up in court."

"What would you suggest, then," Griffin asked, rubbing his chin. "Seems to me you're the law man."

"But you're the law." Both men laughed guardedly, while Lucy sat looking from one to the other, unable to confirm anything, explain anything.

A partnership . . . phrases ran through her mind . . . how long had it been since she had been with a man, a real man . . . She had wanted him ever since she first laid eyes on him. Phrases from that incident in her parlor came back to her, yet she had no proof, no ring. The ring she had was not from him.

After a moment or to while shuffling through a few papers on his desk, taking down a large leather-bound volume from a shelf behind his head and looking through several sections, Geske cleared his throat. "There was a case back in 1855. Somewhat similar to this one. The man died intestate, with a possible heir who couldn't be located. Owned a considerable amount of property and cash on hand."

"What was the decision?" Griffin asked.

"What the court decided was to auction off the assets and put the proceeds in trust in the bank along with any other funds until such time as an heir could be found."

"What if not?"

"Not sure about the time limit. I'll check on that."

Griffin reflected on this for a moment. "That sounds reasonable to me. How about you Missus Dubois? Noel?"

Noel was the first to speak. "This is proper? Legal, this thing?"

"The law acts by precedent," Geske answered.

Lucy hesitated, knowing full well that she had no right to anything of the man's, yet saddened by the thought that all would be dispersed, scattered into a hundred different hands."

"This bonnet—I believe it's yours?" Griffin picked it up. "You have the right to recover it."

She shuddered at the idea of taking it, touching what he had touched. Thinking of when he had touched her body, loosened her hair—her bare feet—She shook her head.

"All right then, we'll keep it with the rest." He rose, Geske as well. "You'll see to it then, John? All tied up legal, like?"

"Of course." Geske bowed slightly toward Lucy. "And now, ma'am, if you would like, I'll eventually send you a copy of these proceedings. For your records."

"Thank you, sir, but that won't be necessary. My connection with mister West is—is over."

On their five-mile ride in Noel's buggy out to see Agnes's children, Abe and Tom, Lucy reflected on the meaning of this past hour. Mattias was alive. The disfigured body was not his. The truth about Homer West and his intentions. The truth about herself.

She felt shaken and confused. A part of her soared with joy over finding the man she'd thought dead still alive. A part of her agonized over the death of Homer West because she had been the cause of it. The agony grew worse with the image of the yellow sunbonnet before her—the poignancy of it, the desperation of the man. She shuddered.

"Are you cold, Lucy?" Noel solicitous, urging the horse on.

"No—yes. How much farther?"

"A few miles. We hurry more."

As the buggy swayed, responded to the unevenness of the rut-torn road, Lucy was forced to recognize another truth. Mattias might as well be dead. She'd rejected him, plain and simple. She'd driven him away, out west to Montana. Most likely he was married by now. It'd been almost six months. He should have kept that ring, with its finely twisted wires. Her life twisted, like the ring.

Pulling up into the yard of the Morton Brick Works, they were met by Tom. "Did you bring Martin, Auntie Lucy?" he cried eagerly

"No, Tom, I'm sorry. I had to leave him in Shakopee. Hello, Abe," she said, as he emerged from the building to join them, then helped her out of Noel's buggy.

"So good of you to come," he said. "All this way."

"It was important to see you, you know that." She took him in her arms, trying to hold back her tears at the sight of him. "Your mother— so tragic, I'm so sorry. And about your father, too."

"We can talk more inside the office. It's too cold out here. Uncle Noel, I'll get one of my men to look after your horse. Tom, go fetch Caleb, will you?"

"You are very busy these days, no?" Noel asked, as they walked toward a large brick building, surrounded by sheds, racks of bricks, wheelbarrows, stacks of firewood, and wagons of various sorts.

"Yes, we are. And I'm afraid the office is rather noisy, with all that brick production going on next door."

As they entered, Lucy noticed several mattresses on the floor, a pile of dirty dishes on a small table in one corner. "You're living here?"

"Tom and I are bunking here, yes. With the house burned down and all—"

"Planning to rebuild soon?" Noel asked while they settled themselves around the pot-bellied stove dominating the center of the office.

"Soon, I hope," added Tom, as he came in.

"Yes, eventually. Soon's we're a little less busy." Abe smiled wryly. "Building a brick house takes a little more time, needs a more secure foundation and all that. Can't work the ground yet, still frozen. Couple of weeks, yet. But you know all that, Uncle Noel, I don't have to tell you."

"You're right. In fact, I'm thinking of that for some of my other property, tearing down a few of the old wooden structures. I'll consult you later, what I need."

"Noel," Lucy said, alarmed, "you aren't thinking of tearing down the DeLaurier house, are you?"

"*Peut-être.* It's seen its day. Already full of bits and pieces from earlier."

That old house, Lucy thought. To tear it down? No longer hers, never was, and yet so much a part of her life. Its memories, whispers, would be stilled.

But talk about bricks was not what they'd come for. "Listen, Abe, my dear, can you tell me more of what happened? It will help me to know. Not knowing about my sister—her last moments—that has been hard."

"Do you really want to hear about it, Auntie?"

"Yes. Tell me how the fire started, tell me what you can."

"Well, there was a big, big fire, and then Ma, she—"

"Hush, Tom, best let me tell it. The fire started in the old fireplace. After we first came off the prairies some years ago, Pa salvaged whatever timber and rocks he could from the old homestead. You'll remember it'd been burned down. Sheriff Griffin's not exactly sure what happened this time. His opinion was that some of the original timbers must've been weakened, and caused part of the surrounding wall to collapse. This may have brought most of the fireplace down. Although we mostly lived in the kitchen where the cook stove kept things more livable, Ma liked a fire in the fireplace, 'specially on cold, dark, snowy days."

"Ma, she'd been real sick—"

"No, Tom, she'd had pneumonia, it hung on for a long time. And what with such a bad winter, she couldn't seem to get over it. Anyways, when the fireplace collapsed, it scattered live embers all over the place."

"But couldn't she have gotten out? And where was Jane?"

"Trapped, that's what she was—"

"Tom! I said I'll do the telling. Well, Jane was down here working in the office. A real help. Tom here was at school. And as for poor Ma, well, you see she was alone, trying to put out the fire. Must've been running back and forth to the kitchen, trying to pour water on the fire. Must've run out of water pretty quick, must've tried to stamp it out with rugs or something."

"That'd be somethin' Ma would do."

"All right, Tom. Well, we think she got trapped as part of the upper floor started to come down. Pa and the rest of us were all down here at the works. Soon's Pa saw smoke he yelled to me and started running. You know it's a fair distance uphill to the house from the works and mill down here on the river."

"Tried to save her—Pa tried to save her," Tom cried. "And I couldn't help!"

"It's all right, Tom. Know it's hard for you to get over that, Jane neither."

"Then she ran off."

"Yes, with Ma gone, Pa in a bad way, she took kind of strange, like. One day she was gone, ran off after that Daniel Benson, like nobody needed her anymore."

"Or that Pa couldn't stop her."

"After a moment or two of silence, the others hesitant to speak, Lucy asked, continued, "Tell me, Abe, where is she buried? I'd like to go there."

"Closest cemetery is the Evergreen in Long Prairie. Pa once said he'd eventually be buried there, a plot reserved for Grand Army veterans. So we put Ma to rest there. Someday he'll be beside her."

Lucy tried to picture it, but all she could visualize was the Prairie Lake cemetery, where Bernard was buried beneath ground now so many times frozen over. "Now Abe, please tell me about your father. How is he?"

"Coming along, I guess. Can't speak, least wise not much, words get all mixed up. Or use his right arm. But he's being looked after well enough. Tom and I try to ride over to the hospital in Twin Falls as often as we can, but it's quite a few miles and things getting busier all the time here, 'specially with spring here and the building season."

He went over to a cupboard along the wall, took out several bottles of ginger beer and some glasses out of the desk drawer. "But here, let me offer you some refreshment, speaking of long rides. You've still got to get back to Little Sauk."

"*Non, merci,*" Noel raised his hand. "Lucy and I need to head home 'fore it gets dark. And you've got a lot of things to do."

"You stayin' long, Auntie?" Tom asked hopefully.

"Only a few days," she said. "I've some things to take care of, too. But perhaps we'll see each other again before I leave. And you must let me know if you hear anythng from Jane." Jane's apparently irresponsible actions lay heavily up her, as if she'd taken over Agnes's responsibility for the girl.

Noel was strangely quiet during the long ride back. Occasionally he'd observe a new house going up, a new wayside store, more land cleared, but his remarks were never on the subjects so disturbing to Lucy. She knew it might have helped to talk about them, perhaps Noel understood that, too. But she could not. Not with him.

As they were approaching Little Sauk and the crossroad leading west toward the DeLaurier place, she had a sudden impulse. "Noel," she said, "keep on going, don't stop. Please drop me off at Maggie Skinner's."

"But Mary —your things—at my place—" he protested

"No matter." Maggie was the one person she wanted to see, the one who might help her make sense out of—out of everything. To come to terms with discoveries so mixed with shock and grief, the overburdening weight of other things. Those things which seemed to define life's contradictions.

Spring Harvest 14

L UCY LOOKED FORWARD TO SPENDING that early spring night with Maggie Skinner, her next to last night in Little Sauk. Tomorrow's transportation to the cemetery in Long Prairie Lem could provide, although she'd miss the luxury of Noel's buggy with its isinglass side curtains, some protection against the cold March winds.

"There's the Skinners' house, Noel, a ways back from the road."

"*Mon dieu*, you think I do not know that house?" he laughed. "My land in front, my land to the west."

She knew that all too well. Maggie and Lem's boundary line lay along the DeLaurier sixty acres to the east. It hurt, that little remark, reminding her of his ownership, her lengthy dependency. But she let it pass. "I hope Maggie's home, doesn't expect me."

"Mary told her."

"I might have known."

Maggie was overjoyed. "Well, well—as I live and breathe. You're sure a sight for sore eyes!" She crushed her in a fierce embrace, Lem standing just behind her. "Mary Dubois hinted you might be coming. So sorry to hear about your sister and brother-in-law, right sorry. But come in, come in. Here Lem, take her things."

"Trip not too tiring?" Lem helped her off with her shawls, her bonnet, hung them on the rack by the back door.

"No more than expected, I guess."

"Well, then, coffee's ready in a minute." Maggie filled the big pot. "Here, then, put your feet up on that fender. I'm sure they're frozen."

It felt good to be in Maggie's kitchen again, its ordered blue-and-white dishes, fragrant herbs hanging in bunches from a rack suspended from the ceiling across one of the big windows. A robust fire burned within the large black-and-chrome kitchen range, its fender along one side just meant for frozen feet. Lucy felt the warmth rising up through her feet, her legs, until it bathed her whole body in an aura of comfort. It was almost like coming home to something she'd missed for a very long time.

Maggie moved deftly back and forth around the kitchen, sliding a pie into the oven where a beef roast was already sizzling in its own juice. Or, as she tested the pot of baked beans, transferring a kettle of boiling potatoes to another burner lid. Lucy half closed her eyes, feeling, for the first time in several years, secure and at peace.

Supper over, Lem protested he had to get an early morning start plowing, the first step toward spring planting, and so headed upstairs to bed.

"That's fine, Lem," Maggie called after him. "You go on. Us women got a lot to talk about. Prob'ly keep us down here half the night." She poured out tea and moved two chairs closer to the range. "Now then, we'll both put our feet up and get comfortable. And talk."

"Tell me your news first," said Lucy.

"I'm mighty certain you've got more to tell and I'm more than anxious to hear it. But, all right, I'll start with your sister and brother-in-law. Hard to know what exactly happened, since poor Henry's stroke left him unable to talk. Able to talk plain, that is. Ain't been out to see him yet. Don't expect I will. That hospital's clear over other side of the county. How're his sons doing?"

"This morning Noel took me up to their place. The boys seem to be doing all right, although I'm not sure what'll happen with Jane gone. They could sure use help."

"Think you might move back with them?"

"I'd considered that, before—before—"

"Before what?"

"Well, before things took a different turn down in Shakopee." How could she explain Patsy's hints about a different kind of job, office work perhaps, further contacts around town? "My other family needs me, too—My mother, father, new sister-in-law and baby." Nor did she feel she could explain they needed her for financial support.

Fortunately Maggie changed the subject. "Anyone heard from Jane?"

"No, not directly. Only that she was last seen in a hotel on her way to Montana."

Maggie stroked her chin. "Hmm, that don't bode well. No tellin' how that'll turn out. Really tragic, 'bout your sister. There was that account in the *Argus*, 'bout Henry tryin' to save her. He charged right in 'mongst those flames lookin' for her, in there a couple of minutes. Finally carried her out, badly burned, some'at burned himself. Seems Abe tried to help, but it was too late. By that time the fire'd drawn couple of neighbors, and they rushed her in somebody's wagon to a Long Prairie doctor. But by then she was gone. House gone, too. Such a pity."

"What about the funeral? Noel's telegram said it was at St. Hubert's."

"Lem went. Couldn't go, myself, was over to Lone Pine with a woman in labor. Heard, though, that it was a pitiful thing, only a few folks. For some reason, Noel and his family didn't make it. Yes, pitiful thing, ground still frozen solid at the cemetery, had to use pickaxes."

Ground frozen solid. Like Bernard's grave. An overwhelming sense of loss. Such a horrible death for poor Agnes.

Recovering herself after a moment or two of painful reflection, she asked, "And the DeLaurier place? Meant to ask Noel, but put it off. A delicate subject, you know, since I left him in the lurch having to look for a new tenant—and at a season in the year when there aren't many folks looking for a place. This spring would have been a better time."

"Oh, it's still down the road a piece. Empty since you left. All these five, six months. Probably taken over by mice, chipmunks—dust by now. An awful mess, next tenant'll have a right royal time. Want to go see it? Door probably unlocked or a window broken downstairs, somewhere. Noel seems bent on lettin' it go, eventually rebuild, replace it with a fancy brick house. Get 'em cheap now from Morton's, I reckon." She opened one of the stove lids, dropped in another piece of wood. "Why? Thinkin' about movin' back there?" She laughed, half jokingly.

"No, of course not. Right now I've got my life arranged back in Shakopee. Might even have Tom come down and live with us. One of these days, Abe'll have his own family. Yes, Maggie, I must say things are working out for me, finally. I've had several jobs, actually looking forward to one when I get back."

"What kind of jobs?"

"Well, you know—working for people." She didn't dare go into detail. "And now my brother Alfie and his wife have a new baby, a new place, a farm just outside town. My other brother George—doing well—actually building a house next door for our folks. I'll be living with them, with my children."

"Sure sounds fine and dandy." Maggie eyed Lucy critically. "You happy?"

"Of course."

"You can't fool me, miss Lucy. Somethin' eatin' on you, can see it a mile off."

"Bit tired, that's all." She could not bring herself to talk about the disastrous incident with Homer West and that shock of discovery this morning. Her repressed feelings about Mattias, her grief at losing him. George's present financial straits and his need for her income. There were so many things she wanted to say, but the hour was late and the entire day had been more than stressful.

"Will you look at that—past midnight! Come along, then, time for you to be tucked up in the guestroom. You didn't bring anything with you? I'll lay out some of my things. Nightdress too big, I reckon, but warm enough and it'll do for tonight."

Just before they went upstairs, leading the way with an oil lamp, Maggie asked, "Say, Lucy, since you're stayin' 'til tomorrow afternoon, how about invitin' some of the old neighbors over for noon dinner? A few still around, would like to see you—Clarks, Schweitzers, a couple of others, maybe even the Johnsons, though they're a bit far down the road. Remember him and his son helpful to you once."

Lucy wondered whether she'd feel up to it. There'd been already too many encounters over the past two days, and far too many efforts to connect with the past. Besides, only tomorrow was left and she wanted to visit her sister's grave. To please Maggie, though, but with little enthusiasm, she said, "Yes, that'd be fine."

Drifting off to sleep, she contemplated her return to Shakopee day after tomorrow. How strange and unexpected that she'd actually be looking forward to her return. Noel would put her on the morning train to Sauk Centre, send George a telegram, and she'd arrive in Shakopee station by late afternoon.

What then? Mike's house next door would soon be finished and she and her children could move in, sharing it with her elderly parents, while George eventually settled in his own house with his family. Abe willing, she'd send for Tom and raise him along with her own children, he and Martin already like brothers. Agnes would have liked that.

Lucy snuggled down deeper into Maggie's thick, warm quilts, the lavender scented sheets and pillowcase exuding peacefulness and serenity. What about Jane? There was nothing she could do about that at the moment. Maybe, she mused sleepily, she'd try to locate that little girl on Homer West's photograph. A woman—a girl—wandering in the wilderness—

And then—and then—Lucy was finding it more and more difficult to think coherently as the lavender sent out its deep, pungent odor. She needed sleep, but there were so many things to work out—so many—She needed to talk to Patsy about what she had in mind about a new job. Hadn't she mentioned some possibilities? Lucy imagined a scene in which she argued her way into working in an office as a secretary of some sort. 'Mister Drouville,' she'd say, 'I'm so infinitely qualified . . . a dedicated worker . . . I can offer you . . .'

Early next morning Maggie was already on her feet, bustling around preparing the noon dinner. She'd sent Lem down the road with invitations. "No, Lucy," she said more than once when Lucy offered to help. "No, you're a guest now. You just sit there in a comfortable chair, put your feet up, talk to me, and tell me about life in Shakopee."

"Don't know where to begin," laughed Lucy. "You wouldn't believe some of it." And some of it she had no intention of relating. "What time are the neighbors coming for dinner?"

"Not for three or four hours yet—give me plenty of time to bake a cake."

"But it's only eight, and I hear someone driving into the barnyard already."

Lucy joined Maggie at one of the big kitchen windows. "Isn't that the Holberg wagon? I recognize its funny blue stripe."

"Reckon so," Maggie replied. "Asked Karin to come a little early. She and Sep not left for Montana yet, although their boys sure anxious for them to come out. Couple of weeks yet, folks need better weather 'cross the prairies. Karin, bless her soul, she's bringing some bread and—not sure what else, but she wanted to bake it here. My range better, you see, 'specially that big oven." She wiped her hands on her apron. "Well, here they come, Sep with her of course, she never learned to drive that rig. Open the back door, will you? My hands covered with flour, and the Holbergs prob'ly loaded down."

With a wave of relief, Lucy realized that, after yesterday morning's revelation, she would not have to face them with the knowledge she'd been responsible for their son's death. She could not have done it. Most likely she'd have rushed out the front door, run all the way down the road to Noel's house, begged to be let in, and caught the next train back to Shakopee.

As it was, however, her uneasiness still prevailed. Most certainly they'd talk about their boys, about Mattias, his marriage. There was, however, not much she could do about it except pretend to listen. Just outside the mudroom door there they were, with a stamping and scraping of feet on the outside stoop. "Coming," she called, "I'll open the door, Sep."

But it was not Sep standing there. It was Mattias, carrying a large basket and looking everywhere except at her.

"Ach, Lucy," said Karin Holberg, pressing in behind him. "Is so good see you. You let us in, no? So cold it is out here, rain comes soon, spring so late this year."

Lucy stepped back and watched Mattias set down the basket, remove his jacket and heavy boots, take his mother's shawl and bonnet, hand them to her along with his own jacket and fur hat, still saying nothing and avoiding looking at her. There was a weakness about her that made their weight almost unbearable, and she set them down quickly on the nearest chair, leaned against the back of it for support.

"Good you could come, Karin—such short notice," said Maggie. "You, too, Mattias, although I know perfectly well you should be out in the fields with your father this morning."

Mattias looked embarrassed, took the cup of coffee she offered him, glanced at Lucy, quickly looked away again. "We'll catch up," he muttered.

"But I thought—I thought—" Lucy stammered.

"Nay, Lucy," said Karin. "Mattias had the plan to go, but at the end—"

"Now, Karin," Maggie interrupted, "why don't you let Mattias speak for himself—he's got a tongue, hasn't he? Although right now I'm beginnin' to doubt it."

She tucked her thumbs in her belt, rocked back on her heels. "No, I've got a better idea. Mattias, lad, you've got your rig here, plenty of warm rugs? Good. Lucy was anxious to ride out to Long Prairie, wants to visit her sister's grave. You've got just enough time get there and back before dinner. We'll wait if you're late. So—off with both of you. And on the way you can talk—both of you! Talk, talk, I said!"

As Mattias steered his blue sided-wagon out onto the main road, Lucy was still in a daze. Alone with Mattias, and she could think of nothing to say. All her imagined conversations, her recriminations, her carefully posed questions, were forgotten. It now seemed they were complete strangers with absolutely nothing in common.

It was Mattias who broke the silence. "Warm enough?" he said. "Hate to think of your being cold." He leaned over, tucked the buffalo robe more protectively around her. A long pause, during which he concentrated on reining around a sharp curve. "This horse better'n your old Blaize for wagon work. Usually leave Blaize back in the barn, 'cept for plowin'."

"You still have Blaize? I thought you were taking the stock out with you to Montana."

"Nope, changed my mind. Brownling, Blaize—well, they stayed behind while Hans, Erik, and I went out to find a spread. Got out there, land looked better for beef cattle raising, not dairy farming. Didn't think that was for me. Came back." Another long pause. "Came back, dunno why. Nothin' left for me here. Besides, something else—" He looked straight ahead. "Yes, somethin' else—"

"Of course, Mattias. Your parents, you didn't want to leave them here on their own? I know at their age, it would be hard for them—my parents the same, one of the reasons we went to Shakopee."

"One of the reasons?" There was a pause. "You mean there were other reasons?" He reflected for a moment or two. "No, it wasn't because of Ma and Pa." Suddenly he jerked back on the reins and stopped the wagon in the middle of the road. "It was you."

"Me?" Things were happening too fast.

"Yes, ma'am . . . Lucy, I mean. I was hopin'—never gave up hope. Attracted to you the first time I saw you. God help me, you standin' on the other side of your husband's grave. Knew what I wanted then. Didn't seem right. Fought off Erik—and yes, Hans, too." He paused. "And yes, fought off myself as well long as I could. Least wise 'til that night of the granary fire."

"But why didn't you—"

"Couldn't find the way, wondered if it was right, didn't know how you felt. You seemed so devoted to your late husband. Almost a sacred thing. And I respected that. What right did I have to come between you and him?"

"But then later—even when we had some moments together. You need to understand, it's hard for a woman to make the first move, not proper at all."

"But first you told me your mind was made up, that you were leavin'. Then there was that gossip in the *Argus*. Thought it was because you were more interested in that old druggist Homer West. From what I saw, too. Then later it seemed you were more interested in finding a better life in Shakopee. Not sure how that DeLaurier house figured in, but I was pretty darn sure you wanted nothing more to do with me—or it."

"Oh, Mattias," Lucy sighed. She was close to tears.

"Even bought you an engagement ring, was about to propose. But you'd already got your ticket bought and all." He shifted his body slightly on the wagon bench. "I did go after you, though."

"You—you came to Shakopee? To Shakopee? When? I didn't—"

"The train came through Sauk Centre on the way back from Montana. Could have got off then, caught the one to Long Prairie which stops at Little Sauk. Or, I said to myself, why not stay on, all the way to Minneapolis, change to H & D line to Shakopee? Weren't easy to decide."

He flicked the reins. "Wait a minute, another wagon comin'. Got to move us out of the middle of the road."

Lucy looked at him in disbelief. "You came to Shakopee? To find me?"

"Got off the train, all right, fairly late in the afternoon. I'd heard your brother worked in a big store, walked down the main street until I found it."

"George? My brother George? You couldn't find George, then?"

"Found him, all right—stroke of luck there, he was just leavin' work."

"Didn't he tell you where I was?"

"Well, at first he acted kind of strange, didn't want to say much. Finally he told me you'd left town, gone into Minneapolis to look for a job. Didn't seem right to me, but couldn't argue with him. And I darn well knew I'd never find you in the big city. So, I caught the next train to Minneapolis, slept in central station all night, caught the first train next mornin' back to Sauk Centre and then Little Sauk. Real mad nothin' worked out." He paused, quickly glanced at her. "Well, maybe mad's not the right word for it."

"You've been here all along? In Little Sauk?"

"Yep, guess so, 'cept for that month or so out west before that. Sure thought I'd lost you for good, until Maggie's husband, Lem, told me only this mornin' that you were at their place." He turned on the bench to look at her intently, "Can't tell you what that meant to me," then stared straight ahead.

Lucy was astonished, that strange tingling sensation beginning to creep down her spine at the implication of this news. That Mattias had come to Shakopee, looked for her. "Why would George make up a story like that? It doesn't make sense."

After a moment's reflection, she said, "Well, yes, it does, come to think about it. You see, I was afraid Homer West might try to follow me to Shakopee. I wasn't sure I loved him. In fact, I think one reason I went to Shakopee was to get away from him. So I warned George that, if ever Homer showed up looking for me, not to tell him where I was."

"So your brother thought I was Homer?"

"I'm sure that's what happened." She fell silent, considering how fortunate it was that Mattias had not been sent to the saloon and seen her working there, or on that particular night, seen her in Petitjean's arms. It was Heinz, the manager at Meyer's Hotel, who'd inadvertently sent West to his death. How ironic. The same man who'd inadvertently sent Lucy earlier to work at O'Grady's after he'd refused to hire her back.

As if following her thoughts, Mattias continued. "Well, Lucy, what about Homer? I'm sure needin' to be clear in my mind 'bout that. I thought it was him you cared about. What could I offer you? He had everything—money, a business. No hope for me. Maybe in time I could have made a decent living as a carpenter, or a roofer. You didn't seem willin' to wait for that."

"But Homer is dead. I only learned that yesterday morning. I'm not sure I ever loved him. No—yes, I'll admit—maybe there were moments."

"That time I saw you together—right there in the hall of the DeLaurier house—"

"I knew you suspected the worst. I tried to explain, more than once. You—me—we seemed bent on shutting ourselves off. And then, our last meeting, when you gave me the ring—you just walked away . . ."

"No, you walked away."

She didn't know what to say to this. They both remained silent for another mile or so.

Finally, she said in a rush of words, "My husband, Bernard . . . oh, Mattias, I must tell you truthfully, that he will always be a part of my past life, perhaps even my future life. I know that's hard for you to understand. Probably unfair to confess to you, but—"

"No, I can respect that, honestly, and respect you for sayin' it. What could I possibly offer you?"

"Love."

"Love? Reckon I don't know too much 'bout that." He shrugged, looking uncomfortable. "Maybe it's always been there, just didn't know how to get it out. Lucy . . . Lucy—please help me—"

Moved by his struggle, Lucy placed her hand over his where he held the reins against his knee. "Don't you think Maggie has already helped you? How else would we be here in this wagon, on this road, talking like this?"

Mattias suddenly stopped the horse and snapped the brake lever forward. He turned toward Lucy and took her in his arms. "Wouldn't put it past that woman to have set this whole thing up," he said in her ear, then kissed her. They sat that way in each others' arms, the buffalo robe around them both, until the horse got restless and rocked the wagon back and forth.

"Better move on," said Mattias. "Getting' colder, rain later. Long Prairie only 'bout another quarter mile. We'll just take care of your business at the cemetery, head back. Bet they're all just waitin' on tender-hooks to know what we've had to say, what we're goin' to say."

The next day, as Noel was going into Long Prairie he claimed on property business, Lucy asked him to send a telegram to George. "Please tell him that I'll need a few more days here to settle matters."

"You're not going to tell him anything else? About you and Mattias Holberg? So sudden—do you think—*peut-être*—" Something about his look expressed—what? Disappointment? Resentment about her decision? Almost immediately, however, he caught himself and gave her a warm embrace. "*Mon dieu*," he said in apparent sudden resolve, "that is right, *probablement*. You have indeed many *matières* to consider."

Around Noel and Mary's formal dining room table that evening, the discussion of matters began. Noel had several plat maps before him, Mary went back and forth serving coffee, buttered scones. "Here's the Holberg property line, Mattias—see, right here?" He pulled out his pocket knife, unfolded it, and traced along the line. "According to the records, 160 acres along the south side of the Narrows road."

"I see that, sir," said Mattias. "And look, along the east boundary line it borders on those twenty or so DeLaurier acres. Never did understand why that spread was broken up like that."

"*Eh bien,* if you look on the other sides, east and south, what do you see?"

"Your spread, or at least the main part of it."

"*Exactement.* And what does that suggest, eh?"

"I'm sorry, sir, I don't see what you're drivin' at."

"I think I do," said Lucy slowly. "Noel, do you mean you're thinking about joining your two spreads?"

"*Mais non,*" Noel interjected. "Not quite like that. No, that would be too complicated, with the road running through them." He pausing, tapping the plat map with the knife handle. "*Voilà,* here is my *propos.*"

He stopped tapping and glanced somewhat annoyed at Mary. "Marie, *ma cherie, pas de serveuse,* sit down and join us. You know you are much involved with this matter. And Marie, *ma femme,* you know we have made an agreement." He looked intently at Lucy as he said this. Somehow Lucy understood what his look conveyed.

Noel now smoothed out the plat map across the table. "You see, after Mattias and Lucy marry—soon, I hope—yes, then they will have the Holberg spread. I understand, Mattias, that he and your mother intend to go out to your brothers? At least Sep believes so."

"Yes, they're already at it."

"So now I ask, what is the good of having all these spreads split up? Here is my propos. Why not trade?"

"Trade? Trade what, sir?"

"Don't you see, Mattias? I will trade you the DeLaurier place for your place—Mary consenting, of course, because, if you remember, it was taken out in her name in case I should ever—But no matter. Mary would have the Holberg place, we would join it with those maverick twenty acres, and so—*voilà!* Our Dubois spread would then be all in one piece." He began retracing the areas on the plat map.

"But Noel," Lucy interjected, "what's the advantage? You once said those acres were too poor for rye."

"Ah yes, but now I think of something else. I think now of wheat, the news of maize—or what is called corn—also good."

"But the DeLaurier acres? What of those?" The thought of the house, the fields, the garden—once hers in essence, now perhaps to be hers and Mattias's in reality, was almost too much.

"What of those, you ask? Eh, what of those?" he asked, chuckling and slapping his thigh. "*Eh bien*, wait, you will see. I have a plan. A big plan."

"But the houses—"

"So, Mattias—you look surprised, eh? You, too, Lucy? One thing, though. Your old Holberg house, not so big as DeLaurier's. But again, no matter. We will not live in it, only one of the children later, perhaps. Think, Mary—when your children are ready, they will be even closer, *n'est ce pas*? Or better meantime, Mattias, your parents Sep and Karin? Why not rent it to them if they decide the trek is too much, too far? With you and Lucy, they will have family here."

"Not to mention four children already," Mary put in, smiling broadly. "Well, well, Mattias—imagine you an instant father! Just think—" A sharp look from Noel cut her off.

Mattias looked flushed as he bent over the table, intently studying the plat map. Finally looking up, he said, "That's fine, I reckon. Ma and Pa'll be pleased. Hans and Erik and me—prob'ly wasted too much time already, tryin' make up our minds 'bout how to make our spread pay. Montana seemed the right choice."

"But your plan, Noel? You said you had a plan?"

"*Eh bien*, Lucy, you remember our talk after the granary fire, eh? Idea of dairy farming took root. Talked to Hans Holberg later about it."

"But you raised all kinds of objections."

"Didn't think you knew much. I know more now. Last week I went into Long Prairie to see Geske about this, some other matters. I told him not to mention it to you the other day —not until I knew—" He gave her a guarded look. "Also a couple of men around town connected with the Mona creamery co-op. Good prospects there, good future. They were convinced, showed me figures. So now I will explain to you—"

"The DeLaurier place—well, well—" Mary interrupted. "Now Lucy, you are to marry Mattias, soon? You are sure of that?"

"Next month—April. When spring has actually come."

"You won't have much time, once you get back from Shakopee. And spring's already in the air—willow trees starting to bud along the river. Now you'll let me plan your wedding, won't you? I'll start a list—"

"Marie!" Noel looked at her reproachfully.

"Of course, if you're willing. Isn't that right, Mattias?" Lucy suddenly felt that Mary's interventions no longer mattered.

"And the DeLaurier house, my my," Mary added again. "We'll have it there. Almost as if we'd kept it ready for you—or rather, that the old house was begging, waiting for you to come back."

Lucy nodded, not prepared to articulate her own thoughts just now, beginning to visualize what she remembered of the house. The long windows of the parlor, the curved stairway leading up from the hall. The spacious front bedroom, the brass bed left in the guest room. The chives, onions, and rhubarb just now sprouting in the kitchen garden. The high roofed barn, with its shafts of golden light and sweet smell of hay, Brownling's warm flank at milking time. Her refuge once, her refuge again.

Now Mattias would share those rooms, they would be filled with the sounds of children. The house had whispered to her, comforted her in ways that made it her own, even as she became more determined to leave it. "Perhaps Agnes's foster son, Tom—"

"Doesn't Abe need him at the brick works? Especially now with his father disabled?" Mary was always practical.

"We'll have to discuss that," Lucy said. "Later."

"But say, Mattias, another matter of business. *Cela veut dire*—I mean, I was about to explain my plan for a dairy farm." Noel paused, absently tracing property outlines on the plat map. "You see, it is like this. *Eh bien, cela veut dire* not only a dairy farm. Long time back, time of the granary fire, Lucy mentioned it. Strange for a woman, *n'est-ce pas?* But you must know by now she is no ordinary woman."

Mattias smiled, nodded as he glanced at her, obviously embarrassed. "Know it now."

"*Eh bien*, farming for cows—did not seem practical at first."

"Now, Noel," Lucy responded, "I've got a confession to make. It came up by accident. Yes, Hans brought it up, explained all that to me. But it was really Mattias I wanted to come back into the house then. I wanted to tell him something. It ended up being Hans—and so I had to think of something to talk about. It ended up being dairy farming."

"Sure wish I'd known that. Hans beat me to it. Yes, Hans did get quite involved with the notion—attended meetings and the like, made all sorts of calculations. We were all enthusiastic, until—"

"What happened?"

"Until we discovered our land wasn't at all suitable for pasturage. We couldn't support a dairy herd, and none of us were very good at figures, keepin' books. It would take a good manager—we didn't think it would work."

"Didn't think much of the idea then, either," commented Noel, "but lately, you know—creameries springing up all over the county, a good investment. For the dairy farmers as well—they buy shares, get a percentage of the profit."

"What makes you think it will work here in Little Sauk, sir?" Mattias asked. "We haven't any experience, the land—"

"Ah yes, the land. Think, now. Your place, *non, non*. The DeLaurier place, *oui*—yes. Rich pasturage down along the river, also over east along the prairie. You buy a herd of dairy cows, you enlarge your barns—and *voilà*."

Mattias was clearly interested, but still seemed hesitant. "Takes capital, sir. Takes organization, management. I'm afraid I haven't any of those, Lucy either, if you'll pardon my saying so. Isn't that true—" An instant's hesitation, as if he wasn't sure yet what to call her, what term of endearment would be comfortable.

Lucy had noticed his hesitancy about using such terms. So reserved, still, perhaps that would come in time. But she needed to challenge him on one account. "No, not exactly true. I do have some idea about business. I've learned things the hard way in Shakopee from mister Heinz, from Patsy—"

"Patsy?" Mary looked curious, suspicious.

"Oh, a business acquaintance," Lucy quickly responded. "And I can learn more. If you could trust me to manage the cooperative, organize the local farmers, the deliveries to the creamery in Little Sauk?"

"There isn't one there," Noel pointed out.

"No, not yet. But Noel, what about that new building I saw going up across from the station? Right at the railroad tracks?"

"Ken Harmon responsible for that. Half of it for the new post office, other half to rent out. Hmm . . . *mais oui*, yes, it might be big enough, Ken owes me a favor—maybe to make the rent reasonable. And on the rail line—important!"

Mattias insisted on taking a hard line. "Well, how about the capital? I have some savings in the bank, but I'm sure it won't be enough. A big business venture like this—well, frankly, I dunno."

"A ha! Now words come out of Geske's mouth. Yesterday, I find out Homer West did leave a will. Lucy I have not yet told. You will not believe where it was found." He paused for effect. "In the store, on the shelf behind some of his patent concoctions." Another pause, looking directly at Lucy. "And now, *faites-vous attention*—prepare yourselves! This man West names Lucy Guette Dubois the beneficiary."

"What? Me?" her hand went to her mouth.

"It will take a while to probate," Noel added. "But even with the fees and so on, that's quite a bit of property—the store, the stock. Will bring in many dollars, enough capital to invest."

"Oh no!" said Lucy. "I can't imagine why—not after what I'd—" She could not finish, overwhelmed by surprise, confusion, guilt. Perhaps he'd made it out when his hopes were the highest, when he was sure he was going to marry her. Then he'd never had the chance to change it. "That little girl—that haunting picture in his pocketbook—" she began. "But there's no need to explain now." She would find her, bring her home to the DeLaurier house. In a series of fleeting images, she imagined what it might have been like had the child been Homer's, had she married Homer, had the child come home to the DeLaurier house by a different way.

"*Eh bien, d'accord?* It is all agreed, then?" Noel folded up his pocket knife, began rolling up the plat maps. "So, that is how we will proceed. And *bien tôt*—very soon, eh?"

"You'll find out about the building—the costs—how to keep the books—and—and—" So much to learn, Lucy recognized from her brief experience with Patsy. "And Mattias—"

"*Precisement,*" commented Noel. "And you, Mattias—I understand, could look after building the barns, buying the dairy herds, and looking at enough pasturage to support the herds." He laughed. "Grass, *mon dieu*, grass they will eat and eat."

"What did mister Geske say about the contents of that will?" She worried about the legal aspects. "And what about the creamery co-operative?"

"He will do what he can—for the family, as he said. As for the creamery, there is need to talk to local farmers, use the *Argus* to promote. For a co-op—*eh bien*, one must be willing to join, know the advantages. Then there is the matter of Articles of Association."

"The what?" Mattias asked.

"Must legalize it, that is, according to John Geske, a form of protection. But he will explain in time. He will prepare the papers. Ah, *oui*, many papers."

"Yes, it will all take time, I'm afraid. So much to think about, to plan."

"Wedding first, my dear," Mary pointed out, already making a few notes on the back of an envelope. "Such a pity you've got to go back to Shakopee tomorrow."

"Much to do there, as well. But I'll be back in a week or so. And with the children."

"Do not worry," said Noel. "The DeLaurier House will be ready. Mary will make certain of that. Maggie Skinner *aussi.*"

The next day Lucy and Mattias stood waiting for the Sauk Centre train on the Little Sauk station platform. "We've only a few more minutes," said Lucy.

"We've waiting so long already, a few more minutes won't matter." He paused, looked off in the distance. "Will it—my—my darling."

He'd gotten the word out. "I suppose not," she said, slipping an arm around his waist and leaning against him as he sheltered her against the sharp March wind.

"What shall we call this business? You'll have to think of a good name before you settle your affairs in Shakopee and bring our children home." It didn't escape Lucy's notice, his use of the word our.

"Yes, we've got to have a good name," he continued. "A name attracting attention, confidence, maybe. Think you can do it before we finish the spring plowing, before the wedding, before expanding the DeLaurier house to build a skimming room, a milking barn, a loading dock?"

He smiled as he brushed away a strand of hair escaping from her bonnet. "You see, I've learned a lot more since yesterday. Lot more 'bout a lot of things."

The approaching train whistle sounded in the distance, followed by the clicking of wheels over the Sauk River trestle. "Almost here," Mattias said.

Lucy thought how different this moment was from her departure so many months ago. So many months, unknowns, hardships, and disappointments ago. Thinking aloud, she said, "I now have so much. So much of everything."

"But the name—you haven't the name yet."

"The name?" She embraced Mattias once more as the train slowly came to a stop along the platform. At the same time, her eye caught the Holberg wagon, tied up at the station barrier. "How about—how about the Blue Line Co-op? "

"The Blue Line Co-op? Well, that'll do just fine," he said. "Just fine. Been there all along."